COVERT KILL

JASON KASPER

SEVERN RIVER

PUBLISHING

COVERT KILL

Severn River Publishing
www.SevernRiverBooks.com

ISBN: 978-1-64875-400-5 (Paperback)

ALSO BY JASON KASPER

American Mercenary Series
Greatest Enemy
Offer of Revenge
Dark Redemption
Vengeance Calling
The Suicide Cartel
Terminal Objective

Shadow Strike Series
The Enemies of My Country
Last Target Standing
Covert Kill
Narco Assassins
Beast Three Six

Spider Heist Thrillers
The Spider Heist
The Sky Thieves
The Manhattan Job
The Fifth Bandit

Standalone Thriller
Her Dark Silence

To find out more about Jason Kasper and his books, visit
severnriverbooks.com/authors/jason-kasper

To Raoul Jacques DeLier

Build me a son whose heart will be clear, whose goal will be high; a son who will master himself before he seeks to master other men; one who will reach into the future, yet never forget the past.
-Douglas MacArthur

Africa is mystic; it is wild; it is a sweltering inferno; it is a photographer's paradise, a hunter's Valhalla, an escapist's Utopia. It is what you will, and it withstands all interpretations. It is the last vestige of a dead world or the cradle of a shiny new one.

-Beryl Markham, *West with the Night*

Pirate ships and guinea pigs from hell: gentlemen, we have officially arrived in Africa.

-Worthy

1

Niger River, Nigeria

Reilly's voice crackled over my earpiece. "*We got a speedboat behind us...no running lights, trailing a hundred meters off our six. I can make out two or three guys at least, possibly more.*"

He sounded more confused than apprehensive, and I grasped my rifle to cross our boat's walkway toward the bridge as I replied, "Let me check with the captain. Sit tight."

The palm trees silhouetted against the sky glowed green in my night vision, augmented by dim moonlight as we cruised north on the Niger River. My only previous foray into Africa had been Somalia, but those windswept deserts were a far cry from the view on the opposite side of the continent.

Here, the coiled mangroves at the river's edge should have been a lush explosion of wildlife, but instead they seemed withered, tinged with a vaguely petrochemical scent that I would have expected in New Jersey. I'd been anticipating a dramatic *Apocalypse Now*-style infil upstream into the heart of the country, but we'd been met with an uneventful boat ride —until now.

I arrived at the bridge and yanked open the door, entering the room and addressing the tall Nigerian man steering the ship.

"We've got a boat following us. Are they pirates?"

His terse reply came in crisply accented English. "Of course. Who else would be in these waters right now?"

I cursed under my breath. Speed was the one thing we lacked—we'd opted for a slow 31-foot vessel in the interests of hiding three white men along with our cargo.

Keying my radio, I spoke quietly to my two teammates. "Definitely pirates."

Then I asked, "How many men on their boat?"

"As few as three, as many as seven."

"Three to seven," I transmitted, releasing my radio switch as I felt the first tugging suspicion that this supposedly-vetted boat driver could be complicit. If he made a wrong move in the coming proceedings, it would be my responsibility to take him out.

"Can we bribe them?" I asked quickly. "Talk our way out?"

The captain shook his head gravely. "They will search this vessel no matter what you say. If it were just me, they would rob any cargo. But with expatriates aboard...they will kidnap you, take you to the mangroves. And try to extort ransom, probably 50 million Naira, from your employer."

Well, wasn't that a subtle irony, I thought. My employer wasn't in the practice of paying ransom, at least not for us—the entire reason my team had been selected for overseas jaunts like these was that we could be completely disavowed. And if denying our affiliation would prevent a major international incident with Africa's largest economy, then that's exactly what would occur.

I swallowed hard, then updated my teammates with the information. "Skin color's working against us here; there's no way to pay off the pirates. We're worth more to them as ransom."

To the captain, I asked, "What are they waiting for?"

"Maybe they are trying to decide how to attack. Or maybe they are drinking cocktails first to ward off evil spirits."

"You're kidding me."

He shook his head again.

"These are primitive people, Mr. Suicide. But dangerous. They have been killing men in the delta for many years."

Well that was too interesting not to pass along, I thought as I keyed my radio.

"Sidenote: the pirates believe in magic."

Nervously clearing his throat, the captain went on, "Any moment now, they will order us to halt."

As if on cue, Reilly transmitted, *"Here they come, making a move for the port side."*

The thin, high buzz of a boat engine roaring to full throttle was the only warning I had to duck before a blinding white spotlight illuminated behind us, its glare slicing through the windows.

"Stop!" a booming, amplified voice shouted over a bullhorn. "Stop, or we will send you to hell!"

"All right," I told the captain, "come to a full stop and let them board."

"What?" He sounded incensed at the suggestion. "Why do you not simply shoot at them?"

"Because," I explained impatiently, "they'd break off pursuit and come back with their friends. It's not the shooting we mind, it's leaving survivors. I need them to get close."

Another prospect was lingering at the back of my mind: this was no accidental encounter. If our mission had somehow been leaked, any number of interested parties would be incentivized to use local forces to kill us all. And before I risked drawing potential threats toward the rest of my team, I needed to know for sure one way or another.

The captain reluctantly throttled down his engine, the boat cruising to a gradual halt as I transmitted to my teammates.

"All right, we're stopping to let these guys board. Stay down until the first ones come over the side. Then we'll hit them."

Worthy crouched against the short sidewall at the bow, peering over the edge as the pirate vessel approached with its spotlight fixed on the bridge.

In hindsight, Reilly's initial report of a speedboat was a bit optimistic. Perhaps twenty feet in length, the battered craft had an open deck bearing masked men wielding rifles, with one at the rear manning an outboard motor.

The pirates slowed alongside them as Reilly transmitted, *"Five men, one on the motor. Looks like they've all got AKs or shotguns, nothing belt-fed."*

"Copy," David replied. *"Doc, I want you to take out the man on the engine— if they manage to speed off, we'll never catch them."*

From the rear of the boat, Reilly transmitted back, *"On it. Looks like they're approaching the bow."*

As the boat captain cut power completely, the sound of the rumbling engine faded to lapping waves and the pirate vessel's approach. Worthy felt the deck beneath him rolling in the current—not the best conditions for accuracy, but this would be a close-range engagement and he trusted his team's reflexes were better than those of the pirates.

He readied the carbine in his grasp, a suppressed HK416 with all the bells and whistles for night fighting. With one hand on the pistol grip and another braced to activate his infrared laser, Worthy listened to the growling hum of the pirate boat closing the distance. He ducked as their spotlight swept the deck from front to rear, then hovered on the bridge where Worthy could make out the captain through the windshield, standing with his hands raised.

He felt the bump of the smaller boat knocking against his own, and heard David transmit between the pirates' shouted orders at the captain.

"Racegun, they're starting to come up right next to you."

Worthy waited a half-second before rising from his crouch—and coming face-to-face with a man who wore a knit cap pulled over his face, two crude eyeholes cut in the fabric and a rosary around his neck as he tried to hoist himself over the rail.

Driving his suppressor into the man's sternum, Worthy fired two subsonic rounds that sent the lead pirate falling back onto his boat. His body collided with a second man trying to board behind him, and Worthy exploited the confusion to swing his infrared laser to a third pirate standing at the bow, this one shirtless and fumbling to bring his shotgun up.

Three shots to center mass caused him to fall forward, almost dropping into the river as the spotlight extinguished from a bullet fired by one of his teammates. As the view through his night vision dimmed, Worthy steadied himself on the rocking deck and angled his rifle over the rail, aiming downward at the second pirate to board who'd been knocked down after the first kill.

He found the man trying to pull himself out from under his friend's body, exposing the space between his shoulder blades to Worthy's laser as he drilled a trio of rounds into him.

Then Worthy swept his aim to the aft section of the pirate boat, finding the next two men that his teammates had already dropped and firing a controlled pair into each as David and Reilly did the same with his own kills, their three lasers crisscrossing over the vessel until the five pirates were thoroughly seeded with jacketed hollow points.

Worthy reloaded, slamming a fresh magazine into his weapon and conducting a 180-degree sweep forward of the boat. He checked the near bank first, then the far one, peering into the labyrinth of mangrove inlets for any indication of onshore observation or, worse still, another pirate vessel.

"*Racegun,*" David transmitted, "*pick up security to our front again and I'll get the rear. Doc, I want you to search that boat—we need to make sure this was as random as it seemed.*"

From his position at the back of the boat, Reilly emitted a loud groan.

He swam about as well as a bowling ball, and as the largest man on the team, he should have been the last one assigned to some parkour bullshit from one boat to another in the midst of this filthy river.

But his team leader had spoken and the Nigerian captain was already firing his engine, guiding his vessel alongside the idling pirate boat that had drifted away in the current. So the medic begrudgingly obeyed, meeting David at the center of the port side and asking, "Sure you don't want to send Worthy?"

David was peering over the rail, hopefully second-guessing his decision to send a guy over the edge.

Instead the team leader replied, "Worthy's the best marksman, so I need him on security. You can swim, right?"

"No, actually, I'm a terrible—"

"You'll be fine," David cut him off. "We need to get this thing searched and sunk. I want to know if they've got any long-range radios, planning materials with a timeline, anything that indicates they knew we were coming. If that's the case, we're in for one hell of a night."

"Well," Reilly remarked, "if I get eaten by a croc or a hippo, the blood will be on your hands."

They arrived at the pirate boat, the hulls clacking against one another as Reilly examined the four-foot drop from one vessel to the next.

"Tick tock," David said, ignoring Reilly's comment. "Over the rail, before we run into any more pirates."

Slinging his long-barreled HK417 rifle, Reilly hesitantly climbed the side rail and straddled it, then stepped down on the far side as he perched for the jump.

He waited until the hulls knocked together again to make his leap, noting with dismay that the pirate vessel bounced off and began drifting away as he was midair.

Reilly landed on the edge of the deck with a thud, the boat rocking under his considerable weight. One leg dipped into the tepid river water up to the knee, and he scrambled forward along a slick of blood between two pirate bodies as the craft rolled in the opposite direction, then righted itself and drifted away from his team's boat.

"Son of a bitch," Reilly muttered, kicking his left leg to shake off the excess water as a polluted stench soaked through his pants and boot. The outboard engine was still rattling at idle, and above the sound he vaguely registered David laughing from the opposite deck. Shaking his head, Reilly rose to a crouch and stood to begin his search.

Approaching the front of the pirate vessel, he flipped up his night vision and turned on the red lens headlamp around his neck. He was about to kneel before the first body when a noise caused him to spin around—gargled breathing from the back of the boat. Its source was revealed at the periphery of his headlamp beam as the rearmost body impossibly began to move, a single arm reaching up to claw at a handle on the outboard engine.

Reilly whipped his rifle into a firing position, but it was too late—the boat lurched forward at full throttle, sending him into a forward sprawl that ended when he crashed onto the deck. Why, he wondered as the boat sped up the river and away from his teammates, did the most ridiculous situations always happen to him and him alone?

Rolling to his side, Reilly recovered his rifle and tried to rise to a knee.

It wasn't an easy process—the boat was leaping over waves and crashing on the far side, veering left and then right as a man who should have been dead somehow maintained his grip on the throttle.

By the time Reilly managed to kneel, desperately trying to steady himself well enough to put his rifle to use, he was shocked to see his boat's running lights already fifty meters behind him, the distance increasing with each passing second.

At that moment he heard David transmit, "*Doc, I think you've got a survivor on board.*"

Very funny, Reilly thought, killing his headlamp and flipping down his night vision. The scene before him blazed to light in mottled shades of green—dead bodies shifting with the boat's movement, and the man at the rear still maintaining his hold.

Reilly quickly took aim, firing two suppressed shots at the engine man as soon as his team's boat was out of his line of fire. He was certain he'd hit him, but the vessel continued speeding forward, cresting a wave and crashing down to knock Reilly on his side. This bastard must have had a postmortem death grip on the throttle, thought Reilly as he started to rise, then thought better of it and aimed his infrared laser at the outboard motor instead.

He fired five shots, the 7.62mm rounds causing the engine to cough, sputter, and finally fall silent. The boat finally—*finally*—came to a stop, and the night fell nearly silent aside from the gentle lapping of waves against the hull.

Catching his breath in disbelief, he transmitted to his teammates.

"Good news: I'm all secure. Bad news: outboard motor is now scrap metal, so I'm kind of stranded out here."

David responded, *"No sweat, we're coming to you. Flex cuff the bodies to the boat, then prep a demo charge against the hull so we can scuttle it. Then finish your fucking search."*

I stood beside Worthy at the bow, scanning ahead as we neared the pirate vessel now adrift with Reilly on board. The big medic was visible on the deck, completing his duties with a light step to prevent the boat from rocking too far in either direction.

Keying my radio, I asked, "They all dead this time?"

It took him a moment to respond, *"I put a 7.62 round into everyone's head and the boat is starting to take on water, so yeah, they're all dead. Just hurry up and get me, this is embarrassing."*

"Or amusing," I offered. "All depends on your point of view."

Reilly let that particular observation go unanswered.

Worthy spoke beside me. "How do you want to play this, boss?"

"Only one way *to* play it. There's room to profit off this."

"I hear you. I'll follow your lead."

As our boat slowed to a halt beside the pirate vessel, I called out to Reilly.

"What'd you find?"

His response came by way of tossing me a rectangular parcel. I caught the shrink-wrapped parcel, then examined it to find the contents were a hard-packed brick of white powder. Turning it over, I found a sticker bearing a ram skull logo.

He said, "There's two more bricks where that came from, both with the same branding. One of them is open, which explains how the guy on the motor managed to survive getting shot so many times. I could probably rub a drop of his blood on my gums and stay awake for three days."

"Cocaine's a hell of a drug," I acknowledged, peeling off the sticker and stuffing it in my pocket before tossing the brick back to Reilly.

He caught it and continued, "Nothing on board to indicate they were coming after our team. Looks like they were just small-time pirates trying to shake down the wrong boat."

"You secure the bodies and rig the demo?"

"Yep."

"All right," I said, "let's get this over with."

Worthy and I straddled the side rail, extending our arms toward Reilly. He pulled the ring on his fuse igniter, then dropped it and took hold of the rail as we helped hoist him up and over. Reilly grunted from the effort, and I caught a whiff of oil residue as he swung his soaked left leg aboard.

As soon as the three of us were on deck once more, I called out to the captain, "Let's go."

The churning buzz of the boat engine increased in volume as we pulled forward, and my teammates followed me back to the stern. There we lined up against the rail, watching the pirate vessel bobbing in the waves.

"That was a pretty bad engagement," I said to Reilly. "For you, I mean."

The medic scoffed. "What? We all shot him."

"We all shot him, but he was *your* target. Take out the man on the engine, remember?"

"David's right," Worthy agreed. "That little mess was on you. Hell, I believe that's the kind of story that would travel forever and a day in the team—unless, of course, no one else was to find out. And for the small price of a case of beer, I can definitely forget to mention this to Ian or Cancer."

"Two cases," I corrected him, reaching up to pat Reilly on his thick, muscled shoulder. "One for each of us. Silence costs, brother. Next time kill the engine before you start searching."

The detonation sent a dull *boom* across the water, its flash of orange light receding along with the echo as the pirate boat tilted on its long axis before slipping downward. I watched its hull slip beneath the surface and vanish from sight as we continued our journey upstream.

2

Cancer bobbed his head in rhythm with the rap song playing over the vehicle speakers, the action mirrored by the Nigerian man in the driver's seat. They'd been parked for over half an hour, all of it filled with rap, most of it quality.

"I like it," Cancer said. "This a local guy?"

Tolu nodded enthusiastically. "From Lagos, like me. Nigeria has the best rappers in all of Africa."

"You listen to Western stuff?"

"All of it," the driver responded.

"Lemme ask you something, Tolu. What's going on with rap today?"

Tolu shook his head. "It is sad, very sad. The mumble raps..."

"Autotune."

"Face tattoos."

Cancer snickered. "Some shameful shit. Thank God we've still got some good lyrical rappers, and the classics."

"Yes," Tolu agreed, "the classics."

Then silence lapsed between the two men, and Cancer could feel the tension rising. He eyed the Nigerian, considering how to proceed without sabotaging the otherwise outstanding rapport between them.

Toluwanimi Layeni was 29 years old, and despite numerous wildly entertaining conversations over the past few days, Cancer still couldn't figure him out. Take this moment, for instance. Here they were, two grown men sitting in a van at four in the morning, and Tolu was dressed like he was about to stroll into a West Hollywood nightclub: garish shirt unbuttoned to the mid-sternum, skinny pants, quasi-dress shoes, and enough gold between his chains, bracelets, and watch to make a pawn shop owner blush.

Speaking with measured candor, Cancer said, "Tolu, I think we both know where this conversation is headed."

The driver nodded solemnly. "We do."

"So as not to make this awkward, we both go on the count of three."

"This is the only way," Tolu agreed.

"One. Two. Three."

Both men spoke their next word in unison, and with equal amounts of conviction. But Tolu said "Tupac" as Cancer said "Biggie," and a look of shock flashed over each man's face before they eyed one another warily.

After a few moments of silence, Cancer said, "I may have to find a new driver for my team. I'm not sure this is going to work out."

Tolu answered, "And I may need me a new team to drive. Tupac is the OG. Platinum status before Biggie's first single."

"Oxcarts were invented before Cadillacs, but that don't make them better. Biggie has the superior flow—"

"And Tupac was a poet, with better lyrical ability."

"Ah," Cancer countered, "consider the storytelling, though. You ever listened to the *Ready to Die* album? I mean, really listened to it?"

"I could ask you the same about *Me Against The World*, my friend."

Cancer was about to respond when David transmitted over his radio earpiece.

"*Cancer, this is Suicide.*"

"Shit, hang on," Cancer said, then keyed his mic and replied, "Send it."

Tolu turned off the radio as David responded, "*We're three minutes out.*"

"All right, I'll meet you at the spot."

Tolu looked over and asked, "You want me to help?"

"No, I got it. Just wait here."

Then Cancer exited the cab into the warm night air, now in the seventies even in February—as close as Nigeria got to having a winter season. By mid-afternoon, he knew, temperatures would easily crest a hundred degrees.

Walking to the back of the panel van, Cancer opened the twin cargo doors to reveal interior walls lined with gear: video cameras, tripods, rolls of extension cord, microphones, and recording equipment. Tolu had carved out a decent living for himself transporting journalists and reporters to various hot spots across his homeland, and that professional capacity gave him the access and placement to have long since been vetted and flipped to a CIA asset. The man's day job also dictated the team's cover: they were posing as investigative journalists for Garrett News, a niche media company that served as a front for select Agency operations abroad.

But Cancer ignored the media supplies for the time being, turning his attention instead to a hidden latch in the floorboard that he pulled open, removing the panel to uncover a cavernous space beneath the false floor.

He descended the dirt slope to a series of wooden slats over the water, then crossed the long dock to its endpoint twenty feet into the Niger River. The chanting warble of night creatures in the surrounding forest was soon drowned out by the approaching boat, which he caught sight of a moment later. Its engine began throttling back as the craft slowed, gradually settling to its stopping point alongside the dock.

In the dim glow of the running lights, Cancer could make out his three teammates as they prepared to transfer the cargo. Turning on his headlamp, he saw David handing down a rucksack.

Taking the heavy pack and setting it aside, Cancer asked, "How was your trip—you guys find Colonel Kurtz or what?"

David clambered off the vessel with a grunt. "Had a scrape with a pirate boat, closed the loop. Anything new on your end?"

"Yeah." He reached for a rifle case from the team medic. "After three days stuck in a safehouse with Ian, I'm ready to retire from this line of work forever. Our driver's cool as shit, though."

David eyed him suspiciously, then took a kit bag and set it on the dock. "It's unsettling to see you in a good mood."

The gear transfer was complete within minutes, after which the boat cast off and continued its churning path upstream. Each of the four men donned a ruck and hoisted the rest of the kit and weapons bags, then began the short uphill trudge back to the van.

A bloodcurdling cry came from the forest, making Reilly jump.

"Rock hyrax," Cancer said with a knowing smile. "Looks like a guinea pig."

Worthy shook his head. "Pirate ships and guinea pigs from hell: gentlemen, we have officially arrived in Africa."

As they reached the van and began piling their equipment into the false bottom, Cancer announced, "Fellas, meet Tolu. Tolu, these are the guys."

The driver turned in his seat and nodded to the men. "Hey, boys, *how far*?"

David squinted at him.

"How far to what?"

Cancer explained, "Pidgin English. *How far* means how are you doing." He addressed the driver. "Don't worry, Tolu. I'll get them schooled."

After replacing the floor panel over the false bottom, the team loaded into the vehicle—David in the passenger seat, and Cancer, Worthy, and Reilly taking up positions among the press gear in the cargo area.

Tolu fired the engine, and Nigerian rap began playing over the speakers.

Cancer nudged Worthy. "I told you, he's awesome."

Worthy raised an eyebrow, looking at Cancer as if he must have been joking. Some people had no taste in music, the sniper thought, turning his gaze to Reilly. The medic appeared to be sulking, having barely spoken since stepping off the boat, and one of his pant legs was soaked from the knee down. Cancer sniffed the air, then tapped Reilly on the arm. "Why do you smell like oil?"

Reilly pulled his arm away and muttered, "I don't want to talk about it."

3

Ian stepped out the front door of the safehouse, shielding his eyes from the sun as he peered across the heavily planted front yard. The gate opened within a few seconds, and he caught a glimpse of the media van rounding the fence and pulling into the winding driveway.

As it approached, Ian glanced around the yard for any signs of observation.

Most of the surrounding homes stood on tree-covered lots with little visibility to the street, their rooftops emerging above the vegetation and driveways blocked by small iron gates. The neighborhood was located in the outskirts of the capital city of Abuja, and its houses were mostly occupied by a thriving community of expatriates from various countries. While the building Ian had just exited was visually indistinguishable from the rest, its interior was where things got interesting.

The van swung in a tight turn before reversing toward the front door where Ian stood waiting, a knot forming in his gut. Cancer had left scarcely eight hours ago to retrieve the rest of the team from their maritime infil, and in that time their entire mission had shifted on its axis. As the team's sole intelligence operative, Ian had monitored the developments first with curiosity, then dread—and he didn't relish having to break the news to his teammates, David least of all.

Reilly was the first to exit through the van's cargo doors, easing his hulking frame onto the pavement as he gave Ian a brief nod and then stretched. Worthy was next, looking as if he'd just woken up—probably the case, after their all-night boat ride—and before Cancer could set foot outside the van, David stepped out of the passenger side, his eyes darting across their surroundings. He was already nervous about the safehouse's proximity to a major urban area, Ian knew, and he considered that the team leader's day was about to get a whole lot worse.

As the team members began unloading their equipment, David approached him with brisk strides.

"Hey, brother, what's good—"

"We've got a problem," Ian cut him off.

David came to a halt, rubbing his eye with one hand.

"All night on a boat and that's the first four words I get from you."

Ian shrugged. "You want me to help get the gear inside first?"

"No, the guys can take care of that. Show me the house and then we can talk business."

The intelligence operative led him inside, scarcely clearing the doorway into the whitewashed interior before David asked, "Security?"

Ian waved his finger in a circle. "Pinhole cameras in every direction, remote feeds piped in through the office monitors and backed by motion sensors. We can get by with one guy on guard duty."

"Good. How are we doing on supplies?"

Ian led him down the hallway. "Full lineup of civilian clothes, formal to informal and everything in between. Backup generator has gotten us through the last two power outages."

David hooked a thumb toward the kitchen on their left and asked, "Food?"

"Kitchen was fully stocked when we got here. We could hunker down here for the first year of the zombie apocalypse without going hungry."

Nodding his approval, David said, "Reilly will be glad to hear that. How's the coffee situation?"

Ian shot a sidelong glare at his team leader.

"Come on, David. Have you ever known me to scrimp on caffeine?" Without waiting for a response, he paused in the hallway and pointed.

"Next door on the left is the debriefing room. Four bedrooms down the hall, plus an unfinished storage space for the gear. And the office is this way."

Stepping into what should have been a living room, Ian paused to allow David to take in the view: tables ringed the space to complete a fully stocked office that included computers, shredders, and a suite of telephones with encrypted lines.

Once David gave a satisfied nod, Ian took a seat before the central monitor and waited for his team leader to pull up a chair beside him. Jostling the mouse, Ian saw the screen come to life with a grainy still frame of a bearded Nigerian man wearing a checkered *shemagh* over his scalp, the excess scarf draped over one shoulder. He had camouflage fatigues and a tactical vest, and one arm hoisted a machete victoriously skyward.

David frowned.

"So you brought me here to show me more pictures of the wonderchild?"

David's moniker was fitting, Ian supposed, in its own perverse way—because while Usman Mokhammed was many things, his status as a prodigy of sorts was irrefutable.

If the extraordinarily violent terror organization of Boko Haram was considered a business, then Usman was the equivalent of an employee who started in the mailroom and was on his way to becoming CEO. As of eight months ago, when Ian's team was deployed to Syria, the young terrorist wasn't even on the Agency's radar. But when the Nigerian military captured Hakeem Salafi, a Boko Haram captain, Usman was promoted to take his place and given command of somewhere between 120 and 150 men. No one was sure of the exact number; what they *did* know was that Usman took the reins with staggering efficiency, elevating the unit under his command from crude terror into a highly sophisticated killing machine.

The first mission he commanded was a daring prison break, raiding a detention facility in Maiduguri and freeing 86 known Boko Haram operatives, along with another 42 inmates who immediately pledged allegiance to their liberator. Having effectively doubled the size of his fighting force overnight, Usman had gone on to target foreign aid workers in Nigeria's besieged northeast, killing two dozen in the first month and effectively severing the distribution of food and medicine to tens of thousands of civilians already displaced by Boko Haram violence.

Then, he'd turned his attention to income.

Bank robbery was nothing new for Boko Haram—it was one of their main revenue streams. But Usman had taken it to a whole new level, targeting not just small local banks in Borno State but also major financial institutions in government-controlled metropolitan areas like Kano and Zaria. He'd used the proceeds to equip his men with a lethal array of belt-fed machineguns and rocket launchers, and the Agency had since intercepted communications of senior Boko Haram leadership appointing Usman as an emissary to travel to Somalia and establish a strategic partnership with their East African counterparts, Al-Shabaab. What followed was a dedicated intelligence effort to track down Usman to his camp outside Gwoza, and once his location had been pinpointed, Ian's team was sent in to conduct a surgical strike against the rising terrorist star.

There was just one problem.

"Usman's gone," Ian said flatly, minimizing the image of the machete-hoisting leader to pull up a digital map of Nigeria.

Beside him, David released a pained exhale and tapped the knuckle of his fist atop the table three times in quick succession, as if trying to defuse his frustration.

"Where to?" the team leader asked.

Ian pointed to the town of Gwoza in the northeast. "At half past ten last night, Usman's cell phone trace departed his camp and moved here"—he slid his finger southwest, coming to a stop roughly halfway to the team's current location before tapping the screen—"to here. A town called Bauchi."

David sounded relieved. "Oh. You scared me for a second there. So he's well outside Boko Haram territory and hunkered down, what, six hours or so from here? That means we can hit him tonight, before he moves again."

The house was now filled with clomping footsteps as his teammates carried gear inside. Ian heard a cry of delirious joy as Reilly discovered the food stockpile.

"It's not that simple," Ian said. "Usman's cell phone went dark on the outskirts of Bauchi, and the Agency doesn't have an exact location. Based on his pattern of life, he won't activate his phone again until after nightfall. But there's a bigger issue at play here."

"Which is?"

Folding his arms, Ian replied, "Usman has spent nearly a month living in the same Boko Haram camp outside Gwoza. The more success his men have had, the less he's personally accompanied the raids—makes sense, because his career is on the rise and he's getting too important to get killed on an operation. But last night, he leaves this terrorist utopia and suddenly travels 350 miles into a government-controlled area. Why?"

David considered the question for a moment.

"Maybe he was tipped off that we were coming. Put his cell phone on a truck to throw us off, then vanished to God-knows-where."

"And if the Nigerian government were aware of our mission," Ian responded, "I'd agree with you. But the only people in this country who know exactly what we're doing here are the US ambassador and his station chief. That's why I think there's a major attack in the works. Something important enough for Usman to personally spearhead it."

David folded his arms and leaned back in his chair. "What does the Agency have to say about all this?"

"They've raised the threat level at the US Embassy, notified the Nigerian authorities that an attack is likely imminent. But between pirates in the south and Boko Haram in the north, that's nothing new. We don't know what Usman's destination is, and he's on a trajectory for Abuja or Lagos. So the real question is, how do we react?"

David tapped an index finger against his chin, studying the screen.

But rather than answer, he produced a sticker from his pocket and handed it to the intelligence operative. "After our little scrape with the pirates, we found three kilos of coke. Those stickers were on all of them—you recognize it?"

Ian took the sticker, examining the ram skull logo before handing it back with a shrug.

"It's not unusual. Lots of producers label their stuff to create brand loyalty, the same as any marketing department would. Most of the time they use logos from major brands—Ferrari, Rolex, Gucci, that sort of thing

—but sometimes it's custom. I don't recognize the ram skull, if that's what you're asking. Could try to run it down if—"

"No." David returned the sticker to his pocket. "Don't worry about it. I was just curious, and besides, I think we've got bigger things to worry about."

Then he stretched, groaning and releasing an exhausted sigh as he concluded, "I've got an idea about how to handle Usman."

4

David's voice transmitted from the speaker box on the desk, *"Raptor Nine One, this is Suicide Actual."*

Duchess grabbed her hand mic and replied, "This is Raptor Nine One, send your traffic."

"Suicide element is consolidated at the safehouse. No complications since our pirate encounter last night. Angel has gotten me up to speed on our target status, and I have a proposed change to our mission plan."

Pausing before she responded, Duchess surveyed the room around her.

The operations center was filled with staff members seated among the tiers descending to the front of the room, where a series of flat-screens displayed digital imagery of Nigeria. The one she was watching at present showed the town of Bauchi, where Usman Mokhammed's cell phone beacon was conspicuously absent.

Feeling the eyes in the room upon her, she transmitted back, "Go ahead."

David continued, *"Recommend I take my team to Jos—it's eighty miles" southwest of Usman's current location in Bauchi, and the last spot along the A3 Highway before he could change direction."*

Duchess located the town on her computer screen, orienting herself as David continued, *"If Usman activates his cell phone before he moves, that gives us over an hour of lead time to set up a vehicle interdiction. Once we have eyes-on, I'll make the assessment on whether he's got more men than we can handle. If he does, we don't spring the ambush but provide exact reporting on his vehicle makes, models, and license plates—everything the Nigerian military needs to find him before he can attack. But if he's traveling with light security, my team can take him on the road, kill him tonight, and be back in Abuja, mission complete, by sunrise."*

"Let me confer with my staff." Duchess set down her mic and called out, "J2, what's the threat level between Bauchi and Jos?"

Andolin Lucios stood at the front of the room, turning to face her as he replied with a trace of Spanish accent coloring his otherwise monotone voice.

"Bauchi is pretty secure; the Nigerian government actually relocated a few hundred schoolgirls there after the Chibok kidnapping. No Boko Haram attacks for years. In Jos, where the team proposes to stage, there have been clashes between Christian and Muslim populations. Some of them fatal. But it's all local ethnic strife, no Boko Haram activity to speak of. Given the large expat community in Nigeria writ large, I don't assess any issues with the team traveling to either town."

"Thank you," Duchess said, and Lucios sat down as she called out, "J3?"

Wes Jamieson rose and answered in a booming voice.

"There are some small villages along that stretch of highway, but the vast majority is open woodland and tall grass savanna. We shouldn't have a problem recommending ambush sites for the team to confirm or deny before nightfall. But I don't think a static vehicle interdiction is our best play. Depending on traffic density, we risk civilian cars in the crossfire."

"Noted," she said. "Then what would you recommend?"

Running a hand through his auburn hair, Jamieson answered, "The team's got multiple vehicles at their disposal. I'd advocate for a mobile ambush, probably tailing Usman out of Bauchi and having the assault elements spread out along the highway. That way they can consolidate and take him on the open road with a minimum of civilian traffic. If Usman is traveling in a single vehicle, it could be as easy as a PIT maneuver and gunning down any survivors. And if he's moving in a convoy, they can transition to surveillance-only and see where he's headed."

Duchess nodded, and Jamieson sat down.

"Legal?"

Now Gregory Pharr rose, attired in a suit as was his custom despite the business casual dress requirements.

He began, "Geographically, we have no restrictions on moving inside Nigeria. The A3 Highway is as good as hitting Usman outside Gwoza as originally planned, and probably much safer for the team."

"Understood. Thank you, Gregory."

But rather than sit down, Pharr continued, "The real problem will be positive identification of the target. Once Usman activates his cell phone, we've got plus or minus five-meter fidelity on his location. When he's out on the open road, that means something—but only if there's not much traffic. Due to the delay in his cell phone GPS reporting, we need to mitigate any possibility of collateral damage. At a minimum, that's going to require a positive identification within our margin of error."

Duchess said, "So you agree with Wes—have a team vehicle tail Usman's tracker out of Bauchi?"

"And then proceed within the five-meter bubble. If we co-locate a team tracker with Usman's phone when there are no other cars in the vicinity, we've done our due diligence for positive identification on that specific vehicle."

"At which point I can greenlight the attack."

"Yes, ma'am. Then we're in the clear, legally speaking. The rest is up to the team's discretion. But to do any less is to put this project into a very gray area—"

Duchess interceded, "I've heard enough, Gregory. No need to push the envelope here."

Pharr nodded, a subtle indication that to ignore his guidance was to jeopardize the Agency's targeted killing program in its entirety, then took his seat.

Then Duchess turned her attention to the woman seated beside her: Jo

Ann Brown, an active-duty lieutenant commander in the Navy and the head military liaison to Project Longwing.

"And what say you, Jo Ann?"

The Wisconsin native shifted in her seat, crossing her legs as she replied, "I think it's got 'clean kill' written all over it so long as we get PID. This has potential to be the first no-strings mission success for our team. But that's only if Usman is traveling with light security."

"Which is possible, given that he needs to maintain a low profile in government-controlled areas."

"Possible," Jo Ann agreed, "but I don't see it. If Usman is conducting an attack it's going to be something big, and that means he's traveling with his troops. So my concern is whether David has the restraint to call off the hit if he finds himself vastly outnumbered. In the past, he's demonstrated an affinity for biting off more than he can chew, and then choking on it."

"Don't I know it," Duchess muttered, then picked up her hand mic to transmit.

"Suicide Actual, this will have to be a mobile vehicle interdiction. My staff will prepare a target packet on the stretch of highway in question. Be advised, I require one vehicle to follow Usman out of Bauchi so we can correlate a team tracker with his cell phone for PID. Then, and only then, will I transmit approval for the kill."

After pausing to take a final breath, she concluded, "Until then, you are cleared to relocate your team to the vicinity of Jos."

5

I watched the headlights crossing the two-lane highway beyond my windshield, the view partially obscured by the patch of trees we'd backed our vehicle into.

Keying my command radio, I said, "Raptor Nine One, this is Suicide Actual. Comms check."

This ostensibly routine procedure was, in this case, code for *do you have a fucking update for me?*

That particular detail wasn't lost on Duchess, who responded in kind, "*Have you loud and clear. When I have an update, you'll know—Usman hasn't activated his cell phone.*"

"Copy. Standing by."

I released my transmit button and breathed a long sigh. We'd staged at nightfall and remained in place for over an hour, and I was growing more uncomfortable with each passing minute.

Behind the wheel of our stationary truck, Reilly looked over and asked, "Why should it be Worthy? I've always wanted to do a PIT maneuver."

"We all did them," Ian pointed out from the backseat, "in our last driving course."

"But that's not real world stuff, man."

I turned to face him in the darkness.

"Worthy's got the most tactical mobility experience. He was a shoo-in. And take it easy, you'll still be in on the demolition derby—"

"As a backup." He shook his head sadly and repeated, "I've always wanted to do a PIT maneuver."

Behind me, Ian said, "At least you got to drive. The backseats in this thing are like asphalt."

Practically every other vehicle we'd seen in Nigeria was some flavor of Toyota, and it was no surprise that the humble Agency fleet we had access to included a selection of Camrys, Highlanders, and 4Runners.

We'd selected the SUV option for tonight's operation, with me, Reilly, and Ian making up the primary assault force. Worthy was behind the wheel of a second 4Runner with Cancer riding shotgun, and they held the unenviable task of following Usman out of Bauchi to achieve positive identification. Once that occurred, my truck would pick up their trail. When Usman was ripe for the picking on the open road, we'd use the same procedure that police used to end high-speed chases.

Worthy would employ a maneuver known as the PIT—pursuit intervention technique—to ram Usman's vehicle into a spin. Then Worthy would pin the target car from one end, while my 4Runner did the same from the opposite side; after that, it was a matter of everyone bailing out and opening fire. In the best-case scenario, the entire takedown would last sixty to ninety seconds.

And in the worst-case scenario, Usman would be traveling with too much security for us to risk engaging him.

Until we found out either way, I felt vaguely troubled that we didn't have Tolu present. Nigeria spoke over 500 languages, and while the official one was English, we were in a sufficiently rural area to make that assurance questionable if we encountered any locals.

But expats were generally not harassed by police, and ultimately I'd made the decision to have Tolu stage in the media van outside Zaranda, a highway town to our southwest. That provided us enough flexibility to exfil the team in the event one or both of our interdiction vehicles was disabled, and given the fact that no one had so much glanced in our direction since we'd been staged, I was feeling fairly good about that choice, if nothing else about this situation.

Before I could ponder that thought any further, Duchess transmitted in an urgent tone.

"*Usman is on the move—he's already on the A3 Highway west of Bauchi, now passing through the town of Miri.*"

Worthy keyed the ignition of his 4Runner before David had finished speaking his transmission.

"*Racegun, get moving—he's already in Miri, headed west. You need to haul ass.*"

Cancer tossed his cigarette out the passenger window, rolling it up as Worthy racked the transmission into gear.

They peeled out of the hotel parking lot, whipping a right turn onto the highway and cutting off a passenger van before Worthy floored the accelerator. He registered Cancer adjusting the HK417 rifle from its barrel-down position between his legs, then consulting his phone as he responded to David over the team frequency.

"We're on the move. Are they going to relay the cell phone location or what? I don't see his tracker on my map."

"*She's working on it; should come through any second now.*"

A moment later, Cancer replied, "All right, I see it now—Jesus, this guy's already cleared Miri."

"*It's worse than that,*" David continued. "*There's a delay on the uplink, so depending on his rate of speed he could be a few hundred meters ahead of whatever you see on your phone.*"

Cancer said to Worthy, "You don't step on it, he's going to pass David's truck before we get to him."

"I am stepping on it," Worthy said, "and I thought he was supposed to turn on his phone before he left Bauchi."

"What's life without a few surprises? Looks like he's four klicks ahead of us, passing through Dungel."

The speedometer needle glided past 145 kilometers per hour, and Worthy whipped into the oncoming lane to pass a commuter van. Traffic was sparse at this hour of night, and Worthy weaved his way around a slow-moving pickup as his 4Runner struggled to gain speed at the upper edges of its range.

He blazed through the highway towns of Miri and Dungel without issue, the clusters of roadside buildings a blur as he maneuvered past civilian vehicles. Then they were in the open savanna, the 4Runner's headlights flaring across clusters of trees and scrub brush. The highway was straight and the right lane clear, so Worthy pushed the truck as fast as it could go—the speedometer reached 170 kilometers per hour before hovering there, the engine maxed out with a steady roar as Cancer raised his voice to be heard.

"Less than a klick remaining—that must be him."

Worthy could see a glinting pair of red taillights ahead, but just barely. He eased off the accelerator, letting the vehicle coast the remaining distance until he was thirty meters off the rear bumper.

Cancer looked from the windshield to his phone, then said, "Looking good so far. Just creep up slow—we need to be within five meters."

Worthy eased forward, holding steady at the appointed range.

Cancer transmitted, "We're inside the bubble of an old Range Rover. This has got to be Usman, request positive identification."

"*Stand by,*" David replied.

Worthy said, "She better confirm fast so we can back off. Otherwise we're going to spook him."

But David's next transmission was, "*Negative on the match—it's not him.*"

"It has to be," Cancer objected. "We're right on top of his signal."

David replied, "*We're seeing a longer transmitting delay than the Agency is. Just pass him and keep going.*"

Worthy accelerated toward the truck's bumper, then pulled into the left lane to pass.

Then something strange happened—the Range Rover pulled left, blocking Worthy's advance. He braked and swung back into the right lane, trying to get around the vehicle, and the process repeated.

Cancer readied his rifle and said, "It's either a dickhead civilian or part of Usman's convoy. Either way, PIT his ass off the road."

Worthy began doing just that, accelerating toward the rear quarter panel of the Range Rover. This time, the SUV didn't try to block his path;

instead, the passenger side windows rolled down in unison and a rifle barrel emerged.

The muzzle flashed as Worthy braked hard, narrowly avoiding a close-range burst of automatic gunfire.

Cancer brought the stock of his suppressed HK417 rifle over his shoulder, then drove the barrel forward and fired three rounds.

The trio of bullets ejected a cloud of glass dust inside the vehicle and blasted a hole through the windshield. Cancer punched his suppressor through the opening, using his next six rounds to blast at the rear window in the hopes of killing the driver.

Worthy transmitted, "Shots fired; the truck is engaging us."

David replied, *"Can you take them?"*

"Cancer's trying to figure that out right now, boss."

As he fired his next volley of rounds at the swerving Range Rover, Cancer's chest was flung forward against the seatbelt. Worthy was braking to avoid a collision—the enemy vehicle was cutting left and right across both lanes, preventing them from passing while simultaneously providing firing angles for the men now aiming out windows on both sides.

Cancer kept his feet pinned against the floorboard, using his legs to brace himself against the seat back as he fired controlled pairs at anything he could—enemy fighters when they were visible and, barring that, in the direction of the driver. His accuracy was complicated by Worthy careening the 4Runner to counter the Range Rover's curving turns, trying to remain behind the rear bumper to prevent them from scoring a direct hit.

The enemy's return fire consisted of wild automatic bursts whenever they caught sight of the 4Runner, and Cancer heard the ominous *thunk* of sporadic rounds punching through the vehicle skin. He continued engaging the best he could, conducting a reload before firing again.

With two car lengths between the vehicles, Cancer could tell this was a losing proposition. If he hadn't scored a shot against the driver with his first 20-round magazine, he likely never would. He called out to Worthy in a strained voice, "Get in the right lane and slow down—see if they keep rolling."

Worthy complied, but as he began braking, so too did the Range Rover, which continued its curving path across both lanes as shooters on either side of the vehicle fired backward.

Cancer heard an audible popping sound that preceded Worthy swerving in the road, and he checked the instrument cluster before announcing, "They hit a tire."

"Run flats should hold for a few dozen miles," Cancer shouted back, firing a three-round volley as wind whistled through the broken glass.

But the 4Runner struggled to maintain speed, becoming less maneuverable as the Range Rover slowed for another firing run. Cancer knew what he had to do; still, even under the present circumstances, he felt a tinge of resentment as he keyed his mic and transmitted.

"We're decisively engaged. Need backup."

"*Copy,*" David replied without hesitation. "*We're on the way.*"

Reilly sped out of his hiding place among the trees, swinging left onto the highway and gunning the engine to full speed.

From the backseat, Ian said, "If we move to support, Usman will get away."

David answered, "Remember the last time Cancer asked for backup?"

"No."

"Yeah, me neither. If he's calling for us, then things have really gone to shit. Ian, try to get some vehicle makes and models from the westbound lane—one of them is Usman."

"What?" he shot back, incredulous. "All I can see are headlights, same as you."

"Well, you're the intelligence guy, not me. Figure something out." The vehicle's speed turned the oncoming headlights into shooting stars in the darkness by the time David transmitted, "Racegun, can you get them to slow down?"

Worthy's response was strained with the effort of steering while under fire. "*Yeah, if we slow down, they do too—they're running a blocking maneuver on top of a spray-and-pray.*"

"Perfect," David continued. "Once we have visual I want you to cease fire and slow down as much as possible. Then we're going to give them the surprise of a lifetime—same plan as before, but we'll swap tasks for each vehicle."

Reilly muttered, "It's not really a PIT maneuver, though, if we're approaching from the front—"

"You want to ram the truck or not?" David testily replied, then transmitted to the other team truck. "After we hit them from the side, box them in and dismount. Duchess says Usman isn't in that truck, but we're not taking any chances. Total annihilation, no survivors, full site exploitation."

Then and only then did he transmit to Duchess, a conversation that Reilly could only hear one side of.

"Raptor Nine One, Suicide Actual," David began. "Be advised, our trail element out of Bauchi is decisively engaged by what I assess to be a rear security element of Usman's convoy. My truck is moving to their location on an urgent call for backup, over."

Duchess's response was a mystery to everyone in the vehicle but David, and a few seconds later, he transmitted, "I'm not hanging two of my men out to dry over a chance to get Usman. We were supposed to let them pass if they had too much security; well, I'm telling you they *do* have too much security, and your PID criteria forced us to find out the hard way. Going off comms until the situation is resolved, over."

Swerving ahead of a Mercedes sedan, Reilly commented, "She's not going to like that, bro."

David backhanded him across the arm.

"Focus. I want that enemy truck spinning so hard that everyone inside is in a coma by the time we get around to blowing their heads off."

Reilly heard the tinny *click* of Ian putting on his seatbelt and answered, "Don't worry, boss. They'll be brain-dead by the time I'm done with them."

His team leader didn't respond, instead flicking his gaze from the phone in his palm to the road ahead. Then he said, "Should be within a klick—"

"There they are." Reilly nodded to the twin sets of headlights coming toward them, both careening from one side of the road to the other.

David transmitted, "Racegun, Cancer, hold your fire—we have eyes-on."

Reilly decelerated his 4Runner from the upper limits of its speed in anticipation of the coming impact. Every second counted now as they proceeded within five hundred meters of the oncoming Range Rover, then four hundred meters, and Reilly gauged the distance by the spread of oncoming headlights before finally braking hard and swinging his truck across the lane divider.

The Range Rover swerved too late to avoid the strike, and the bumper of Reilly's 4Runner smashed into its rear quarter panel as the medic maintained acceleration, causing the enemy vehicle's rear tires to lose traction and sending it into a skidding flat spin.

Then it was gone from view, reduced to a circling blare of headlights in his rearview as Reilly spun his steering wheel hard left to miss a patch of trees beside the highway. Hitting the gas, he steered his 4Runner back toward the highway to see the outcome of his impact—the Range Rover was now stationary and facing the opposite direction. He accelerated up to its rear bumper before slamming on the brakes and coming to a full halt so the enemy vehicle couldn't reverse.

David was scrambling out of the passenger side by the time Reilly detached his seatbelt and, with the enemy vehicle blocking his door, clambered over the console. He was halfway through the maneuver when he felt the thud of Worthy and Cancer's vehicle slamming into the Range Rover's front end, boxing the enemy vehicle in for the coup de grace.

I leapt out of the 4Runner, rounding the hood to assume a perpendicular angle on the stationary Range Rover. Ordinarily I'd have preferred to take cover behind an engine block, but the danger now was friendly fire more than enemy contact—the enemy wasn't shooting at present, their disorientation evidenced by the slow, groggy movement of human silhouettes dimly lit by the ambient headlights.

Coming to a stop between the driver and passenger doors, I heard men skidding to shooting positions beside me—Ian and Reilly to my left, Cancer and Worthy to my right—and by the time I activated the red laser on my weapon, it was one of five gleaming across the Range Rover's interior.

My team opened fire in unison, blasting subsonic bullets into the enemy vehicle from front to rear and rear to front, our lasers crossing over one another. I let the melee continue for a few seconds longer than necessary before shouting, "Cease fire!"

We descended upon the Range Rover, ripping the doors open and pulling bodies onto the highway. Any minute now we'd have civilian traffic bearing down on us, and the hasty search consisted of little more than confiscating cell phones as Ian photographed faces of the dead in the hopes that one could be confirmed as a high-ranking Boko Haram official, if not Usman himself.

That latter hope was dashed when Ian announced, "He's not here."

The emotion that ran through me at that point was somewhere between exhilaration that everyone on my team had survived the encounter and crushing defeat that we'd failed our tactical mission. But Cancer and Worthy had survived a potentially fatal engagement, and that counted for something.

At that moment, Cancer approached me and said, "Boss, one of our run flats got shot out."

"Make it as far back to Abuja as we can before changing it," I replied, scanning his vehicle to see the cluster of bullet holes on the glass. "And take care of that windshield."

Cancer and Worthy did the latter remarkably fast, using their rifle butts to smash the pane of laminated safety glass and tossing the excess in the back of their truck. In Nigeria, having no windshield at all was far less conspicuous than one shattered by bullets. We left the enemy weapons in place—the last thing we needed was for anyone to think we shot up a carful of civilians—and my team was back aboard their respective trucks within seconds of my exfil order.

I slid back into the passenger seat, transmitting my update to Duchess as Reilly pulled away from the wreckage of the enemy truck.

"Raptor Nine One, engagement complete with four EKIA, no friendly casualties. We're headed westbound on Highway A3 at this time, moving to pick up the tail on Usman and determine the make and model of a vehicle in the convoy for interdiction by Nigerian authorities. How copy?"

I expected Duchess's reply to be conciliatory if not elated—despite the unexpected development, my team was still in the fight, and if we couldn't kill Usman, then the Nigerian government could, at a minimum, capture him on their own turf.

But her response sounded disappointed, forgoing the radio protocol of callsigns.

She said, "*Negative, return to your safehouse as soon as possible. You must not be looking at your phone.*"

"I'm pulling away from a murder scene on the other side of the world, so no, I haven't checked," I responded, fumbling for my Android.

My effort was halted when Duchess replied, "*The enemy you killed didn't just block your attempt; they reported your interference.*"

Before I could pull up the map on my phone, she continued, "*Usman is in the wind. His cell phone signal went dark.*"

6

Morning sunlight streamed through the safehouse windows as Ian sipped his coffee, watching the team leader seated at the desk beside him.

David looked pensive, uncertain—and though neither man said it, he had good reason to be. As the minutes ticked down to eight a.m., both men alternated between watching the silent desk phone and engaging in sporadic bouts of conjecture.

Sensing Ian's eyes upon him, David looked up and asked, "You're sure about Usman?"

"Yes," Ian said, "I am. Think about it: if you're a terrorist leader traveling in a convoy, the rear security says they're taking fire and then goes off the grid, what would you do?"

David's shoulders sank. "Assume my cell phone is compromised, kill it, and continue the mission."

"And that's exactly what Usman did. The question now is, what's going to happen when Duchess calls?"

The team leader drew a long breath. "Well, since it's Duchess we're talking about here, I'm assuming she's going to be pissed."

Ian set down his mug and conceded, "That's a good assumption, but don't place all the blame on her. She's got her own oversight to worry about, and from their optic we had a lethal confrontation with a few foot soldiers at the cost of one Agency vehicle and a very near compromise of the entire mission."

"Well that's, like, your opinion, man."

Ian checked his watch. "Any minute now, you'll see that I'm right. What I can't predict is what our marching orders will be."

"Marching orders?" David said incredulously. "We continue the mission."

Ian wasn't sure how to respond to that—whether David was being naive or ignorant, the intelligence operative couldn't say. It wasn't that the mission itself was particularly sensitive; they were in a permissive area where a group of white men could roam more or less freely, which was a far cry from their last operation in China four months earlier.

But the previous night's outcome was far from ideal, and the team was only one small cog in a very large and extremely politically sensitive machine. The US didn't take targeted killings lightly, and his nation's experience in that endeavor was a spotted and inflammatory history in contrast to Israel, for which such operations were more or less a way of life and had been since the country's inception.

So Ian said nothing, instead waiting for the inevitable—and within ten seconds of muted silence, the desk phone rang.

David inhaled deeply, readying himself for whatever was about to occur. By the second ring, Ian said, "You going to pick that up?"

Instead, the team leader pressed a button to take the call on speakerphone.

"This is David. I've got you on speaker with Ian."

Duchess was quiet for a moment, then said, "Fair enough. I've got you on speaker with the entire OPCEN staff. How are your men doing?"

"We're good," David replied. "No injuries, we're refitted, and our local driver took the damaged vehicle to a friend who runs a chop shop in Abuja. It should be mission-ready within a few days, and my team has conducted refit and are prepared to flex as soon as our target surfaces. Since I haven't heard from you prior to our scheduled call, I'm guessing that hasn't occurred yet."

She replied, "We notified the Nigerian government of Usman's convoy —they claimed they'd set up some checkpoints to intercept him, but since he's still at large, that clearly didn't occur as planned. The only feedback thus far is their announcement that the Nigerian police killed four Boko Haram fighters on Highway A3 last night."

David snickered. "We saw that in the news. At least someone got to take that gunfight for a victory lap."

"Concur," Duchess said wearily. "But that's probably our last point of agreement on this call."

"What's that supposed to mean?"

"I have orders to pull your team out of Nigeria. Your main body personnel will link transport all military hardware to the dock site at 2100 West Africa Standard Time tomorrow. Advance party will fly commercial out of Abuja the following morning—"

David slammed a fist on the desk. "We did *everything* you asked us to do. Following your PID requirements shouldn't be grounds to boot us off the mission."

Ian put a hand on David's shoulder, an attempt to calm him that went unnoticed as Duchess calmly responded.

"And there's little question that Usman is orchestrating a terrorist attack-in-progress. I'm not disagreeing with you, David. The decision wasn't mine to make."

"Then whose was it?"

"People above my pay grade."

Ian leaned forward. "Duchess, I understand the concern. But an imminent attack is all the more reason we should remain in Nigeria. At a minimum, get us authorized for a 72-hour holding pattern. If Usman hasn't surfaced by then, we'll go."

Her voice remained placid as she said, "It's *because* of the probable attack that you need to go. We've had to provide the Nigerian government multiple warnings of Usman's movements. If he's suddenly found dead, it points the blame back on the Agency."

"Behind closed doors, sure," Ian replied. "But the news this morning is proof that the Nigerian government will gladly take credit for Usman's death."

"The Nigerian government has more leaks than a wicker canoe. When the media comes looking for facts—and they will—some official will sell them fact-based speculation. And the current administration is unwilling to risk that."

David interceded, "We weren't sent here by accident. After the July 4th attack, you followed the money trail to a banker in Abuja. Let us go after him, at the very least."

"You are not authorized to take *any* action against that banker," Duchess replied hotly, "and I won't divulge his identity until that changes, which it won't. Usman's sudden movement into government-controlled territory wasn't your fault. Neither was last night, so don't turn this into grounds for disbandment. Start packing your bags, gentlemen: it's time to come home."

The team leader opened his mouth to respond, but it was too late—Duchess had ended the call.

Cancer spoke from the doorway behind them.

"Ian, you thinking what I'm thinking?"

Both men spun their chairs to face him. Ian shook his head and David searched Cancer's face for insight as the sniper clarified, "Two words: Gateway Zuma."

Rolling his eyes, Ian turned back to the desk.

David asked, "What the hell is that?"

"A restaurant," Ian explained, lifting his coffee mug from the desk. "It's in downtown Abuja. Before you guys got here, Tolu took me and Cancer."

David shot back indignantly, "How can you think about eating right now?"

But Cancer was unrepentant.

"Because everyone's tired after last night and we're getting kicked out of Nigeria, for starters. But mainly," he concluded, "because the food was amazing."

Ian, nearly cringing in anticipation, knew what David's response would be—the team leader was going to go off on some knee-jerk tangent objecting to Duchess's order, then propose some harebrained scheme that Ian would have to temper with the cold facts of reality, hopefully aided by Cancer. If there was one thing David was remarkably consistent about, it was having a problem with authority; particularly, Ian thought, when it pertained to hampering his team's operational leeway.

And David, for his part, didn't disappoint.

"Forget the restaurant. That banker is the reason we scored the Nigeria mission in the first place. That gives us"—he checked his watch—"about 36 hours to do a little detective work and figure out who he is."

Cancer responded before Ian could.

"Hundreds of bankers in Abuja, boss, if not a thousand or more. I don't care if we have 36 hours or 36 days, it ain't gonna happen. Let's eat."

7

Worthy entered Gateway Zuma to find the restaurant's massive interior nearly filled by eleven a.m., a solid indicator that whatever they were about to eat, it was going to be good.

The interior boasted high ceilings and tall windows overlooking a crystalline blue pool that was lined with palm trees and outdoor seating areas. Inside tables were well-spaced between potted ferns and leather couches, exuding a nightclub setting, and the white-aproned wait staff delivered trays overflowing with food.

As soon as they entered, Tolu made a move to leave. "Where are you going?" David asked. "Have lunch with us."

The driver slapped David on the shoulder and said, "You men have things to discuss, brother. Besides this, drivers eat together at the bar. This is custom."

Then Tolu departed, making his way to the bar as a hostess led the team to an open table overlooking the pool.

They took their seats, and Worthy found himself sitting across from an enormous framed painting of what appeared to be a rounded hill of dirt. He squinted at it, then asked, "Why's there artwork of a termite mound?"

Ian glanced over his shoulder to see what Worthy was looking at, then raised his eyebrows and replied, "That's Zuma Rock, just west of the city.

Nigeria's most iconic landmark. It's a thousand feet high and takes five hours to climb—not exactly a 'termite mound.'"

Reilly was oblivious to the proceedings, his eyes fixed on the menu as he asked Cancer, "What's good here?"

David replied, "If the Niger River was any indication, I'd stay away from the seafood."

Before Cancer could respond, a waiter appeared and, without taking his eyes off the notepad in his hand, asked gruffly, "What do you want to drink?"

Worthy was somewhat alarmed by this rude introduction, and to his surprise, Cancer of all people took the comment in stride, smiling at the waiter and replying, "We're Americans."

The waiter's expression brightened. "Of course. For a party of your size, may I recommend our off-menu chef's special: a platter of Nigerian specialties including Garri, Gala sausage rolls, Suya, Isi Ewu, and fufu with plantain and crushed cassava. More meat and vegetables than six people could eat, along with a selection of four traditional soups and Jollof rice."

"Sold." Reilly slapped his menu shut. "Let's do that. And a round of beers, please. Your best local brew."

The waiter collected their menus and left, and Worthy waited until he was out of earshot before asking, "Why was that guy a dick until he found out we were American?"

Ian explained, "He assumed we were British, and Nigerians aren't big on colonialism. They even switched to driving on the right side of the road after gaining their independence."

"Good for them," Reilly remarked. "Limey bastards."

The beer arrived in record time, delivered by a female server balancing the uncapped green bottles on a tray. She set one before each man, and with a word of thanks, Worthy lifted his to find that it was ice cold, the blue label bearing a gold star and a lager designation.

After the server left, he hoisted his bottle over the center of the table and said, "Gents."

The team clanked their beers against his, then took the first sip in unison.

David was brooding, looking sullen as he took a second long pull from his bottle.

Worthy asked, "What's eating you, boss?"

"Oh, I don't know," David said. "Maybe the fact that we're getting sent home after losing Usman."

Cancer offered a rare comment of consolation, waving his hand dismissively. "Don't beat yourself up too bad. We're five guys; the entire Nigerian government wasn't able to catch Usman when Duchess handed them his convoy on a silver platter."

"Yeah," Reilly muttered. "And now a lot of Nigerians are probably going to die because of that."

Worthy frowned, the aftertaste of beer turning bitter in his mouth. "I'm not disagreeing with you, but Usman was never the real issue—whoever conducted the July 4th attack was. The money trail led to Nigeria, so Duchess picked the only target here she could in the hopes that we'd find some intel along the way."

Ian raised his eyebrows at the point man and set down his beer. "What makes you think Usman isn't tied to the big picture?"

"How could he be?"

"I'm not sure," Ian allowed, "but if you think Duchess is telling us everything she knows, you're out of your mind. I wouldn't be surprised if her target selection wasn't as random as she'd have us believe."

For once, the presence of alcohol didn't improve David's mood in the slightest. He replied, "But her decisions are only as good as the intel she's getting, and we have no idea what 99 percent of that consists of. Where's she getting it from, and how accurate is it?"

Ian gave a sigh of resignation. "Hell if I know."

"What about you?" Worthy asked Cancer. "You seem to be way too comfortable about cutting slingload on Usman."

The sniper considered the comment, then answered, "I'm not any happier about it than the rest of you."

Reilly noted, "You don't seem to be bothered, either."

Cancer rolled his eyes. "Let's not pretend this is any different than the military. Doesn't matter who we're working for; we're soldiers. That means we go where they tell us to go, and do what they tell us to do. You guys are overthinking this."

Ian took on an accusatory tone as he said, "You're *under*thinking it. Everything we've done so far has taken us one step closer to a larger terrorist conspiracy—the real people behind the July 4th attack. Nigeria was the only lead we had left, and make no mistake, now that the mission's aborted we've lost it for good."

"Not for good," Worthy corrected him. "Erik Weisz will rear his ugly head again. But when he does, it might be another attack on US soil. I'd say that's pretty good reason for us to be concerned about pulling out of here tomorrow."

"Heads up," David said quietly, cutting his eyes to the door.

Both the team leader's tone and subtlety matched what most men reserved for the sudden appearance of an attractive woman, or several attractive women; but that had never been at the forefront of David's agenda, and Worthy glanced over to find his explanation.

A group of white men were entering the restaurant—they wore suits, though that was the only commonality linking two otherwise distinct subgroups in their party.

Two of them were slight of build, moving within the perimeter of four bulky men who Worthy could identify at a glance as bodyguards— earpieces, suit jackets unbuttoned and clearly worn over sidearms, scanning the crowd as they moved. He momentarily wondered if his team had somehow had the ill fate to end up sitting beside some VIPs from the US Embassy.

But he quickly dismissed the notion as a waitress approached the empty table before they were even seated, delivering a pair of shot glasses and filling them from a bottle of vodka that she took with her as she left.

Worthy looked back to the men, seeing the bodyguards moving in a four-man wedge formation: one man in the lead, and two spread out in the rear. The two principals were within that triangle, flanked by the remaining bodyguard—the shift leader, Worthy knew, who was the most senior and in charge of the security detail.

Reilly observed, "Not half bad."

Worthy gave a slight shake of his head as he watched the men approach on their way to the table.

"Shift lead doesn't trust his guys—he's paying more attention to the diners than his own formation."

Cancer seemed concerned only with his ability to kill the principals, noting after another second of evaluation, "We could take them."

As if he'd heard the comment, the last bodyguard in the procession happened to clip the toe of his shoe on the leg of Cancer's chair. Whether the move was accidental or an intentional response to the team's more than casual observation of the bodyguard procedures, Worthy couldn't be sure. But he cringed nonetheless, keenly aware that he'd never met anyone so eager to incite conflict as the teammate who'd just been provoked.

Cancer, for his part, didn't disappoint. Looking over his shoulder, he said, "Watch where you're going, asshole."

The bodyguard stopped abruptly and turned to face him. "What did you say to me?" he asked in a thick Russian accent.

It was less a question than a threat, and given his size, one that would probably make most men on the planet mutter an apology. But Cancer wasn't most men, and he draped an arm across the back of his chair and clarified, quite casually, "I said watch where you're putting your size thirteens before I take this chair and break it over your face."

The Russian took a step forward, an action that caused Cancer to stand and with him the entire team, each ready to intervene in the upcoming brawl. At the instant this occurred, the bodyguard seemed to forget about Cancer altogether; his focus was drawn to sizing up Reilly, by far the largest member of the opposition. There wasn't much of a disparity in terms of muscle mass, but Reilly stood perhaps an inch taller than his Russian counterpart, and that miniscule difference was exacerbated by the cool confidence with which the medic approached, his smiling eyes imparting a silent dare for the bodyguard to go ahead and try throwing the first punch.

To Worthy's surprise, Ian pushed his way between the two men and said, "*Bez problem, drug moy. Pozvol' mne kupit' tvoim druz'yam raund.*"

The intelligence operative snapped his fingers at the waiter, who was standing at a distance, watching the scene unfold with wide eyes. Then Ian pointed to the table of Russians and said, "Another round for my friends, please. On my tab."

The burly Russian remained focused on Reilly; then, determining that discretion was indeed the better part of valor, he broke eye contact with the medic to give Ian a nod before departing.

Cancer turned to Ian with disgust. "Well look at the happy little diplomat. What's the matter, you don't feel like throwing down?"

"Have a seat," Ian said firmly, finding his chair as the team returned to their places at the table.

Worthy narrowed his eyes at Ian. "I didn't know you spoke Russian."

"A little bit."

"So," Worthy asked, "who are those guys?"

Lowering his voice, Ian replied, "The guys at the main table are oil executives from a company called Gradsek. They've got onshore and offshore drilling operations. With all the multinational oil companies pulling out of Nigeria, Gradsek has been acquiring market share. They've got a lot of economic and political pull around here, and are too high profile for us to be messing with. It's not worth it."

"Yeah?" David asked. "What about the four gorillas they brought with them?"

"Chalk them up as the only reason why Gradsek can continue expanding—Nigeria produces two million barrels of oil every day, and 300,000 of them are illegally siphoned. Then you've got pirates and vigilante groups hitting the oil companies however they can, on top of prices per barrel falling almost every year. Private security is the only reason there's any foreign investment left in Nigeria."

Ian sighed and turned up his hands. "So they're assholes, yeah. But necessary assholes."

8

Duchess strode down the hall at a determined gait, narrowing the distance between her office and the OPCEN as a pair of staffers jogged past her on the way back to their workstations. Her duty staff had been reduced to a skeleton crew overnight; after all, there was no need for everyone to be present with the Nigeria operation officially being shut down. But the one a.m. call with a single brevity code—*Lovelace*, shorthand for "all personnel required"—had resulted in a full spin-up that was still in progress.

She watched the staffers run past, resisting the urge to match their pace. No one wanted to see the boss moving at a panicked run, a lesson she'd learned over and over in her many years at the Agency. When the winds were changing, it paid to be viewed as the center of the storm. The very fact that she'd been selected to head the fledgling Project Longwing was testament to her career to date—they needed someone who wasn't afraid to play in the mud, someone possessing both the operational experience to lead and the expendability to be cut loose if this preliminary foray into targeted killing went politically awry. And given Project Longwing's short and inordinately volatile history, that latter eventuality had very nearly come to pass several times already.

But the call summoning her back to the OPCEN brought with it the certainty that after two years of her program operating in the shadows, she was about to be thrust into the political limelight whether she wanted it or not.

She badged herself into the OPCEN to see the newly arriving staff getting hasty backbriefs by their colleagues. Jo Ann was already seated at her desk, feverishly typing an encrypted chat exchange with, Duchess presumed, the Joint Special Operations Command. Lucios was also at his station, and Duchess called out to him as she approached her seat.

"J2, what do we have?"

The intelligence officer didn't shift his eyes from the computer screen before him. "ExxonMobil got hit last night in Lagos—three security guards killed, six oil executives kidnapped. All Americans."

She lowered herself into the chair, considering this for a moment before asking, "Location of the hostages?"

"Unknown." He turned to face her. "No one's claimed responsibility yet, and the media is assuming this is the work of pirates or a vigilante group such as the Niger Delta Avengers. Both have kidnapped extensively for ransom in the past."

"And your assessment?"

"The scope and planning of this attack exceed what either group is historically capable of. That being said, Lagos is well outside Boko Haram's area of influence, so if they are responsible, this indicates a major shift in their tactics. But given what we know of Usman's movements over the past 48 hours, I simply can't believe this is a coincidence."

Duchess leaned back in her chair. Any minute now, her phone would ring with someone wanting answers—and with a dearth of assets in West Africa, her tactical command of a five-man ground team was about to catapult Project Longwing into the bleeding edge of US response.

Choosing her words carefully, she said, "If this is the work of pirates or vigilantes, the hostages will remain in the delta and the Nigerian government can lock that area down."

"Concur."

"But if this is the work of Boko Haram—and I agree, that's perhaps not such a big 'if'—I think it's safe to assume the hostages would be moved north, back into terrorist-held ground."

Lucios nodded without speaking.

"And if that's the case," Duchess continued, "where would they go?"

Lucios blinked, consulting his computer screen and tapping the mouse to pull up a report. "We've had two independent human source reports in the last twelve hours indicating a buildup of Boko Haram forces in the Sambisa Forest. It covers thousands of square miles, contains an unknown number of terrorist camps, and Boko Haram has taken captives there before—most notably some of the Chibok schoolgirls."

"Do you have a specific location?"

"I do, ma'am. Well, sort of—one of the reports referenced Location Mijad, which I cross-referenced against an old SIGINT hit. I've got a grid, but no further means to corroborate the validity. And even if—"

Before he could finish the thought, Duchess's desk phone rang.

Holding up a finger to silence Lucios, she lifted the phone to her ear and said, "Duchess."

"This is Senator Gossweiler. I need everything you have on the situation in Lagos."

Given the late hour, this was a remarkably swift response from the chair of the Senate Select Committee on Intelligence, but as the main political oversight to Project Longwing, particularly with a team in a country with a late-breaking hostage crisis, Duchess knew she wasn't the only one being pressed for answers.

She replied, "Senator, based on the recent movements of Usman Mokhammed, we believe this may be a Boko Haram operation. If that's the case, there's little doubt the hostages will be moved to the northeastern portion of the country."

"What's the military response?"

Duchess looked to Jo Ann, who had already tilted her computer screen in anticipation of the inquiry. Scanning the information, she replied, "A Delta troop plus enablers is standing by to forward-stage in Germany, with a full suite of JSOC intelligence assets ready to go wheels-up provided they get approval."

"They'll get the approval," Gossweiler replied. "It's in the works as we speak. How long until they're boots on the ground inside Nigeria?"

"At a minimum, sir, we can plan on 24 hours to arrive, and 36 to 48 hours before they're set to take action."

"Why so long?"

Clearly, Duchess thought, the senator was unaccustomed to the tyranny of distance as it pertained to Africa. Since the equator shrank on global projections, most people assumed Africa to be far smaller than it actually was; the true size was larger than the US, China, Japan, Mexico, Europe, and India combined. Somalia's coastline alone was as long as the entire eastern seaboard.

But she wasn't about to explain that to him, and sided with a hollow platitude instead.

"Travel time for personnel aside, Senator, the surveillance aircraft they'll require to do their job will have to make a long multi-leg journey, even if we can reroute some from the Middle East. And there's very little Allied presence in West Africa, so our intelligence assets will have to start their operation from scratch."

"Not from scratch," he corrected her. "Your team is already in-country. Now how can we put them in play?"

Well, Duchess thought cynically, they weren't an intelligence asset at all, but a paramilitary one. In truth, they were little more than a kill team to be sent only after a vast intel effort had pinpointed a target location, and even if she knew exactly where the hostages were at that moment, it would take a hell of a lot more than five men to overcome an enemy force in possession of six hostages—at least if any of those hostages were to make it out alive.

Still, if she could parlay this situation with Gossweiler, she could keep her team on the ground and in the hunt for Usman. Given that she was less than a day removed from being ordered to send them stateside, that was no small victory.

She said, "Senator, we received corroborated intelligence of a location that is being reinforced by Boko Haram personnel. It's in the Sambisa Forest, which is within enemy-held territory and about as remote as Boko Haram can get for hiding American detainees. With your permission, I recommend retasking our Longwing team to that area to conduct a recon effort. Given the imminent arrival of JSOC assets, that's the best use of the team given the situation. It'd be a stretch of their charter, but—"

"Forget the charter," he snapped. "The administration wants a full-court press—get them moving."

9

Reilly's first shout sounded distant, his voice distorted as it echoed through the safehouse walls.

"All hands on deck!"

The second time he shouted the words, I was reasonably confident I wasn't dreaming. Blinking my eyes open and sitting up, I saw the room was largely dark—sunrise had yet to arrive in full, and I checked my watch to see that it was just past six in the morning.

Reilly burst into my room a moment later, speaking breathlessly.

"Duchess on the line for you, boss."

Sliding out of bed, I asked, "What for?"

"Dunno. She said to spin up the whole team, though. It's something urgent."

I followed him into the hallway, moving quickly as the rest of our team emerged from their rooms and followed suit.

We met in our ad hoc operations center, the team converging in a mix of boxer shorts and T-shirts except for Cancer, who strolled in groggily in his old-man briefs.

Worthy was the first to speak.

"Usman must have surfaced."

"We've already been fired," I answered.

"Maybe someone had a change of heart."

Ian pushed his way through our ranks, taking a seat before the computer as I pulled up a chair in front of the conference phone whose blinking red light indicated Duchess was still waiting.

By the time I reached for the phone, I felt the team clustering in tight behind me. Ian opened the classified email along with a string of intelligence databases on the secure computer. Shifting to the next keyboard with surprising dexterity, he opened a series of browser tabs linked to open-source news websites as he spoke.

"We knew Usman left Gwoza to conduct an attack. Whatever that was, it's already occurred."

I tapped the button to put Duchess on speaker.

"David here," I said.

Duchess's voice held a measured tension as she replied, "Have you seen the news?"

Ian tapped my shoulder and nodded toward the unclassified computer monitor. A muted pair of news correspondents were engaged in a heated discussion, and the graphic in the corner of the screen showed a map of Africa with one country highlighted.

At the bottom of the screen, a blue banner read *BREAKING NEWS: ATTACK IN NIGERIA.*

"I'm looking at it now," I answered, analyzing the ticker feed scrolling across the bottom of the screen: *3 Americans dead in Lagos, 6 ExxonMobil executives missing.* Then I added dryly, "Does this mean we should stop packing?"

Duchess wasn't amused. "You're still packing, but not to come home. We've got a tip on a location in Sambisa Forest, and it's possible the hostages will be taken there. It's thin, but right now it's all we've got. I just sent over the grid."

I raised my eyebrows at Ian, who had received her message and plotted the point on our mission planning software. He thrust a finger at his screen to orient me, pointing to the far northeast border of the country, the sloped offshoot of Nigeria's boundaries almost entirely run by Boko Haram.

"Is that our destination?"

"It is now," she said. "I need you to get moving asap."

Cancer grabbed Reilly by the shoulder and whispered, "Start packing the van."

The medic departed as Cancer snatched a notepad and pen off the desk and began to scrawl something as Duchess continued, "You are tasked to conduct special reconnaissance and confirm or deny the presence of hostages at that location in advance of JSOC arrival in-country."

My stomach sank at the words.

On one hand, we'd gone from being forced out of Nigeria to becoming the lead element in an international hostage rescue effort.

But on the other, we were in no way equipped for a special reconnaissance operation. Our original mission had been a paramilitary incursion into a Boko Haram camp, an in-and-out affair to kill Usman in his sleep at a precise grid location.

Still, I responded quickly, falling back on the adage known to everyone in a leadership position for a ground team: when in doubt, feign confidence.

"We're on it," I said. "Will get moving and report back with an ETA."

Duchess sounded unimpressed. "I've got to feed the beast here at Langley. I need your ETA now."

I heaved a sigh, then said, "Wait one," and put the phone back on mute.

Ian spoke without prompting. "Driving route is twelve, maybe thirteen hours to the nearest dismount."

"We'll plan for thirteen," I said.

"So if we leave now, we can step off on foot around 2000—two hours after sunset."

"How long's the foot movement?"

Ian consulted his screen. "8.2 klicks straight-line distance. Worthy?"

The point man was leaning over Ian's back, staring at the screen. "What do we know about the Sambisa Forest?"

By now, Ian looked considerably more pale than he had at the start of the call. "It's a nightmare. Close to 40,000 square miles, who knows how many Boko Haram camps. It's their ultimate stronghold, very few roads, lots of hills, and between military bombings and failed raids, a hell of a lot of people have died there."

Cancer didn't seem to be listening, continuing to scrawl on the notepad in his hand. But Worthy was focused, his eyes darting across the satellite imagery as he concluded, "Minimum six hours to walk all but the last klick. After that it's anyone's guess on how long it'll take us to get eyes-on—enemy's going to get a say in that. But I'd say we can be one kilometer out from the camp by 0300 tomorrow."

This answer was satisfactory to me, but not to Cancer; as I reached forward to take the phone off mute, the sniper swatted my hand away.

"No way," he said. "We're not considering the equipment we need to get before we roll out."

I paused, trying to determine the best response. As a trained sniper, Cancer had more experience in reconnaissance than the rest of us put together.

"What do you suggest?"

"We go shopping. Spend two hours getting what we need, hit the forest by 2200, and have seven hours for a dismounted movement before the sun comes up again. Mark my words, getting the supplies we need will be the difference between a successful recon and us getting captured or killed."

"So what do we need?" I asked.

Cancer consulted the notepad.

"Sewing kits, fishing net, rope, lots of burlap, sandbags, zip lock bags, and tarps. Hand tools, some shovels and hacksaws. Plus scissors, shoe glue, spray paint, newspaper, tent stakes, lime, and binoculars. We'll have to split up to get it all."

Looking up from the pad, he concluded, "And that extra two hours puts us one klick out by 0500."

"All right," I said, reaching for the phone. "Any more objections, speak now or forever hold your peace."

When no one spoke, I tapped the button to take the call off mute.

"We can be boots on the ground in Sambisa by 2200, and be in proximity to the objective by zero-five. Expect to have visual on the camp sometime tomorrow afternoon."

Her reply was almost instant.

"My operations officer says you could be one klick out by 0300."

"Your operations officer," I said hotly, "isn't going eyeball-to-eyeball with Boko Haram. We came here for a surgical strike on Usman, not to crawl around one of the worst hotspots in Nigeria with a dagger in our teeth. I'm looking at a guy who's forgotten more about reconnaissance than I'll ever know, and we need to get the right supplies before we can head out. If he says zero-five, it's zero-five."

There was a long pause before she replied, "Understood. I'll send over all data on your objective along with hostage profiles and update en route. And David?"

"Yes?"

"There are a lot of eyes on this one. The hostages are from a private corporation, but I shouldn't have to tell you that US interests are clearly enmeshed with our oil supply abroad. That's to say nothing of our economic involvement serving as a stabilizing force in West Africa. The entire administration is taking the gloves off to get this resolved as quickly as possible. Whatever you do, don't screw this up."

10

Ian reached for a final section of black fishing net, the material cut two squares wide. Placing the end against a sleeve of the fatigue jacket in his lap, he began sewing the netting strip to the fabric.

There were, however, a few factors complicating the procedure.

First was the bouncing suspension of the media van as it cruised up the highway to Borno State, which bordered Chad and Cameroon on Nigeria's northeastern corner. Then there was the fact that Ian had—quite regrettably—left his headphones in the safehouse, thus subjecting himself to Tolu's never-ending soundtrack of rap music.

The final factor that had slowed Ian's otherwise fairly proficient sewing was addressed now by Worthy, who knelt in the far back of the van.

"On the plus side," he said in his Georgia drawl, "I've never gone into a mission high before."

The point man was only half-joking. Even with the driver and passenger windows rolled down and wind whipping through the cargo area, the smell of paint fumes was enough to make Ian loopy.

Their weapons were already painted mottled tan and brown as a matter of standard practice. But the rucksacks and tactical vests had to be modified on the fly, every exposed surface spray-painted with grass and leaf patterns as Worthy used paper overlays to complete the effect, consulting images of the Sambisa Forest that he'd prepared prior to their departure.

Sitting next to Ian, Cancer replied, "And you better hurry up and finish so that all has time to dry, otherwise they're going to smell us coming a mile away."

"Yeah," Reilly added. "Besides, if you could sew, you wouldn't be on spray paint duty in the first place."

Worthy completed another pass of spray paint over a rucksack, then peeled his patterned cutout off the surface.

"How would I know how to sew? How do any of you?"

Reilly shrugged. "I'm a medic, bro. Stitches."

Cancer spoke without looking up. "Sniper. Not my first time making a ghillie suit."

This left Worthy to cast an accusatory glance to Ian. "What about you? Lots of sewing required in the intelligence business?"

"High school," Ian explained, completing his stitches on the fishing net and applying a few dollops of shoe glue to seal them in place. "The redheaded twins in my class took Home Ec."

Worthy was quiet for a moment before calling up to the cab.

"David?"

In the passenger seat, the team leader was balancing a laptop over his thighs, using satellite imagery to plot their infiltration corridor based on the information Duchess had sent.

He said, "Don't interrupt me, I'm planning." Then, looking back at the cargo area, he admitted, "But I can't sew worth a shit."

"See?" Worthy said. "And this seems excessive, is all."

Ian reached for a handful of burlap fibers from the box at his feet, then girth-hitched the mass around the strips of fishing net that now dangled from the fatigue jacket. He'd never considered the particulars of *how* snipers built the ghillie suits that made them look like piles of leaf litter, and was somewhat mortified when Cancer matter-of-factly explained that unweaving individual strands of burlap was standard procedure—which, after an hour of practice, made Ian desperately regret not simply buying a suit in the States for this eventuality.

Responding to Worthy, Cancer said, "We'll be on target for at least 24 hours. At a minimum we'll be in close proximity to Boko Haram in broad daylight, and that's even if none of them manage to step on us in the course of their security patrols. You want to take your chances with the camouflage pattern on our fatigues, be my guest."

Reilly grabbed a pile of burlap strands and added, "If the Sambisa Forest is as badass as Ian says, odds are we'll be found and killed either way."

Ian completed another girth hitch of fibers around the fishing net, ensuring it overlapped the one beneath it before commenting, "After two hours of nonstop rap, I can't say the prospect bothers me as much as it normally would."

Cancer raised his voice and declared, "This is Wu-Tang Clan, you cultural swine. And rap is an art form, *na so,* Tolu?"

Tolu shouted back in pidgin, "*Make you no vex me!* Best music in the world. Talk smack in my van, I *go land you slap.*"

Cancer cut his eyes to Ian and said menacingly, "That means he'll slap you, Ian."

"Yeah, I got that," Ian replied, continuing to work on the fatigue jacket. "Thanks for the translation."

Reilly looked at Ian and asked, "You think the hostages will be there?"

Ian shook his head slightly. "I have no way of knowing how Duchess got that location, or how reliable her source was. But even she said it's thin. If it's a dry hole—which it probably will be—then our team is irrelevant because the JSOC hordes are probably descending on Nigeria as we speak."

Looking up from the ghillie-suit-in-progress, he concluded, "And I can tell you one thing for certain: if the hostages don't end up at that exact grid, we'll never find them. The forest is massive, and if Boko Haram was able to hide a few hundred kidnapped schoolgirls there, they'll have no problem making a half dozen hostages disappear."

11

Worthy rounded a tree, attempting to pick up his bearing when he spotted a patch of bushes rising to knee height, appearing almost black in his night vision. In any other forest, he'd push through them without a second thought.

But these particular plants had razor-sharp thorns nearly an inch in length, a lesson he'd learned the hard way shortly after Tolu dropped them off at the outskirts of the Sambisa Forest. After lacerating his calves and spending precious minutes trying to disentangle his fatigue pants, Worthy had avoided these dark patches like the plague.

He diverted to the right, straying farther off course in an attempt to make headway toward their objective. It hadn't taken long to realize that thorn bushes were only half the battle—the Sambisa held open clearings at fairly regular intervals, and anything easily trafficable to his team was equally so to the hordes of Boko Haram fighters swarming across this swath of forest that had somehow risen out of the otherwise arid savanna in northern Nigeria.

So Worthy drifted farther east, leading his team through a grove of low trees whose canopies interlocked to obscure the sky almost completely. That was what made this forest such a refuge for terrorists—impervious to satellites and aerial surveillance, Boko Haram could easily hide an army in the Sambisa, and that's exactly what they did. So far Worthy's duties as point man had allowed him to detect three separate encampments whose fires provided the only early warning that he needed to change course immediately. His normal vigilance had transcended to a hyper-alert state as he scanned the vegetation ahead, fearful of treading near a more disciplined enemy camp whose occupants didn't have a bonfire burning at this hour of night.

He was halfway through the grove of trees, circumnavigating the thorn bushes to his left, when he heard something arguably worse.

A chorus of eerie, high-pitched chuckles punctuated by nasal screeches reverberated in waves to his front.

"Hyenas again," he transmitted in a whisper. "Ten o'clock."

A charging lion, Worthy thought, would be an easy day by comparison —see the animal, shoot the animal. But if a clan of twenty or thirty hyenas surrounded his team, their suppressors would do little to discourage an attack. They'd heard the hyenas at several points so far, but had yet to actually see any of the slimy creatures, which, to Worthy, made the situation worse.

David replied over his earpiece, *"If they haven't tried to eat us yet, they're not going to. Besides, the only thing our weapons can't handle is an elephant."*

Continuing to move, Worthy keyed his mic and said, "No elephants out here."

"Actually," Ian clarified in a helpful tone, *"there's a small bush elephant population in this area. Sambisa was originally a game reserve—"*

David cut him off, transmitting, *"Would you shut. The fuck. Up."*

Worthy reached the end of the tree grove, arriving at a more open patch of ground that flanked the thorns on its way to his intended heading. Ordinarily he'd bypass anything this open, but they were already far off course and the risk was worth it to reach their destination before daybreak. Given that the current heat was as cool as Nigeria ever got this time of year, he couldn't imagine how much this little adventure in the Sambisa would suck in the daytime—particularly once he donned his ghillie suit.

His first indication of an abnormality in the terrain ahead came with the appearance of an open patch between the bushes—possibly another clearing, though something caught his eye and forced him to proceed out of a morbid sense of curiosity as much as anything else.

Stopping at the edge of the trees, he keyed his mic and said, "Hold up a second—I've got UXO up here."

David transmitted back, "*Landmines?*"

Not a bad guess, Worthy thought, considering that the forest was supposed to be littered with them.

But the visible portion of an aerial bomb at the center of the jagged clearing was ringed by three enormous craters. "Looks like a Mark 82."

Cancer replied, "*500-pounder? Go give it a good hard kick, see if it's still good.*"

Worthy's attention drifted away from the torpedo-shaped bomb casing rising from the earth, its tail fins suspended three feet in the air.

At the outskirts of the craters, he made out the skeletal remains of multiple bodies—five or six by the looks of it, though some were sufficiently dismembered to make an exact count futile short of a forensic analysis. Ribs were interspersed with the concave shells of partially intact skulls, the pale remains glowing a surreal shade of seafoam green in his night vision.

He transmitted, "Probably a half dozen bodies, too. No weapons. Survivors must have recovered those. I'm taking us around."

Reilly replied by the time Worthy had begun moving around the bombing site.

"*Nigerian tax dollars at work. Frankly I'm pleasantly surprised their air force managed to hit anything.*"

Worthy made his way through the brush, pausing mid-step to make out a long, irregular object beneath his boot—a human femur, probably flung through the trees from the bomb blasts.

Diverting around the remains, Worthy continued leading his team deeper into the Sambisa Forest.

12

I trudged through the trees, doing my best to follow Worthy's path lest I take an errant step onto a landmine.

It was easier to follow him with the approach of nautical dawn. Birds were beginning to chatter, their calls increasingly taking the place of nocturnal insects. The scene through my night vision was bright green and staggeringly clear, allowing the best view of the Sambisa Forest since we departed the van the previous evening. That fact provided limited comfort, however, given that we were now within ninety minutes of sunrise and still had yet to reach our destination. At the very least, the improved visibility should have allowed us to speed our pace, but even that was a pipe dream because we were simply too worn out to do so.

We'd been on the move for over six hours, placing us an hour behind even my most pessimistic projections. Between the impenetrable walls of thorn and the clearings that pervaded the forest, we didn't have much say in the matter. Add in the dehydration and muscle cramps associated with any foot movement of this duration, and were all in the hurt box. The Sambisa had dictated innumerable adjustments to our intended azimuth, and by now I thought it was no wonder the Nigerian military could do little to control this vast swath of wilderness—if we could barely make our way as a highly trained five-man team, I shuddered to think what an actual clearance operation would require.

Worthy came alongside a thick tree trunk that had been split, presumably by lightning. Turning to face me, he circled a hand over his head and then pointed to it, and I silently mirrored the motion before he turned forward and continued walking. Once I was abreast of the tree, I repeated the procedure for Ian's benefit—the poor guy was more exhausted than any of us, and it took him a moment to notice the hand signal before I saw his return confirmation. The tree was now an en route rally point, a spot where we'd meet up if we became dispersed by enemy fire or something as mundane as a break in visual contact from one another. Worthy had been establishing them all night, at intervals every few hundred meters, using whatever notable landmarks he could find among the seemingly endless forest.

This was part and parcel of every foot patrol, which was, by my estimation, the worst part of every mission.

While we had yet to put on the sweltering ghillie suits, our rucks were stuffed to the bursting point and had taken their toll on our stamina. We had no idea how long we'd be out here, and absent any ability to resupply, we had been forced to pack as much food and water as we possibly could.

The water in particular had taken up an inordinate amount of our packing space—we were now a few months into Nigeria's dry season, and had to assume a dearth of local water sources. If our all-night patrol was any indication, this was a wise precaution; we'd yet to tread through anything more substantial than a few dried-out streambeds, and once in position, we would have to ration our supply accordingly in the interests of maximizing our time on target.

Within half an hour, Worthy transmitted, "*Major clearing ahead—I'm going to skirt it to the right.*"

As I followed in his footsteps, I glanced left to see that it wasn't just a clearing, but a vast field extending hundreds of meters to the next patch of forest, an area so wide and open that Boko Haram could have camped a battalion there. But that would have removed the overhead cover they relied upon to remain hidden, and the massive clearing appeared to be completely free of people.

That didn't mean it wouldn't be traversed by enemy fighters looking to move quickly when there was no sound of aircraft overhead, however, and I remained unsettled by the presence of such a key terrain feature so close to our destination.

I considered how defensive the Boko Haram forces would be. On one hand, it was a miracle that an American team happened to be in close enough proximity to respond as quickly as we had. On the other hand, any terrorist organization that had survived as long as Boko Haram, fractured or otherwise, might just as easily assume that a military presence was never too far away. That was, of course, if the hostages were present in the Sambisa Forest at all.

My thoughts were interrupted by Worthy's next transmission.

"Boss, I'm about ten meters out from the destination."

"Copy," I replied, relieved that we'd nearly made it. "Take us all the way in."

I spent the remaining distance scanning the surrounding landscape. Without any significant hills to place between us and our objective, I'd instead chosen the stopping point more or less arbitrarily based on its distance one kilometer from the target. If I was going to call an audible and shift that position based on the ground-level view, it would have to be in the next few minutes.

But I was satisfied to find us in a thick swath of vegetation, complete with a semicircle of thorn bushes to the west that would prevent anyone from approaching from that direction. There were no water sources nearby and we were far from any natural lines of terrain drift that the enemy would be likely to follow, and I deemed this as good a stopping point as any other. I even spotted a sharp depression in the ground that would save us some digging time, though my decision was hastened by the fact that within half an hour or so, our night vision would be useless until sunset arrived.

Keying my mic, I said, "All right, this is our MSS."

While the purported enemy camp was a thousand meters ahead, a sufficiently distanced MSS, or mission support site, was a key prerequisite for any reconnaissance effort. This would be the command hub from which Ian and I would piece together a complete picture of the objective based on the surveillance teams' observations, while maintaining the standoff required to send that information to Duchess without alerting any enemy on target.

I tried not to relish in the fact that the foot movement had come to an end for me and Ian. The other three men would still have to cloverleaf around the objective to establish their surveillance sites, and that entailed a lot more foot movement under considerably greater risk.

But first we all had to don our homemade ghillie outfits, a reality spoken by Cancer a moment later.

"*All right, boys,*" he transmitted, "*time to put on the old Sasquatch suits.*"

13

Reilly took another step, pausing as Worthy halted in place to listen before taking his next tentative footfall. If patrolling with a heavy ruck was agony, then shouldering the same pack while taking three or four steps per minute multiplied the effect by a factor of ten.

Still, they had no choice; they were now moving without cover of darkness, the forest's depths unfolding before them in a mix of murky shadows penetrated by occasional beams of blinding sunlight. It had taken the two men well over three hours to complete a semicircular route to the east of the objective, and they were now headed straight toward it at the conclusion of their initial cloverleaf maneuver. Every step now brought them closer to a possible enemy stronghold, and they had slowed their pace in favor of stealth.

Meanwhile, the air temperature had seemingly leapt from the seventies to the nineties in a five-minute span. It was as if the moment the African sun had sufficiently cleared the horizon, it began beating the entire continent into submission.

And of course, the fucking suits didn't help. Reilly had never worn a ghillie suit, and after the last few hours of painstaking foot patrol, he desperately hoped he'd never have to again.

Heat retention was only the first problem—unsurprisingly, being draped in overlapping strands of burlap fibers was about as serene as walking with a king-sized comforter set over your head. Second, and debatably worse at present, was the sheer weight.

His fatigue jacket and pants alone were burdened with somewhere around eight pounds of burlap, and that was before he took into account the hoods covering his boonie cap and rucksack. And given the fact that the latter was already packed to the bursting point with food and water, Reilly was actually grateful they hadn't been able to weigh the complete setup. He felt better off not knowing.

Even so, the medic had to admit the ghillie suits served their purpose remarkably well. On a typical daylight patrol through the woods, losing sight of the nearest man in formation was almost impossible.

But with his silhouette now obscured by piles of draped material, Worthy had practically transformed into a bush with legs. The effect was amplified by them taking the time to pluck leaves and lengths of dry grass along the way, supplementing the ghillie suits with vegetation that would have to be replaced when it wilted. All Reilly could make out at times was the point man's movement, the vague shifting of a shape in the forest to his front. And if Worthy suddenly stopped moving when Reilly's eyes weren't fixed upon him, as had occurred on two occasions so far, the medic actually had to scan closely to see where he was.

Worthy stopped again and glanced back at him, tapping his ear and then pointing forward. Reilly nodded, listening intently through the scattered bird calls until he could hear it too: human voices.

They sounded like they were at least twenty or thirty meters ahead through the forest, and all he could make out were the occasional snippets of emphasized words or a short burst of laughter. Reilly noted two things distinctly: first, they were close, and therefore he'd soon be able to get this rucksack off his back. Which was a good thing, because at this point he felt like there was no fluid in his body left to sweat out.

And second, the voices sounded relaxed, more like men at a backyard barbeque than bloodthirsty terrorist lunatics. Reilly hadn't expected that, feeling somewhat reassured that they weren't expecting a team of Americans to show up at their doorstep.

Worthy unslung his ruck from one shoulder, lowering himself to the prone before setting it down completely. Reilly closed the distance to him and followed suit, careful to set down his pack as gently as he could to avoid making noise.

He watched his point man make the final adjustments to his ghillie suit, ensuring the burlap strands from his boonie hat were sufficiently draped around his shoulders. Then Worthy looked back to the medic for a buddy check of his camouflage, and Reilly had to suppress a laugh.

Worthy looked like some kind of swamp monster that had risen up from the depths, the visible portions of his face caked with dried mud that had partially washed away from rivulets of sweat. Reilly looked no better, he supposed. Camouflage face paint looked great in the movies, but the team hadn't anticipated a need for it in Nigeria. Since that wasn't the type of thing you could easily acquire in a city like Abuja, they'd opted for the next best thing—mixing water with dirt to form a mud paste, then smearing it over every patch of exposed skin.

The men both smiled at the ridiculousness of the other, and without speaking, freshened up their appearance in tandem.

Reilly brushed aside a small patch of leaf litter, exposing the soil below. With one hand he collected a scrape of dirt and whatever bacteria and parasites it contained, then used the fingers of his opposite hand to smear the soil over his sweat-soaked face until he was reasonably certain it was covered.

Worthy did the same, then looked back to Reilly for approval. If he looked like a mud monster before, now he looked like one that was trying too hard. Reilly gave him a thumbs up, and both men carefully pushed the leaf litter back over their hasty dirt scrapes.

Then Worthy set off, beginning a meticulously slow crawl through the underbrush. Reilly repositioned himself ahead of the abandoned rucksacks, keeping his rifle poised across their backtrail. He felt his heart thudding as he waited—the shuffling sounds of Worthy easing his body face-down across the forest floor had disappeared completely, as had any visual of his departing figure. The wait was, in a way, worse than the entire movement up to this point. Reilly listened to the distant murmur of men's voices, dreading the sudden cry that would indicate someone had spotted his teammate. If Worthy became compromised, he'd be returning at a sprint, and as soon as he passed Reilly it would be up to him to lay down enough suppressing fire to cover the point man while he donned his ruck, then reversed roles.

And then they'd be fleeing the area in a panicked rush, making their way to a pre-designated emergency linkup point well clear of the MSS while transmitting the total mission compromise.

But the first aberration in the noises of the forest was the rustle of leaves, and Reilly turned to see Worthy's face appear through the undergrowth, the shifting mass of his ghillie suit sliding across the ground as he returned. This wasn't good, Reilly knew; he'd been hoping that Worthy would transmit from some successfully attained vantage point, summoning the medic forward to join him.

His return seemed to indicate the worst-case scenario short of compromise, though Reilly didn't receive his confirmation until Worthy advanced to within a foot of him, then whispered, "There's a wall of thornbushes blocking any view of the objective. Looks like it extends twenty meters in either direction, at least."

Reilly felt his spirits deflating as Worthy concluded, "We're going to have to do another cloverleaf."

The medic nodded, and together the two men donned their rucksacks and prepared to withdraw the way they'd come. One more semicircle through the forest, Reilly thought, before they could attempt a head-on approach in the hopes of catching any sight of their reconnaissance target.

As they began pulling back into the woods, Reilly considered that it could have been worse—he could be Cancer right now. After all, that poor bastard was operating entirely on his own.

Cancer continued his sniper crawl, pulling his body in measured strokes across the ground.

He proceeded with a metronome-like regularity, keeping each movement slow and fluid enough to go unnoticed by a casual observer. The effort was complicated by weight—he was dragging his rucksack by a four-foot length of webbing secured to his rigger belt—but anything wide enough for his shoulders to pass through would suffice for his equipment as well. The more uncomfortable Cancer felt, after all, the less risk he had of being spotted by the enemy.

Less than a foot over his sniper hood were the savagely sharp thorns that had threatened to shred his skin at the slightest opportunity. He'd been passing between these merciless bushes for the better part of an hour, trading twenty minutes of his life for seven to ten feet of progress. He was undeterred by this lengthy crawl, however—frequent checks of his wrist compass ensured he was staying on azimuth as he approached the target grid, and if he couldn't pass through this vegetation at a walk, neither could the enemy. That was particularly important when he didn't have a teammate backing him up, much less a trained spotter obscuring his backtrail.

Dust coated his nostrils as he slithered over the hot ground, betraying every human instinct to lift his head as he clutched the closed bipod of his G28 sniper rifle, its weight hoisted over his prostrate arm. Roughly half of all his sniper training had been dedicated to stalking, and right now, that was proving to be a wise investment.

He paused before a thorny tendril blocking his path and set down his rifle to unsheathe his fighting knife in a laborious, minute-long process of rolling halfway to his side. Once the knife was in hand, he used the blade to slice the vine, then set the severed length to his left. Within a few days it would shrivel to a dead brown remnant that put it at odds with the surrounding vegetation, but no one would see it unless they crawled across the same path he just had—and if that occurred, he was fucked anyway.

Then Cancer resumed his grip on the rifle bipod, shifting the weapon over his forearm and bicep before continuing his slow crawl as he considered the effort ahead. The planning maxim was that two men could effectively rotate surveillance for 24 hours, while three could remain in place as long as their food and water supplies held out. Four men, if you had that luxury, could actually resupply their own position by sending two of them back to the MSS when needed.

But there was no rule of thumb for sending one man off on a surveillance element; a two-man element was the minimum for any part of military operations from recon to room clearing, and for good reason.

Yet here he was, off by himself—and frankly, there was no other way.

This wasn't a carefully planned and resourced reconnaissance effort; it was a knee-jerk, half-assed response to an emerging crisis, putting his team in harm's way because the lives of American civilians were suddenly at stake. When it came to surveillance positions, two was one and one was none. No one was getting a God's-eye view of the objective without getting caught—in reconnaissance, the commander painted an overall picture by piecing together the reports of multiple elements, each with their own sliver of visibility on the target. To combine himself, Worthy, and Reilly into a single element was to doom the recon effort to failure because the objective called for three or four surveillance teams, not one.

So Cancer had made the argument to split the difference and set off on his own. He was a seasoned-enough sniper to assume this risk simply because there were no other options.

He continued his stalk, thinking that he actually preferred this sort of thing during the day—moving close to an objective at night risked watching the sunrise to find his seemingly perfect surveillance position was actually exposed to enemy view, and by then it was too late. But daylight hours allowed him to scan every inch of foliage, a painstaking approach made more so by the knowledge that whatever ground he gained in full sunlight, he could hold for the duration.

Cancer arrived at the space between the thorn bushes, a smile spreading across his lips.

He shifted the rifle to his front, ensuring the netting was in place over the weapon with the slit in alignment with the objective lens of his scope. Then, and only then, did he lower the bipod legs and bring the G28 to a firing position, aligning his right eye behind the optic as he scanned the terrain ahead.

The visual angle extended down what appeared to be the center of the enemy camp. He shifted left, then right, taking in the benefit of this vantage point with the knowledge that it would serve him well in the coming reconnaissance. Then he instinctively began breathing using the Buteyko method, a technique to slow his oxygen intake with long exhales and control pauses to calm his mind and body for the long haul.

Snipers had all kinds of tricks to remain in position for long periods of time: pissing into bags with sponges, surreptitiously eating field rations with their face to the ground. Cancer, however, had always preferred to exclude every possible distraction by eating and drinking as little as possible, removing every bodily requirement through a single-minded focus on the sight through his scope. To that end, there was one supplement he never traveled without.

Slipping his fingers into a vest pouch, he procured a round white tablet and deposited it into his mouth, using his tongue to tuck the chalky mass into his cheek. He immediately began to feel the dull tingle of the lozenge, which would deposit four milligrams of nicotine—about two cigarettes' worth—into his bloodstream in the coming half hour or so as it dissolved. While he vastly preferred the substance in its most ancient and civilized form of smoking, the tablets designed for people trying to quit provided him with a welcome source of consumption when the alternative would result in him getting shot in the face.

Keying his radio, he whispered to David, "I've got eyes-on the target."

Ian flipped open the ruggedized laptop, the screen coming to life with a soft glow that illuminated David in the shadows beside him.

Lying shoulder to shoulder beneath the tarp, both men momentarily locked eyes. David looked bewildered, and for good reason—they hadn't expected anyone to reach the target so soon, much less establish a feasible surveillance position.

David arranged a notepad and pen over the maps and protractors spread out on the ground, transmitting back, "Cancer, MSS copies. Send your grid."

Then he jotted down Cancer's response as Ian typed the grid. They'd transcribe every scrap of information in this manner, then cross-check the data against each other's notes to construct an overall map of the objective.

While their three teammates had been cloverleafing the objective in an attempt to gain visual, David and Ian had remained at the MSS a full kilometer away, spending the vast majority of that time constructing their current hide site at a naturally occurring depression in the earth. Building it in broad daylight had been a hair-raising proposition, but they had little choice in the matter.

First they'd had to remove a wide swath of groundcover consisting mainly of leaf litter and fallen branches, relocating it to ponchos spread for the purpose. Then they'd dug using sawed-off shovels from an Abuja hardware store, storing the removed dirt in sandbags until they had a scrape large enough to fit both men and their rucksacks. After lining the hole's perimeter with tent stakes, they'd used rope to form a crisscrossing web at ground level, staking down a tarp over it and redistributing the excavated dirt atop it before spreading the piles of leaf litter and deadfall.

The end result wasn't exceptional in terms of comfort, but Ian had to admit it served their purposes well: both he and David had walked around the site until they were confident it blended with the surrounding terrain, the only distinguishing feature being a foot-tall gap at the entrance that a passerby would almost have to kneel down to see.

Now both men took their notes while breathing the tiny hide site's sweltering, earthy air as Cancer finished transmitting his grid. Then the sniper continued in a whisper, *"Limits of visibility are as follows: left 55 degrees, right 137 degrees. SALUTE report follows."*

As Ian typed, he considered that he wasn't particularly surprised that Duchess's grid had proven to be an accurate Boko Haram location—dozens, if not hundreds, of them were scattered across this sprawling forest. But the confirmation of enemy fighters didn't mean the American hostages were present or ever would be. In the search for the kidnapped Chibok schoolgirls, the Nigerian military had raided the Sambisa Forest en masse, finding and freeing almost 300 women from Boko Haram captivity—none of whom were the intended hostages.

"Send it," David replied.

Cancer spoke in a hoarse whisper. *"Size: four military-age males. None of them look like they're starving; all are reasonably alert so we can rule out significant dehydration. That means they're either new arrivals or receiving regular resupply, in which case there's an avenue of approach for vehicles that we couldn't make out from the satellite imagery. Break. Activity: they're standing in a group in a clearing, bullshitting, smoking, look like they're waiting around for something. No defensive posture, no indications that there's a high-*

value individual or hostages to protect. Break. Location: 50 meters to my twelve o'clock."

Ian typed quickly, completing an almost word-for-word description of Cancer's report as David continued taking analog notes via pen.

"Unit: dressed in a mix of woodland camouflage fatigues and brown Arab-style thawb garments with headscarves. Combat boots on three of them, sandals on the fourth. Two of them are wearing the Soviet surplus AK racks you'd expect to see in a third-world area, olive drab, three mag pouches and a grenade pouch on either side. Mag pouches look full, which indicates the guys who aren't wearing them have kit located outside my POV."

Legitimate point, Ian thought; in many regions of the world, extremists wore these seemingly ubiquitous chest racks whether they had anything to put in the pouches or not. To them, in lieu of any formalized training, it was often the status symbol of a warrior.

Cancer continued, *"I can't tell if anyone's got grenades. Time: now. Break. Equipment: one AK-47 and two AK-74s worn on slings. One unmanned PK machinegun with a hundred-round drum sitting in the open, oriented north so we can safely assume there's a road or trail approach somewhere in that direction. Break. Let me know when you're ready for the camp layout, over."*

"One sec," David replied, finishing his notes and receiving a nod from Ian before he continued, "All right, send it."

"I can make out four tents. Three are A-frames, canvas material, five feet in height and seven feet in length, probably capable of sleeping three to four men. Tent one: distance 55 meters, azimuth 67 degrees, long axis oriented northeast to southwest. Tent two: distance 47 meters, azimuth 82 degrees, oriented east to west. Tent three: I can only see a partial, distance 52 meters, azimuth 200 degrees, oriented north to south."

"Got it. What about the fourth?"

"It's a dome tent, canvas, seven feet in height, eleven-foot diameter, probably sleeps ten people. Azimuth 62 degrees, distance 70 meters, and I can't make out the opening from my position."

"Copy all. What else you got?"

"Thorn bushes end one meter to my front, and the terrain descends approximately 15 degrees into a bowl-shaped clearing three meters after that. Far treeline is 85 meters to my front, looks passable for an assault force. I can't make out the

entire camp, but from my optic it looks like the clearing runs roughly northwest to southeast."

"Got it, wait one." David raised an eyebrow at Ian.

The intelligence operative winced, then said, "Four guys isn't enough, and American hostages would be accompanied by some level of Boko Haram leadership. If this were legit, the security posture would be much higher. I'd also like to see some food and water provisions if nothing else; they can't barter for ransom if their hostages have starved to death, so the camp would be fortified with more than a handful of blue-collar guys with one crew-served weapon."

"Bottom line?" David asked.

Ian shrugged. "Based on his report, this sounds like a dime-a-dozen terrorist placeholder in the Sambisa. Boko Haram spreads their guys out, so for all we know this is a team- or squad-sized outpost no different from a few hundred others in this area."

David looked pained, but his voice was cocky and casual as he transmitted back, "First eyes-on the target is a case of beer to you."

Cancer replied, *"Suck it, Doc and Racegun."*

Then David asked, "How's your position? You safe, or do you need to pull out and relocate?"

The question elicited an equally confident response from the grizzled sniper.

"I'm up their asses right now, crawled through eighty meters of thorns to get here. They're not going to make my position, and if anyone steps on me they're already gonna be bleeding out from the thorn bushes. Advise I remain here for the duration—I could make three more approaches and not match this view."

"Understood, just sit tight." David hesitated, then asked, "One more thing: any sign of hostages?"

Cancer responded without hesitation.

"None whatsoever."

Worthy slipped between two trees, peering over the bushes to his front before dropping to a knee, then the prone, and low-crawling forward on his second attempt at a cloverleaf maneuver.

Through the leaves he could make out the clearing Cancer described: oblong and dotted with tents, with four men standing at the center, puffing on cigarettes and continuing what appeared to be an animated conversation.

Pulling himself forward to achieve a better line of sight through the underbrush, Worthy appraised his surroundings to find he was in a densely packed cluster of bushes, impenetrable to foot movement without crawling or breaking brush, with sufficient screening of vegetation between him and the objective.

He transmitted in a whisper, "MSS, this is Racegun—surveillance site established."

"*Send your location,*" David replied.

Worthy consulted his GPS and recited the ten-digit grid, hearing a low rustle of brush as Reilly appeared behind him, alternately dragging both rucks forward.

David said, "*Copy all, send SALUTE when ready.*"

Worthy barely heard him—Reilly had just grabbed his ankle and given it a shake, and a moment later the point man could make out a distant buzzing in the forest to the north.

"Stand by," he transmitted, "I can hear a vehicle approaching."

David didn't answer, and didn't need to—at that moment, everyone was holding their breath, Worthy most of all.

The fact that the hostages hadn't been sighted yet didn't mean the reconnaissance mission had been a wash. After all, the missing Americans had been captured on the far side of the country, in Lagos, and there was no telling how long their transport would take. The sound of a vehicle engine in the Sambisa Forest was the first indication that the hostages might be here, and Worthy only needed to wait and see if that was coming to fruition.

A motorcycle rolled into view at the north end of the camp, piloted by a single rider with a compact assault rifle slung across his back. Worthy recognized the weapon as an FB Mini-Beryl, a Polish weapon used by the

Nigerian military that stood in stark contrast to the Soviet-block firearms that Cancer had already identified among the occupants.

The guards' reactions were telling. They quickly readied their weapons, the unarmed man lifting his PK machinegun off the ground as the group formed a sort of muster line before the motorcycle pulled to a stop.

The rider dismounted, addressing a guard who stepped forward with an AK-47— must have been the camp's top leader—and Worthy watched their brief exchange in an attempt to discern which man was being deferential to the other.

He received his answer when the motorcycle driver raised his voice, shouting something indiscernible before belting the camp leader across the face.

Then he mounted his bike, firing the engine and wheeling back the way he'd come, leaving a cloud of dust drifting across the camp as its occupants scrambled into action.

Reilly whispered, "What the hell did we just witness?"

Worthy shook his head slightly. "I have no idea."

14

Duchess leaned forward at her desk, listening closely as her intelligence officer spoke.

Lucios was as monotone as ever—for all the man's strengths as an intelligence officer, he was quite possibly the least compelling public speaker she'd ever encountered.

He continued, "Tech division pulled a video down from an Islamic extremist site. They're trying to block it everywhere, but it's already popping up across the internet and the major networks are spinning up for a breaking news report. We've got half an hour before it goes live worldwide."

"Put it on the main screen," she directed.

The central flat-screen flashed to a close-up of Usman Mokhammed, who was dressed in military fatigues and a tactical vest. He was unmasked, lips moving in what was surely a prepared statement as Lucios narrated the muted proceedings.

"There's the usual anti-Western rhetoric, with some commentary on foreign oil companies bringing poverty to Nigeria while the politicians profit. He's demanding the release of two senior Boko Haram leaders currently in Nigerian custody, his own predecessor included."

The camera angle zoomed out then, revealing a second man kneeling with his back to Usman, hands tied behind his back.

Duchess immediately recognized the man as Anthony Walters.

When an American citizen was taken captive by a terrorist organization, their photograph became a permanent installment on the daily intelligence briefings until they were either declared deceased or recovered alive. Along with the rest of the counterterrorism community, Duchess had spent the past day working against an almost constant backdrop of the hostages' faces displayed on a screen at the front of her OPCEN.

But the smiling employee photograph of Walters stood in stark contrast to the video before her now—the portly man in his mid-forties appeared disheveled, his lower lip split and right eyelid swollen and bruised. He wore a polo shirt and khakis, likely the same clothes he'd been captured in, and despite Usman Mokhammed now brandishing a knife behind him, he appeared calm and strangely dignified as he faced the camera.

"Timeline?" she asked.

Lucios continued, "Twenty-four-hour deadline for the prisoner release, which puts us at 1400 Nigerian time, 0900 EST tomorrow. That's when the next hostage will be killed, with an additional hostage every two hours until their demands are met. He says all deaths will be videotaped and the footage released on the world stage."

On screen, Usman grabbed Walters's hair, twisted his head back, and began sweeping the knife in sawing strokes across his throat.

The torrent of blood that flooded from the wound, spilling across Walters's shirt, made Duchess cringe. It was the stuff of Hollywood slasher films, though anyone who'd viewed the ISIS decapitation videos ad nauseum—as Duchess had—knew at a glance that it was authentic.

Usman succeeded in severing the vertebrae, kicking the dead man's body forward and hoisting his head aloft for the camera. The screen went black.

The entire OPCEN went quiet then, the hushed silence broken by Jo Ann at the adjoining desk.

"Administration is going to be playing for keeps after this."

The sound of Duchess's phone ringing almost made her jump, eliciting a primal response in the wake of the horrific video she'd just seen. She felt sick to her stomach, more so with the knowledge that the caller was almost certainly Senator Gossweiler demanding an update that Duchess didn't have. What else could she tell him that he didn't know already?

After a moment of hesitation, she lifted the receiver.

"Duchess here."

To her surprise, it wasn't Senator Gossweiler but a female Agency switchboard operator who responded, "The ISA has just landed in Abuja, and their team lead is requesting an update. Ground Branch requested I route the call to you."

"Put him through," Duchess said, putting the phone to her chest as she said to Jo Ann, "Line two, ISA."

Jo Ann lifted her phone and tapped a button to patch into the call, and Duchess knew the connection was complete when she could hear the muted background noise of people conversing on the other end—the ISA team setting up their command post.

Duchess began, "This is the project chief for the Ground Branch presence in Nigeria. I've got you patched in with my head military liaison. How can we help?"

Despite her cordial tone, Duchess knew this was a delicate matter; even though the Intelligence Support Activity was unarguably the most elite and secretive intelligence unit in the US military, Project Longwing's existence was compartmentalized down to a handful of politicians and top Agency officials.

A man with a pronounced New York accent replied, "Thank you for taking my call. We're just getting set up at the embassy, and—"

Jo Ann cut him off, asking incredulously, "Bailey?"

The man went silent. "Who is this?"

"Jo Ann Brown, we met when I was with JSOC. The Somalia rescue."

"Jo Ann—I didn't know you went over to the Agency. I hope this means we won't have the black hole of information that I usually get."

"I was going to say the same."

"How many people do you have in Nigeria?"

Duchess intervened, "We've got the usual staff at the embassy that you'll meet soon if you haven't already, and some local sources mostly focused in the northeast." Frowning, she added, "We're also overseeing a five-man team from the Special Activities Center, currently performing special reconnaissance at a Boko Haram camp in the Sambisa Forest."

He asked, "You think they'll be taken there?"

Jo Ann and Duchess answered "No" in unison, and Duchess hastily added, "We corroborated source intelligence about a buildup at the location in question, and that was and remains our only possible lead. The ground team has since denied that any hostages are present, and we expect it will remain a dry hole."

Bailey responded, "Well my people are awaiting the arrival of our SIGINT birds, but that won't be until tomorrow. Until then, we're trying to run down facts from a few hundred intelligence reports."

Jo Ann set a hand on Duchess's shoulder, then pointed to herself and tapped her sternum twice. Duchess nodded.

Then Jo Ann said, "Bailey, let's trade direct lines. If I get any information ahead of the curve, I'll keep you linked in. I hope," she added, "that will be a two-way exchange."

15

I stuck my head through the hide site's narrow entrance, looking and listening for any sign of enemy presence.

After Ian and I spent the past nine hours trapped under a reinforced tarp roof, the sunlight was blinding. Despite the hide site's hot, stagnant air, at least there was shade—the forest floor was blazing hot, though the cries of birds in the trees overhead provided some assurance that there was no imminent danger.

Nonetheless, Boko Haram owned this entire forest and could appear anywhere at any time. And while my team were no strangers to operating behind enemy lines, doing so in the service of our primary mission—assassinating low-level terrorist leaders before they became too powerful and difficult to find—was one thing. Being thrown off course to operate far outside our realm of expertise, as with the current reconnaissance mission, felt altogether more dangerous. If we died now, it would be in the act of being the eyes and ears for a dedicated hostage rescue force, and even that to save members of a swollen US corporation.

As I exposed myself outside our hide site, the thought of endangering my life for that latter cause seemed all the more ludicrous. I'd accepted the sacrifice of being away from my family to find and kill enemies of the

United States, had, in fact, been willing to die for that cause. But the potential of getting smoked right now seemed an asinine way to go, and I had a hard time suppressing a deep sense of dread spreading by way of a tightness in my chest.

It only took a moment, however, for me to mentally curse myself for the emotion. Three of my guys were on the frontlines of that camp, a stone's throw from four enemy fighters, and here I was a thousand meters away, fearing for my own safety. As if the fact that I had a wife and kid back home should make my life in any way more valuable than the lives of my teammates. Besides, I thought, the temporary exposure was absolutely necessary: sending a data shot over satellite communications, as I was about to do, took both time and a clear signal.

I pulled myself forward with my weapon in one hand, extending the other back to the hide site entrance. Ian reached forward and handed me the fully assembled satellite antenna, which I set up on its tripod and angled upward at the preordained azimuth. Next Ian passed me the ruggedized laptop, connected to the antenna via a coil of wire that I hastily arranged on the ground.

Flipping the computer screen open at a 45-degree angle to keep it from reflecting light, I initiated the transmission and watched the status bar fill from zero to three percent. Then I took one last look at the screen display with a sense of astonishment that we'd accomplished as much as we had. Particularly, I thought, on a shoestring shopping trip and given the fact that most of our preparations had occurred from a moving van as we headed toward the Sambisa Forest.

Cancer's first visual report from the camp had seemed miraculous at the time; that alone was enough to plan a hasty raid. But as soon as Worthy and Reilly established their surveillance site, it opened up a whole new world of information.

With two perspectives, we'd been able to plot the grids and use azimuths of visibility to triangulate the camp, and in Ian's capable hands that resulted in the digital graphic that I observed now—a bird's-eye depiction with every tent numbered, distances and directions annotated, and the surrounding terrain marked with impassable thorns and areas of loose vegetation that would allow an assault force to approach. The two surveillance positions had even weighed in on recommended sniper positions based on lines of sight to the objective, and Ian had plotted them on the graphic along a fan of shooting angles and ranges to each tent.

As an appendix to the presentation, we'd prepared a consolidated timeline of every detail from our ground infiltration to the present moment, detailing the enemy numbers, their equipment, and every action observed by the surveillance positions. Most notably was what occurred in the camp after the motorcycle departed an hour and a half earlier. The remaining fighters had hastily cleaned up the camp, hidden a pillowcase-sized sack in the bushes—presumably narcotics or alcohol—and then assumed a security posture at the perimeter.

Ian seemed to think that indicated the imminent arrival of some Boko Haram VIPs and, if we were lucky, the hostages. As I watched the status bar of my data shot to Duchess, I wondered when and if additional fighters would arrive at the camp. Even the guards probably hadn't been informed; as foot soldiers, they were probably told to clean up their shit and stand by. We could easily be on target for another 24 to 48 hours, and if we pushed past that point, we'd be running perilously low on water.

The status bar finally filled to completion, ending the satellite transmission. I quickly handed the antenna back to Ian, followed by the laptop. At that moment I became aware that the birds to my right had suddenly gone silent, an eerie quiet falling over the forest. Instinctively glancing that direction, I saw someone slipping through the trees twenty meters away.

My blood turned to ice as I registered a second man behind him, both appearing as little more than shadows through the foliage. They were headed straight for our MSS, the kind of direct trajectory that assured me we'd been detected much earlier and were now about to face the wrath of a dedicated force sent to finish us off.

There were only two choices: either tuck my rifle under my chest and put my face to the dirt, hoping that my ghillie suit would serve its intended purpose, or ease back into the hide site and hope they didn't spot me.

I opted for the latter, sliding backward on my belly. My boot caught Ian's shoulder and he pushed it aside, causing me to angle in that direction until

I passed back underneath the overhead cover with the desperate hope that I didn't disturb the ground outside.

As soon as I was concealed, I faced Ian with a finger to my lips. He looked confused, and I pointed to my eyes, then to the right, in an indication that I'd spotted enemy fighters.

Our next actions were performed with a synchronized fluidity: we assumed prone firing positions, aiming out the low entrance to our hide site.

Standard procedure at a time like this would be to zero out our radios along with the laptop data, using purpose-built mechanisms to leave the enemy no information to exploit. But there was no time, and if I was in the final moments of my life, I was going down fighting, not tinkering with electronics.

I braced my rifle buttstock against my shoulder, holding my aim steady as I waited for the inevitable: the first enemy combatant to crouch down and look inside, an easy headshot that would kick off a supremely short gunfight.

My earpieces crackled to life with Duchess's voice, which seemed deafening at this particular juncture.

"Suicide Actual, this is Raptor Nine One."

I keyed my radio three times, transmitting bursts of static to indicate that I could hear but not give a verbal response. Duchess must have taken the hint, because there was no follow-up to her attempt at radio contact.

Then I heard the men approaching, the snap of a branch outside indicating that we were seconds from being discovered.

They were moving quickly, quietly, a seasoned force who knew the terrain far better than we did. I heard no talking or clanking of unsecured equipment, merely the crunching of footsteps on dry leaf litter growing in volume until a set of combat boots passed five meters ahead of the entrance, moving from right to left as the man negotiated the depression and climbed to the opposite side.

Another set of boots appeared, then another, and while I had no idea how many men there were, the tension of the moment was almost unbearable in its intensity. Our hide site was well-concealed, but at this range the slightest sideward glance could easily reveal the shadow of our entrance, the dispersion of top cover over the section of tarp appearing at odds with the rolling terrain's natural crests and ridges. We might be able to take out one or two men, but a single burst of automatic fire would easily kill Ian and me—and with dead Americans in such close proximity to the Boko Haram camp, the rest of my team was one enemy radio call away from a comprehensive search that would uncover both surveillance positions and result in the execution of anyone who survived the inevitable compromise.

I watched a fourth man pass in front of the MSS, followed by a fifth, before the sounds of their movement faded. Impossibly, they had slipped past without pause, but our troubles were just beginning. I simply couldn't accept that they hadn't spotted our hide site, well camouflaged or not, and kept my focus riveted out the entrance, weapon poised for them to circle back—though if I'd noticed a hide site in passing, I wouldn't approach it from the front. Instead I'd pass out of earshot, let the hide site occupants think they were in the clear, then circle from the six o'clock to finish them off.

And that was exactly the eventuality I braced myself for. We had nowhere to run, no means of speedy retreat that wouldn't expose us further. There was only one thing left to do.

Turning to Ian, I whispered, "Zero everything out."

He shook his head. "David, relax. They're gone."

"They know we're here. That wasn't random."

"You're right," Ian agreed, "it wasn't random. But Boko Haram owns the entire forest, so they don't need to patrol it."

"Bullshit. That was a dedicated patrol, not some new recruits on basic training. They knew what they were doing."

Ian, astonishingly, flashed a grin. Then he squeezed my shoulder and whispered, "Don't you get it? This is a good thing—a *very* good thing. It means they're ramping up patrols on the far perimeter of the camp we were sent to surveil. You see what I'm getting at?"

I swallowed and replied, "You think the hostages are en route."

"Yeah, David. I do."

"You sure about this? I mean, if they come back—"

"David," he said forcefully, "just tell the guys."

Keying my mic, I transmitted, "Net call, be advised the MSS just had a five-man enemy patrol pass within a few feet of us. Any closer and they would have stepped on the roof of our hide site. No indication that they were looking for anything in particular, and Angel assesses they were likely part of increased security patrols in the vicinity of our objective. If that's the case, our odds of that camp receiving the hostages just went up threefold." I released my transmit switch for a moment, then keyed it again. "And if outside units are patrolling a full kilometer outside the target, the camp guards will probably begin some local security patrols as well. Stay sharp, and stay hidden."

Cancer replied in remarkably short order.

"Guess I'll put my pants back on. What do you think we've been doing out here while you and Ian are honeymooning at the love shack?"

I transmitted, "Don't make me revoke your case of beer, you fuck."

"You don't have the balls."

"Then push your luck and see what happens."

After a beat of silence, Worthy added his contribution.

"We've got good eyes-on, Suicide, and the only way they're finding us is if they step on our backs. Just make sure you guys stay safe at the MSS. You let Duchess know about that little complication?"

"No," I replied, "but I'm about to. Stand by."

Then I keyed my command radio and transmitted, "Raptor Nine One, this is Suicide Actual."

"Raptor Nine One," Duchess responded. *"Confirm receipt of your data shot, send any further traffic."*

"A Boko Haram patrol almost walked on top of our MSS," I replied. "From the looks of it, they're beefing up peripheral security around the camp."

Swallowing hard, I spoke cautiously. "We haven't been in place long enough to say for sure, but between this and the motorcycle courier delivering a message to the camp this morning, we think things are looking pretty good for your tip on this camp location to pay off in the next day or so."

"I hope you're right," she answered, then assumed a sterner tone. *"Usman*

executed one of the hostages in a graphic video that is now circulating on international news media."

I locked eyes with Ian, my heart sinking as she continued, *"The administration is highly motivated to put an end to this situation as quickly as possible. If the remaining hostages do arrive at your target, plan on immediate approval of a fully resourced hostage rescue, with your team at the tip of the spear."*

16

Cancer felt a hot pulse of fear at the sudden noise beside his sniper position. The quiet, slithering rustle was almost indiscernible above the birdcalls yet grew subtly in volume with each passing second. Flicking his eyes right, he stared into the underbrush until he succeeded in locating the source.

A yellowish reptilian head emerged from the brush, its wide eyes unblinking as it approached and trailed a slender body. He could tell at first glance that it was a cobra; what kind, he couldn't say for sure, though he felt relatively certain that Ian could have launched into a verbal dissertation if the sniper transmitted a basic description.

Cancer remained frozen, his blood pressure continuing to mount. In the long list of things he hated, few ranked higher than snakes—but in training, he'd once held a firing position near a red ant pile, sustaining bite after stinging bite over the course of three hours without moving. At least if the cobra sank its fangs into him, things would be over quickly.

The reptile paused, flicking a black tongue at him for a moment before proceeding, undaunted, over his rifle barrel.

He watched the snake glide in front of his face, estimating that four feet of smooth golden scales had passed before he caught sight of the tail, which fell to the ground on the opposite side of his G28 before drifting out of sight.

Cancer breathed a long, weary sigh of relief, coming to the end of his exhale when Worthy transmitted.

"Vehicle inbound from the north, can't see it yet."

Focusing through his scope, Cancer saw the camp guards maintain their security perimeter before he also heard the faint rumble of a large engine. A moment later, Worthy transmitted again.

"Looks like a Deuce and a Half, entering the clearing now. I'm about to lose visual."

"I got it," Cancer intervened, watching the large cargo truck rumble into view.

At first glance, he thought that Worthy was correct: the six-wheeled truck appeared to be of the two-and-a-half-ton, medium-duty family of vehicles that had originated from a WWII US Army predecessor before spreading in military and civilian variants throughout the world. This one was painted a nondescript shade of tan, free of license plates or identifying markings. "It's pulling up to the dome tent now," he transmitted. "Stand by."

He sent that message by way of telling everyone else to keep the radio net silent—after all, he'd need all the focus he could manage. After sweltering hours of sipping water between nicotine tablets, Cancer had yet to move more than an inch in any direction and was running on zero sleep; and now, he'd have fleeting seconds to analyze and interpret whatever was about to transpire.

The truck swung back north, coming to a stop facing away from the dome tent. Within seconds, the tailgate dropped and three armed fighters scrambled out. A fourth man rounded the side after exiting the passenger door—this one bearded, strolling with the authority of command, and Cancer saw at a glance that it was Usman.

He aligned his scope, fighting for any view of the truck's contents as the camp guards and incoming fighters crowded around the tailgate. Their bodies blocked his view, but not completely—he caught sight of a terrified Caucasian face at the rear of the truck, a man with a handlebar mustache being forced off the back with his hands and feet bound before the Boko Haram fighters muscled him into the dome tent.

Other restrained passengers followed them, and Cancer ticked off their distinguishing features—one man had silver hair, another was bald—but the swarm of camp guards shifted until it was all he could do to count bodies.

The scene ended as quickly as it had begun, the hostages now inside the dome tent and out of sight along with Usman. A guard closed the truck's tailgate, and it rumbled off as quickly as it had arrived, moving north and away from the camp. Cancer felt his heart slamming as he processed the sight, swallowing hard before he keyed his radio.

"A truck just dropped off four additional enemy fighters, including Usman. I have positive identification of Hostages Two, Three, and Four. Another white male that I couldn't PID, possibly Hostage One. All are inside the dome tent, along with Usman."

David responded excitedly, "*Any sign of the fifth hostage?*"

"Yeah, about that..." Cancer hesitated before continuing his transmission, replaying the mental images almost in an effort to convince himself he was wrong. But the sight had been clear enough, and with a final, steadying breath, he keyed his mic again.

"There aren't five hostages on target. There are seven—and at least one of them is a woman."

17

I watched the night sky from the edge of the clearing, scanning the cloudless starscape for any signs of movement. I couldn't hear or see any aircraft, but I knew they were up there somewhere. Then, turning my attention to ground level, I saw the tall grass drifting gently with the nighttime breeze, but no sign of life beyond the rolling symphony of insects. The sight was familiar: this was the enormous field we'd skirted on our infiltration the previous night. At that time, I'd seen the clearing as an enormous liability, a massive danger area far too close to our MSS.

But after the hostages arrived, it had become a godsend.

I checked my watch, expecting to be within range for a radio transmission any minute now. Then I quite abruptly realized I had to pee, and that this was my absolute last chance to do so. For a moment I prepared to take a bathroom break where I stood before looking at the night sky again, thinking better of it, and taking a few steps into the woods instead.

Somewhere overhead was an unseen fleet of aircraft surveilling the field and transmitting the footage to a host of locations from the Agency to JSOC, to say nothing of the Pentagon and White House. That level of scrutiny made me a little self-conscious about my last-minute urination, so I did my business under the cover of the forest canopy.

I was so dehydrated that I could smell my urine, and just as I noticed this peculiar detail, my earpiece came to life with the staticky voice of a man.

"*Passing through 4,000 feet on a nine-zero bearing. Suicide, throw me a visual.*"

Shaking off, I quickly recovered the strobe from my kit and returned to the edge of the field, turning it on and holding it aloft. The blazing pulses of infrared light came to life at six-second intervals, and I keyed my radio to say, "Strobe up."

Within seconds, the man replied, "*I have your strobe at the north end of the DZ. Kill it.*"

Turning off the device, I pocketed it and transmitted, "Ground winds are five knots from the north, gusting to ten."

I had enough skydiving experience to make the estimate reasonably accurate; still, I cursed myself for not having the foresight to purchase a simple handheld device to measure wind speed while we were in Abuja. At any rate, my estimate didn't matter much now—the train of a massive military operation was already in motion, and nothing would stop it.

The biggest wild card so far had been the appearance of two additional hostages, one of them female. According to my updates from Duchess, no one thus far had figured out who in the hell they were. Without reports of missing American citizens beyond the six oil executives, one of whom had been executed and three of whom had been positively identified on our target, there was no telling who the woman could be. But as with many terrorist groups, Boko Haram were no strangers to kidnapping foreign nationals. They could have snatched a few expats off the street for all I knew, and until a concerned family member or employer reported their absence, we'd be none the wiser.

I caught sight of the first incoming man a moment later—the silhouette of a body suspended beneath a rectangular parachute crested into view as he turned into the prevailing wind. He was followed seconds later by a second man, then a third, as a file of jumpers guided their canopies into the landing area.

Adjusting the rifle in my grasp, I watched the proceedings with a profound sense of awe.

The assault force was massive. With eight enemy fighters on the objective, I'd expected Delta Force to drop in a dozen of their superhuman shooters and call it a day.

So I'd been shocked to learn that they were inserting a staggering 23 men. The vast majority were Delta assaulters and snipers, but they also had three Air Force personnel—a combat controller to manage aircraft, and two pararescuemen for treating the hostages—along with an Explosive Ordinance Disposal specialist.

The parachutists lowered their rucks on retention lanyards, and the first one to land did so a few seconds after his pack thumped to the ground. He was only a few meters from my position in the woodline, having flown close to the edge to leave room for the waves of shooters flying in behind him.

Others began landing in roughly ten-second intervals, and after clearing the woods behind me to ensure there were no approaching enemies, I watched them assemble. It should have come as no surprise that they were supremely efficient; they were, after all, the apex predators of special operations for a reason.

They worked in pairs, with one man pulling security as his buddy stripped off his parachute, along with the oxygen equipment and cold weather gear required for a high-altitude parachute flight. Then they began laser-checking their weapons, the treeline glinting with infrared beams as each shooter confirmed his sight alignment survived the landings.

As the troop of men continued landing, the first two jumpers to touch down approached me, both toting their kit bags before depositing them at the treeline.

"Suicide?" one asked, watching me with his four-monocled night vision device.

"In the flesh," I said. "You the point man?"

"Yeah. Bronson."

I'd done my best to map out a series of checkpoints between this clearing and the MSS, planning a route that would keep the assault force out of the thorns and away from clearings. Those points were now loaded on the wrist-mounted GPS he checked presently, orienting himself in the direction we'd be moving as his partner pulled security.

I cautioned him, "After the MSS, best route is anyone's guess—my guys cloverleafed to the objective, so I'm not sure what the terrain will be like."

"No sweat, we'll find our way."

The final jumpers were touching down as a new trio of operators approached, dropping their kit bags on top of the pile as the point man turned to them and called out quietly, "Right here, boss."

The central figure stopped in front of me and said, "Danforth, GFC. How'd you guys get on target so fast?"

"We were in the area for another thing. Got lucky."

Turning to appraise the drop zone, where waves of shooters were hauling in their parachute equipment, he responded, "I want you to stay behind me in formation. We'll be following a recce element and a few assault teams."

"You got it. Once you're in position, my surveillance positions can open fire on your mark—"

"Hell no," he said. "We're going to get as close as humanly possible before we start shooting. Then we'll be moving through the camp at a sprint. I want your surveillance positions to hold their fire, *period*."

I recoiled at the comment, then realized that for all these guys knew, we were a few cowboys from Ground Branch with questionable marksmanship abilities. Given that this was a hostage rescue, every shot had to be surgical, and no one in the world did it better than Delta.

"No problem," I said, watching the operators consolidate in a perimeter around us. "It's your show. Just let us know how we can help."

"My guys are tracking your men's surveillance positions and will control their fire accordingly. But I don't want your people to move until I get the all-clear, then direct you to have them activate strobes and consolidate on the objective. Any updates at the camp?"

I lifted my ruck from the ground beside me, worming my arms through the straps as I replied.

"None of the hostages have moved from the dome tent. No piss breaks, nothing. My guys believe Usman is with them. Still three guys in perimeter security out of eight total, and I can get any updates you need en route."

"Good," he said, "hang on a sec."

Pausing to listen as various callsigns checked in over their radio frequency, the accountability ended with the commander transmitting, "Recce, lead us out."

Their point man led the way, trailing a wedge formation of assaulters.

Another wave of shooters filed into the woods before the commander took his place in the patrol, waving at me to follow. He was flanked by a unit radio operator on one side and an Air Force combat controller on the other, both of whom made quiet transmissions at various points to carry out his guidance. An hour ago these guys were leaping off the ramp at 20,000 feet to begin a high-altitude, cross-country canopy flight to the landing area, and now they were en route to the objective as casually as if this were a routine training patrol.

Staying a few meters behind the commander as the assault force slipped north through the Sambisa Forest, I keyed my team radio and whispered, "Assault force is on the ground. We're beginning movement."

18

Ian remained under the cover of the hide site, now its sole occupant.

He'd offered to accompany David to the drop zone, of course, but his team leader had been adamant that the hide site was a much safer place to wait. If he got smoked on his way to meet the incoming Delta shooters, he said, the assault would proceed regardless—and there was no need for Ian to risk his life.

So Ian waited alone in the darkness, acting as an observation post to listen for enemy movement ahead of the assault force. As he did so, he felt a mounting sense of unease.

Everyone on the team had their concerns, but Ian's had nothing to do with the tactical situation ahead and everything to do with the appearance of seven hostages on their objective. They'd only expected five, of which only three had been positively identified; a fourth was very likely the remaining oil executive that Cancer had spotted but been unable to confirm. Even if the fifth hostage was one of the two that Cancer had been unable to see clearly—a very big *if*, in Ian's mind—then who were the additional two hostages, one of them a woman?

But when Ian proposed questions about the two additional captives, the general consensus from his teammates had been, who cares? They'd come for five hostages and would help save seven instead. Sweet.

For Ian, however, that abnormality marked the onset of a disturbing series of questions that had no answers. Sure, it was theoretically possible that Boko Haram had snatched two targets of opportunity somewhere between Lagos and the Sambisa Forest. That wasn't, however, what had occurred—Usman had taken a substantial force across Nigeria, far from their secure territory in the northeast, to the delta region where his organization rarely operated, all to conduct a remarkably sophisticated kidnapping attempt that indicated weeks if not months of detailed planning. He'd even lost a trail vehicle in his convoy to Ian's team, ditched his cell phone, and still proceeded.

Nowhere in that chain of events was there room to seize a pair of accidental hostages, particularly when the consequences risked Usman exposing his entire operation. No, Ian thought, the terrorist leader knew exactly who he was snatching and why, and the explanation would only become clear if and when Delta succeeded in securing the camp.

Cancer transmitted then, speaking in a tone of disbelief.

"They really said we're not supposed to shoot anybody? Like, zero shots fired?"

Ian shook his head. Even now, no one but him cared about anything other than the tactical particulars.

David replied, *"The commander was very clear on that point. They're going to assault directly between your surveillance positions. And you need to stay in place until I direct you to come out—then you'll follow their people off the objective and link up with me for the return trip."*

Now Cancer sounded professionally offended.

"What, they think we're some kind of amateurs?"

Worthy replied, *"No, they think we're not Delta Force. And we're not. Just let them do their thing—this isn't their first rodeo."*

Then David transmitted, *"Angel, point man is a hundred meters out. Kick on your strobe."*

Ian crawled out of the hide site with his weapon, hauling his rucksack out behind him. Strapping on the pack, he fired his infrared strobe and held it aloft, scanning the forest to his south for any sign of the approaching force and finding none.

But within seconds, David came over the net again.

"All right, he's got you. Turn it off."

Ian complied, donning his ruck before waiting nervously with weapon in hand until he discerned movement through the trees. At first he only saw the hints of a few shadowy figures passing among the forest, then made out more people until he realized he was looking at the lead assault team in a tight wedge.

For a moment, he thought the formation had missed the MSS entirely. The formation of shooters breezed straight past him, ten meters away from the hide site, as if there had been no mention of a linkup at all. They moved remarkably quietly, their footsteps guided by the best night vision that money could buy.

An infrared laser appeared on a tree to his side, then traced downward through the undergrowth back to its source in the formation as David transmitted, *"Angel, come to me."*

The intelligence operative did as he was told, moving laterally to the assault force until he met up with David, following silently in the footsteps of the ground force commander.

19

"*Objective rally point established 500 meters south of objective,*" David said.

The transmission caught Cancer off guard—the assault force had already made shockingly fast progress through the forest. Now that they'd dropped off their rucks at an ORP, Cancer thought, this thing was going to kick off sooner rather than later.

David continued, "*GFC requests a final update before proceeding with assault. Cancer, send it.*"

The sniper scanned the objective before replying, "Still got a guard outside Tent Two oriented north, and a guy west of Tent Three oriented south."

"*Stand by.*" There was a pause as David relayed the information to the Delta commander, and then he continued, "*Racegun, go ahead.*"

Worthy answered, "*PK gunner still facing north beside Tent One. A single roving guard came out of Tent Four a few minutes ago; he's currently stationary next to the road at the north edge of the camp.*"

After another brief pause, David transmitted, "*Copy all, assault force is moving out to the target. Clear the net for emergency updates, and stand by for the raid to commence.*"

Sure thing, Cancer thought, continuing to scan the camp for any changes to enemy disposition as he waited for the assault to commence.

Cancer had been trying to reconcile why the Delta guys wouldn't let his team open fire on the enemy in conjunction with their own snipers. It wasn't as if his team couldn't distinguish friendly from enemy; hell, they'd been the ones with eyes-on the objective, and that was the only reason anyone knew the hostages were here in the first place. To be relegated to the status of impotent observer in the wake of a historic hostage rescue seemed like a slap in the face after all the work, and frankly luck, leading up to this point.

And yeah, he got it. They were Delta Force, the intergalactic ninja death squad. Neurosurgeons of hostage rescue and all that. If they didn't want his team shooting, they surely had reasons of their own, and naivety wasn't one of them.

Still, Cancer decided, being a lone sniper had its advantages. His team had been sent to Nigeria to bag Usman Mokhammed, and that little shitbag was still camped out in the dome tent alongside the hostages. Cancer resolved to keep a close eye on that structure. In his experience, terrorist leaders tended to embrace their inner Olympic sprinter as soon as the shooting started, leaving it to their underlings to fight and die as they escaped.

And when Usman burst out of that tent to flee, Cancer was going to drop him like a sick animal.

He continued to lie in wait, expecting the fireworks to begin any moment now, but nothing happened. The visible guards continued to mull around the camp, the minutes seeming to stretch on endlessly as Cancer waited for the first shots to break out. He supposed that made sense; the assault force was probably creeping forward as silently as they could, closing the final distance with measured footfalls to keep from being compromised.

Cancer could tell the exact moment the enemy detected them.

There was a shout from the south side of camp, and the guard force began scrambling into position to face the woodline. Men were spilling out of the A-frame tents, emerging shirtless with a rifle in one hand and their magazine carriers in the other.

Delta's response was equally abrupt. Within a second of the initial shout, every visible enemy was glowing with a constellation of infrared laser dots. Cancer was certain the melee would begin then, but none of the assaulters or their accompanying snipers took a shot. Instead, the enemy continued taking up fighting positions at the south side of the camp, yelling to one another and aiming their weapons in fear and uncertainty.

What was the assault force waiting for? Hostage rescue wasn't Cancer's forte, but this was insanity. They had seemingly every bad guy in their sights, yet held their fire for reasons that he couldn't fathom.

Ultimately, it wasn't until the first guard opened fire with his AK-47 that anyone from the Delta formation took action. But when they did, it was a thing of beauty.

The roaring burst from the assault rifle ended when the shooter's chest split apart from return fire, and the sweeping rays of infrared lasers trembled with suppressed shots that decimated the enemy force. Standing enemies were falling dead before they could shoot, and those in the prone were slumped over their weapons as volley after volley of incoming fire laced through their bodies.

Only then did the assaulters storm out of the woods, the sheer immediacy of their arrival a shock even to Cancer—they must have been barely hidden in the vegetation at the camp's fringes.

This thing was going to be over as quickly as it began, Cancer thought, and swung his aim to the dome tent as he waited for Usman to emerge.

Reilly watched the assault proceed through the screen of his night vision, the dark figures of Delta operators swarming across the camp with blinding speed.

The enemy force had simply wilted under their gunfire, and the medic only spotted one who survived long enough to run—an act he performed with impressive speed, legs pumping, his rifle in one hand as he sped north into Reilly's line of sight.

Reilly knew he wasn't supposed to shoot, but he'd be damned if he was going to risk that man flanking his position. Tracing the fighter's path with his HK417, he fired three suppressed shots that ended his departure attempt. The fleeing enemy staggered and fell, hitting the ground with his legs spasming. The medic kept his aim but didn't fire—unless the fighter was able to reach for the rifle that had fallen from his grasp, Reilly would let Delta finish him off.

As it turned out, that didn't take long to occur.

A pair of infrared lasers met the downed man almost as soon as he fell, and apparently these Delta guys didn't like to take chances. Two of them fired a combined total of six to eight rounds into his figure, at least two at his skull, before racing past the body and setting up security at the north woodline.

They were followed moments later by a swarm of shooters establishing a perimeter in all directions from the camp, including one who knelt beside a tree and faced Reilly and his partner in the brush. The medic wasn't afraid of friendly fire per se, but erring on the side of safety, he twisted a knob on his night vision to send two infrared flashes in a momentary designation of his position.

The nearest shooter responded in kind, two blinks of an IR flash to indicate he'd seen the signal. No sooner had that occurred than David transmitted the impossible.

"*All secure,*" he said. "*The seven hostages are alive, no friendly casualties, and they're prepping for exfil. Activate your strobes and consolidate on the objective.*"

Reilly could barely believe what he was hearing—the assault had just begun, the entire sweep from first shot to last occurring over the course of two minutes at most.

From his position beside Reilly, Worthy said, "Let's do it."

Then the point man activated his infrared strobe, reaching for his rucksack as Reilly did the same.

Worthy shouldered his pack and took the first tentative steps toward the clearing, shouting, "Friendlies coming out!"

After 28 hours of not speaking above a whisper, the announcement felt almost alien to him, his parched throat straining at the effort.

But the nearest operator responded in kind, "Come out," and when

Worthy and Reilly emerged from the woods, turning off their IR strobes, he pointed to their left and said, "Command cell is at the south woodline. Link up there, we're stepping off in five mikes."

Worthy nodded in gratitude as he made his way to the center of the objective, hearing Reilly address the perimeter operators as they passed.

"Nice work, fellas."

His comment went unanswered—these guys were all business. As Worthy made his way through the camp, he took in the frenzy of post-assault activities around him. While much of the visible force was occupied with securing the camp perimeter, those who remained were moving with a choreographed fluidity. Some operators were searching the tents and bodies for intelligence, others consolidating the enemy weapons in a pile where an EOD man was preparing a demolitions charge on a time delay to blow them in place.

Cancer came slogging past the final few bushes at the western edge of the clearing, hissing in pain as his legs collected thorns. Worthy turned his attention to the dome tent, where he saw operators pulling out the hostages one by one.

It was hard to quantify the immense relief he felt at the sight; three men were already lined up outside, clearly in shock and recognizable from the hostage profiles he'd studied as the missing oil executives. The hostages were getting the VIP treatment—operators were addressing them by first name, asking if they had any injuries and assuring them they were safe. Worthy actually saw an operator handing the men water bottles and Snickers bars, which seemed ludicrous until he considered their blood sugar was probably at rock bottom after two days of Boko Haram hospitality.

A fourth man was escorted outside next—another executive, this one shaking badly—and as Worthy slowed his pace, he watched for the fifth and final ExxonMobil employee to appear.

But a woman was led out of the tent next: dark hair, maybe mid-thirties, and very fit. She was sobbing as she joined the others for processing, and Worthy was horrified to see that the next hostage wasn't an oil executive at all, but a second female.

This one was more composed, arms folded tightly across her chest as she was questioned. Then, impossibly, came a *third* woman, beautiful even from a distance, and Worthy realized that they were still short one known hostage...his first indication that something had gone horribly awry.

His second indication came a moment later, causing him to halt in his tracks with disbelief.

"Let's go," an operator called to them. "All OGA to the command cell. We've got to move."

He was using the acronym for Other Government Agency, the catch-all military term for CIA personnel, but Worthy was only half-listening. He watched another man being escorted out of the dome tent, this one with his hands restrained behind his back and a Delta operator holding each arm.

Worthy felt his jaw drop, unable to process the sight.

The captive was Usman.

20

I was slogging through the brush, keeping a tight interval behind the Delta commander, when the distant blast reverberated on the objective.

Whatever weapons the Boko Haram fighters had in the camp just went up in a fireball, and as the echo faded, my attention returned to the exfil-in-progress: a boring march through the forest, the assault force entirely uncontested. To say it was a letdown was an understatement. I was hoping to serve as a rear vanguard for the withdrawal, perhaps sent to deal with an enemy force while allowing the hostages to proceed toward the clearing unhindered.

But these guys wanted us to stay in the center of the formation with our mouths shut, and the last thing they needed was any more shooters. Over the entire course of the mission, I hadn't even gotten to see the objective—the GFC and his accompanying radio operator and combat controller had remained ten meters back in the woodline, coordinating aircraft and relaying to their command.

The movement out couldn't have been more at odds with the movement in—while their approach had occurred with painstaking stealth, their exit was only quasi-tactical. Hostage escorts were using their taclights to illuminate the ground for the newly-freed Americans, while a file of shooters moved on either side in a formation that could best be described as forming a human shield. Noise discipline was a distant afterthought to moving as quickly as possible—a fitting compromise, I thought. While the night had been almost silent prior to the assault, now it sounded like we were on the flight line of an airport.

The sky hummed with multiple levels of support aircraft that had swooped into audible range the moment the hostages were recovered, least of all the unmistakably low roar of fighter jets orbiting above the Sambisa Forest. They were joined now by a thin buzzing noise that sounded almost comically understated by comparison, at least to anyone who didn't know what it was. Seen from most angles, the AC-130 gunship looked like any other cargo plane; but when it banked left, the business side of the bird tilted an array of deadly cannons and missile pods toward the unfortunate souls on the receiving end.

So many aircraft orbited overhead that I had to strain to hear the radio transmission over my earpiece—Cancer speaking in his usual pissed-off tone.

"Can't believe the one fuck we were sent here for in the first place was the only bad guy to survive."

Keying my radio, I asked, "What are you talking about?"

Worthy replied, *"Commander didn't tell you?"*

"The GFC hasn't told me shit," I said. So far he'd been too occupied with running communications—to his troop sergeant major via his own radio, to his command via the unit radio operator, and to the aircraft by way of the Air Force combat controller— and even if that weren't the case, he didn't seem interested in my team beyond knowing we were all within the formation prior to leaving.

Worthy's response caught me off guard. *"Usman is in the formation—they took him captive. He's walking out with the hostages."*

My gut response to the news was revulsion. The man had decapitated an American citizen on camera, then distributed the footage along with his demands. If there was one person Delta should have shot in the face at the first available opportunity, it was him.

But there was a plus side to having him alive, and I pointed it out on my return transmission.

"At least they'll be able to interrogate him. It's not like we had the manpower to pull off a snatch operation on our own, or the legality."

Reilly pointed out, "*That didn't stop us in China.*"

"The exception that proves the rule," I said. "My guess is the Agency interrogators will convince Usman to renounce his wayward path. Who knows, maybe he'll provide some good intel."

"*I hate to break this to you,*" Ian broke in, sounding irritated, "*but Usman's captivity is going to be short-lived, and in the meantime, he's going to be eating filet mignon under the capitol building in Abuja.*"

"What's that supposed to mean?" I asked.

"*Do the math. Six oil execs were captured, and only five of them survived until the rescue. Delta just freed four, along with three mystery women—I have my theories as to who they are—which leaves at least one hostage in the breeze. And if you think he's dead, think again.*"

Threading my way between the thorny bushes on either side of me, I said, "Why don't you spare us the dissertation and get to the fucking point."

"*You want the point? Here it is: the US will transfer custody of Usman to the Nigerians.*"

"No way," I said, crouching and pushing a vine away from my face as I cleared a low swath of tree cover.

"*Think about it. America just launched a knee-jerk hostage rescue to the tune of a hundred million dollars, and one of the execs is still missing. You think they won't give up Usman in a heartbeat to get him back?*"

Cancer pointed out, "*America doesn't negotiate with terrorists.*"

Ian was undeterred.

"*No, America doesn't* publicly *negotiate with terrorists. They'll work through proxies all day, though, and in this case let Nigeria do it for them. Nobody knows that better than Usman himself.*"

"Bullshit," Cancer said.

"*Think I'm wrong? Suicide, ask the GFC how they rolled up Usman alive. Want me to spoil the surprise? He hid out with the hostages, and surrendered unarmed.*"

I hesitated for a moment, then keyed my mic and said, "Stand by."

Closing the distance with the Delta commander, I tried to ask what had happened, but the combat controller spoke first. "Sir, Warlock has eyes-on six armed men skirting a field eight hundred meters to our northwest. Well outside minimum safe distance."

"Legal?" the commander asked.

"Absolutely."

"Hit them."

The combat controller's tone went from conversational to clinical as he transmitted, "Warlock Three Two, this is Anarchy Two Seven. GFC assesses imminent threat to friendly forces; you are clear to engage PAX in the open, request two-by Hellfire and clean up with 30 mike-mike, send battle damage assessment when able."

I couldn't hear the aircrew's radio response, but the outcome was clear enough. The distant screech of two missiles was followed by their near-simultaneous explosions and then the low, rhythmic *thunk-thunk-thunk* of a 30-millimeter chain gun firing.

"Roger all," the combat controller transmitted, then, to the commander, said, "Six EKIA."

The GFC relayed the development over his own command frequency, and I waited for him to finish before asking, "How'd you guys manage to roll up Usman?"

Seeming inconvenienced by my interruption, he answered, "Usman surrendered, unarmed."

"So?"

"So," the commander continued impatiently, "he was with the witnesses —er, hostages."

I knew what he meant. These guys could have smoked him under any number of perceived-threat justifications—maybe he had a suicide vest, for example—but not in front of seven civilians who could report a question-able kill, potentially to the media.

Falling back to my previous interval, I transmitted to my team.

"Angel, you're right."

"*I know I am,*" Ian shot back, "*and here's another thing no one is considering. The missing hostage we know about isn't the only one. Otherwise, there wouldn't have been women on the objective.*"

"What do you mean?"

"*Because of the number three.*"

Before I could ask him for clarification, we'd reached the clearing, and the lead elements in the formation began fanning out to secure it for exfil. I'd barely arrived at the edge of the field when I heard the first Marine Osprey thundering in to land. The long fuselage was suspended between stubby wings whose tilt rotor assemblies were angled upward, the shadowy discs chopping the air as the bird spun in place and touched down with its ramp facing us.

I could make out a field surgical team in the open cabin, prepared to treat the hostages and any casualties from the assault force. My view of the men aboard was obscured by the first contingent of Delta operators crossing in front of me, escorting the hostages to the aircraft. It was my first clear look at them the entire mission, four men and three women shuffling forward beside a corresponding shooter clasping them by the arm.

At the end of the row was an eighth passenger, this one with his hands bound behind his back, a soldier on either side of him. Usman passed within a few feet of me, his expression clear in my night vision—the smug bastard looked completely at ease, walking casually, as if his escorts were personal aides.

The procession marched forward and onto the bird, the ramp closing after them as its engines spooled to full power. Then the aircraft lifted straight up, wobbling slightly as it rose to a hundred feet and then drifted forward, passing out of view over the trees.

Three more Ospreys glided into view, landing in an echelon formation as the Delta operators hoisted parachute kit bags and lined up in chalks to load. My team each grabbed a kit bag to lighten the load from the missing hostage escorts, then took our place in the rightmost line of shooters. We filed between two operators that formed a chokepoint, slapping the shoulder of each man as he passed to maintain a running count. Then our file jogged across the field, following the lead operator onto the Osprey's ramp, then into the narrow cabin where the lead shooters were dropping their kit bags into the center before stripping their rucks and claiming drop seats. I looked toward the open ramp, counting off the other four members of my team as Cancer gave me a thumbs up to indicate everyone was accounted for.

We didn't take off immediately; some of the Delta guys had to shuttle a

few more kit bags aboard while the final contingent maintained local security. Above the idling roar of the engines, I heard Reilly shouting out to the
Delta operators seated around us.

"Hey, you guys got any of those Snickers left?"

It seemed like a badly timed joke that neither I nor anyone aboard
would understand; but to my surprise, one of the assaulters procured a
candy bar and passed it down the row to him.

"Sweet." Reilly ripped apart the wrapper. "Thanks, bro!"

Then the ramp closed halfway, the engine noise growing louder as we
lifted off and began a vertical ascent.

I caught a final glimpse of the Sambisa Forest out the ramp, a black
swath that vanished from view as the Marine pilots banked the Osprey into
a hard left turn, toward Abuja.

21

Ian watched David closely, waiting for some response to his extended explanation as they sat in the ad hoc operations center of their Abuja safehouse.

David, for his part, looked like shit—unshaven, bags under his eyes, hair disheveled as he sat there in his T-shirt and boxers.

Ian knew he probably looked just as bad, but sometimes the devil lay in the details.

While everyone else in the team had slept in ahead of Duchess's call, Ian had been the first one awake. He'd used his time wisely, first calling Tolu to place his order, then making the first pot of coffee and drinking three cups by the time the Nigerian driver arrived with the goods: three dozen eggs, bacon, sausages, and fresh cheese.

Ian hadn't cooked, of course, leaving that to the next two men awake, both having slept until close to noon: Worthy and Reilly, who began preparing breakfast as Ian pored over intelligence reports, drank more coffee, and grew increasingly confident in his theories, which he'd just finished briefing to David.

Finally, the team leader responded, "I don't know, man. Seems far-fetched, is all."

"You're under-caffeinated," Ian replied, checking his watch, "and under-fed. Go get some food and coffee before Duchess calls."

David rose and shuffled off, leaving Ian to face his computer and the latest news from this corner of the world—breaking reports of a joint US-Nigerian raid yielding seven hostages and thirteen enemies dead, along with the capture of a high-ranking terrorist. Having been on scene, Ian concluded that the "joint" specification was a concession to the Nigerian government, which was probably notified last-minute of the arrival of US forces to their airspace, then kept completely in the dark as to the target location lest their political staff let the details slip too soon.

Ian took another sip of hot coffee, considering the previous night's festivities.

The reception at Nnamdi Azikiwe International Airport outside Abuja was carefully orchestrated chaos—an entire terminal had been shut down by the Nigerian government, with two Air Force C-17 cargo planes staged on the runway. One was for the Delta Force shooters to return to Fort Bragg, North Carolina, where they'd immediately refit and stand by for the next international crisis. The second bird was for the hostages, who would be transported stateside under the care of a full onboard medical and psychiatric staff, along with military and CIA intelligence personnel to conduct debriefs in the hopes of obtaining any information on the remaining hostage's whereabouts.

Where Usman had gone remained to be seen—Ian's team had quietly boarded an unmarked vehicle that the Agency had sent for them, then returned to their Abuja safehouse to await Duchess's next call. And while Ian remained confident in his assessment that Usman would be transferred to Nigerian custody, he had no earthly idea what his team's next tasking would be. An American oil executive was still missing—along with, Ian speculated, at least two other unidentified hostages—and while his team's charter had nothing to do with searching for captured Americans, they'd succeeded in executing an impromptu special reconnaissance mission that resulted in a successful hostage rescue. For that, if nothing else, they should have been justified to receive an assignment in the collective effort that was sure to follow.

Cancer entered the room then, and the sight of him almost made Ian startle with disgust.

He looked about as bedraggled as David had, with a few notable exceptions. While his team leader had the self-awareness to pull on a T-shirt over boxers, Cancer was both shirtless and wearing tighty-whities, with a lit cigarette dangling from his lips as a final affront to any sense of professionalism.

Cancer pulled back a chair and took a seat beside Ian, lifting one sandal-clad foot onto the desk and exposing a pale, hairy thigh crisscrossed with lacerations from the thorn bushes as he spoke with an exhaling puff of smoke. "What's good, Ian?"

"Please put your leg down. Have some respect."

Squinting at the computer clock, Cancer took another drag and said, "We've got twelve minutes before the call. Fill me in before then, or I'll hang brain and make you really regret not telling me."

Aside from not knowing—or particularly wanting to know—what that meant, and having received a less than enthusiastic response from David, Ian spoke quickly.

"Usman may be a sociopath, but he's smart. I told you last night, it's all about the number three. He initially demanded the release of two Boko Haram leaders, but surrendered to the Delta guys rather than put up a fight. He wouldn't do that unless he had an insurance policy in place, and since he wouldn't go back on his previous demand, that means he staged three hostages in advance to cover the possibility of him being captured."

Cancer looked unconvinced, taking a leisurely exhale of his cigarette.

"But there's only one missing executive."

"You saw those women on the objective," Ian pointed out. "Mark my words: there are two more where those came from."

"Who were they, anyway? ExxonMobil would've known if any wives went missing."

"They weren't wives."

"Three of those guys were married—"

Ian snorted a laugh. "They were girlfriends."

"Girlfriends?"

"Mistresses."

"Mistresses?" Cancer scoffed. "How'd you arrive at that?"

Leaning forward in his seat, then back again in consideration for the proximity of Cancer's nether regions, Ian said, "It's the only logical explanation. These guys are big oil executives working in Nigeria while their families are back in the States, right? Even under night vision, those women were not unattractive. No way Usman got distracted from his core hostage-snatching mission to roll up a few expats, particularly after we knocked out his tail vehicle on our first attempt to get him. Conclusion? He targeted the oil execs, and the women were targets of opportunity at the same location."

Cancer took another puff of smoke. "Son of a bitch. So that's how you know—"

"That there are two more? Yes. Otherwise Usman would have covered their bases by separating two more oil executives from the main group of hostages."

"Why not do that anyway?"

Ian shrugged. "Female hostages will incur more international outrage. Especially since rape and sex slavery are cornerstones of Boko Haram's corporate policy. Remember all the hashtags when they captured those schoolgirls? More pressure to recover the hostages equals a greater likelihood of their demands being met, albeit through third-party channels."

Nodding in silent consideration, Cancer asked, "You tell all this to David?"

"Yup."

"He believe you?"

"Nope. Doesn't matter—he's going to hear it all from Duchess in a few minutes. The question is, what's she going to do with us?"

Cancer eyed Ian warily, a tendril of smoke rising lazily from his cigarette. "For someone with pronounced tactical ineptitudes, you can be pretty smart at times."

"Someone's got to be the brains of this operation, no?"

"And someone's got to be the looks," David called out from the doorway as he entered the room with coffee in hand. "Sure as shit not going to be either of you two. Cancer, put your old-man balls away before you scare Ian into therapy."

Cancer took his leg off the desk somewhat self-consciously and asked, "You really don't believe this clown?"

David pulled up a chair and said, "It's a fine working theory, I suppose. But Ian's not telepathic, so there's no way he's right about all of it. I wouldn't be surprised if there's a completely different explanation we haven't considered."

Before he could speak further, the desk phone rang.

Ian checked his watch, then raised his eyebrows at David. "Duchess is early."

22

Duchess held the receiver to her ear, listening to the male switchboard operator say politely, "It's ringing now, ma'am." She took a sip of tea from the mug on her desk as she waited, then set it beside her keyboard as she studied the photograph of a man on her computer screen.

She'd retreated to her office for the call, the only place she could have a candid conversation away from the OPCEN's prying ears.

And the call she was about to have was particularly candid.

It wasn't just the new tasking for her Longwing team, but the *why* behind it. Political approvals often moved at a snail's pace, and right now she had no time to spare. When the current administration said the gloves were off, they meant it—but the moment their goal was attained, the free rein would end.

In between those two moments, though, was a twilight period where Duchess could further her own agenda, one focused less on the current hostages and more on pursuing a new global terror organization that could easily kidnap hundreds more in the coming years.

Project Longwing had been creeping incrementally closer to uncovering that network, first by disrupting its earliest known effort—the July 4th attack—and then, in China, by attaining the first pseudonym linked to one of its agents: Erik Weisz.

That name, and the money trail leading to a Nigerian bank official, had led to Duchess selecting a Boko Haram target in the first place. The ongoing hostage crisis was merely a coincidence, and while she'd never admit this, a lucky one in the grander effort to track down Weisz and his people. Her personal theory of a new terror organization, however, hadn't yet translated to additional operational authorities, so she had to make do with the limited resources at her disposal. At the moment those consisted chiefly of a single ground team, and with the current situation in Nigeria, she could now justify using them however she damn well pleased.

But only until the hostages were recovered.

After that, she'd be back to grasping at straws. As she waited for the call to connect, Duchess decided that she was going to make the most of it while she still could.

Finally the switchboard operator said, "It's connected, I'm patching you through."

Duchess waited a moment and heard a new voice on the line.

"David here. I've got you on speaker with my guys."

Drawing a breath, she replied, "Then let me congratulate your entire team on a successful reconnaissance mission. If you hadn't been able to pull that off, it's very likely we'd be weeks from locating, much less rescuing, those hostages."

"Speaking of hostages," David countered, "my understanding is that we're still down one oil executive, and up three women the US didn't even know were missing. News reports have been pretty vague about the women, though—who are they?"

A wry observation, Duchess thought. "Two Americans and one Canadian, all expats with dual citizenship living in Nigeria. News reports will remain vague because as it turns out, all three were shacking up with married ExxonMobil employees during their lengthy stay in the country."

David snickered. "If you can't trust wealthy oil company executives, who can you trust?"

"It gets worse," she said. "The rescued hostages confirmed that an additional two women were captured and are still at large. Both Americans."

The slapping sound of a high five came over the line then, though David sounded disappointed as he continued, "Well, I have to say that Ian predicted all of this, so let's see if he's right on one more point. Where is Usman?"

Duchess reached for her mug, then thought better of it and cleared her throat instead.

"He was transferred to Nigerian custody last night."

He shot back, "Why would we give him to the Nigerians?"

"What an excellent question," Duchess responded dryly. "Short answer? Due to rampant corruption, the Nigerians weren't notified of the hostage rescue effort until the last possible minute. They are deeply embarrassed, and the transfer of Boko Haram prisoners was part of the arrangement in allowing the US to take over the airport in Abuja to facilitate repatriation."

A new voice spoke, this one slightly more nasal.

"Duchess, this is Ian. Usman's surrender along with three hostages being kept offsite indicates that Boko Haram will demand a three-for-three exchange, and when that happens, we both know the Nigerians are going to give it to them."

Duchess nodded. "I think that's exactly why the administration agreed to hand over Usman. They want the hostages back, and if they can do that without launching another costly and high-risk military operation, so much the better."

David interjected, "If everyone's expecting Usman to be released, then we should stay in the country to carry out our original mission. Maybe hit him before he disappears in Boko Haram territory for another six months or more."

"We still don't have any official statement from Boko Haram," Duchess said. "Forget about Usman for a moment. The administration has ordered a military and intelligence free-for-all to find the three remaining hostages, and the priority is locating them before another decapitation video surfaces. They're giving the green light to everyone who's offering their services, which means I can keep you in play—but only until the clock runs out."

"Which means what," David asked, "we go back to some grid in the Sambisa?"

She felt a vague smile playing at her lips.

"We were lucky to have the lead we did, and there is no other verifiable intelligence that would justify another special reconnaissance mission. No, David, I've got something much more interesting in mind for your team, and a very finite span of time where I can act on it."

Ian spoke again, preempting her revelation. "We're going back to the reason you sent us to Nigeria in the first place: the money trail. You're giving us the banker."

Her smile abruptly turned to a frown.

"'Giving' him to you implies a targeted killing operation. That's not what this is."

David asked, "Then what is it?"

"The banker has been linked with transfers of terrorist-related funding, to include acting as a courier for paper money. I've gained approval for an intelligence-gathering operation, on the basis that any materials recovered can be traced toward Boko Haram and provide possible leads to the hostage location or locations."

"And if we get any intel on this Erik Weisz figure in the process—"

"So much the better," she replied. "But that's not our official justification, nor can it be. The point remains that we may have lost Usman, but we can continue following the lead of something bigger—albeit only until the hostages are recovered. After that, the long leash I've been granted gets tightened, and you're back on a plane to the US."

"So if we can't kill the banker, then what can we do?"

Duchess's gaze flicked back to her screen, where the man's face stared back in a snapshot from his employee identification badge. She said, "He travels to and from work with a laptop in addition to one or more cell phones. You are authorized to use only non-lethal—I say again, *non-lethal*—force to recover those devices, along with anything else on his person. As ever, there must be nothing to indicate that the US had a hand in it."

David sounded ambivalent. "People get mugged every day in Abuja. Push us whatever you've got on this guy, and we'll get surveillance up and running by this afternoon."

"There's no need for that. We've already obtained a pattern of life based on the historical picture from his cell phone GPS. I'm looking at his full target profile, home and work addresses, and real-time cellular tracking."

The team leader's voice became wary. "A few days ago it was a stretch to follow Usman's cell phone, and you'd been monitoring him for months. Where are you suddenly getting all this real-time capability?"

Duchess didn't want to say too much—the truth was, Jo Ann's friend in the ISA, one Ben Bailey, had been more than eager to help. The man with the New York accent hadn't simply delivered, he'd overdelivered, using his team's resources in Abuja to obtain local data in record time.

She admitted cautiously, "We've received some assistance from a forward-deployed Activity team." Then, lifting her mug of tea without taking a sip, she continued, "And that element is monitoring phone activity from the banker's office at this time. However he reacts to a theft of possibly incriminating devices could be just as telling as whatever you take from him—who he reports the loss to, and what he says about the theft. None of that happens unless you move on this asap; with Boko Haram likely moving for a hostage exchange any day now, we have no time to spare. Because once those American citizens are recovered, there's a very high likelihood that the administration will pull everyone out of Nigeria, your team included. I can't do anything to stop it. This banker represents our one and only link to Erik Weisz, and if we lose that now, we won't get it back."

23

Worthy sat in the passenger seat, watching the twin iron gates of the Central Bank of Nigeria building from his vantage point in a parking lot across the street.

The gates were staffed by a quartet of uniformed security officers who serviced incoming vehicles, checking identification and running a mirror wand across the undercarriage before waving drivers through. Far more prevalent at this early evening hour, however, were cars leaving the compound rather than entering. They proceeded past an automatic exit gate before turning onto the side street and disappearing from view; and so far, none of them had been Olapido Keyamo, the corrupt Nigerian bank official Worthy's team had been authorized to shake down for intel.

Tolu spoke from the driver's seat. "Why you not just walk up in there, take what you need like a real bank robber."

Worthy glanced at the building, a concrete leviathan contained by a solid perimeter fence boasting all the barbed wire and security cameras he'd expect from a major financial institution located in a country with a thriving terrorist population.

"Not sure that'd work out so well. You trying to get rid of me?"

"No, I *dey miss you* when you go. Just tired of sitting is all."

Worthy, for his part, had no complaints. After a long recon mission of lying in the bug-and-snake-infested brush of Boko Haram country, doing his best to ration a dwindling water supply, this assignment was like a trip to the spa. He was fed, showered, and sitting in the relatively comfortable passenger seat of a climate-controlled vehicle. Even the rap music that Tolu kept humming through the speakers didn't bother him, which was a big leap from what he could have said on their previous drive toward the Sambisa Forest.

David transmitted, "*Heads up, looks like he's on the move.*"

Worthy checked his phone display, seeing that Keyamo's tracking beacon had indeed shifted position outside the building.

"Copy," Worthy replied, "will advise when I get visual on the target vehicle."

Then, to Tolu, he said, "Looks like you're getting your wish. Should be any minute now."

Clapping his hands together three times, Tolu gripped the steering wheel and said, "I keep my eyes out for the Benny."

Worthy continued watching his phone, seeing that the beacon remained stationary.

Duchess had assured them that with the Intelligence Support Activity's wealth of surveillance equipment in Abuja, the tracking data following Keyamo's phone should occur in near-real time.

That much was of little consolation to the team, however, and after the debacle of trying to roll up Usman along the highway, David had wisely mandated that a team member follow the banker as soon as he left work. Worthy couldn't argue with that—if the timeline on this kind of free-range operation was as tight as Duchess seemed to think it was, rolling the mission to the next day could cause it to not occur at all.

The beacon suddenly began moving, each blip bringing it closer to the compound exit—too fast for a walking man, Worthy noted with pleasure.

"Here we go," he said to Tolu, looking up to see a pair of slightly oval-shaped headlights gleaming from either side of a massive front grill approaching the exit gate.

Worthy transmitted, "Eyes-on a black Bentley sedan exiting the compound; vehicle make and phone tracker check out. We're moving now."

Then Tolu began driving, but not in pursuit of Keyamo's Bentley;

instead, he took a circuitous route toward Ahmadu Bello Way, the four-lane road their target used to get home.

Ideally they'd have a rotation of two or three cars to maintain continuous visual on Keyamo without arousing suspicion during the three-kilometer drive to his residence, but the mission ahead didn't leave that kind of manpower to spare.

So Tolu sped down the side streets instead, moving toward an intercept point along the main route as quickly as he could—which, given the number of other cars on the road, turned out to be one hell of a lot slower than Worthy would have preferred.

"This traffic is terrible," Worthy muttered.

"You think this is bad? Never visit Lagos."

"I thought you liked Lagos."

"Like?" Tolu echoed, sounding irritated. "LOVE. Lagos is my home, the greatest city in all of Africa. But a ten-minute drive takes an hour, and this is because everyone wants to live there."

Then, his tone growing more playful, he added, "Lagos is also where I learned to drive like this."

He swerved around the vehicle to their front, accelerating toward oncoming headlights before cutting back into his lane. Worthy's passenger mirror nearly clipped a bicycle piloted by a woman who, to the point man's alarm, didn't seem to notice.

Then Tolu careened right, speeding through a parking lot before re-entering the side street ahead of two slower vehicles. Bracing a hand on the door panel, Worthy watched his phone display and said, "Just take it easy. He hit a stoplight; we've got time."

"Listen *well well*," Tolu answered him, maneuvering the car around their next corner, "I know we got time. Because you got me at the wheel, no *wahala*."

No sooner had the sentence left his mouth than he slammed on the brakes, screeching to a halt in front of a man pushing a shopping cart loaded with bags.

Tolu laid into his horn, shouting, *"Comot for road!"*

Then he floored the gas, narrowly missing the passing man as Worthy's back was thrust into the seat from the acceleration. They were rapidly approaching the intersection with Ahmadu Bello Way, and Worthy watched Keyamo's beacon heading northwest as Tolu stopped at the corner.

"Just wait here," Worthy said, continuing to watch his phone as the car behind them laid into its horn, the driver incensed as Tolu let several gaps in traffic slip by.

Looking up, Worthy saw the sleek black sedan glide past a moment before the tracking beacon arrived at their location. He said, "Go, go," and Tolu hit the gas, cutting off a vehicle in the nearest lane by way of merging with traffic. They barely avoided a collision but Tolu didn't seem to care, weaving through traffic as he called out, "I see the Benny, right lane. Three cars ahead."

Worthy checked his phone again and then squinted ahead, trying to locate Keyamo's vehicle but finding it hard to distinguish from the other cars on the road.

"You sure?"

"The taillights," Tolu said. "Yes, I am sure."

Sure enough, Worthy saw the red glow from a pair of oval-shaped lights ahead, then transmitted, "Re-acquired visual on Ahmadu Bello Way, we're three cars back approaching the intersection with Gimbiya Street, break." Pausing to check his phone again, he continued, "Minimal tracker delay, almost negligible."

"*Got it,*" David replied. "*Then keep your distance, and don't get spotted. As long as he goes straight to the house, we're home free.*"

Worthy watched the Bentley slow before the intersection, then slide into the right turn lane. The cars between them proceeded straight, eliminating any visual gap as Tolu asked, "You want me to go straight?"

"No," Worthy replied in a split-second decision. "We've got to be sure. It's only one turn."

Tolu steered into the turn lane then, putting their vehicle directly on the Bentley's bumper for an uncomfortable few seconds before the final car crossed the intersection and Keyamo took the corner.

"Right turn," Worthy transmitted. "He's now eastbound on Gimbiya, final stretch."

Tolu hung back a few car lengths, negotiating the final stretch of their surveillance route as Worthy tried to process the sight before him.

Most of what he'd seen of Abuja had been incredibly modern: sleek buildings and tree-lined boulevards, with far more commonalities than differences with any major American city. He was abstractly aware that roughly half the population of Nigeria lived without electricity on less than a dollar a day, but he hadn't seen that reality firsthand—until now.

To his right were hotels and apartment buildings, restaurants and bars. But to his left, a row of street vendors peddled their wares beneath sloppily erected tarps and bedsheets, and beyond them, what appeared to be an open field served as a dumping ground for piles of trash. The de facto landfill was lit by sporadic cooking fires, and he could make out clusters of homeless families picking through the garbage, many of them children.

To his front, Keyamo glided along in a twelve-cylinder Bentley sedan that retailed for a quarter million in the US, and probably contained an additional six figures' worth of optional features—and that extravagant vehicle now took a right into the entrance of his neighborhood.

Tolu proceeded straight, leaving Worthy to take in a fleeting glance of the Bentley's taillights slipping past a guardhouse and down the residential street.

Watching sidelong as the car faded from sight, Worthy transmitted, "He just turned into the neighborhood. I'm staging for exfil."

David replied almost at once, *"Copy, we'll take it from here."*

I was flat on my belly, able to ignore—somewhat, after the Sambisa thorns —the shrubbery looming overhead as I awaited Cancer's confirmation that the Bentley was passing his lookout position two blocks away. Reilly and Ian lay in wait beside me, the three of us utilizing Keyamo's abundant landscaping to conceal ourselves along the walkway stretching from the driveway to his front door. Just getting onto his property had been an achievement unto itself.

It wasn't that the neighborhood was particularly secure, although judging from the lack of anyone but my team negotiating the tall brick fence and crossing the patch of woods leading to our target's house, I could only assume that the neighborhood's security force and frequent police patrols had made a practice of cracking skulls known well enough that local incursions were sufficiently discouraged.

That wasn't to say that we were completely safe, per se. After infiltrating the residential area, we'd still had to scale another fence just to attain our current position on Keyamo's property. Still, I thought, this should be easy. Keyamo wasn't known to be armed, and the element of surprise—which we currently held in spades, thank you very much—went a long way in ensuring a successful outcome.

Cancer transmitted, "*I've got eyes-on the Bentley, approaching my lookout position now.*"

His next message took a full ten seconds to arrive. Judging by the wait, he must have had a considerably long line of sight down the residential street.

"*He's passing my location at this time, thirty seconds out from arrival.*"

"Copy," I replied, releasing my transmit switch to roll a balaclava down over my face. There was a slight rustle in the bushes beside me as Reilly and Ian did the same. With Keyamo arriving in the next 30 seconds, this was our final opportunity to conceal our identities—with any luck, he'd assume the night's events to be the work of local bandits. Still, our current situation was a distant consolation prize from any semblance of a preferred scenario. Ideally we'd surveil the site for two or three days before striking, examining Keyamo's dismount procedures and ensuring there'd be no surprises before we committed our small force.

But Duchess had been adamant: the clock was ticking, and both the US and Nigerian governments would play ball at the first prospect of a clean hostage exchange. The Nigerians would shoulder the blame for negotiating with terrorists, to be sure: they'd done as much before as a modus operandi. And if Duchess was even half correct in her assumptions, tonight could easily be our one and only shot to advance the ball before being recalled stateside for reassignment.

I caught sight of a bright glow in the cul-de-sac at the far edge of the yard, rising in intensity until glaring headlights turned into the short driveway. As the Bentley approached its stopping point before the looming residence that rose three brick stories to a peaked series of rooftops, I transmitted my last call.

"Bentley is stopping now. Stand by."

After the tremendous idling of the twelve-cylinder engine fell silent at last, I forced myself into a steady, consistent breathing cycle until I heard a vehicle door slam and the loud chirp of the car locking as a man's rhythmic footfalls approached.

But the sound of Keyamo's march was broken by a new transmission: Cancer, his tone as urgent as it was frustrated.

"Cop car inbound, no sirens—decide fast."

And that was all the notice I had to make a split-second choice forced upon me at the worst possible time. The lack of sirens meant the police were probably conducting a routine neighborhood patrol, and while that shouldn't have been concerning, the fact that Keyamo lived on a cul-de-sac was. Those cops would make a counterclockwise turn in that circle of pavement, casting their headlights directly upon the house. Even if we managed to tackle Keyamo and try to hide him in the bushes, there was no guarantee we wouldn't be spotted; to the contrary, it was hard to imagine them failing to notice three masked men holding down a neighborhood resident, particularly when their eyes would naturally be drawn to one of the most expensive cars in Nigeria parked a few meters away.

With no time to roll the mission until the next day, I considered that we'd positioned Cancer for two reasons, and acting as a stationary lookout was just one of them. The other was diversion, and while I desperately hoped he wouldn't be needed in that capacity, now we had no choice. The clicking footfalls of Keyamo's leather-soled dress shoes were growing closer by the second, and I spoke my return transmission as quietly as I could—the last thing we needed now was for Keyamo to hear someone speak in an American accent.

"Hit them."

Cancer heard David's order with a mixture of relief and anger—relief that he'd be able to do something more than sit in the trees and crush bird-sized mosquitoes while most of his team got in on the real action, and anger that once he did, he'd have to run. If there were two things he hated, it was snakes and running.

To be fair, it hadn't taken David long to make his decision. The Nigeria Police car was cruising slowly, still five or six seconds from crossing in front of his position. That gave Cancer ample time to execute his next move, which in terms of tactical sophistication was firmly on the caveman end of the spectrum.

He burst out of the trees, face covered in a balaclava, left hand raised as if flagging down the officers. With his right hand he drew the Glock 19 at his side and, stopping just shy of the road—after all, if they made the wise choice to try and run him over, he needed the ability to retreat into the wooded patch behind him—leveled the pistol and opened fire.

The sound of unsuppressed gunshots shattering the residential calm was startling even to Cancer, and certainly to the occupants of the patrol car. He wasn't trying to kill them, of course, instead doing his best to present the appearance of a deranged lunatic picking a fight for no apparent reason. The first two rounds sparked between the headlights; a third punched through the hood and caused the engine to hiss and emit a low whirring sound.

And by his fourth shot, he saw that he succeeded—the patrol car screeched to a halt, both doors flinging open. Whether he'd disabled the vehicle or the cops were simply making the absurd strategic blunder of coming to a full stop while being shot at, Cancer didn't know and didn't have time to find out. The first muzzle flashes of return fire sparked so quickly from behind the vehicle's open doors that Cancer's first thought was that the officers might have been cruising with their guns in hand, which, given that this was Nigeria, might have been the case.

Cancer took off running, though not into the woods.

Instead he paralleled the road away from Keyamo's house, a course designed to draw the officers' focus away from the real target that night. He couldn't maintain the ruse for long, however; despite turning himself into a moving target, he was still a target, and after a few meters Cancer cut into the trees and fought the whipping branches scraping across his face and body.

He heard the officers giving chase on foot—maybe he'd succeeded in disabling the vehicle after all—one cop speaking what must have been a radio call a moment before the other shouted at him.

"*Stop!* Stop, you fucker!"

Another gunshot rang out, and while Cancer didn't hear the impact, he had no intentions of pushing his luck with Nigerian police marksmanship. Satisfied that he'd succeeded in diverting the officers away from his team-mates' operation-in-progress, he continued threading his way eastward to break their visual contact. The wooded swath lining the southern edge of the neighborhood would soon thin out to his front, and before that occurred he'd have to complete a buttonhook and change course. That effort would be aided by the night vision device in his pocket, which he'd utilize to go full stealth and easily bypass the flashlight beams that appeared behind him now.

In the meantime, it was all he could do to outpace the determined cops behind him. Extrajudicial killings were more or less a routine occurrence for the Nigeria Police, and Cancer considered that the biggest difference between himself and anyone else they'd shot at previously was the fact that he wasn't currently in handcuffs.

And if he intended to keep it that way, he'd have to complete the race of his life all the way to his eventual fence crossing point.

Keying his mic on the run, he said, "Moving to alternate exfil."

No response—the interdiction element probably had their hands full with Keyamo, or at least he hoped so.

Sliding to a partial halt beside a tree, Cancer grasped it with one hand and swung a 90-degree turn to change course to the south. Then he began running again, weaving his way through the brush in a desperate attempt to get the hell out of this neighborhood while he still could.

Reilly heard Keyamo's footsteps halt abruptly at the first popping gunshots in the neighborhood, the banker seemingly frozen with fear on the walkway between his Bentley and the entrance to his house.

But the inaction didn't last long, and when the footsteps resumed, they did so at a run. He was making a panicked break for his front door, and if

Reilly didn't act fast, the man would pass him by. So he pushed himself upright between the manicured bushes on either side, preparing to take a darting leap into the footpath to clothesline Keyamo with one massive arm swing.

As the team's largest member and—judging by physique—the only amateur bodybuilder, all tasks of Herculean strength fell upon him and him alone. After all, the next closest team member was Ian, an intelligence operative who was in no danger of prevailing in a chance barfight, much less a critical hand-to-hand engagement like the one that approached at a run now.

That wasn't to say Reilly didn't relish his assignments, particularly the task at hand. After all the hard, laborious hours at the gym, there was a certain sense of both justification and catharsis in using his physical attributes to accomplish a key task for the benefit of both his team and the overall mission. Short of a medical casualty, this was the singular task to which he and he alone was suited.

But as Reilly rose above the bushes and stepped into the path, he saw that he wouldn't be able to clothesline Keyamo after all. The terrified banker was moving far too fast for that, was already too close, and Reilly barely had time to use his body as a physical obstacle blocking the walkway.

Then he got his very first up-close, in-person view of Olapido Keyamo, now fumbling with his keys in preparation to unlock the front door. The man was tall and birdlike, the only fat on his entire six-foot-four frame a spare tire around his midsection, which was all Reilly could see in the split second before he ran headlong into the target.

They collided with enough force to fall to the ground like bowling pins.

Hitting the ground on his back, the medic saw Keyamo impact the walkway with a grunt as the air was knocked out of him. A briefcase Reilly hadn't noticed until now tumbled from his grasp as the strap of a leather satchel, previously hoisted over one shoulder, now pulled at the prone man's neck. Before Reilly could scramble forward to straddle the man's back and administer a chokehold, Keyamo was crying out in some Nigerian dialect—since English was the country's official language, that indicated the banker had made some key assumptions about who was robbing him and what they would understand or otherwise empathize with, and that was a very good thing for the team.

But a moment before Reilly pounced upon the man, he managed to roll to his side, appraising Reilly's masked face with terror as he emitted a gasp of surprise and abruptly switched to English.

"Please—do not hurt my family!"

Ian stepped out from the bushes, watching Reilly mount Keyamo's backside and wrap an arm around his throat.

A sense of near-panic racked the intelligence operative upon hearing Keyamo's sudden shift in language—he'd no doubt seen white skin at the periphery of Reilly's mask. Ian responded instinctively in the only way he could.

Whipping a kick across Keyamo's face, he hissed the first Russian phrase to come to mind.

"Zatkni past!"

Then he descended upon Keyamo's restrained body, reaching around his teammate to strip the essentials with gloved hands: phone, briefcase, and laptop satchel for intelligence purposes, gold wristwatch and wallet to disguise the effort as an act of robbery. Ian hastily deposited each item into a sack carried for the purpose, hearing a final, more distant gunshot as Cancer's diversion drew the cops away.

Ian proceeded to pat down Keyamo for any additional material, hearing the man sobbing against Reilly's chokehold as he recovered a silver cigarette lighter and the Bentley keys. Palming the key fob in his hand, Ian unlocked the vehicle and carried his sack to the driver's side as footsteps approached behind him.

He paid the approaching man no mind—Ian knew full well that David was rushing in from his vantage point to gag and flex cuff the restrained banker before they made a hasty getaway.

Cancer spoke over the net then, his words breathless.

"Moving to alternate exfil."

Ripping open the driver's door, Ian ducked inside a supple, diamond-quilted seat to the smell of conditioned leather inside his mask. He checked the glove compartment first, emptying the contents—which appeared to be an envelope of registration and insurance information, along with a leather-ensconced owner manual—into his open sack on the ground outside the car.

Then he checked the center console, snatching the loose cash, Chap-Stick, and breath mints he found while leaving the spare change behind before searching for secret compartments. He started by feeling for concealed switches on the steering column before moving to the cuphold-ers, which he pressed for false bottoms before turning his attention to the stereo and navigation displays. These were probed with gloved fingertips before he determined Keyamo hadn't installed a hidden switch, and then Ian pulled back the sheepskin floormats, scanning for irregularities in the bodywork below.

Then he moved to the backseats, repeating the process and finding nothing beyond English-language copies of *The Economist* stuffed in the seat pouches. The magazines went into his bag as well—he'd search them later for coded shorthand or slips of paper handed off in a brush pass— before he popped the trunk and searched that as well.

He'd studied the digital manual for the Bentley Flying Spur that after-noon, and knew where to direct his efforts as he pulled aside the floor mat to check the spare tire compartment. Upon finding it empty save the expected equipment, he determined his search was complete.

There were many other possible hiding places, of course; drug smug-glers would code vehicles with endless combinations of dash and brake inputs to open secret compartments within the interior, or hide items within the taillights or against the underbody. That was to say nothing of replacing airbags with kilos, or intrepid human smugglers who would replace upholstery with bodies. A full inspection would require the use of partial disassembly along with sonar equipment and borescopes—but given the time available, Ian was satisfied with his search.

Besides, he thought, a more invasive search could reveal a level of sophistication beyond the average Nigerian stickup crew, and that could result in attention they didn't need.

He turned his gaze to David and Reilly, who were now dragging

Keyamo's gagged and bound form into the bushes. Approaching his team leader at a jog, he grabbed David's shoulder and whispered in his ear, "Get his belt."

David did so in record time, delivering a kick to Keyamo's ribs before flipping him sideways. Then he stripped the belt from his waist and handed it to Ian, who stuffed it in the sack, then zipped it shut and threw it over his shoulder as police sirens wailed at the entrance to the neighborhood.

I followed Reilly at a sprint as he led the way across the front lawn. He was first to clamber over the fence at the edge of Keyamo's property, and after landing on the far side, he turned to receive the sack of intel that Ian hurled over before starting to climb.

I was atop the fence as Reilly caught the package, then leapt down to the edge of the cul-de-sac. Ian made landfall a few seconds after me, and the three of us darted into the edge of the wooded area ringing the neighborhood's southern boundary.

Stripping off my mask, I transmitted in a whisper.

"Cancer, we're in the woods—what's your status?"

It took the sniper a moment to reply, and while he was panting, his tone now held enough composure to assure me he'd transitioned to night vision and was in the process of stealthily bypassing whatever pursuers he'd gained.

"Think I lost them, but there's plenty more on the way. I'm probably ten minutes out from alternate exfil."

Keyamo's wife would locate him any minute now—while the gunshots had been distant, easily missed by someone cooking inside the massive house, the police sirens now flooding into the neighborhood would surely draw her attention. As soon as she looked out a front window, she'd notice her husband's Bentley in the driveway, and the first step outside would reveal his muffled cries from the bushes. Not exactly a story for the grandkids, but fuck him—he was facilitating payments to a major regional terrorist group, letting others bear the brunt of their kidnappings and suicide bombings while he padded his personal accounts in Abuja. Had Duchess given us the legal authority to kill him, he'd have considerably more to complain about.

A more pressing consideration at present was the imminent police response. I could hear their sirens tearing through the neighborhood's central street, which was precisely why we'd chosen to cross the woods to an adjoining road instead.

Reilly was on point with Ian picking up the rear, and we used our night vision sparingly to make our way through the darkening woods. Aside from our radios and concealed handguns—plus, of course, the spoils we'd just stolen from Keyamo—the movement was swift without rucksacks.

I checked my GPS and transmitted, *"Racegun, we're a hundred meters out."*

Worthy's response was immediate.

"Ready when you are, boss."

We covered the remaining distance in record time, reaching a tall brick perimeter fence as I transmitted, "Need pickup in thirty seconds."

"Roger," Worthy answered.

We used a two-man technique to negotiate the wall, with me bracing my back against the brick fence as Reilly clambered over me to reach the top with the intel sack in hand. Ian repeated the process, and the two extended their arms from the top as I jumped, walking up the brick wall as they hoisted me from above.

Now with all three of us awkwardly straddling the fence, all that remained was to examine the far side—no pedestrian foot traffic on the sidewalk, just a few cars passing on the road. Reilly tossed the sack down and we lowered ourselves to the far side, making landfall as a van turned on its four-way flashers and slowed beside us.

Reilly pulled open the cargo doors, and the three of us piled inside as Tolu killed the flashers and accelerated forward. "Cancer, we made linkup," I transmitted. "Where are you?"

"One minute out from alternate exfil."

"Got it, we'll meet you there."

Worthy turned from the passenger seat and asked, "How'd that go, boys?"

"We had an easier time than Cancer," Ian answered, beginning to unpack his large bag. He was in the process of stuffing the digital devices into a Faraday case to block any tracking signals as Tolu turned down a side street and began a circuitous route back the way we'd come. A cop car sped toward us, its light bar glaring red and blue as it roared past before I allowed myself a sigh of relief.

I couldn't help feeling that the entire foray had been fun—after the grueling reconnaissance mission that ended, regrettably, without any payoff of a gunfight for my team, a hasty throwdown against a corrupt financial officer was almost a night on the town by comparison. Both figuratively and literally.

I'd long harbored a curiosity about exactly how far removed personality types such as these were from becoming career criminals versus career soldiers, whether military or paramilitary. And in the end I hadn't come up with any good answer; if you were an adrenaline junkie as I was, or simply enamored with guns and gear, the line between knocking over banks or armored cars and special operations seemed at times to be perilously thin. Sure, people could moan about patriotism and duty all day—but while those notions had succeeded in getting me to eagerly sign an Army contract as soon as I turned eighteen, after a couple deployments I was locked into the job for the rush, *period*.

Working with magnificent assholes like these didn't hurt, either. I turned and slapped Ian's arm, grabbing hold of his sleeve and shaking him.

"That phrase in Russian—a stroke of genius."

Ian, startled, pulled his arm away and shrugged. "Thought we could cast some suspicion on those Gradsek mercs, since Keyamo clearly saw we were white."

"Brilliant. What did you say?"

Ian shrugged again. "I said 'shut the fuck up.'"

I jabbed an index finger at his face. "You little genius. What did I do to deserve you?"

Reilly was far more solemn about the whole affair, looking uncharacteristically brooding.

He said, "I just—I just wish we could've, you know..."

"What?" I asked.

Reilly hung his head. "...used the Bentley for exfil."

I frowned. "Well, thank the powers that be that we've got Ian on our side. He brings a thirty-pound brain and spits Russian off the cuff. You're upset we didn't steal the car and get rolled up by the cops three minutes later."

Tolu called back from the driver's seat, "Me friend's chop shop, boys. Would make fast work of it and we could split the money, *notin spoil.*"

Then he braked the van to a halt, Worthy climbing in the back with us as Cancer slid inside the passenger seat.

As Tolu pulled away to begin the route to the safehouse, Cancer looked back to the cargo area with his face flushed and glistening with sweat as his eyes darted across the massive yield from Keyamo's interdiction.

"Well, that sucked. Looks like it worked, though."

Ian looked up from his trove of stolen items. "Don't celebrate just yet—we still have to find out what intelligence is here."

24

Cancer cracked open another beer, tossing the cap beside its comrades littering the safehouse kitchen countertop. After taking a long swig, he deposited the bottle opener beside the pile and turned to saunter back to the team's operation center, AKA the living room.

A promising sight greeted him—a foldout table erected for the purpose was now covered with Keyamo's possessions, none of which Ian would allow anyone to touch until he'd completed his meticulous inventory. His teammates had initially sat around the table at rapt attention, eager to see what mysteries would unfold, and the interest had peaked when Ian forced open the briefcase to reveal close to three hundred thousand USD worth of non-sequential Nigerian naira currency. That particular revelation elicited a few low whistles and suggestions they hit the Abuja casinos rather than report the findings to Duchess.

But morality had taken precedence, if morality meant that Duchess was now monitoring Keyamo's communications and would, therefore, discover exactly how much money had just been lost.

Besides, after opening the briefcase, Ian had taken so goddamned long to piece through everything, searching for hidden papers and SIM cards in every fold of material, that most everyone had soon lost interest. Worthy and Reilly had drifted off to bed, while David nursed a beer while transmitting detailed photographs to Duchess—for all the team knew, some seemingly innocuous item could hold greater intelligence ramifications to one nerd or another at CIA headquarters.

Cancer, for his part, had never been big on intel. Tell him who needed to be hit and when, and he'd get it done. Or if his duties as a sniper required comprehensive reporting on the layout of an objective as the mission in Sambisa had, he'd gladly relay details all day in the hopes of getting to shoot someone at the end of it.

The current situation, by contrast, was so far outside his give-a-fuck o'meter that he ordinarily would have left David and Ian to their own devices long ago.

But Cancer remained awake, incrementally chipping away at his sobriety while he watched the intelligence operative and team leader process their findings, for one reason and one reason only: after his desperate sprint through the woods with cops in pursuit, he was simply curious to see what the corrupt banker had been hiding.

To that end, he noted that Ian had hooked up Keyamo's laptop and cell phone to devices that would clone their contents, simultaneously screening for and suppressing malware before the files could be transmitted over a secure government connection.

After taking another pull of beer, Cancer asked, "You sending the digital shit to Duchess?"

Ian didn't break stride, continuing his pat-down of the now-empty laptop satchel. "Yeah. She'll let us know if the analysts find anything interesting."

"Lemme ask you something. Why not just give all this shit to the ISA team who handed us Keyamo's pattern of life on a silver platter? We're four shooters and one brain. From what little I know of the ISA, they're basically all Ians, right?"

Ian looked up quizzically, as if he hadn't considered that as an option.

"You know, that's not a bad question."

"Because," David said over his shoulder from the computer, "Duchess probably wants to vet everything we recovered before deciding what to pass along to outside parties. Pretty standard CIA practice."

Now on Cancer's side, Ian countered, "Sure, but the ISA gave us Keyamo."

"They absolutely did," David replied, "and we'll probably never know how Duchess pulled that off. But we work for the Agency. Whatever she worked out on the back end is her business. Duchess says clone and send everything to her, that's what we'll do. Besides, you want those ISA dudes to know who we are and where we're hanging our hats in sunny Abuja? What if one of them gets rolled up?"

Cancer let the inquiry trail off without a response, scanning the table contents as David resumed working at the computer. This had been a pretty solid excursion, Cancer reasoned. According to Duchess's ISA contact, Keyamo had been maintaining the same routine for months on end, and was thus ripe for the picking from any number of greedy parties. And if Ian's use of Russian served its purpose, it would throw Keyamo—and whoever he was in bed with, financially speaking—off the scent of American involvement.

But so far, the looming question remained: what intel had they actually harvested? And to Cancer's dismay, the unenviable answer could be summed up in two words:

Not much.

To be fair, Ian's search effort was valiant, to say the least. If the team's goal was to create a psychological dossier on the banker based on his physical possessions, he'd have a hell of a lot to work with.

But as for intelligence? Well, Cancer thought, let's see. The man's Chap-Stick—which Ian had taken on the assumption that it could have been a clandestine USB stick, instead turned out to be, well, fucking ChapStick. Not that it did anyone on the team a lot of good at present, because after a brief analysis of his cell phone contacts and seeing how many mistresses the man juggled outside of his marriage, no one particularly wanted to risk skin contact with an item that had come anywhere near his mouth.

Cancer's eyes fell upon the only useful item from the pile, which he snatched up as Ian protested, "Hey! I haven't searched that yet."

"Keep your pants on," Cancer replied, cracking the lid with a cursory glance to confirm there was no concealed microchip. Lo and behold, there wasn't. The container of breath mints was, predictably, filled with breath mints.

At least the night wasn't a total wash, he thought, tossing a mint into his mouth and nodding with approval.

Extending the container to David, he said, "Mint?"

"Screw it," David muttered, "why not."

Cancer shook out a second mint and tossed it to his team leader, then offered the package to Ian. After a moment of hesitation, he declined, and Cancer set the pack down among the table's yet-unsearched contents.

Well, that was that, Cancer thought. Five Agency contractors and one host nation driver asset had targeted a known scumbag, taken everything he had, and the final mission outcome was that two people now had fairly fresh breath. Wonderful.

25

Duchess tapped a finger against her lips, mulling over the contents of her OPCEN computer screen.

Beside her, reading over the same report, Jo Ann said, "Other caller on the line seems a little well-educated to be Boko Haram."

"To say the least," Duchess muttered.

"So who do you think it is?"

"I have no idea," she allowed, "but the real problem is that no one else does, either."

Half the reason they'd shaken down the banker, she thought, was to collect intelligence. But the other half was to see what he did afterward—and with Bailey's ISA team monitoring his communications ahead of the robbery, everyone in the Project Longwing OPCEN was expecting some particularly juicy information to surface immediately afterward.

And to an extent, it had: one phone call, a quick and suggestive exchange, and then total silence from Keyamo. No attempts to contact anyone else, least of all the police, to report the theft.

And despite the best efforts of her own people as well as the ISA team over the past thirty-five minutes, no one had yet been able to run down exactly where the other phone number led to. She'd expected to find some immediate link to Boko Haram, but whoever Keyamo had spoken to didn't seem concerned with systematic violence—instead, he seemed concerned with money.

She scanned over the transcript of that phone call again, searching for any connection and finding none.

[call begins]

KEYAMO: *Sir, I was robbed tonight. Outside my home.*

UNKNOWN: *The payment?*

KEYAMO: *Gone. Along with my phone, wallet, and computer. It is no longer safe—*

UNKNOWN: *I will assign bodyguards to you, and cover the lost payment as a sign of good faith. But you will continue the arrangement, Mr. Keyamo. Nothing stops the transfers.*

KEYAMO: *Sir, I believe the thieves were white. And one...one spoke Russian.*

UNKNOWN: [inaudible] *not confuse yourself. I do not know who robbed you, but I know exactly who did not.* [end call]

She looked up to see Andolin Lucios ascending the tiered levels of OPCEN seating, carrying a tablet at his side.

"Tell me you found something," she said as he approached.

His face was expressionless, but that told her nothing. Whether delivering groundbreaking news or notifying her of some catastrophic setback, the intelligence officer's face and voice rarely betrayed any semblance of emotion.

Stopping beside her desk, he said, "We couldn't find the number in the public directory because it wasn't there—it was in the government directory."

There it was, Duchess thought, feeling the tingling sensation that always followed some new twist in intelligence. She asked, "You have an ID?"

Lucios consulted his tablet.

"Chukwuma Ndatsu Malu. Permanent Secretary for Nigeria's Federal

Ministry of Petroleum Resources, which makes him God as far as joint venture oil and gas contracts go."

"Is the ISA tracking that?"

"Yes, ma'am, we're keeping them looped in as per your guidance. Now an initial scan of Malu's financials reveals that he's been receiving regular deposits from Gradsek in varying amounts, usually on a monthly basis."

"Outside of government channels?" she asked.

Lucios gave a curt nod.

"That's right, the money goes directly to a personal account. Now that's not very surprising, to be honest. Political corruption is systematic in Nigeria—their elected officials have siphoned hundreds of billions from the national bank in the past few decades alone. Based on the amounts we're seeing from Gradsek, it looks like they're just keeping the wheels greased for political approval on their expansions, based on some kind of a fixed percentage for each new contract. Any oil company worth its salt is probably doing this at every level in the chain of approval."

Duchess felt her shoulders sag. "So this is nothing to get worked up about."

"Sadly, not at all. Actually pretty conservative for what we'd expect from a man in Malu's position, but the forensic accountants are just getting warmed up and this guy has more accounts than an offshore bank. The money is hidden between business holdings, shell companies, charitable foundations, and family assets...that's just considering his official portfolio. There could be any number of additional accounts under proxy names."

"Keep digging, and let me know what else you find out."

"Yes, ma'am," Lucios said, turning to depart.

Waiting until he was out of earshot, Jo Ann asked, "What do you make of that?"

"Nothing yet," Duchess replied. "But the China mission linked us to international terrorist financing through the Central Bank of Nigeria, and that just led us to Keyamo. Now there's a high-ranking politician in the mix, so our next play is to see how Malu reacts to the theft."

She lifted her phone from the receiver as Jo Ann asked, "Who are you calling?"

"Your friend at the ISA."

Jo Ann shook her head. "Bailey will call as soon as he has something."

"You sure about that?"

"I've worked with him before. I'm sure."

Jo Ann was a sharp woman—overly optimistic and harboring an almost naive idealism at times, but sharp nonetheless—and she seemed to view Duchess's suspicion as borderline offensive. Reluctantly, she hung up the phone.

It rang a moment later, and Jo Ann lifted her eyebrows as if to say, *I told you so.*

Snatching up the phone, Duchess heard a switchboard operator say, "I've got the ISA rep in Abuja."

"Put him through," she replied, then put the receiver to her chest and whispered to Jo Ann, "Fine. You were right."

Jo Ann picked up her phone, listening in as Duchess began, "Ben, I've got Jo Ann on the line with me. You've been getting everything you need from my people?"

He chuckled, then spoke in his booming New York accent.

"For the first time in a long time, yes. Thank you for that, ladies. Now I'm calling to return the favor."

"We're all ears."

He continued, "My people are starting to work a remote tap on Malu's office and cell phones, but it's going to take time. However, we were able to pull his phone records and I think you're going to like this: after speaking with Keyamo, Malu only placed one call. Based on the previous transcript, I think it's safe to say he was reporting the missing payment and declaring he'd cover it himself, possibly with a delay in the transfer."

Duchess mulled over that comment. "I'd say that's a reasonable assessment. The question is, who did he report to? We've been holding our breath for some Boko Haram connection."

"That's the kicker," Bailey continued. "He didn't call Boko Haram at all. It was a Gradsek line."

Jo Ann spoke up then.

"Bailey, our people have found initial evidence that Gradsek has been paying Malu to secure contract approvals."

"I can't say I'm surprised," the New Yorker quipped, "given this is

Nigeria we're talking about. But Malu notifying Gradsek about the robbery is still an irregularity. The lost payment he's referencing wasn't a direct deposit to himself, it was the three hundred grand worth of non-sequential bills that your team rolled up. That means it's a separate transaction altogether, which is indicative of Malu brokering some agreement between Gradsek and an outside organization."

Jo Ann said, "We've previously tied Keyamo and his bank to terrorist financing. You think Malu is paying Boko Haram?"

"Too soon to say. But if Malu is fronting the missing cash just to keep the wheels turning, it's something important. I'm not going to sign off on known terrorist involvement by any stretch, and given that Gradsek is focused on the delta while Boko Haram operates on the opposite side of the country, it's unlikely at best."

"So we're dead in the water," Jo Ann noted.

"Not necessarily. The best thing we have going is the number that Malu dialed to report the theft, which traces to a Gradsek facility. More specifically, it's a landline to one of their port operations on the coast. Why a landline and not a cell?"

Jo Ann was silent, and Duchess swiftly filled the void.

"Because it's an unregistered landline at a continually staffed office. If it's a port operation, that means they may need to alter logistical considerations at the drop of a hat when complications arise."

Bailey sounded pleased with the deduction. "That's more or less the size of it, I imagine. Implication: we run down that location, you could determine who else Gradsek is paying and why. It's too early to rule out Gradsek involvement in the ExxonMobil kidnapping, and with every other JSOC and intelligence outfit scouring Boko Haram, I'd say we just stumbled upon a thread that no one else is following."

Duchess asked, "Do you have any people near the Gradsek facility that Malu called?"

Bailey gave a weary sigh. "We're centralized in Abuja, and unfortunately I don't have the manpower to flex there given our commitments to locating the hostages. But I'll be able to remotely tap Malu's communications and pass anything significant along to you, and if you can get your people inside that Gradsek facility, I'd love to be a second set of eyes on anything they find."

Duchess nodded slowly. The CIA usually prided itself on the careful compartmentalization of intelligence, and this kind of real-time, free-flow information sharing was normally reserved for the final phases of tracking down a high-value terrorist target or rescuing hostages.

Or, in this case, exploiting what little time remained before Project Longwing's involvement in Nigeria was shut down completely, and losing the presence of a ground team at the heart of a grander conspiracy. Besides, she thought, Bailey had proven remarkably useful so far—and if he could manage a tap on Malu's phone lines before the Agency could, then she'd need his information as much as he needed hers.

"Done," she said. "Where is the facility located?"

"The place where this whole thing began—Lagos."

26

Reilly was sleeping soundly, dreaming of his college days and California coeds, when a slap to the shoulder spurred him to half-consciousness.

He responded by groping beside himself in search of his rifle, mumbling, "What is it? A...a checkpoint, or, like—"

Ian slapped his shoulder again.

"Not a checkpoint. Dude, you're missing Lagos."

Reilly sat up, rubbing his eyes as he took in the sight of the media van interior where he'd been peacefully sleeping since...well, at this point, who knew anymore.

He objected, "You fuckers woke me up at four a.m. to start driving."

"Yeah?" David replied from the passenger seat. "That was about twelve hours ago. Get your fat ass up, we're almost there."

Yawning, Reilly stretched and offered, "It's muscle mass, man. Muscle weighs more than...you know"—another yawn—"fat, and stuff."

Squinting around the van's interior, he saw Cancer seated in the back, looking almost absurd in civilian clothes as he stared at Reilly in disgust.

"You better hope one of us needs you to save our life tonight," Cancer said to the medic, "or I'm going to seriously question why we even bothered bringing you."

Reilly's first observation, before he'd even mustered the energy to rise to a knee, was that for a city that existed in perpetual gridlock, he'd never heard so many car horns blaring simultaneously.

Peering out the windshield, he saw sloppy outcroppings of sheet metal and cardboard shading the street-level vendors hawking bead jewelry, shoes, and watches, while every balcony and window above them was brimming with racks of items for sale: clothes, towels, hats, flags. Any vehicle capable of threading the needle between traffic and human beings did so at maximum speed, and the motorized rickshaws were only slightly less terrifying than the motorcycles, most of which had at least one passenger clinging on for dear life.

He yawned again and muttered, "It's like a shanty town had a baby with Times Square."

Tolu said from behind the wheel, "Home at last. Getting paid for it, too. God *don butta* my bread."

Nearer to the road were food vendors and men pushing wheelbarrows loaded with fruit or flour bags, and every square foot of space in between was flooded with a visually impenetrable swarm of people in flashy, colorful clothes.

"Huh," Reilly said to Tolu, "they're all dressed as obnoxiously as you are. It's like a gay pride parade out there."

Whether the driver didn't hear him or chose to ignore the observation, he proudly continued, "These my people, Yoruba people. We ain't all lame like the stiffs in Abuja. In Lagos we do it right, have the best *owambe*—the best parties—in all of Africa. You want me to take you to one?"

Ian responded matter-of-factly, "Tolu, we'd definitely like to *owambe*. But we've got a lot to do tonight."

"Yeah," Reilly added, "you know, invade a port facility and probably get captured and tortured by former Spetsnaz mercenaries. Our schedule is packed."

Then David said abruptly, "Shit, get ready—we've got cops coming up on our six."

Reilly angled his view to take in the passenger mirror, seeing that traffic was indeed parting to allow a black SUV with a flashing red lightbar gleaming from its roof to pass.

"No cops," Tolu said, pulling to the side of the road. "These are the rich in Lagos."

The SUV was followed in short order by a Mercedes G-Wagon, Rolls-Royce, Porsche 911, and finally a black sedan equipped with a sparkling light bar that would pass for a police car in the States. After the procession passed, the vehicle and human traffic immediately reconverged on the road as if nothing had happened.

Ian asked incredulously, "They use sirens just to get through traffic?"

"Like Moses parting the Red Sea," Tolu said with more admiration than judgment, then added, "probably rappers. Although the *real* real rich"—he craned his neck to look at the sky beyond the windshield—"use those."

He pointed to a helicopter crossing overhead, its rotor blades forming a blurred disc against the sunlight as it vanished behind buildings on the far end of the street.

Tolu clearly loved his hometown, Reilly thought—and how could you not? Aside from the crawling traffic flow, widespread poverty, and financial elite treading across the poor while impersonating law enforcement, it was a veritable paradise.

Tolu nodded to himself. "And I cannot let you boys leave Nigeria without trying some palm wine—"

David asked, "Anyone here but Ian look like they drink wine?"

"I *danno* say wine, I say *palm* wine. Completely different, you will see."

"Right," Reilly said, lying back down to situate himself on the van floor. "I'm going back to sleep."

27

Worthy hauled his gear bag down the hallway, following his team toward an open doorway. Then he came to a halt, taking in the view with the absurd sense that of all the places he'd hung his hat in global travels, this may have been the most ridiculous.

The central feature of the apartment's living room was a comically over-sized bar cart, brimming with bottles and a decanter set. It was positioned in a way that led Worthy to believe it was the first stop for the returning occupant, placed on a direct trajectory to a faux leather couch in front of an enormous flat-screen TV surrounded by speakers. He barely noticed the kitchen in the corner; his attention was distracted by the posters that covered the walls like something out of an inner-city high schooler's fantasy: gaudy images of rappers and their album covers, the lone standout a movie poster for *Scarface*.

He said, "So this is the view that makes these poor Lagos girls turn and run the other way."

Tolu laughed loudly, tossing his bag on the couch before turning to extend his arms up and out.

"To the contrary—your old friend Tolu does quite well with the ladies."

Worthy slipped inside and set his gear bag next to the others, as Tolu continued, "My shit is your shit. Make yourselves at home, have a drink."

David didn't take much convincing, descending on the bar cart and examining the bottles with such eagerness that Worthy half-expected the team leader to knock back a cocktail on the spot. Instead he nodded with approval, replying without diverting his eyes from the liquor supply.

"When we get back, maybe." Then he turned to face Tolu. "And thanks for letting us stay here."

Cancer was less amicable, his gaze shifting across the rap posters with a look of disdain.

"I notice you forgot to include Biggie Smalls."

Tolu folded his arms unapologetically. "No wall space left."

Appearances aside, the next thing to strike Worthy was the noise—Tolu had said that Lagos was the New York City of the African continent, and that was true if the chief basis of comparison was constant racket from the street. The third-floor apartment may as well have been on ground level, with every car honk and siren piercing the thin walls. Worthy would have to sleep with earplugs here, if he slept at all.

For the team, these living accommodations were about as suboptimal as they could be.

It wasn't that the Agency didn't have safehouses in the coastal city— according to Duchess, three existed between Lagos and the surrounding area. But with the influx of American personnel sent to Nigeria to search for the remaining hostages, the safehouses were each filled to varying capacities with people from the intelligence community. And while the space technically remained to accommodate Worthy's team at one safehouse or another, the problem with being part of a highly compartmentalized targeted killing program was that cohabitation was, more or less, completely forbidden. Since the sudden occupation of multiple hotel rooms by five white men would test their cover story as investigative journalists to the max, the team had settled for the most discreet option remaining: their local asset's personal residence. And to Tolu's credit, he'd been all too eager to host them.

Reilly moved to the kitchen as Ian set off to scout the apartment with a compass, searching for a window where he could establish an encrypted satellite link. Worthy had expected the intelligence operative to be more apprehensive about the coming mission than any of them;

instead, Ian sounded almost giddy as he reappeared and pointed to a doorway.

"Found a perfect shot—I'll set up in here."

Tolu threw up his hands. "My bedroom? Any other room, no *wahala*. But you cannot take a man's—"

"It's the only good angle," Ian said apologetically. "Nothing I can do."

How Ian was so at ease with the current situation, Worthy wasn't sure. Usually it was the team who circumvented official authorities. This time Duchess was fully complicit, not only supporting the effort but moving the team around Nigeria like pawns on a chessboard. That was fine by Worthy, of course—he hadn't signed up for this outfit because he wanted the nine-to-five. But the possibility of himself or his teammates getting captured or killed was very real on every mission, and Worthy took issue with assuming those risks on an increasingly vague and half-formed chain of intelligence and assumptions. Which summed up the team's experience in Nigeria thus far.

Worthy moved to a side table, lifting a framed photograph and examining it.

The backdrop was a dramatic rock formation rising against a cloudless sky, and Worthy recognized the monolith as Zuma Rock. In the foreground was a teenage version of Tolu—or at least Worthy thought it was Tolu. The younger boy he had his arm draped around could have just as easily been him as well, the resemblance uncanny between the two kids.

Before he could ask the question, Tolu snatched the frame away from him, pulling open a drawer in the side table and depositing it before slamming the drawer shut.

"I'm sorry," Worthy said, taken aback by the first sign of aggressiveness he'd seen from the otherwise lackadaisical driver. "Didn't mean to go through your stuff."

Tolu drew himself up to his full height. "But that did not stop you, did it?"

Nodding toward the drawer, Worthy asked, "That your brother?"

"Yes. Yewande, my little brother."

Ian took a step forward and asked, "Is he in Lagos?"

Worthy heard the concern in his teammate's voice, and felt his own stomach tense with the same recognition. As an Agency asset, Tolu was vetted with a thorough background check; at least it was supposed to be thorough. In truth, that job was well outside his team's purview, and all they ultimately received was a basic profile.

But Ian had clearly remembered the line of Tolu's profile that read *SIBLINGS: NONE.*

Now there was a discrepancy between Agency and asset information, and that presented a security issue that needed to be resolved at once. Because if their driver had lied during the vetting process, it could indicate any number of unenviable possibilities.

Tolu seemed to realize this at the same time, and rather than answer Ian's question, he replied, "I did not report having a brother because I do not anymore. He is gone."

Worthy asked, "What happened?"

Tolu lifted his chin, cutting his eyes to them and then David, who had come to a stop a few feet away. Then he spoke unrepentantly, as if to make it clear that he was judging the team and not the other way around.

"Yewande became an addict. The people he ran with, they introduced him to some very bad men. And through this..." He paused, then injected a measure of forcefulness to his next words. "He joined Boko Haram."

Ian cocked his head, genuinely curious. "I thought they recruited from—"

"The north?" Tolu said. "Yes, mostly. But they also send preachers to the cities. To find the lost souls, the most poor. The boys from broken families."

The driver suddenly appeared self-conscious of the admission, and hastily added, "This was not the case with Yewande. We had a good family, and he was *smart* smart—never needed to study. But when he started using, my father was too hard on him. *I* was too hard on him."

After a beat of silence, Worthy asked, "How did he die?"

"I did not say he died," Tolu snapped. "I said he was lost. Yewande left for the north almost ten years ago. He asked me to go with him, and I said he would burn in hell for what he was about to do. That was the last I saw him. Probably he is already gone, but I will never know." Then Tolu swiftly reappraised the men standing around him, his shoulders tense, as if prepared to come to blows at the first sign of irreverence toward his brother.

But he found none among the three Americans, each of them rendered silent by the admission. Tolu relaxed somewhat, his voice low and measured as he continued, "So I help you people because it is the right thing to do. Also for the money, of course."

After a slight shrug, he added, "But mostly, I help because I hate Boko Haram. They took Yewande, and for that...the more of them you kill, the better."

28

The blast of a ship foghorn echoed across the dock, causing Reilly to strain to hear David's transmission.

"Loading crew is still in the area. Stand by."

Kneeling in the shadows, Reilly kept his gaze fixed to the front, toward his destination.

They'd packed night vision, but it appeared they wouldn't need it much tonight; the ambient glow from various security lights around the massive facility provided more than enough illumination to guide their movement.

It also, regrettably, made them highly visible during this particularly painstaking endeavor. The air was thick with the smell of petroleum, corroded metal, and seawater; that latter scent, however, wasn't as desirable as Reilly would have wished. His initial hopes of a sexy and glamorous coastal raid with a view of the waves were dashed the moment he looked at a map.

The Duniya Port Complex was nowhere near the Gulf of Guinea—incoming ships had to travel north along the Lagos Lagoon, passing several miles of beaches and mangrove swamps before reaching the cluster of ports on either side of the harbor. That meant the scenery was more industrial than anything else, and even if Reilly had a view worth enjoying, it was disrupted by the near-paralyzing fear of getting caught.

The shipping port where his team now staged was the biggest and most active in West Africa, utilized not just by Nigeria but also the landlocked countries of Chad and Niger beyond its borders. Every shipping company and maritime logistics organization for thousands of miles had a facility along the harbor, where loading and unloading occurred 24/7, 365 days a year, under the scrutiny of Nigerian Customs officers who had free rein to conduct random inspections. That meant a free-for-all of dock workers and security personnel moving at all hours of the day and night, and Reilly—the first of the team to expose himself in the coming fiasco—was flying blind, at the mercy of radio transmissions telling him when to move.

And with little more than a suppressed pistol, a backpack, and a gear bag slung over his chest, Reilly felt particularly vulnerable.

David's next order was spoken with the urgency that indicated the window of opportunity was short.

"Doc, you're clear to set up on Crossing Point Alpha—get moving."

Reilly didn't reply, instead darting across the open space toward the evening's first obstacle: a twenty-foot-tall chain link fence topped with a roll of concertina wire. He moved to the corner post, glancing with dismay at the pinnacle where a quartet of CCTV cameras were angled to cover both sides of the fence as well as the perimeter in between. Coming to a stop at the base of the fence, he unfolded the metal device in his hand.

The two metal slats slid apart, forming an inverted V with a footpeg at each tip. Reilly slid one footpeg through a gap in the chain link and then lowered the device until it sat flush. Stepping atop the newly emplaced foothold, Reilly pulled himself up the fence and withdrew a second step from his gear bag, then unfolded it and slipped it through the chain link a few feet above the first.

He repeated the process four more times before reaching the top of the corner post, where his next obstacle hovered near his face: a menacing coil of razor wire.

For this he resorted to another item from the gear bag, withdrawing a folded fire blanket and shaking it open by a corner. The fiberglass cloth unfurled below him, and after tightening his hold on the chain link, he flung the flame retardant material up and over the concertina.

Adjusting the fabric over the wire, he carefully pulled himself atop it, holding the camera post with one hand to steady himself as he felt the wire sag beneath his considerable weight. Reilly was no incredible fan of heights, and reasoned that the delicate crossing twenty feet over the concrete below would have made anyone second-guess their resolve. Nonetheless, he mustered the composure to blow a kiss at the nearest CCTV camera lens before lowering a leg down the other side, where he probed for a footpeg. Once he found it, Reilly transitioned his bodyweight to it and began his descent.

The process was considerably faster than climbing up had been. Reilly simply had to keep his boots parallel to the fence, gripping the chain link for stability as he lowered himself down from peg to peg.

Finally he alighted on pavement inside the perimeter fence, then darted to his next piece of cover in the form of a row of shipping containers stacked four high.

He arrived at the corner and peered around the side, seeing that the thirty-foot-wide expanse before the next row of containers was free of wandering dock workers. At the sound of jangling chain link behind him, Reilly glanced over his shoulder to see Cancer ascending the fence crossing setup with Worthy in pursuit.

Returning his attention to the task at hand, Reilly slid around the corner and knelt at the base of the container beside him, searching for the first available forklift pocket in the metal.

Procuring a wireless internet travel router from his bag, he slid it into the forklift pocket and then situated a wireless camera in the gap, just enough that the lens was exposed to the empty row between containers.

Then he transmitted in a whisper, "Camera One, in position."

"*Signal is weak,*" Ian replied. "*Try moving the router closer to the edge.*"

Reilly slid the device closer to the camera before Ian spoke again.

"*We've got signal—shift the camera ten degrees to the right.*"

Reilly obeyed, making a miniscule adjustment to the angle only to hear Ian scold, "*I said* ten *degrees. Come back halfway.*"

The next adjustment hit paydirt, with Ian confirming, "*Keep it right there. That's perfect.*"

Running footfalls approached behind him, ending when Cancer stopped and knelt.

"You good?" Cancer asked.

"Yeah."

"Then cover Worthy."

Reilly left Cancer alone to evaluate the next leg of their movement, returning to the corner of the container stack in time to see Worthy setting foot inside the fence, removing the lowest footstep from the chain link and stashing it in his bag before racing to join them.

The fire blanket was gone, leaving the concertina at their crossing point looking surprisingly unmolested—it had been compressed a bit relative to the remaining wire spanning the top of the fence, but only a pinpoint examination would reveal that.

Worthy slowed his run, and both men fell in at Cancer's backside as he transmitted, "Entry team inside the perimeter, beginning movement down Route Red."

"They're clear," Ian said. "Unfreeze CCTV Four through Eight, and Ten."

Sitting beside him in the media van, David relayed the command to Duchess, who was pulling the strings for this little venture all the way from Virginia.

"Raptor Nine One, unfreeze CCTV Four, Five, Six, Seven, Eight, and Ten. Entry team proceeding down Route Red at this time."

Duchess transmitted back, her voice tinny over the speaker box. "*Copy all, restoring feeds. Stand by.*"

Ian checked the computer screen to his left, scanning the series of boxes representing gridded subdivisions of CCTV camera feeds. Four were on the camera post that Reilly, Cancer, and Worthy had just climbed alongside, while another provided peripheral coverage of the crossing point. The footage on all three was identical to what the live operators in Gradsek's security control room were watching at that moment.

There was the faintest change in the quality of light, a minor flicker that was hardly noticeable unless you were watching for it: the result of the feeds being restored to real-time. The clocks in the corner of each had never stopped ticking—a slick piece of work for which he could take no credit.

Port complexes like Duniya covered a massive amount of real estate, with the ground subdivided between companies that often had their own security—and in Gradsek's case, that meant fences like the one their entry team had just negotiated.

But not even Gradsek had the manpower to have guards along their entire perimeter at all times. They could have, of course, if they hired and trained Nigerians for pennies on the dollar by international standards— but foreign oil companies universally refused to hire local labor. It was one of the chief grievances of vigilante groups like the Niger Delta Avengers: multi-billion-dollar companies polluted the inland water supply, exterminating the livelihood for riverside fishing communities while refusing to employ the newly jobless masses. It was a recipe for a thriving trade in illegal oil siphoning and piracy, and that was exactly what had occurred and would continue to with no end in sight for Africa's largest economy.

For Ian and his team, however, the disparity spelled opportunity. Gradsek relied on roving patrols to secure its facility, paired with an extensive system of building sensors and alarms and backstopped by internal and external motion sensors. Since all were controlled via a wireless digital interface, they were no match for CIA hackers clearing the way for the entry team.

A greater challenge was the CCTV network being manned by live operators. And despite the CCTV system being closed circuit by definition, the Agency technicians were nonetheless able to find a way to bypass it. The key was the Gradsek CCTV system's use of online streaming cloud backup, which provided a vector for Agency hackers to access system administrator privileges on the DVN server. From the comfort of their office in Langley, Virginia, they could now selectively freeze camera feeds on cue without disrupting the entire network.

But the CCTV cameras were justifiably focused on monitoring the perimeter, leaving vast swaths of the facility itself outside Ian's remote purview. As with their recon in the Sambisa, the team hadn't come to Nigeria prepared for a clandestine penetration—and to ensure a roving patrol or random dock worker didn't stumble upon the team as they departed, they'd had to bridge the gap using an unorthodox solution that came into play now for the second time that night.

Reilly transmitted, *"Cameras Two and Three are in position."*

Ian consulted the computer to his right, seeing the live feed from the first camera Reilly had set up. After a brief delay, two additional feeds came into view—the wireless connections to both were weak but stable, and Ian could make out the angled image of two new corridors between rows of shipping containers, one looking south and the other eastward.

He transmitted back, "Cameras Two and Three are good. You're clear to proceed."

"Beginning movement on Route White."

David relayed the development to Duchess, and Ian saw their figures onscreen a moment later, jogging swiftly down the corridor under the watchful eye of one of the cameras they'd just emplaced. The other was in position purely to detect incoming traffic along an intersecting corridor, and despite the obvious challenges involved in pulling this off, Ian felt satisfied with his setup so far.

He'd acquired the wireless cameras in Abuja, using his travel time to Lagos to configure them in a single network. Together with staging portable routers alongside the cameras to leapfrog a signal on their way in, the entry team was slowly building the network of visual angles inside the Gradsek facility. Once it was time to exfil, Ian would be able to tell them when to move—and, perhaps more importantly, when not to.

The setup was far from perfect, of course. Ian had suggested to Duchess that the ISA team accompany them or at least provide some suitable equipment, only to be told that he was severely mistaken about what the men and women of the Activity did for a living. So he'd done the best he could, but retrofitting components from a commercial security system to assemble real-time surveillance during a clandestine penetration was like playing flag football with a brick: doable as a last resort, but with a much higher potential for disastrous consequences than the alternative. It was, however, sufficient for a temporary solution to the problem.

At least, Ian hoped.

He gave another scan to the perimeter CCTV cameras, ensuring no new personnel were inbound through the main gate before checking the wireless cameras for new activity. Other than a forklift sweeping past Camera One, everything was clear.

Next he turned his attention to the laminated imagery attached to the side of the van: a detailed overhead view of the objective and surrounding area, overlaid with angles of visibility from the CCTV cameras, accurate to within two degrees. Then there were the three legs of their infil, comprising rows between stacked shipping containers: Routes Red, White, and Blue. That much had all come courtesy of the CIA—oh, how Ian wished they received this level of direct support on a regular basis—and the team had added the numbered angles of coverage for their own wireless cameras.

He checked that reference graphic frequently, keeping himself oriented to the overall mission schematic. David was doing the same beside him, for largely the same reason—if there was suddenly some security response or unexpected movement of Gradsek personnel, they'd have precious little time to relay instructions for the entry team to avoid being seen.

Reilly had positioned an additional two cameras within the next few minutes, checking their effectiveness with Ian before continuing their infiltration along the final leg, Route Blue.

Ian's gaze flicked between the camera feeds and the objective graphic with increasing frequency, his heart rate quickening with each passing second. Any moment now the entry team would arrive at their stopping point, and that would put them at the literal and figurative back door to the Gradsek office that the Permanent Secretary for Nigeria's Federal Ministry of Petroleum Resources had personally called after the banker shakedown in Abuja. What intel that would yield, Ian couldn't begin to speculate. But the chances of compromise had gone up with each leg of the infil, and once they reached the threshold of a Gradsek office known to be continually manned, those odds would be catastrophically high.

The moment arrived sooner than he expected, Cancer's voice coming over the radio with an almost uncanny degree of control.

"*Doc is prepping Cameras Four and Five, staging for lookout. Confirm security alarms disabled in Building 13.*"

David answered, "Affirmative, I confirm Building 13 security has been disabled."

"*Copy,*" Cancer whispered. "*Me and Racegun are preparing to make entry.*"

Worthy stood ready with his suppressed Glock 19 pistol, covering Cancer's actions at the door behind him.

Aside from a rolling service door that would be far too noisy to penetrate, the office building had two entrances: one on the northeast corner and another at the center of the south wall. All else being equal, they'd planned on avoiding the center door—despite a lack of blueprints to work from, that entrance's orientation spelled a greater likelihood of opening into a central hallway with multiple doorways.

But a partial sweep of the building exterior revealed lit windows along the north side, the view obscured by lowered blinds. That eliminated the corner door from consideration, forcing the trio to converge at the south wall for their surreptitious breach.

As Reilly stood by as a lookout with Worthy pulling local security, Cancer used two tools for the task: a tension wrench, and an electric pick gun designed for covert entries. That latter device functioned the same as most others on the market, save the small detail that it was extremely quiet. While Cancer unlocked the door handle and transitioned to the deadbolt, Worthy could hear little more than a faint whirring sound.

Everyone on the team had practiced the craft back in the States, though no one was as proficient as Cancer, who'd begun his lockpicking career with B&Es in high school. The crusty old bastard could generally pop a lock cylinder in half the time it took anyone else, and was the obvious choice for breaching the building's outer door.

After that, the immediate danger would fall to Worthy.

In truth, a physical entry like this was an absolute last-ditch option, the highest risk and therefore least preferred method of gathering intelligence. It was reserved for extreme cases where all other options had been exhausted—which, regrettably for Worthy, had already occurred.

He heard the flat *click* of the deadbolt a moment later, turning in time to see Cancer slide the tools into his drop pouch and pull open the door for him to enter.

Worthy did so with his suppressed Glock tucked into his chest, elbows low to his sides as he anticipated obstacles in his path. Instead, he found a center hallway opening into a lit room at the far end of the building.

He moved forward into the hall, seeing an open doorway on either side as he instinctively cut right, tucking his body near the wall and maintaining forward security for Cancer to enter behind him. With his senses on high alert, he detected no movement but immediately heard the faint sound of classical music playing from the room at the end of the hall, along with the distinct scent of fresh coffee brewing—so much for their hopes of catching the building's sole occupant asleep.

Part of the Agency's cyber assessment had been analyzing Gradsek's shift rosters for the entire dock facility. That had led them to yet another glaring discrepancy—despite this building comprising 3,200 square feet, only four Gradsek employees had access. All of them were high-level officials in the company's import and export branch.

Because of that, and the fact that those four individuals maintained continuous rotation in six-hour shifts, Worthy knew that only one man would be present in the building, though both his exact location and level of vigilance remained to be seen.

He held his position as Cancer gently closed the door behind them, then moved to his backside. This was a tactical nightmare, betraying every instinct of close-quarters battle training, but with Reilly posted outside the building to cover their backside, the entry team was reduced to two men conducting surreptitious clearance, and that involved a different set of rules entirely.

The moment he felt Cancer's hand upon his shoulder, Worthy flowed forward and slipped into the room to his right.

Moving slowly and methodically to minimize the sound of his footfalls, he cleared the doorway, then pivoted right and extended his arms into a firing position. He swept the room from right to left, collapsing his sector with Cancer mirroring the process on the opposite side.

The room was empty, at least of people.

But they'd come for intelligence and this space revealed a treasure trove, too much for them to possibly exploit. One wall was lined with file cabinets, more than they could search under the circumstances. Another wall, however, held paydirt—a massive dry erase board split into rows and columns by strips of electrical tape, the lines filled with neat text that appeared to denote shipment and container numbers, contents, and dates.

Cancer rotated to pull security on the doorway, leaving Worthy to holster his pistol and replace it with the Android phone in his pocket. He held it steady and took a snapshot of the board, the room momentarily illuminating with a blinding camera flash. Checking the display to ensure that the text was clearly visible, he texted the image to Ian and then performed a hasty visual sweep of the room, looking for any exposed documents to photograph.

There were none, the remaining information safely ensconced in the row of file cabinets that Worthy couldn't check. Even if they were unlocked, the racket he'd make in trying to open and close drawers was too risky.

Worthy pocketed his phone and drew his suppressed pistol as he moved to Cancer's rear and whispered, "Done here."

He waited for the sniper's response, wondering what was about to transpire. While the lit office emitting classical music was obviously off limits, they still could potentially enter the room across the hall. It was on the west side of the building, meaning it had the rolling service door on its far wall, presenting tantalizing prospects for what cargo might lay within.

But examining it presented a higher risk of compromise, and the fact that they'd snapped a photo of the dry erase board was a victory in itself. After all, they had no specific intel parameters beyond securing whatever they could without getting caught. Because if they were found, they'd have no choice but to render the offending Russian unconscious and restrain him. With over three hours remaining before the next shift change, that scenario would hold the singular advantage of allowing Worthy and Cancer to collect more intel, possibly going so far as to break into the file cabinets.

The catch, however, was that the value of any intel was only as good as Gradsek's continued ignorance that anyone else had acquired it. Once that happened, they'd suspend all illicit activity and cover their tracks however they could.

As the entry team's senior man, Cancer would make the call on whether to exfil now or press their luck in moving to the next room. He did so with three whispered words.

"We're taking it."

Worthy gave his shoulder a squeeze to indicate he was ready. A moment later Cancer swept into the hallway, rotating right to assume a firing position facing the end of the hall and pulling security for Worthy to cross.

The point man took slow, measured steps toward the opposite doorway, turning right and searching for targets. Cancer flowed into the space behind him, clearing the left side of the room as Worthy swept his aim across his sector. All but a narrow swath of the room was filled with wooden shipping crates atop shipping pallets, and the far corner held a half-open door. Advancing toward it, Worth angled his aim to visually clear the space beyond, which turned out to be a small bathroom.

Spinning in place, Worthy saw that Cancer had picked up security at the doorway, leaving him to search for intel.

The wooden crates before him were four-foot cubes, and Worthy began photographing the room to document the total number packed in front of the rolling service door. They were lined up four across and three deep, and Worthy momentarily regretted not bringing a tape measure to get their exact measurements.

That regret dissipated with a closer look at the nearest crate, which held a stamped label containing the unit's outside and inside dimensions, weight capacity, stacking strength, and weight. He photographed that with his phone, checking that the text had been captured clearly against the camera flash. Showing the picture to Ian would have to wait; now that Worthy had obtained evidence of the number and size of crates, only one thing remained.

But determining the contents proved troublesome—the top panels were sealed on each crate that he swept with his phone flashlight. Worthy hit paydirt at the far corner of the room, finding a single crate whose lid was ajar. He approached to see that this one alone had numbers written on the side with marker, and he knelt to snap a picture of the sequence: 250, 246, 238, 222, each crossed out except for the final number, 216. So they'd kept this crate open for transfer of smaller units of whatever was inside, he thought, standing.

Then, phone in hand, Worthy eased the lid aside to view the contents.

The rectangular, brick-shaped parcels were covered in packaging paper wrapped in cellophane, filling the crate to three-quarters capacity in a staggered array. He photographed the crate interior with one snapshot, then pocketed his phone and lifted a brick—it weighed around two pounds, but Worthy didn't have to be an intelligence expert to know that he was holding a kilo.

Withdrawing his pocketknife, Worthy turned toward the hallway light, flipping the blade open and using the tip to make a miniscule puncture through the cellophane and packing paper. The gash revealed a powder packed within, almost white in color, but closer examination revealed it to have a trace of beige.

This was heroin, he knew, and a hell of a lot at that.

Worthy found a zip lock bag in his pocket and used it to collect a small sample of the powder. Sealing the bag, he moved to the crate and pulled three kilos aside, stuffing the brick he'd cut into the space below before replacing the others atop it and carefully shifting the crate lid back to its original position.

Then he heard a terrifying sound—a chair scraping at the end of the hall, followed by a man's footsteps. Worthy felt a hot pang of adrenaline, considering whether he'd made some noise that alerted the office occupant of their presence; but they'd remained quiet, definitely below the audible thresholds of the man's classical music.

It took him a split second to recall the bathroom in the corner, and Worthy realized two things at the same time: one, that the Russian was coming to use the facilities, and two, there was no place to hide.

Cancer sidestepped next to the door, tucking his back to the wall in preparation to attack the incoming Russian. They had no choice but to fight the man—no choice, Worthy thought, except one.

He ducked away from the doorway, then keyed his radio in bursts without speaking: three short presses, three long, then three short. Then Worthy repeated the sequence continuously, transmitting gaps of static in the universal Morse code signal for SOS.

The footsteps continued their approach as Worthy feverishly punched in his signal, hoping against all odds that it would achieve its intended effect in time to save them from compromise and derail their entire mission in Nigeria.

The Russian was now within feet of the doorway, and Worthy almost cringed at the prospect of what was about to occur; then, just as the man was about to clear the doorway, a shrill sound pierced the building.

It was the phone ringing loudly from the office, its chime echoing throughout the building as the footsteps stopped and abruptly shifted course.

Worthy breathed a sigh of relief, reminding himself not to relax just yet. Suddenly Ian's idea of a contingency plan—carrying a burner phone with the Gradsek office number programmed into speed dial, having been acquired from the ISA trace of a Nigerian politician's call history—didn't seem as inane as it had when the intelligence operative proposed the idea earlier that day.

The classical music stopped, and the phone's ring ended as the distant sound of a man's voice filled the void.

"*Privet?*"

No words were spoken between the two team members, no squeeze of the shoulder needed to communicate that they were ready to move in unison.

Instead Cancer rushed out of the room, quietly opening the door and allowing Worthy to dash outside. As he ran, he heard the Russian man repeating, "*Privet?*"

Then Cancer eased the door shut, turning to follow Worthy as both men moved at a sprint, retracing their steps to Reilly's concealed lookout position.

I held my breath as Ian pressed the burner phone to his ear—his end of the line was muted from transmitting sound, but the incoming voice was audible in the silent media van as the man politely repeated a single word for the third time.

"*Privet?*"

Then Reilly's voice came over the speaker box, transmitting on our team frequency, "*Racegun and Cancer are out—we're good.*"

Ian ended the call, tossing the burner phone beside his computer as both of us looked to one another with expressions of shock mingled with an emotion bordering on bliss. Neither of us had expected to actually utilize the SOS contingency, and the fact that we weren't getting notification of a total compromise was almost unbelievable.

Lifting my hand mic, I transmitted back, "Copy, call ended. Return to Crossing Point Alpha, collect all cameras and routers on the way. *When able*"—I emphasized the words, knowing full well that the luxury of the team relaying any additional information would occur only when they were far from the office—"send any indications of compromise and additional intel, over."

To my surprise, Cancer replied almost at once, "*I can't risk re-picking the locks to secure the entry door. Aside from that, we're clean.*"

I set down my hand mic, almost shuddering with relief as I tilted my head back to look at the ceiling before turning my gaze to Ian. Sure, the Gradsek man in the office might notice the locks were open, but that was a far cry from sounding the alarm of discovering two Americans inside his building.

Ian had apparently recovered his wits far sooner than I had—he was back to analyzing his phone, zooming in and panning across the image of a shipping schedule that Worthy had texted.

"David," he said, "I think we've got something significant here."

I shook my head. "No time for a preamble—what is it?"

"The dry erase board indicates exchanges of cargo, both incoming and outgoing, marked by date. All but line eight have transpired already."

"What cargo?"

"That's the thing," he said in frustration, "they're coded with alphanumeric identifiers, but the locations are identified. On the line in question, I see 2500 units of T74, which are to be shipped tomorrow on an outgoing container. Whatever that cargo is, it's being traded for 1800 units of L13 and 900 units of Y210 that arrived at port two days ago and were diverted from the rest of the load for storage in Building 8."

I identified the building on our reference graphic—it was massive, and one of several lining the north edge beside the waterfront. All of them had CCTV cameras oriented both outward to the water as well as inward to the Gradsek compound.

"Warehouse?" I asked.

"Definitely," he said, "and that's cause for suspicion—if that offloaded cargo was legitimate, it would be sitting in the container yard right now along with everything else from the ship. The fact that it's not indicates they're breaking down the load inside the building to avoid overhead surveillance, preparing the cargo for some kind of follow-on distribution."

"You have a point of origin for the incoming ship?"

"Not yet. Even the ship reference is coded, but with dates of arrival and departure, the Agency will be able to run it against the port records."

"Then where is the outgoing cargo located? The T74 they're trading."

Ian blinked quickly as he replied, still staring in disbelief at his phone screen. "That's the thing. It's supposed to be in Building 13, which our entry team just departed."

I lifted my mic and transmitted, "No rush, guys, but any chance you came across signs of an unspecified cargo inside the office building?"

"*Yeah,*" Worthy whispered over the speaker box, "*a shitload of heroin. Twelve crates' worth, each four-foot cubes and all but one sealed and probably full to the brink. I examined one kilo and pulled a sample before we had to bail. Have pictures of everything.*"

Before I could respond, Ian reached for his mic and said, "What color was the powder?"

"*Very light brown, kind of beige.*"

Ian looked at me and shook his head. "High purity, probably refined in Southwest Asia."

"So?" I shrugged. The source of a narcotics load seemed the least of our concerns, but Ian's eyes darted across the CCTV and wireless camera feeds as he replied, speaking quickly.

"So it takes ten tons of opium to produce one ton of heroin. You're talking about over 2,000 kilos of almost pure product from a major laboratory. By the time it gets diluted with additives at the destination, purity decreases to anywhere between ten and sixty percent. That means the hundred million or so of heroin they just found amounts to a street value in the *hundreds* of millions."

Ian's ability to calculate those estimates in his head nearly took my breath away, but not so much as the final figure he mentioned. It was so staggering in scope that I had trouble contextualizing it into some commercial equivalent in terms of legal products, and before I could, Ian spoke again.

"The question is, what is Gradsek getting in return?"

That sent me into a whirlwind of guesswork. If the hostage timeline was as tight as Duchess seemed to think, then we probably wouldn't get a second chance at infiltrating the Gradsek port complex.

And even if we did, I thought, what were the risks? We'd be repeating the same cycle 24 hours from now at best, subject to the same or worse threats of being detected, particularly considering that Cancer hadn't had time to re-pick the office building locks. Once someone noticed that, they could easily assume the worst.

On the other hand, we more or less had what we came for: evidence of a Gradsek conspiracy of some kind, albeit none relating to the three missing hostages. Still, we now owned photographs and a heroin sample, both irrefutable in the CIA's eyes. A single question loomed large over my psyche: should I pull my men out now, or commit them to additional risk in the hopes of further illuminating the intelligence picture?

The mission creep had gotten out of hand in Nigeria. Since arriving, our attempted interdiction of Usman's convoy had been the only excursion that was remotely within our wheelhouse, and at this point we were routinely endangering our lives on the scantest chance of acquiring new information. Our team existed to fulfill a very specific mandate, and part of that was to live as ghosts with the knowledge that our own country would not save us if we got caught. My initial enthusiasm in pursuing the Lagos lead was fading to a very real sense that Duchess was using us as pawns to trade political favors at Agency headquarters, putting us under immense risk for increasingly nebulous goals.

Ultimately, however, it wasn't any particulars of the mission or even the hostages that drove my decision.

Instead, I thought of my wife's scar from the July 4th attack, paired with the horrors my daughter had witnessed. We had exactly one lead from that day, pursued from America to China with a single name emerging from that vast ether: Erik Weisz, now trailed via money flow to West Africa. Now, the only thing standing between following the thread or losing it altogether was my team.

Still, the decision wasn't easy. I wasn't on the ground inside the Gradsek facility; my men were. Any decision I made short of an immediate exfil would further endanger their lives.

Keying my radio mic, I transmitted, "Entry team, halt movement. There's one more location I need you to scout."

I felt Ian's eyes upon me during the long pause before Cancer replied gravely, "*What is it?*"

Consulting the laminated objective graphic, I replied, "Building 8, a warehouse north of the Gradsek office. Two loads of outbound cargo are set to ship in exchange for most of the heroin you just found, cargo codes Y210 and L13. I need to know what they are."

The *I* was the imperative part of that last sentence, I thought, knowing my motivations were more personal than professional at present.

Then I continued, "Send your current location, and stand by for guidance."

Cancer replied, "*We're halfway down Route White, have recovered all cameras up to this point.*"

Ian, also scanning the objective imagery, transmitted, "Head northbound once you get to Route Black. That will end at a paved road, Route Green on our reference graphic, which you'll need to follow about fifty meters east before hitting Building 8 on the north edge of the harbor. Due to CCTV angles and probable alarm systems at the warehouse, you'll need to hold short of Route Green until we receive confirmation that the techs are on top of it."

"*Copy,*" Cancer growled. "*Moving now.*"

The route was the least of our issues—Cancer and his entry team could access the same central reference imagery on their Android devices, and for now I had no choice but to provide our CIA handler an update.

Transmitting over the command frequency, I said, "Raptor Nine One, Suicide Actual. Be advised, entry team has completed their mission uncompromised and undetected. Twelve crates' worth of heroin found and documented along with a coded trade schedule indicating presence of two unspecified import loads diverted to Building 8 in exchange for the drugs. I'm sending the entry team there for a follow-on exploitation, request alarms in Building 8 be disabled along with all CCTV cameras that have angles of visibility on the path between Route Black and Route Green leading up to the target."

Duchess responded, *"Copy all, stand by for confirmation."*

I set down my mic, then looked at Ian helplessly. "Well, here goes nothing."

Reilly trailed behind Cancer down the row of containers, both men following Worthy to Building 8.

Emplacing new wireless cameras wasn't a problem—Reilly had brought three extra camera and router setups, though they were intended as a backup for any technical issues with his primary units. He'd already set up two of the three spares and would need the final one to cover the road leading up to their new target building; but his preparedness with technical equipment was about the only good thing he could say about the matter at hand.

There was also the small issue of recovering each set on their way out, increasing the length of an already perilous exfil for an adjustment to the stated mission that he was already pissed about. David had an uncanny ability to push things too far, never wavering in his desire to ensure that no matter how bad a situation got, he could find a way to make it worse.

Take the current redirect, he thought. Before moving to Lagos, the team found themselves at an intersection where their own audacity and Duchess's willingness to assume risk were aligned for the first time. They'd infiltrated the Gradsek facility, made their way into an inner office, and miraculously escaped with both intel and, apparently, evidence of international heroin trafficking.

Most team leaders of sound mind would consider that an ideal time to cut their losses and get out of Dodge. Not David, Reilly thought sardonically, because why settle for an impossible victory when you could taunt fate yet again on the same night?

The medic knew from Cancer's tone over the radio that he was no more thrilled about this little diversion than Reilly himself, and Worthy was nothing if not a pragmatist. Were the Georgian just a hair more willing to voice his opinion rather than stoically follow orders, Reilly was certain he'd have whispered some complaint during their brief halts to peer around the stacked containers.

But neither Worthy nor Cancer had said a word beyond tactical particulars, instead leaving Reilly to pick up rear security as he followed—and brooded—in silence.

David urgently transmitted, "*What's your current location?*"

Worthy halted the small formation as Cancer replied, "*Route Black, approaching the intersection with Route Green.*"

David replied, "*Take cover now.*"

They were too far down the parallel rows of containers to backtrack and round a corner, so both Worthy and Cancer found the only available hiding place, slipping sideways into the narrow gaps between storage containers as David continued, "*Car inbound from the main gate down Route Green, looks like Nigerian Customs.*"

Reilly tried to follow suit, only to find that the nearest container gap was fractions of an inch too narrow to accommodate his considerable size. He took a panicked glance forward, seeing the glow of vehicle headlights increasing in brightness as they approached. The routers and cameras weren't a problem—unless some intrepid customs employee went crawling on the ground shining a flashlight into forklift pockets beneath the containers, they'd never be found.

Reilly, however, was another story altogether.

He could run, but the lines of sight extended for eighty meters to his rear. Climbing was out of the question—the corrugated siding was unscalable, and it would take an expert climber to shimmy up the metal framework of the container door assemblies rising over thirty feet above him.

Reilly was neither a sprinter nor a climber, and his bulk worked against him in both endeavors as much as the option he chose now.

Exhaling all the air from his lungs, Reilly lifted his arms overhead, stretching high to assume the thinnest profile possible as he shuffled sideways into the gap. The metal to his front and back scraped painfully against him as he wedged himself inside, shimmying ever further into the narrow space until finally clearing the edge as the sound of a vehicle rolled by to his front, then faded.

"*Should be past your line of sight on Route Green,*" David transmitted, "*and Duchess has confirmed that all alarms and CCTVs on your route have been frozen. You're clear to proceed to Building 8.*"

The announcement was of little consolation to Reilly, whose lungs were now screaming for air. He tried to sidestep back the way he'd come, making incremental progress before getting stuck and forcing his arms higher in an effort to maintain an even slimmer profile.

Perfect, he thought, all the way from the US to Nigeria only to suffocate between a couple of containers. Could there be a shittier obituary?

Reilly was seeing stars now, struggling to force his body back through the gap. He found the edge of the container with prying fingers, using his arm strength to pull himself obliquely sideways. Finally his head cleared the edge of the containers, where his first ragged inhale caused his torso to become inextricably wedged once more. This was getting absurd, he thought.

Exhaling again, he managed to slide out completely and take his first gulps of air.

If Worthy were filming this with the same phone he'd used to photograph their infil, Reilly knew he'd never hear the end of it.

No such luck—both of his teammates were already continuing to the end of the container row, completely unhindered by his absence until Cancer transmitted, "*Doc, we need a camera up here—get your fat ass moving.*"

Cancer swept his suppressed Glock across the warehouse interior, moving slowly on his entry team's initial clearance of the building.

He'd wanted to roll out the second they left their initial target, but David had said to move to Building 8 so that was what he'd do. What drove David to assume that massive risk, Cancer had no idea—but who knew what Ian was whispering in his ear, the slimy bastard.

At any rate, getting into the warehouse was a cinch. Those Agency hackers operating from the other side of the world had removed any sense of accomplishment from the feat, leaving Cancer to pick a few locks before entering alongside Worthy, both men using their pistols to perform a surreptitious clearance.

The warehouse's overhead lights were on, a disquieting observation until the silence in the building assured him they were alone: a patchwork of cameras mounted along the ceiling framework indicated those lights were on to illuminate intruders, the alarms aided by a network of prominently mounted motion sensors. Both of those systems had been temporarily disabled from afar courtesy of the Central Intelligence Agency, but nonetheless, Cancer took his first cautious footfalls with a better-than-passing expectation that an alarm would blare at any moment.

When none did, he picked up his pace, clearing his sectors for any sign of Gradsek employees and finding none. That provided precious little consolation that no one else would be arriving in the imminent future, however, and he felt his back rippling with gooseflesh as he moved.

Worthy transmitted, "*I think we're clear.*"

"No shit," Cancer replied. "This time, you and Doc have got security. I'm going to find the cargo."

He expected some objection warranting an angry response—after long minutes of pulling security on the office building doorway while Worthy got to prance about and find the motherlode of heroin shipments, Cancer was prepared to solidify the order with ironclad justification.

But instead Worthy answered, "*We're on it. Happy hunting.*"

Now that Cancer was beginning his formal search for the cargo, though, he faced another dilemma: how in God's name was he supposed to distinguish Y210 and L13 from the seeming miles of shelving and containers packed into this space?

The task seemed a fool's errand, but he continued searching anyway, expecting that he'd make the judgment call to exfil within the next few minutes unless something was found.

And when he saw the answer to all his concerns, it was with a sense of absurdity—there on the floor, not ten feet to his front, a traffic cone bore a taped piece of paper reading L13.

The load that it marked, however, raised its own questions.

He shouldn't have been dismayed to see the 55-gallon oil barrels filling a vast swath of the warehouse floor—his worst fear was finding a weapon of mass destruction, if not actual terrorist operatives awaiting transport to conduct an attack. Nonetheless, the sight of oil barrels triggered a deep-seated instinct that something was very wrong with this picture. Nigeria produced oil in vast quantities; why would Gradsek be *importing* it?

Nonetheless, he transmitted his findings.

"I got oil barrels here, marked as the L13 load. Gotta be a couple thousand."

Ian sounded confused, even dismayed, as he replied, "*Wait, barrels as in —what, like 55-gallon drums?*"

"That's what I just said. There a problem?"

"*The problem,*" Ian clarified, "*is that oil isn't shipped in actual barrels. Maritime transport occurs in purpose-built tanker ships with enormous capacity; for the past fifty years or so, the barrel has just been a unit of measurement.*"

"Well I'm looking at fuckin' barrels," Cancer said testily as the thought dawned on him that there was only one explanation for the disparity: the barrels didn't contain oil at all.

Cancer keyed his mic again before Ian could beat him to the chase. "I'm going to open one, see what's inside."

For the first time in their existence as a team, the nerdy intelligence operative actually agreed with him.

"*Good idea. Keep me posted.*"

Selecting a barrel at random, Cancer examined the rectangular sticker affixed to its side. It bore the title *SCEPURA ENERGY SERVICES LIMITED* above a block of safety disclaimers for moving the product, followed by a product code, batch number, net weight, and volume. Nothing suspicious there, and Cancer snapped a photograph before continuing with his examination.

He opened his Gerber multitool to use the pliers, prying a round plastic seal to expose the metal cap below. Bracing the tips of his pliers against the inner tabs of the metal cap, he twisted counterclockwise until it was loose. Then Cancer spun the cap with his gloved fingers until it cleared the threads and came free.

Setting it aside, he replaced the Gerber with his fighting knife, then opened a zip lock bag, turned it inside out, and wrapped it over the handle.

Delicately holding the knife by the flat part of the blade, he dipped the covered handle into the barrel opening until the hilt prevented it from going further. Then he withdrew it slowly, grasping the bag by its seal and setting his knife aside to examine the results.

The bag interior was covered in a viscous, yellow-black fluid that drizzled back through the cap opening, and he brought his face close to sniff it —definitely oil. He secured the sample anyway, reaching inside the bag to pinch the bottom between his fingers and pull it right side out before sealing the slick of oil inside and stowing it.

So the barrels didn't conceal anything at all, Cancer thought as he sheathed his fighting knife. That should have made him feel better, but it had the opposite effect—he was more deeply unsettled than ever, and now he wanted nothing more than to see what the rest of the cargo contained.

Before continuing his search, he transmitted, "Pulled a sample. Be advised: the oil barrels contain oil."

For reasons Cancer couldn't understand, Ian sounded unsurprised. "*Did you smell it?*"

"Yeah, I smelled it."

"*Describe the smell—sweet or sulfury? Any traces of diesel or kerosine?*"

"Kind of a fuel smell," Cancer replied. "Traces of diesel, maybe, but not like you'd get at the pump."

"*Then it's not crude oil—someone refined it and shipped it to Gradsek. The question is who, and why?*"

Cancer shook his head and keyed his mic again. "Keep your pants on, dickhead. Let me find the other cargo—what's the other code I'm looking for?"

"*Y210.*"

"Good. Now shut up for a minute."

Drawing his pistol, Cancer moved deeper into the warehouse until he stumbled upon another traffic cone labeled Y210, though this patch of floor space bore not one cargo, but two.

The first three containers were ajar, their contents scattered on the ground in an orientation that didn't make sense. Each container's customs seal—thin metal bands stamped with serial numbers—was broken. That shouldn't have come as a surprise, since any enterprising smuggler would have the means to produce a duplicate and re-band them at will.

He moved swiftly between the three containers, photographing the laminated signs with addresses of destination and noting that while one was located in Nigeria, the remaining two were in Chad and Niger, both of them bordering, landlocked nations. Upon taking the pictures, he noted a secondary issue with the containers' contents, partially unloaded: large cylinders labeled as canned corn, though the first one he picked up was empty, as were the others he tested.

His explanation for the disparity came in the form of the fourth container positioned parallel to the first. This one was partially loaded with what looked to be 30-gallon blue plastic drums, the labels identifying their contents as 1-Propanol. When Cancer attempted to lift one, expecting to find it empty, he instead found the weight too unmanageable for a single person.

A cursory examination revealed that the contents of the propanol barrels were in the process of being transferred to the corn cans for export; and, upon closer look, Cancer found exactly what those contents were.

He reached into an open propanol barrel, lifting a kilo-shaped brick from the many shrink-wrapped bricks below it. The brick was labeled with a distinctive sticker that struck Cancer as somewhere between curious and ridiculous, but he pushed aside the thought as he drew his fighting knife once more.

Driving the tip of the blade through the shrink wrap, he knew what he would find before seeing it.

The white powder was glistening, pearlescent. Cancer knew without a doubt that he was looking at either pure, uncut cocaine, or a product so close to pure that it had barely been touched after being processed from coca leaves. Nonetheless, he tapped some of the powder into a zip lock bag, sealed it, and continued photographing the contents until he'd documented them in full.

Then he transmitted, "Y210 is cocaine, 800 kilos or so, maybe more. Looks pure or nearly pure. It's arriving in 30-gallon barrels labeled as 1-Propanol, whatever that is, and being transferred to empty corn cans from another shipment destined for multiple places in Africa."

Ian replied, *"Nigeria imports close to a million dollars' worth of corn every year. It's a smart play: not expensive enough to be targeted for theft, and able to be shipped anywhere without raising suspicion. In stark contrast to, say, their other leading imports of computers, vehicles, pharmaceuticals."*

"Yeah?" Cancer asked. "Then where did all this coke come from—all I've got are tracking numbers, no point of origination for the shipment."

"We'll figure that out in time. Anything else?"

Cancer debated whether to send the final detail rather than wait until he was back, then decided in favor of the former. "Just one thing. All the kilos are labeled with a sticker, a ram skull."

There was a long pause before someone responded, and this time it wasn't Ian but David.

When he did reply, Cancer had no idea why the team leader sounded so haunted by the information.

"Get the fuck out of there and move to linkup."

29

Tolu keyed the ignition and the van's engine rumbled to life. I glanced over to Ian, who gave no indication that he'd heard the transmission that our entry team was now less than a minute out—he was seated at his computer, still poring over the photographs from the objective. Cancer had texted a highlight reel of new images from the warehouse, and it had taken Ian all of five minutes to decipher the seemingly glaring contradiction of oil barrels alongside a major narcotics shipment. The intelligence operative was now riding an emotional high, almost giddy with excitement.

And while I wished I could have shared his sentiment, my mood was considerably darker—the second discovery of a ram skull logo bothered me to no end.

The first time we'd seen it had been on infil up the Niger River. Had the pirate attack been a deliberate interdiction to stop us, paid for in coke? If that was the case, we definitely had a leak. But that explanation didn't hold up to further scrutiny: if the pirates had known a paramilitary element was onboard, they would have come at us with far more people. So at present, Cancer's confirmation of the ram skull logo seemed to indicate some connection I couldn't divine.

Still, the thought vanished under a euphoric wave of relief when Ian opened the van's cargo doors and our other three team members piled inside. Worthy was the first to climb in, followed by Reilly—covered in sweat—and Cancer looking like he'd just finished a particularly irritating day at the office.

He closed the doors, and I called to Tolu, "Let's go."

The van pulled forward as I turned to face my team. "You guys up on equipment?"

All three shot me a thumbs up, and Cancer added, "Could have been a lot worse after Building 8 got added to the agenda."

I ignored his comment, noting that all three men looked none the worse for wear. Their nerves were clearly rattled after the hair-raising penetration effort, but no one had been compromised, and that was the best outcome I could expect.

Keying my command mic, I transmitted, "Raptor Nine One, all personnel and equipment accounted for, beginning our final leg of exfil now. Only known signature on the objective was inability to re-pick door on Building 13 to locked position due to tactical necessity. Will send consolidated intel once we get back, estimate two hours' time."

Duchess's voice came over the speaker box. "*Copy all, CCTV footage shows no increased security activity. Assess your incursion was undetected. Nice work out there.*"

I set the mic down in time to hear Cancer say, "I don't get it. Why import oil to Nigeria—don't they have plenty of their own?"

"To say the least," Ian replied. "Their production is twelfth in the world. But they still rely on oil imports because they don't have sufficient refining capability. The real key, however, was in the register of shipping that you photographed."

"You gonna fill us in, or am I supposed to guess?"

Ian said, "The freighter that transported that oil is registered in Russia, at the Port of Vladivostok. That load of oil was officially registered as agricultural machinery, and it was picked up at the Port of Puerto Cabello, which is in Venezuela."

"So?"

"So Venezuela's dictator of a president has killed close to 10,000 of his own people to stay in power, to say nothing of his ties to narco-terrorism and drug trafficking. He's under international oil sanctions, which Gradsek is bypassing by laundering Venezuelan oil into ostensibly Nigerian product."

"Oil laundering," Cancer muttered, shaking his head. "Why didn't you just say so?"

Worthy offered, "So the drugs are just the icing on the cake."

Ian nodded, explaining eagerly, "Gradsek is functioning as a transit hub. South American-produced cocaine comes into Nigeria to be funneled into South Africa and Europe, while Asian-produced heroin gets sent out to South America so it can make its way into the US. Pretty ingenious when you think about it."

Reilly piped up then, sounding confused about this new information.

"So to be clear—and please let me know if I'm missing anything—we've uncovered a pretty vast international conspiracy."

"Uncovered," Ian replied, "and documented thanks to the pictures. Drug samples don't hurt either, because maybe the CIA can test them to determine the country of origin."

"Right," Reilly said cautiously, "but what has any of this got to do with Boko Haram or the hostages?"

Cancer answered for him.

"Not a single. Goddamned. Thing."

Reilly threw up his hands.

"Great. So I almost suffocated between shipping containers over some bullshit that has nothing to do with us."

Ian raised an eyebrow. "What do you mean, almost suffocated—"

"I don't want to talk about it," Reilly snapped. "Just seems like this entire thing was a waste of time."

Cancer nodded. "Time, money, effort...pick your cliché. And the worst part is, we didn't even get to shoot anybody."

Worthy patted him on the shoulder. "Life can be cruel sometimes. Still, that was a job well done any way you slice it. Bad guys always get a vote, and I for one am glad their vote tonight didn't involve us getting rolled up or killed on the harbor."

The speaker box crackled to life as we approached the highway back to Tolu's apartment.

"*Suicide Actual, Raptor Nine One.*"

"Go ahead," I transmitted.

"*Send SITREP*," Duchess said, then clarified, "*a complete SITREP.*"

Her tone gave me pause, but I quickly responded, "No change from my last, over."

"*Sure you don't want to revise that statement?*"

"Stand by," I told her, lowering my mic to survey my team.

"Everyone sure they've got all their equipment?"

They responded in the affirmative, without hesitation. Before transmitting again, I asked, "Anyone shoot some people and not tell me about it?"

All eyes turned to Cancer.

"Why are you fuckers looking at me?" he protested. "If I shot someone, I'd be in one hell of a lot better mood than I am now."

Ian turned to me and confirmed, "That checks out."

Keying my mic, I transmitted, "That's a negative, Raptor Nine One. My report stands—we are proceeding on final leg of exfil, no issues."

Duchess, for some reason, sounded furious when she responded.

"*Report back to me the second you get to a safe area.*"

30

Ian watched the data upload on the computer, then turned to face Worthy, who was seated on the mattress in Tolu's bedroom.

"Ninety percent," Ian said, "and I'll need Cancer's phone next."

Worthy grunted, never removing his eyes from the phone in his hand. He'd been assisting Ian with transferring all the photographs from the team's Android phones to the secure laptop via specialized cables in preparation for a data shot to CIA headquarters. In doing so, Worthy scrupulously analyzed each image with an intensity normally reserved for Ian alone.

Cancer and Reilly entered the bedroom then, each with their vice of choice: a lit cigarette for Cancer, and Reilly holding a sardine sandwich—a Nigerian specialty, they'd been assured—which he took a bite of before speaking.

"You get everything sent, or what?"

"Not yet." Ian saw that the upload was complete and addressed Worthy. "Your pics are complete, go ahead and hook up Cancer's phone next."

Cancer tapped his cigarette ash into a nightstand ashtray and said, "You better not send that until David checks in. God forbid Duchess finds out we take a minute to relax before calling her." Taking a drag, he concluded, "Not that any of this matters anyway."

The jaded sniper would have found something to complain about no matter what—that was his nature.

But regrettably, in this case he was right.

The mission had been a tactical success, no question. But strategically, it was an abject failure: no evidence of the hostages, and certainly no definitive links to Boko Haram. In that sense, they'd sunk a significant portion of their dwindling time in Nigeria to arrive at a dead end, one that might influence some political or trade negotiations behind closed doors but nothing that would achieve their stated mission of degrading terrorist leadership or, for that matter, pursuing the lead to Erik Weisz.

David entered the room, holding a rocks glass filled with amber liquid.

Ian asked, "You ready to get this over with?"

"Not yet," David replied. "Tolu's got something for us."

The Nigerian man appeared a moment later, speaking around the lit cigar clenched between his teeth.

"All right, boys, time to drink up."

Tolu held a large green bottle in one hand and a cluster of small mason jars in the other. He passed the jars to everyone but David, and Ian held up a hand to defer. "None for me, thanks."

Undeterred, Tolu set down a jar on the windowsill before him and said, "You boys are in my crib, taking over my bedroom. Least you can do is play by my rules."

He poured from a green bottle, filling each jar with milky-white liquid. "Besides, you do not take time to celebrate, life will pass you by."

Ian reluctantly lifted his jar, sniffing the palm wine and detecting an unpleasant bittersweet aroma before nodding to David's glass. "How come you don't have to drink this?"

"Because I raided his bottle of Jameson as soon as we got back," the team leader replied. "Next time, take some initiative."

Then David raised his drink and said, "To Gradsek."

"To Gradsek," the men murmured, clanking their drinks together and taking a sip.

The palm wine was sticky-sweet but left a yeasty, sour aftertaste in Ian's mouth—if he'd encountered this drink under any other circumstances, he'd have thought the bottle went bad. It tasted like day-old ginger beer laced with pineapple juice.

"So what you think?" Tolu asked.

Ian swallowed, wincing slightly. "On a scale of one to ten, I'd rate that as an acquired taste."

Then he took another small sip—when in Rome, after all—and said, "Second one goes down easier."

"Second drink is always better," Tolu said, taking a puff from his cigar. "Third, smoother still. You boys handle your business. I'll be in the living room, catching up on football."

Ian watched the man depart, wondering for a moment what tumult existed beneath his aloof veneer. Tolu had lost a brother to Boko Haram, and while that had justifiably incentivized him to help America's covert counterterrorism efforts, it also meant that any enemy fighter his team killed could be his missing family member. If that thought gave Ian reason for pause, it must have been an internal crisis of sorts for Tolu—but the man sauntered easily out of the room, leaving a lingering cloud of cigar smoke in his wake.

David addressed his teammates. "All right, you guys can clear out too—I've got to call Duchess."

No one made a move to leave.

Taking another bite of his sandwich, Reilly mumbled, "And miss the chance to hear you get crushed by our boss? No way."

Cancer shrugged. "I want to see what she's worked up about."

Worthy said nothing, instead remaining totally focused on the intelligence pictures he was transferring to the computer.

Finally David acquiesced, extracting the radio from his kit and hooking it up to the satellite dish Ian had erected at the window. Then he switched his radio to speaker mode as the others huddled around to hear.

"Raptor Nine One, Suicide Actual. All men and equipment back at the apartment, we're preparing to transmit our consolidated intel findings."

Duchess responded at once, sounding remarkably alert given that it was approaching midnight on America's east coast.

"*Suicide Actual, this is Raptor Nine One. I've received multiple corroborated reports that contradict your previous SITREP, and you have thirty seconds to explain yourself."*

David cut his eyes to Ian, who gave an exaggerated shrug. Whatever Duchess was talking about, it was beyond everyone in the room.

Keying his radio, David replied, "My reporting has been timely and accurate, and the information stands. What's the problem?"

"The problem is that Gradsek reported an attack on their facility at the Duniya Port Complex. An exchange of gunfire resulting in minor injuries to two personnel."

"So?"

"The attack occurred at 0223 West Africa Time, coinciding with your team's entry to Building 8."

Cancer tapped his cigarette into the ashtray again, shaking his head resolutely as David scanned him for some response.

Then he replied to Duchess, "Well it wasn't us. Check your CCTV footage."

"It was outside of the CCTV fan, so there's nothing for me to check. And the timing is too precise to be coincidental."

David asked the assembled team, "You guys hear anything on the objective? Any gunfire?"

"No," Worthy replied, looking up from the phone in his hand, "and it wasn't because we weren't paying attention. I was on security and pretty well freaking out about getting caught—if shots were fired, I would've known."

Ian considered that, unable to reconcile Duchess's accusation with his present confusion. If the entry team had gotten into a scuffle or even detected one, they would have reported it immediately—their tactical frequency was unmonitored, and any stretches of truth were conducted as a team, with David filtering ground reality as necessary in his transmissions to Duchess.

But Gradsek was deeply involved in such a carefully orchestrated smuggling operation that they'd have no reason to call attention to their port facility; Ian wouldn't have been surprised if they left pirate and vigilante attacks unreported just to fly beneath the radar of suspicion.

That thought made him bridge the mental gap between these irreconcilable truths as he finally recalled the ram skull sticker and gave a sudden gasp of realization.

"Of course," he said, looking to David. "I've got it. May I?"

David offered the hand mic. "Well I'm not making too much headway in convincing her, now am I?"

Accepting the mic, Ian keyed it and said, "Duchess, it's Angel. None of our guys heard any gunfire, but I think I can explain."

"*Then start explaining.*"

Ian resisted the urge to inject a measure of defiance in his voice as he responded, "Whoever shipped that cocaine, we found enough of their product in the Gradsek facility to reasonably conclude they don't have a secondary import location in Nigeria. Would you agree?"

"*Tentatively, yes.*"

"So all that coke," Ian continued, "was branded with the ram skull logo. That's the same logo we found aboard the pirate vessel during our infiltration."

"*Your point being?*"

"The river pirates weren't high-level traffickers. How are they in possession of near-uncut kilos straight from the Gradsek facility? All that wholesale product should be moving along international distribution corridors, yet we've got indicators of limited local distribution. Add that to our hard evidence of an open crate of heroin, where a number of kilos were removed from the pipeline to South America, and you've got your answer."

Duchess replied snarkily, "*The only answer I have right now is that your incursion wasn't as undetected as it seemed, and until I can reconcile the news reporting with your account of the penetration, our mission in Nigeria has come to a permanent halt.*"

Ian scoffed. If she hadn't understood his point yet, he was going to have to spell it out for her. Lifting the mic to his lips again, he transmitted, "Gradsek isn't in the retail narcotics business; they're paying for protection from the vigilante and pirate groups. Definitely with drugs, likely with cash as well, and in doing so they're protecting the expansion of their operation while every other oil company is pulling out of Nigeria. And since they can't tie themselves to funding organized terror, how do they explain the fact that they're the only ones not getting attacked on a routine basis?"

A pause before Duchess addressed his leading question.

"*They spare themselves the trouble. Fake the attacks, and do so in a manner that can't be confirmed or denied via their CCTV footage.*"

"Exactly. All they have to do is file reports that they're getting hit along with everyone else, and no one is any the wiser. The fact that we were inside their facility and didn't hear any gunfire is proof of that."

As he finished his transmission, Ian noticed that Worthy alone gave no indication that he was listening to the proceedings; instead, he was alternating his attention between a picture on his phone and a laptop beside him on Tolu's mattress. Ian caught a glimpse of a map of Nigeria on the screen, the image from their mission planning software.

Before Ian could speak again, David snatched the hand mic back from him and transmitted.

"This all seems pretty obvious to me, Duchess. You're supposed to be the intelligence agency, so why does Angel have to do all the heavy lifting here?"

"*Don't push your luck, David.*"

"Look," he continued, "if you find any hard evidence that an attack occurred, we'll talk. Until then, why don't you stop accusing my team so we can all get back on track doing what we came here for?"

"*Small issue with that,*" she replied coolly. "*Until we can analyze the intelligence you collected, we have nothing further to go on. The oil and drugs conspiracy doesn't have any ties to Boko Haram, much less the hostages, short of a few phone calls between a politician, the banker, and Gradsek. Right now we're at a standstill.*"

Behind Ian, Worthy spoke for the first time.

"I wouldn't say that."

"Stand by," David transmitted, and the entire team turned to face Worthy as he stared at the phone in his hand.

"The Venezuelan cocaine arrived in barrels labeled as propanol," he said. "But they were being transferred to empty cans of corn for export, and there are three destinations listed on the form I'm looking at. The majority of coke is being split for rail distribution between Niger and Chad. But a small amount is slotted for vehicle transport within Nigeria." He broke his gaze to point to the computer map beside him. "The town of

Maiduguri, which is in the northeast. That puts it in Boko Haram's backyard."

Then he looked at Ian. "That's a serious load of dope, so that location has got to be a major logistics hub for Boko Haram, right?"

"Not just logistics," Ian replied. "If they're receiving the shipment, it's got to be at least a semi-legitimate operation, which means there's some link to their strategic leadership if not a full command-and-control hub. That means we could run the same play we just did—infiltrate, gather intel, and find out what we can. It's unlikely the hostages will be there, but at a minimum they'd have lines of communication to the key players who know where they're located."

David was hesitant. "It sounds like a stretch."

But Ian pressed him, pointing out the obvious. "Everything since the hostages were taken has been a stretch, and right now we don't have anything better to go on. Until we do, I'd say our best bet is to collect some intel on that location and see if we can find a link."

Cancer groaned, then took a drag off his cigarette and blew a long plume of smoke toward the ceiling.

"This is chaos," he said. "We infiltrated from the coast on the way to Abuja. Then to Boko Haram's backyard. Back to Abuja, back to the coast. Now we're supposed to head into Boko Haram territory on the opposite side of the country?"

"Relax, buddy," Reilly reassured him. "It's a terrorist paradise out there; odds of us getting in without a gunfight are minimal, especially after Delta schwaked one of their camps a couple nights ago. My money says we're looking at major enemy contact if this gets approved."

That seemed to cheer up Cancer somewhat. He took another puff, nodding thoughtfully as he exhaled. "You know what? I agree with Ian. Probably some link to the hostages there."

Leaning forward, David keyed the hand mic.

"Duchess, I think we've got an idea."

31

Worthy poured himself a final cup of coffee from the freshly brewed pot, then made his way back to the operations center.

He almost spilled the steaming contents of his mug when Ian brushed against him in the hallway, the intelligence operative struggling to carry a pair of fully loaded tactical vests on one shoulder with his suppressed HK416 slung over the other.

"Sorry," Ian said.

Worthy stepped out of the way and asked, "You need some help?"

"No, we've got it." Ian continued down the hall, followed in short order by Reilly with a kit bag in each hand. Worthy let the medic pass before continuing to the living room-slash-office, appraising the building interior with a certain sense of fond familiarity. After all their travels across Nigeria, the safehouse felt like home—and, he thought wryly, a home that they were about to leave once more.

They'd slept in at Tolu's apartment the previous day, recovering from their lengthy incursion at Gradsek's port facility before making the road trip back to Abuja. Much of their planning occurred in the back of the van, allowing them a six-hour rest cycle before departing for the next leg of their journey: a hair-raising twelve-hour jaunt northeast along Highway A3 toward the capital of Nigeria's Borno State, Maiduguri.

Setting down his mug beside the keyboard, Worthy took a seat before the route imagery on the computer screen. He zoomed in on their location in Abuja, using the mouse to pan across their route a final time as he absently wondered what would be more dangerous, the 500-plus miles of road stretching into terrorist country or the destination itself.

On one hand, Maiduguri was the largest city in the northeast, equipped with its own airport, university, and even a zoo. But it was also the birthplace of Boko Haram, and while that explained why a major logistics and possibly command hub would be located there, it also meant that secretive strongholds of the terrorist organization were present in the city. Those pockets of safe haven didn't stop Boko Haram from attacking other areas of Maiduguri, however, and they routinely conducted bombings and shooting attacks that had left a death toll of over a thousand within the city limits alone.

Besides, he thought, the real adventure would begin once they reached the target building.

He lifted his mug and took a sip of coffee. It was like a sucker punch to the throat—Ian had made this last batch, and nobody brewed it as strong as guys from the intelligence community. Still, this would likely be his last good cup for the foreseeable future, and Worthy intended to saturate his bloodstream with caffeine while he had the chance.

He continued panning across the route, finally arriving at an overhead view of Maiduguri and zooming in on their target building. If all went according to plan, he'd be inside it before sunrise tomorrow and, should his luck continue to play out, leaving alive.

This mission, like Lagos, was a clandestine intelligence collection, but it would be nothing like the Gradsek incursion. That had entailed tiptoeing through a facility with suppressed pistols while Agency hackers selectively deactivated cameras and motion sensors.

No, this time they'd be on their own—and the location dictated they come prepared for an all-out war.

Cancer, Reilly, and Ian were loading the van with the bulk of everything they'd brought into the country: weapons, ammunition, the full military arsenal that a five-man team was capable of employing. If Boko Haram detected their presence, they'd need all of it. Even with their loose cover as reporters for a niche news agency, any self-respecting terrorist element would be weighing the potential upside of spreading their message to major media channels against the benefit of trying to capture American hostages. The team would have to shoot their way out either way—the only question was when, and how long they could maintain the ruse.

That reality brought with it an odd juxtaposition of civilian and paramilitary elements. While everyone was attired in plainclothes rather than fatigues, David alone would be riding in the passenger seat with nothing more than a concealed pistol for immediate protection.

The rest of the team, however, would be in the back in "full battle rattle," kitted out in anticipation of enemy checkpoints. After their last mission, the procedures to deal with those in remarkably fast and violent fashion had become almost second nature to the team.

He was surprised when David spoke behind him; Worthy hadn't even heard him enter.

"How do you feel about this?"

Worthy turned to the team leader, attired in khaki cargo pants and an off-white safari shirt with the sleeves rolled halfway up his forearms, hands in his pockets. Just another reporter on assignment getting ready for the day, he thought as he looked back to the screen and replied.

"Everything past Potiskum is going to be the Wild West. Terrorist activity on the roads is sporadic, but with multiple Boko Haram factions operating as they please, anything is possible. Maybe no one messes with us, or maybe we're slinging lead in a few hours. And that's before we even get to Maiduguri, which is a whole other ball of wax."

"Good," David said, taking a seat beside him. "I was afraid this was going to be boring."

"Well, it won't be. That's the one thing I can say for certain." Pausing, he added, "This feels weird, doesn't it?"

"What?"

Worthy looked at his team leader. "Getting such a long leash from Duchess. Usually we have to hide half of what we're up to just so she doesn't lose her mind. This time, she's all about it."

"Yeah," David muttered, cupping his chin with one hand and going silent in an apparent moment of consideration. "And who knows what the fuck she's up to. If we didn't know what we were walking into before, then right now we're flying completely blind."

32

Reilly jolted in his seat as the van hit another highway pothole, then readjusted his position before peering through the windshield at the road ahead.

The woodlands and tall grass fields had long since slipped away to arid terrain that ranged from short grass savanna to sandy expanses mottled with patches of exposed stone. What little greenery remained consisted of sparse woods, scattered scrub brush, and patches of agricultural fields. Villages had been few and far between, and for the most part Reilly felt that making the trip in full kit—a mandate from David and Cancer for everyone in the back of the van—was overly cautious given the tremendous visibility in every direction. If any Boko Haram fighters happened to appear, the team would spot them a mile away.

Still, he couldn't complain. Despite the long ride, he was basking in the air-conditioned vehicle interior while the sun-baked countryside roasted at a hundred degrees. If his team did get into enemy contact, Reilly only hoped it would occur after sunset when the temperature dropped to a far more civilized range.

Yawning, Reilly leaned his head against the wall behind him and had just closed his eyes when David announced, "Looks like a checkpoint ahead—get ready."

Those words caused a jolt of adrenaline in Reilly's system, and as he leaned forward to peer out the windshield again, David pulled the folding partition shut, isolating any view of the four men now readying their equipment in the back.

Reilly grasped his suppressed HK417, bracing himself for what was about to occur. David would first try to talk his way through the checkpoint using their official cover and, if that failed, attempt to pay a bribe. The odds of either playing out well against a group of savage Boko Haram terrorists were slim to none, and that meant they'd probably have to employ their third option: the shootout.

The medic's role in this scenario was to be the first out the back, engaging any immediate threats behind them before moving to the driver's side and orienting his field of fire to protect Tolu. Cancer would back him up while Worthy and Ian took the passenger side position, after which the battle would unfold in a fluid reaction to the enemy positions, which David was presently trying to announce.

"Two hundred meters ahead, looks like five or six with long guns."

Reilly listened closely to Tolu's response through the partition as the driver objected, "These are not Boko Haram—look at the tuk-tuks."

"The what?" David asked.

"Motor rickshaws," Tolu clarified. "Boko Haram uses motorcycles, and that is why the government has banned them in the northeast. So these people are lawful, you will see."

"Well they're not military or cops, so who are they?"

Tolu hesitated. "This I cannot say."

David's next statement was directed to the men in the back. "Fifty meters out, stand by."

Reilly's pulse was hammering as the van slowed to a halt and Tolu spoke to some unseen party outside his window. He sounded casual, although Reilly could only discern two English words amid the long greeting—Garrett News—and the seamless delivery of their cover story elicited an excited, rapid-fire stream of Nigerian dialect.

Then Tolu translated for David, "Civilian JTF: Joint Task Force. They are hunters, volunteering to help the government fight terrorists."

David asked, "They mind if we ask them a few questions?"

Another exchange of Nigerian dialect ended with Tolu relaying their response in the affirmative, and David quietly transmitted over the team frequency.

"*I want Cancer and Racegun to stay in the back, kitted up if anything goes wrong. Angel, see if they've got any intel on our route. Doc, you keep him safe.*"

Reilly quickly stripped off his tactical vest, setting it on the floor and laying his suppressed HK417 atop it as Ian did the same with his own kit. Both of them wore holstered Glock pistols concealed in their waistband for just such an eventuality—although if this went bad, Reilly thought, the handguns would be a desperate half-measure to buy time until Cancer and Worthy dismounted with their long guns.

When Ian nodded that he was ready, Reilly cracked a cargo door just enough to slip out, then stepped into the blinding African sunshine.

The heat hit him like a freight train, and he felt like he was sweating before his boots hit the ground. That discomfort was quickly forgotten as he got his first clear sight of the tuk-tuks—motorized rickshaws as Tolu had indicated, all of them a uniform shade of bright yellow— followed in short order by the half dozen people clustered at the rear of the van as Ian stepped out and closed the cargo door behind him.

And when Reilly first processed the sight of the Civilian JTF members, any concerns he had for his team's safety dissipated as he struggled not to laugh.

They were all males, though that wasn't to say that all were men; the youngest in their group appeared to be nine years old. All were clad in black from head to toe, and all were armed...if, Reilly thought, you could call what he saw now as weapons.

Each held what appeared to be antique black powder rifles, some with crudely carved wooden stocks and others wrapped in duct tape to keep them from falling apart. They were certainly an upgrade from spears and arrows, but not by much. Some wore sheathed machetes on slings, others had knives tucked into their belts, each grinning at Reilly as they chattered in their local dialect.

This was total insanity, the kind of shit you could only find in Africa, and yet Ian reacted as if the sight were the most normal thing in the world.

"Good afternoon, gentlemen," he greeted them warmly. "Anyone speak English?"

Their confused glances made it clear that none did, but it was no matter. Tolu appeared a moment later, addressing the group in the same dialect as he pushed his way through them to translate for Ian.

Reilly moved toward the driver's side of the vehicle, scanning the surrounding countryside for threats, and David did the same from the opposite edge of the bumper. If the converted muskets this group of hunters had was any indication, the pistol in his waistband wasn't as trite of a defensive measure as he'd felt before exiting the van.

Ian began speaking through Tolu, making veiled inquiries about dangers the team may face. "You hunt Boko Haram? Have you encountered any of their fighters today?"

"Not yet," came Tolu's translated response, "but in the past they have conducted raids in the Sambisa Forest. Today they are searching for resupply trucks."

"Do they know of any Boko Haram activity on this highway? Perhaps on the stretch between here and Maiduguri?"

Tolu relayed the question, followed in short order by their response.

"The rebel attacks occur in towns. Against civilians, police stations. Or in the country villages—rarely on the road. The rebels kill children, burn people alive."

"I see," Ian continued. "How terrible."

"He asks if you know of the kidnapped schoolgirls."

"From Chibok. Yes, we do."

"Half of them are still missing. Hundreds more girls have been kidnapped, including—*mi faamaay?*"

The man provided some additional clarification, and Tolu continued, "One of these men married a woman kidnapped by Boko Haram. She refused to marry a fighter, so they made her put on a...a vest, with a bomb."

"A suicide vest." Ian nodded. "I understand."

"Yes, this. But it did not work, and she escaped."

Reilly was getting the distinct sense that, left unchecked, this exchange could go back and forth until sunset. He glanced over to see that Ian had apparently concluded the same, checking his watch and explaining, "Gentlemen, I'm afraid we have an appointment to make."

But this excuse was met with another wave of questions, which Tolu summarized in one sentence.

"They would like to know who you are meeting with."

"The mother of a senior Boko Haram leader. She's given us permission for an interview, and we don't want to be late."

Another flurry of responses before Tolu spoke.

"They want to know which leader."

Ian gave an apologetic shrug. "We're not at liberty to say until the piece is approved for post-production editing. But she hasn't seen her son in over a decade, and wishes to speak about the evils of Boko Haram. As they know, that's an important message to get out into the world."

Upon seeing the crushing disappointment in the hunters' faces—everyone wanted their fifteen minutes of fame, Reilly thought, even counterterrorism vigilantes—Ian added, "However, we will be passing back this way. Perhaps my assistant could get a contact number, and we could do a short session tomorrow or the next day?"

This seemed to appease the men and boys alike, and Reilly begrudgingly produced a notepad and jotted down the cell number provided by a man holding a single-shot, breech-loaded shotgun that looked like it dated back to the American Civil War.

Ian bid the men good luck and happy hunting, assuring them that he'd reach out. There were sweaty handshakes all around, the hunters seemingly starstruck to meet a reporter team, and both Tolu and David hastily boarded the van.

Reilly cracked a cargo door to allow Ian to slip inside, then waved a final goodbye and climbed back in with the peculiar thought that this entire exchange was inspiring, in a way. The police and military weren't even out here, and yet this ragtag group of hunters was doing what they could, using weapons that looked like they'd been passed down for a century.

Slamming the door shut behind him, Reilly turned to see Cancer nodding toward the van wall as he asked, "So how'd that go?"

Reilly knelt beside his kit, pulling on his tactical vest as Tolu steered the van back onto the highway and accelerated.

"If they do find Boko Haram," he said, strapping down his personal kit, "those hunters would be better off using their guns as clubs. Some real archaic shit."

Then he settled back into his seat, relieved to be back in the air-conditioning as he arranged his HK417 barrel down between his legs. No sooner had he gotten comfortable than he heard David up front, responding to a transmission from Duchess.

After acknowledging the message, David called back to the cargo area.

"Agency has reports of Boko Haram activity about 25 miles up the road. Worthy, can you find some local roads to get us off the highway for a bit?"

Pulling out his Android to access the route planning software, the point man leaned forward in his seat and replied, "On it."

33

"Turn that fucking rap off," Cancer hissed.

Tolu almost recoiled at the comment from the only other fan of that particular musical genre. To be fair, the Nigerian driver had been playing his usual soundtrack at a volume level so low that most of the team now regarded it as white noise.

But still, Tolu protested, "My vehicle, my rules—"

"I don't give a shit whose vehicle it is," Cancer replied. "Turn it off."

Tolu complied without further resistance, reducing the sound inside the van to the engine and rumble of tires over the bumpy dirt road.

Cancer knelt at the helm between the cargo area and the cab, peering between the driver and passenger seats to scan out the windshield.

The view beyond the narrow, sandy road was only slightly different in terms of natural terrain from what they'd seen for the past few hours—more wooded areas and scrub brush, to be sure. But the villages they'd passed through were a far cry from the urban sprawl that dotted Highway A3 to their south. Those highway towns were replete with commercial venues for travelers—restaurants, hotels, and retail establishments, however rudimentary—while the small village his team now approached was uncannily similar to the others they'd seen since diverting off their main route.

Sand-colored buildings were just as likely as not to be pockmarked with bullet holes, partially-built walls of cinder block emerging amid the dumping grounds for trash where clusters of long-eared goats fed on whatever they could find. Some of the buildings were homes, and yet people were a rare sight, more often than not scuttling out of view at the sound of the van's approach as they carried jugs of water or burlap sacks of food.

Where the children were in this early-afternoon hour was a mystery, and that bothered him regardless of the oppressive heat outside. These natives were no strangers to the sun's effects less than 800 miles north of the equator, and the rarity of his fleeting glimpses of any discernible humanity made him all the more unsettled about the prospect of enemy presence.

David hadn't said a word to his second-in-command since Cancer had taken up the sole vantage point for cargo area passengers in the media van, seeming assured that if there was a problem, he'd mention it to the team leader at once.

But within thirty seconds of Cancer demanding Tolu turn off the music, David finally looked over and asked, "What's wrong?"

"Nothing," Cancer replied without breaking his scanning effort beyond the windshield. It was a bald-faced lie, of course, and whether or not David discerned that was anyone's guess. The one thing Cancer knew for sure was that the signs were all there—a tightening in his throat, a slight constriction in the lungs, the reptilian alertness that took hold in his brain. And the ominous sense that something was going to occur at any moment.

He couldn't say why to David or anyone else, of course.

Premonition could be a dangerous thing for any soldier, even a covert one. Back when Cancer was cutting his teeth in the profession of arms—how long ago that had been, he thought—he'd gone into some missions with the sense that his own death awaited, and others where he felt an easy victory lay ahead. Rarely, however, did his premonitions have any correlation with what actually occurred; at least until he'd amassed significant experience in combat.

Once warfare became more or less routine for him, well before even his mercenary days, Cancer began to hone an almost frightening instinct that proved accurate more times than not.

The van left the village and entered another swath of rolling scrub brush and low trees, more than enough to conceal an endless number of possible threats to the team. There was limited visibility to their front and none to the windowless rear, leaving Cancer to zero in on the dirt road and its surrounding area with a laser focus, looking for where he'd set up an ambush position if he'd been born in this savanna wasteland and signed up with a terrorist outfit to satiate his need for conflict instead of entering the world in New Jersey and having to join a formal military force to accomplish the same.

His ambush paranoia was reaching a fever pitch as he watched for the spark of muzzle flashes, or the streaking smoke from an incoming rocket. They were six men packed into an unarmored vehicle; they'd be sitting ducks for anyone who wanted to pick them off. Instinct told him something terrible was about to occur—the only question was what.

And yet when it did happen, Cancer felt completely unprepared.

The woman was running straight down the road toward them, bare feet slapping the dirt path. She was waving her arms over her head at the sight of their vehicle, of *any* vehicle, so terror-stricken that she was willing to take her chances with anything and everything except, presumably, whatever occurred where she'd just come from.

Cancer's experience told him to look for the true intent of this obvious distraction—the machinegun team lying in wait, the lone sniper watching from the trees.

And while the twenty-something woman was empty-handed, seemingly unarmed, so too did she wear a long patterned shawl over her clothes, which concealed her hair and descended to mid-thigh, trailing behind her as she ran.

This told Cancer the woman had been called in from some unseen observation post, moving to detonate her explosive load against the van's occupants. His fear wasn't grounded in some anti-Muslim paranoia; he'd previously lost three teammates, one of them a close friend, to a pregnant woman in a burka who raced toward their position, crying for help. Not faking pregnancy, he later learned, but actually seven months pregnant with an unborn child, a life she was willing to extinguish to kill Americans in the process.

In that split second, Cancer knew he couldn't risk explaining all that to David and the others. So, in one climactic moment, he cashed in every ounce of credibility he'd established over God-knew-how-many missions on God-knew-how-many continents, shouting, "Stop the van!"

Tolu screeched to a halt, and by the time David looked over to ask Cancer for some explanation, it was too late—the sniper was pushing past Worthy, Ian, and Reilly on his way to the rear cargo doors, which he flung open before readying the suppressed G28 in his grasp.

He cut right, instinctively flanking the driver's side; if anyone provided immediate support, it would be David stepping out of the passenger door. Whether or not that was about to occur didn't matter much at present; Cancer moved toward the woman with his sniper rifle at the ready, shouting, "Pull up your shirt!"

She didn't respond, and Cancer used his non-firing hand to pull his own shirttail upward as he closed the distance. When she didn't instantly do the same, he dipped his suppressor and ripped a subsonic bullet into the dirt ten feet to her front. If he had to pull the trigger again, she'd be dead or bleeding out.

This wasn't about her religious sensitivities, which meant nothing to him; it wasn't that he was woke or enlightened to the human condition. Instead, it was the fact that he literally *didn't give a shit*, his only concern at present residing in the lives of the men in the van behind him and, as a distant afterthought, the families they'd be leaving behind. He'd seen that all play out before, had held in his arms the weeping widows and children of men who perished while trying to provide some semblance of human kindness in a region that warranted anything but.

The warning shot succeeded in causing her to abandon any inhibitions of modesty or religious commitment, and she yanked up her shawl to uncover her bare abdomen.

Cancer advanced regardless, his weapon poised to drive a bullet through her heart at the slightest indication of noncompliance, every instinct of his experience in more countries than he cared to count telling him that things were never this easy, that there was never a literal or figurative damsel in distress crying for help in any of these third-world shitholes where foreign military presence was required, much less welcomed. That shit all played out well and fine in a Disney cartoon, he thought, but never, *ever* in the real world, where so much as a half-second's delay had caused the loss of lives of far better men than himself.

She hesitated before dropping to her knees in the dirt road, keeping her hands raised, tears streaming down both cheeks. Even then, Cancer watched her fingertips—extremist fighters in far-flung lands had long since learned to build handheld initiation devices, and gone so far as to route exposed wires across their palms, which upon connection would detonate an explosive payload.

But he saw no warning signs, the sole reason that he converged on her while possessing the restraint to mash a palm against her face, flinging her backward into the sand before tossing her sideways onto her stomach. Cancer pushed his weapon aside on its sling to straddle her backside, groping her body from top to bottom with gloved palms to check her for explosives. She was sobbing, chattering incoherently in a local dialect that Cancer couldn't begin to understand. He ignored her cries, continuing his pat-down until he'd reached her ankles and satisfied himself that she didn't pose a threat—at least, not an immediate one.

Keying his mic, he transmitted, "I need Tolu to translate."

34

Ian steadied himself as the van lurched forward and David spoke quickly to Tolu.

"Pull right behind them," he said, then turned to address the men in the back. "Tight perimeter around the woman until we figure out what the fuck is going on."

Behind Ian, Reilly and Worthy had kept the cargo doors open since Cancer's departure. As the van braked to a full halt, both men leapt out with rifles raised, and Ian followed behind them, scrambling around the side of the van.

He didn't need David to tell him what to do—the team leader would expect Ian to be present alongside him for any interrogation, sifting the translated words through a mental database of the extensive regional research he'd conducted prior to departing for Nigeria. Ian rounded the front bumper to find Cancer climbing off the prostrate woman, who was now crying hysterically as Tolu knelt beside her, helping her to sit up.

The driver spoke quickly, trying greetings in various dialects until one caused the woman to respond in kind.

Once she did, Tolu launched into a brief diatribe, to which the woman responded at length.

"The rebels have raided her village," Tolu said, "less than half a kilometer up the road. She escaped and ran for help."

David looked not to Ian but Cancer, and then asked, "What do you think?"

It was a valid question, Ian thought, given there was some possibility of this being a pre-staged ambush.

Even if that wasn't the case, they were, above all, a CIA paramilitary element officially tasked with locating US hostages. Unofficially, however, their greatest purpose was hunting an emerging international terror threat that had already struck at the US with devastating effectiveness, and surely would again. Every diversion from one or both missions increased the likelihood that someone in their ranks would be grievously injured or killed, taking their small force out of the fight that mattered most in the early days of Project Longwing, when there was no alternate team to take their place.

Cancer was still kneeling, looking through his rifle optic at the road ahead as he replied, "We can't stop every crisis in Africa, but we can stop this one."

David withdrew his Android phone, holding it up to the woman as he zoomed out to reveal the imagery of her village.

"We are here," David said, pointing to the lower left edge of the screen. "How many bad guys, and where are they located?"

Tolu translated, and the woman took only a moment to orient herself before responding.

Ian watched her point to the road on the southern edge of the village, explaining through Tolu that the enemy trucks and motorcycles had parked there before their occupants corralled the villagers into a clearing in the north that served as a soccer field. How many enemies there were or what was happening now, she didn't know—she'd been retrieving water from a local well when the attack occurred, allowing her to escape.

David cut his eyes to Ian and asked, "What's happening in the field?"

Ian frowned. "They're probably dividing the families up. Men who resist are being killed, women and girls restrained for forced marriages or use as suicide bombers. Young boys, kidnapped as new recruits."

The rest of the team was clustered around him, pulling security outward as David announced, "Outskirts of the village are three hundred meters ahead. We're conducting an emergency assault. Cancer, get over here."

The sniper turned and knelt beside David, analyzing the phone screen as his team leader said, "Soccer field is our kill zone. I want you setting up at the southwest corner; hold your fire until the assault is ready and then your field of fire is northeast to southeast edges of the field. Get moving, I'll brief the rest en route."

Cancer raced toward the brush north of the road as David called Worthy and Reilly over.

Both men dropped to a knee and directed their attention to the phone screen as David continued speaking, keying his mic so Cancer could remain apprised of the proceedings.

"You two are the assault element. Haul ass to the northwest corner of the soccer field; sectors of fire are the northern field boundary to the southeast corner. I want stationary shots from covered positions—the goal is to flush them back to their vehicles. Anyone who flees north or east gets a free pass. Once the field is clear, move back down the west side to link up with me and Ian."

Worthy asked, "Where will you and Ian be?"

"Isolating the western edge of the village, maintaining fields of fire east down the road to pop any enemy fleeing to their vehicles."

"Got it," Worthy said. "Anything else?"

Holding up a finger so they wouldn't leave, David asked Tolu, "Ask her for a building in the village that can fit a lot of people. Someplace that every resident knows."

After Tolu relayed the question in her native dialect, the woman pointed to a comparatively large structure on the screen, located alongside the road near the center of the small village.

"The mosque," Tolu said.

David nodded. "Reilly, the mosque will be our CCP. Go."

The medic and point man moved out into the treeline, leaving Ian with his team leader, driver, and the woman as David grabbed Tolu by the arm.

"I want you to stay here, with her. When I give you the all-clear, pull the van right up to that building and cut her loose. Then the two of you will direct any casualties to the mosque where we'll have a medic waiting. Got it?"

"Yes," Tolu replied. "I understand."

David pushed himself to his feet, then looked at Ian. "Let's go."

———————

Worthy threaded his way through the low trees and scrub brush, periodically referencing his location on the Android phone imagery as he led Reilly toward the northwest corner of the soccer field. This part of the assault was a delicate balance—engage too soon and the enemy would scatter; too late, and innocent civilians would be killed. And if Cancer had to take the battle's first shots from the southwest corner, he'd risk sending the enemy north into the woods where they could disperse before flanking the team, turning an already bad situation into an unwinnable one.

The only solution was for Worthy and Reilly to begin firing from the north side, driving the bad guys first into Cancer's line of fire, then David and Ian's. Because if they botched this, they could easily be overrun—hell, the odds of that were already high enough considering the single dirt road they'd have to take back to the highway.

That reality was brought into sharp focus as Cancer transmitted, "*I've got eyes-on. I count nine enemy manhandling a few dozen civilians. Looks like five or so have already been executed. The young are being divided: young women and girls in one group and the boys in another.*"

"Shit," Worthy transmitted back, "I'm almost there. Suicide, do I have control to initiate?"

"*In every sense of the word,*" David replied. "*Me and Angel are getting set in the isolation position, ready to intercept any runners. Bunch of abandoned motorcycles and a few trucks, only one lookout that I can see. As soon as you have clean shots, start taking them.*"

"On it." Worthy quickened his pace along his assigned vector of approach.

Reilly moved to his rear right, maintaining a loose echelon formation as their small assault element proceeded toward the target.

Cancer reported, "*Gunfire is them intimidating civilians. But it looks like they're lining up an old man to execute, so you better hurry.*"

"Coming into position now, stand by," Worthy replied, catching his first glimpses of the clearing as the vegetation began to thin out.

Dropping to a knee beside a tree at the last stand of bushes, Worthy brought his rifle optic in alignment with his line of sight as he swept from left to right to scan the field.

The sight was even more horrifying than he'd imagined—a row of dead bodies was lined up face down, all men, while the screaming girls were being herded into a prisoner file at gunpoint. Then there were the boys, some as young as five or six, being kicked and thrown into a separate group while enemy fighters stood scattered in a loose perimeter around the atrocity.

The last thing he saw before taking aim was that the old man Cancer had noted wasn't being executed at all, though that fate may have been preferable over what occurred in the next half second.

With two enemy fighters holding him down and forcing his arm outstretched, a third kneeling man swung a large machete in a savage arc, severing the man's hand as he cried out in a bloodcurdling wail.

Worthy pivoted his rifle to the north edge of the field, toward a pair of enemy fighters standing less than ten meters distant.

They were facing away from him, watching the action in the clearing. One shouldered an RPG-7 launcher from which protruded not the bulbous, pointed nose cone of an anti-tank rocket, but a narrow spike of a fragmentation round that was far more dangerous for the tightly clustered villagers—a single shot from that could wipe out dozens of them.

Worthy used a thumb to flick his selector lever from safe to semiautomatic as he aligned his sights at the center of the RPG gunner's spine, then loosed two suppressed shots before transitioning his aim to the next man in line to die.

Both trigger pulls felt natural, automatic, and in light of the current situation, fully justified.

He fired another pair of shots by the time his first kill of the day hit the ground, sending the second fighter falling forward on his final collision course with the earth as Reilly opened fire on a third man with a double tap of subsonic rounds.

Worthy was about to key his radio when he saw that there was no need—an enemy machine gunner on the far side of the clearing dropped dead, felled by the hidden sniper who was probably all too eager to begin the slaughter.

Cancer registered a satisfying glimpse of pink mist through the scope of his G28, immediately transitioning his rifle right to acquire a second man who looked over in confusion as his friend fell.

The sniper squeezed a second clean trigger pull, watching the figure in his scope lurch in place before dropping straight down, dead before he knew what had happened to his friend. And now, Cancer thought with relish, the real killing could commence.

He felt unrepentant about his initial reaction to the woman on the road, but now knew he'd responded to the tactical necessities while missing the bigger picture. Once again, his instincts had not only paid off but come full circle—in the van he'd sensed that something horrible was about to occur, only to learn from the woman that it already had.

The fact that his team had arrived too late to stop the execution of innocent civilians pained him to no small end; although now that he'd dropped two of these bastards with the full knowledge that Worthy and Reilly were dealing death from the opposite end of the soccer field, Cancer had to admit he was starting to feel somewhat better.

Each trigger pull brought with it the rush of exaltation that he was ending this massacre by replacing it with a brand of justice of his own design, dropping one untrained enemy fighter after another in a race to kill these bastards before they could slaughter or reduce to slavery the innocent masses now screaming in the field.

There was an added bonus that, tactically speaking, these monsters had to be the least trained terrorists on the continent—Cancer was not only able to dial in on a third target, this one a teenager with the buttstock of his assault rifle poised on his hip like he was fucking John Wayne, but also drill a subsonic bullet into his sternum before an alarm was raised in the slightest.

Regrettably, however, once the enemy fighters started shouting to one another, all hell broke loose.

Cancer had initially planned on targets at the most distant corner of the clearing, letting Worthy and Reilly drop the close-range fighters in an attempt to push them south, directly into his immediate line of fire. Anyone who survived the sniper's onslaught would reach their vehicles only to, presumably, be shot dead by David or Ian, most likely David.

But after the first terrorists started dropping dead from suppressed gunfire that they couldn't determine the direction of, the team now faced a second problem—the response of the villagers who'd been turned into cattle by their oppressors.

In the ideal scenario, these innocent people would have hit the deck at the first sign of rescuers. In practice, however, they went absolutely apeshit; apparently, Cancer thought, being sprayed with hot blood pumping through a recently exploded heart had a way of causing innocent bystanders to lose their composure.

He struggled to dial in on a fourth enemy, this one scrambling for cover in the trees, as the villagers rose to their feet and began a desperate sprint back to their homes.

His target's effort was a different story, occurring in seeming slow motion; his movements were delayed and disjointed, indicating that he was either drunk, high, or both, and Cancer sent a bullet through his torso before he fell out of sight. Then the sniper directed his barrel to the three-man amputation team who'd chopped off the hand of an old man who was still screaming at the center of the soccer field. All three seemed riveted in disbelief at the fact that their wanton and indiscriminate attack was being met with any resistance whatsoever, much less suppressed gunshots whose origin they couldn't determine and therefore couldn't react to in any way other than sheer panic.

Those three were standing almost shoulder to shoulder over their still-screaming victim, and out of principle, Cancer targeted the machete-wielding man in the center, who thought himself a badass and was attired in sloppy fatigues. He drilled the man with a bullet to center mass before directing his aim to the counterpart now lunging into the prone as if that would help. Cancer shot him twice, the third round going wide right by the time he realized it wouldn't be necessary. The terrorist was dead before he hit the ground, and Cancer swept his barrel left to drill the remaining enemy fighter before he could muster the composure to move.

Now the events assumed a surreal tinge; in his experience shooting untrained motherfuckers, Cancer knew there was always a coward in the bunch who would distinguish himself by his actions. But here, everyone's actions were distinguishable—not by any discernible will to live, but by their delay in responding to the obvious fact that they were getting massacred.

And to his eternal regret, even these people singled out for death by the natural selection of combat were surviving.

Now they were intermingled with civilians in a race southward by all survivors—the civilians to their homes, the enemies to their vehicles. Cancer locked his aim to the far right of his sector of fire, where the panicked masses disappeared into the cluster of buildings, yet he was unable to engage any armed targets without endangering the men, women, and children obscuring his view. So Cancer did the hardest thing that could be asked of him under the circumstances, and held his fire.

Instead, he keyed his radio and transmitted, "They're running like cockroaches...Suicide, get ready."

Cancer's transmission struck me with an almost palpable sense of disbelief —I'd received no radio confirmation of the assault until now, having been apprised of its execution only by the screams and shouts past the buildings to my left.

I responded in an immensely satisfying manner, firing an easy three-round volley into the sternum of the sole fighter who'd been assigned to watch over the enemy's many abandoned vehicles, most of them motorcycles. The bullet impacts induced a ripple of movement on his shirtfront, the effect of a light breeze between the straps of his magazine carrier.

My target wasn't even of legal drinking age in the US, I thought with a sense of embarrassment that was exceeded only by the fact that I didn't kill him outright.

Instead he screamed, his shrill cry reaching me as he staggered forward, as uncomprehending as I would have been if suddenly shot after two or three stiff doubles of bourbon—what substance exactly, I wondered, was this person using? Before I could squeeze a follow-up shot, I saw a fatal bullet impact his chest with a puff of blood that caused him to fall at last. It was fired by Ian at my flank, adding another embarrassment to my growing list in the course of this emergency assault.

I was about to transmit that Cancer's message was received at the exact moment when it was no longer feasible to do so. Men appeared in a racing scramble between the buildings, one hauling an RPG loaded with a frag-mentation rocket, and they were feverishly trying to mount their motorcy-cles as Ian and I engaged in our pre-ordained sequence, me from left to right and him in the opposite direction.

That wasn't to say things proceeded as planned; my next target wasn't running away, but directly toward me down the dirt road. He didn't bother clutching his rifle, now bouncing on its sling as he ran, desperate to flee the sights of unseen shooters as I nailed him with two shots to the chest, his body falling out of sight.

Good riddance, I thought with a grim sense of validation as I searched for another target.

I heard the thudding footsteps of someone emerging from the building behind me, and I spun in place too late to survive the threat. A wiry thirty-something man with bloodshot eyes was already taking aim at me, not with a battered AK-47 but a pristine Heckler & Koch G3 rifle that must have been stripped from a dead Nigerian soldier at some point in the not-too-distant past.

He'd already beaten me to the draw, and time ground to an impossible slowness as his forearms tensed for the trigger pull.

My weapon was only half-raised by that point, and I instinctively fell backward as the swath of flame emerged from his barrel along with a deaf-ening roar of automatic fire. I squeezed the trigger as I fell, saw my rounds ticking in the dirt road between us as the hissing snaps of his rounds whipped through the air around me. I felt an odd tugging sensation on my left thigh a moment before I hit the dirt, landing hard on my back as my surroundings vanished in puffs of dirt from the incoming bullet impacts.

At this range, his automatic burst should have turned me into a cheese grater. I was certain I'd been hit a half dozen times and simply not registered it, and I aligned my rifle before squeezing the first semi-accurate shot of this close-range engagement.

Before I could pull the trigger, his gunfire went silent, though whether from a malfunction or because he had reached the end of his magazine, I had no idea. The clouds of dust cleared to reveal an answer I hadn't considered: the terrorist lowered his barrel, pirouetting gracefully forward with a tight cluster of three bullet wounds marring his shirtfront as a fourth round clipped the side of his head and sent a spray of pinkish-orange mist flying.

The mist hovered for a moment as he fell, then vanished by the time his body struck the ground and shuddered violently with some postmortem reflex.

I was panting hard as I remained on my back, sweeping the buildings for other threats, unaware of any emotion beyond a blinding fear of imminent death and unable to comprehend what had just happened. I knew beyond a doubt that I hadn't shot the man, but had no explanation for his death until a euphoric voice cried out beside me.

"Man, that was some real *Pulp Fiction* shit right there!"

It was Ian, racing up to appraise me before spinning away to pull security. As he did so, he gave a short, high-pitched laugh.

"Your leg, David. Look at your leg."

Ian sounded far too bemused to be indicating a wound, unless he too was in shock. I looked to my right leg and found no blood, then scanned my left to see the source of his comment.

There was no blood there, either, though my left cargo pocket bore a neat bullet hole. I pressed my finger into the space, probing for an injury and instead finding a gap in the fabric on the opposite side. It was the shooter's lone hit, a bullet so close to my thigh that it passed through the side of my cargo pocket without breaking skin.

Cancer transmitted over my earpiece, "*Soccer field is clear. If anyone's left alive, I haven't seen them.*"

I pushed myself into a sitting position, then shakily rose to scan for additional targets and concluded there were none. Raising a hand to my transmit switch, I tried to key my radio but failed—my fingertips were trembling, and it took me a second attempt to mash the button before I spoke.

"Looks like we're done at the isolation position." My voice cracked on the last word, and I swallowed before continuing. "All elements, strongpoint around the mosque to establish CCP—I'm calling in Tolu."

Reilly ran between the village buildings with Worthy behind him, both men feverishly trying to make their way to the casualty collection point.

They passed the woman who'd warned them of the attack—she was moving in the opposite direction, crying out in the local dialect, directing wounded toward the mosque. Reilly picked up his pace, fearing that he'd be late for his own party as he heard David transmit.

"Doc, hit the road, then cut left. Van is parked directly in front of the mosque; me and Angel have already cleared the building."

"Got it," he replied.

He reached the road a moment later, hooking left past a row of motorcycles and trucks until he spotted the team's van. Ian was climbing out of the back, shouldering Reilly's two aid bags—his primary and a spare—and running them into a low, squat building of mud brick on the north side of the road. David was pulling security at the door, his oddly fearful gaze falling on Reilly and Worthy as he waved them in.

Reilly charged toward the building, arriving to hear David ask, "What do you need?"

"Everyone," the medic answered, cutting left into the doorway to examine his treatment area.

For a moment Reilly thought he'd entered the wrong building. This was a place of worship by designation only—other than a floorspace covered in pillows and prayer mats, there was precious little in the large room to designate it as a mosque.

Ian deposited the two aid bags in the center of the room, and Reilly descended on his primary pack to recover three colored placards.

Handing them to Ian, he said, "Door is the chokepoint, you're on Urgent," and then pointed in a separate direction as he spoke each color.

"Green...yellow...red."

No further explanation was necessary for Ian, who moved out to set up the placards around the room. each color distinguishing patient priority. Green was Delayed, the minor injuries that didn't require critical aid. Yellow was Urgent, for patients whose care couldn't be put off for nearly as long. And the red meant Immediate, for casualties whose wounds were both life-threatening and able to be treated given the medical supplies on hand.

Reilly unzipped his aid bags, spreading apart flaps with bulging pouches marked by glow-in-the-dark patches reading AIRWAY, SPLINTS, MEDICATION, BLEEDING, and MINOR SURGICAL, among others.

Behind him, Worthy asked, "Where do you want me?"

"Immediate," Reilly replied without looking, assigning the point man to the highest level of care. Reilly conducted frequent cross-training for his team back in the States, and developed a keen eye for each man's medical aptitudes. As the team's lone medic, this was critical—the more casualties there were, the less actual treatment Reilly would provide. Circumstances were far different with only a single casualty, especially a team member— he'd gladly walk through the fires of hell to save any one of them, as they would for him.

But when the situation was a mass casualty event, or MASCAL, the roles reversed.

The sheer number of casualties changed everything; as the team member with the greatest degree of medical training by a long shot, Reilly was of greatest use in a managerial position, screening incoming patients and assigning a priority status before sending them to one side of the triangle for treatment by another team member.

As Reilly moved to the door, Cancer was the next person to enter, his clothes and kit covered in tiny brambles. He was breathing hard, having recently extricated himself from whatever tangle of brush he'd chosen for a sniper position.

"You're on Delayed," Reilly said, and Cancer moved out to the green placard. No further explanation was needed; this was standard MASCAL procedure, and now that the site was fully prepped and manned, only one thing remained: to get some actual casualties inside.

When that didn't immediately happen, Reilly wondered if this entire thing had been a waste of time. Maybe the villagers didn't trust them, or maybe they were all gathering at the home of some witch doctor for superstitious backwater cures, he thought as he moved outside to scan the street.

His first step beyond the door brought him into a near-collision with a young woman carrying her four-year-old son. The boy's forehead was lacerated by what he guessed was the buttstock of a rifle, blood running down the side of his face in torrents.

But Reilly focused on the boy's eyes, finding one pupil dilated—a possible brain injury, but no immediate respiratory distress. Not much they could do but stop the bleeding and monitor his vitals, ensuring his breathing didn't become compromised enough to require an artificial airway.

He directed them both inside and shouted, "One Minimal."

Cancer waved them over, and no sooner had Reilly turned to the door than he saw his next casualty—another woman, this one in her twenties, with tears streaming over her face rather than blood.

She clutched a shawl tightly at her chin while holding a fist over her abdomen. Definitely in shock, but breathing and relatively alert—probably a rape victim, he assessed at a glance.

"One Minimal," he called out, directing her toward Cancer.

Things happened quickly after that: a forty-something man arrived while holding one arm at the elbow, the upper sleeve distorted and malformed but no blood seeping through—proximal bone fracture.

Reilly shouted, "One Delayed," and sent him to Cancer.

Next came an injured man clinging to a friend for support, holding a blood-soaked hand over a probable gunshot wound in his abdomen. He was gasping for air, gut shot with uncontrolled hemorrhaging, and he was going to have a rough ride if he survived.

"One Immediate," he called, extending an arm toward Worthy as the two men struggled across the mosque.

Tolu entered then, followed by David, who quickly spoke.

"Villagers have a truck ready to evac casualties once you give the word.

Nearest hospital is Damaturu, just over an hour from here. Driver's waiting in the vehicle. What else do you need?"

"Just Tolu for now," Reilly replied, and David ducked back outside the doorway to pull some semblance of security for the rest of his team while directing the remaining casualties inside.

A teenage boy appeared next, half-carrying and half-dragging an older man into the mosque. Reilly saw at once that the casualty was alive, but just barely. The terrorists hadn't just used a buttstock to crack his head; they'd tried to kill him and damn near succeeded, a gaping wound in his shattered skull revealing traces of visible brain matter.

His escort was speaking in a panic to Tolu, who replied with some supplemental guidance in the local dialect before explaining to Reilly, "He was defending his wife—"

Reilly pointed them toward Worthy and called out, "One Expectant. Racegun?"

Without looking up from his treatment of the gut-shot man now laid on the ground before him, Worthy echoed, "One Expectant."

The confirmation was, in this case, necessary.

While the man with the head injury would join the side of the triangle formation for Immediate casualties, Reilly's designation told Worthy that this new patient would very likely die. As such, the point man should lay him down, keep him as comfortable as possible given the circumstances, but not waste any medical supplies or time treating him. Other patients with a chance of survival desperately needed both, and as far as the supplies went, so did the team.

Reilly's two aid bags only held so much equipment, and every scrap of gauze or tourniquet that the team committed to saving these locals was one less than they'd have for themselves in the mission ahead. The upcoming night raid in Maiduguri had tremendous potential to take a turn for the worse, and Reilly would be left to treat any team injuries using whatever supplies remained.

If the man with his brain exposed were the only casualty, Reilly could dedicate his full medical resources to saving him. But in this case, doing so would endanger many others, and he was forced to maintain a measure of objectivity in the interests of a greater good that was, at present, hard to discern.

Grabbing Tolu by the arm, Reilly said, "Anyone who brought in a casualty but isn't injured, get them out of here through the back door. They need to wait outside until we're done."

Tolu set off to comply while Reilly turned to appraise a man who'd walked in under his own power—but just barely. He staggered toward Reilly without any visible injuries but almost doubled over wheezing in an attempt to breathe. The medic stopped him before conducting a hasty visual sweep of his back—one side bore what looked like a stab wound. His respiratory distress indicated a developing tension pneumothorax, which would quickly prove fatal if untreated.

"One Immediate."

He pointed the man toward Worthy, who was still treating the abdominal gunshot as he called out, "Support!"

Cancer abandoned his two Minimal patients, moving to assist with the new casualty.

The next incoming patient should have been the first one into the mosque—a man in his sixties with a missing hand, being escorted by two villagers. They'd ratcheted a belt around the man's forearm in an attempt to save him, and the stump at his wrist was, at first glance, bleeding remarkably little.

They probably thought their impromptu tourniquet had succeeded, but Reilly knew better. He recognized at a second's glance that the radial and ulnar arteries had simply shunted themselves, retracting inside the wrist. It was clear from the volume of blood on his forearm that the wound had bled profusely before that occurred, the remaining hemorrhage mitigated only slightly by his elevation of the cut, the application of a belt, and a one-handed attempt to maintain pressure by clasping his wrist.

But with the minutes that elapsed between now and the man's amputation in the soccer field, Reilly knew that the pendulum was about to swing the other way, with the severed veins undergoing vasodilation and causing him to bleed out in the next ninety seconds or less if left untreated.

As if there wasn't enough urgency in the situation, Tolu arrived beside him and translated their words. "Last casualty. This is the village elder."

No further explanation was needed—as a man of great influence in this limited sphere, the victim warranted an otherwise unprecedented level of care by the senior medic on scene, least of all for his ability to inform and influence the greater strategic situation at hand. The fact that he'd waited until last to enter the mosque was a well-intentioned move, but one that could nonetheless cost him his life.

Reilly responded accordingly, making the decision to personally treat this elderly Nigerian out of consideration for both the broader implications and medical necessity.

The medic ripped a tourniquet from the front of his kit and applied it to the man's mid-forearm in an attempt to preserve as much of the radius and ulna bones as he could— who knew if prosthetics were possible in this part of Nigeria, but Reilly would treat him the same regardless. Then he wrenched the windlass in a series of clockwise turns until it was impossible to tighten it any further as he spoke to Tolu, who attempted to relay the words.

"He says that—"

"Get his escorts out of here," Reilly ordered. And while Tolu translated that instruction and the two men gradually complied, the village elder continued speaking with a renewed sense of determination.

The medic ignored him, securing the windlass in place as the elder continued chattering urgently. Finally Reilly resorted to telling Tolu to translate seven simple words.

"Tell him to shut the fuck up."

After securing the windlass, Reilly dipped into his personal aid supplies to recover a wad of Kerlix and stripped it from its wrapper, pressing the gauze atop the stump with care. The bizarre truth about such amputations was that shards of exposed bone could slice your hand apart as easily as a razor, and with two million Nigerians living with HIV, Reilly was cautious while holding the gauze in place. He used his free hand to unroll an Ace bandage and wrap it over the dressing to hold it in place.

Once complete, Reilly finally stripped the belt from the man's arm, tossing it aside.

"One Immediate," he shouted, pointing the village elder to Worthy and Cancer, where he'd await transport while having his vital signs continually assessed. But the man was speaking more insistently now, each ragged word coming across as gibberish to his savior—though not to Tolu, who insisted on translating the man's words.

"He says there is still a rebel."

"What?"

"One of the invaders. He is alive...and hiding among the people."

Reilly was silent for a moment, processing that information with the feeling of a hot coal simmering in his gut. Most of his combat time had occurred with an almost clinical sense of detachment—he was there to do a job, and took no pleasure or sorrow from the act of killing.

But the effect of warfare on innocent civilians was a hardship he'd never grown accustomed to, and the man's comment elicited a peculiar sense of rage in the normally easygoing medic.

He gave the man a reassuring attempt at a smile, then replied in a low tone, "Can he assign someone to point him out to us?"

Another exchange before Tolu responded, "Yes, one of his men can do this. But he is afraid his people will be punished—"

"Believe me," Reilly cut him off, his expression hardening, "once we get ahold of the bastard, revenge will be the furthest thing from his mind."

35

Ian felt a knot of dread forming in his stomach as he stepped outside the mosque with Tolu, responding to David's request that both men help him in the upcoming proceedings.

The casualty situation was, by now, well in hand—Reilly had released the two Minimal patients, while the Delayed casualty with a broken humerus had moved to the village's ambulatory vehicle, which only needed the three Immediate patients to arrive before setting off for the nearest hospital. Those latter three were now receiving Reilly's direct care before being moved; the Expectant casualty with the shattered skull had, by then, expired.

As would the man Ian located to his left, he suspected.

David and Cancer were practically dragging the restrained captive through the streets—he looked to be in his mid-twenties, and had taken the precaution of stripping his fatigue shirt before trying to hide among the populace.

Now he was in camouflage pants and a sweat-stained T-shirt, hands flex-cuffed behind his back as the team leader and sniper alternated between shoving and kicking him from behind as they made their way down the street. Ian took a moment to try and assess how cooperative the prisoner would be, only to come up uncertain—he was bleary-eyed, head hung as he struggled to maintain his footing.

David and Cancer dragged the captive into the alley beside the mosque, and Ian tapped Tolu on the shoulder with the words, "Let's go."

They arrived in time to see David push the captive into a stone wall, pinning him against it with a hand on his neck as he said, "Cancer, go help with the casualties."

The sniper objected, "Boss, I can—"

"Go," David insisted, waiting until Cancer departed before nodding toward the prisoner and asking, "He drunk, or what?"

"Tramadol," Ian replied. "It's an opioid painkiller, and they mix it with alcohol and every other drug they can get their hands on. Bad guys use it to numb themselves to killing, and the civilians use it to cope with the violence. Half the region is addicted."

"Will he be able to talk?"

Ian paused before providing an honest reply.

"Yeah. He will."

His hesitation wasn't based on uncertainty—the man would be spilling his guts in no time flat, he was sure—but out of fear for what was about to transpire here. If his long history with the team leader was any indication, then this interrogation was going to get ugly fast.

Tolu asked, "What are you going to do?"

"I'll show you," David replied, flipping the captive around to face him.

Then, without a word, David belted him across the face with a hard right cross, causing him to drop in place before he drove a wild kick into his ribs.

Ian grabbed David by the shoulder, intending to halt the attack only to receive a curious glance from his team leader, who said, "You're playing good cop. Did I mention that?"

Ian fell to his knees beside the captive, rifling through his pockets and coming up with a handful of flyers printed on strips of paper. The text appeared to be Arabic, though Ian only needed a hasty phonetic reading of the header line before understanding the significance.

He held up the papers to David and said bitterly, "Now we know why

Duchess missed this. They're not Boko Haram, they're ISWAP—Islamic State West Africa Province."

"You've got to be shitting me," David replied angrily. "This is the group that split from Boko Haram?"

"Yeah."

"So they have no idea where in the fuck the hostages are."

"None at all."

David responded by kicking the man again, this time across the cheek-bone—the restrained captive grunted in pain, spitting a dark stream of blood into the dirt. The team leader's anger wasn't entirely misplaced, Ian thought; at best, the team had ended an attack against civilians, somewhat miraculously without taking any casualties themselves. That reality was doubly unlikely given David's close call with the final enemy fighter, and Ian suspected that if David were capable of any compassion under the circumstances, his near-death experience had removed it entirely.

But the irrefutable fact that there was no strategic intel to gain didn't stop David from yelling at Tolu, "Tell him he cooperates or I turn him over to the villagers, and they'll do worse things than I could dream of."

Tolu hesitated before translating the statement, which caused the man to curl into the fetal position, sobbing as he delivered a lengthy reply in the local dialect.

The driver said, "He was taken from his village at the age of eight. Says they gave him alcohol, drugs, and blindfolded him. Put a rifle in his hands and told him to pull the trigger. They removed the blindfold, and his best friend was dead at his feet. He begs mercy."

Ian was moved almost to tears by the admission—which, by his extensive research into the systematics of African warfare, was nothing less than the complete truth. In the Congo, after all, warring factions did far worse to the child soldiers they forced into slavery.

David, however, was unmoved.

Ian had known the man for years, throughout circumstances that far preceded their Agency affiliation, and saw not the slightest indication of sympathy in David's face as he replied, "I'll be sure to shed a tear for him later. Right now, I want to hear anything he knows about an ISWAP or Boko Haram presence between here and Maiduguri."

Tolu relayed the inquiry and listened to the response. "He does not know. His men came from a camp to the north, far from the highway."

Ian closed his eyes and pinched his fingertips against the bridge of his nose—he had no doubt the man was telling the truth, and that alone sealed his fate.

Advancing a step toward David, Ian said, "Come on, man, please..."

"Please? *Please?* You see what they did to these people?" David drew his pistol. "He wants mercy? This is mercy."

Then he dropped to his knees before the flex-cuffed prisoner, driving the muzzle of his pistol into the man's right eye as his captive cried out in protest.

David spoke in a low voice. "Believe me, this is better than you deserve."

He pulled the trigger as the man's head rocked against the ground, one eye transformed into a gaping entry wound as a pool of blood and brain matter began to spread at the base of his skull, soaking through the arid Nigerian dirt.

I stood and holstered my pistol, turning to see Tolu looking like I'd just shot his puppy instead of a terrorist. No matter, he'd get over it in time—or not, I thought. At the moment, I didn't particularly give a shit either way.

Grabbing him by the sleeve, I gave my next order.

"Go back inside the mosque and find the village elder. Tell him we're foreign military looking for the US hostages, and find out if they know where they might be located. They won't, but you're going to ask anyway. Once we're gone, his people need to load up the dead terrorists in an ISWAP truck and get rid of it."

Tolu looked at me resentfully—what a joke, I thought. This guy spent all day listening to musicians rap about shooting people, and the sight of a single execution hurt his feelings. Giving his arm a shake, I asked, "You got it?"

He pulled his arm from my grasp, giving me a curt nod before departing.

Then I glanced at Ian, who looked only slightly more composed than our driver. At least the intelligence operative knew the score, whether he agreed with it or not. We weren't taking prisoners, and the very act of treating casualties could turn out to be a lethal decision if an ISWAP counterattack managed to arrive before we pulled out. Not only did we have no perimeter security, but we couldn't even establish it without pulling team members out of the casualty collection point. Short of abandoning the wounded altogether, the best thing we could do was to leave this village as quickly as possible.

I told Ian, "Keep the ISWAP propaganda, and let's get these trucks searched."

Then I stepped into the dirt road and jogged east, past the abandoned motorcycles on my way to the first truck belonging to the now-deceased enemy force.

As I moved, I transmitted over the command frequency, "Raptor Nine One, Suicide Actual."

I wasn't keen on reporting this incident at all, but now that the cat was out of the bag, it was unavoidable. We'd just shot up a significant terrorist element, and the odds of Duchess finding out from some intel report correlated with our route was too great for me to ignore. So I decided to provide a quick update—after all, she couldn't order me to abort the assault if she only found out about it after the fact.

Duchess spoke from the far side of the world, her voice grainy over the satellite connection.

"*Suicide Actual, send your traffic.*"

By then I was closing with a covered flatbed truck, pointing at Ian to search the cab before I visually cleared the cargo area before climbing into the back.

"Our adjusted route took us past an ISWAP village raid-in-progress. We conducted a hasty assault, assess we killed all the enemy but the entire village has seen us in action. Told them we were foreign military searching for the hostages, over."

The back of the cargo truck was empty aside from some foldout benches—this must have been the dedicated prisoner transport vehicle. I lowered myself to a crouch at the rear before leaping back into the street.

"*Which village?*" Duchess asked.

Ian appeared beside me, shaking his head to indicate that his search of the cab had yielded nothing of use. We began moving to the next vehicle, an abandoned pickup truck.

"Stand by," I replied to Duchess, reading off the ten-digit grid from my wrist-mounted GPS. That was the sickest joke of this entire event—the village was so obscure that its name wasn't even listed on our mission planning software. The only location that would mean anything to the CIA was the alphanumeric grid identifier that I rattled off now, which in their hands probably wouldn't even help our team, much less the locals. It would be a data point on an intelligence report, perhaps, but nothing more: these kinds of atrocities happened every day in Africa. They had long before we arrived, and would continue long after we'd gone.

We reached the pickup and repeated the procedure, with Ian diving into the cab as I climbed into the back and began rifling through the containers I found—some fuel cans, food provisions, and water jugs. Useless.

I was climbing out of the back when Duchess replied, "*Copy all, what's your current location?*"

"Still on scene," I answered, moving to the final truck. "Treating some casualties before we move out."

She knew better than to question me on that point—if we were remaining in place after being compromised to the local populace, it was for a damn good reason. Instead, she asked, "*How many EKIA?*"

"Unsure," I replied quite honestly, climbing up the rear bumper to find a wooden crate in the back. "Maybe a dozen."

"*Did you say a dozen?*"

I flipped open the rusty metal clasps securing the crate lid.

"They were heavily drugged. Probably the easiest firefight we'll ever have." I deliberately left out the fact that I'd very nearly been gunned down, escaping death by mere inches only through a combination of a reflexive fall, an untrained opponent, and the fact that Ian had responded more quickly and effectively than I was able to manage under the circumstances. "Will provide further information when able, need to finish site exploitation at this time."

Then I flung the crate lid open, my heart seizing up at the sight before me—which would very likely be the last thing I saw in this lifetime.

But instead of being killed, I heard Duchess's monotone reply in my earpiece.

"Understood. Standing by."

My next breath took considerable effort to summon, and it took the sight of Ian exiting the pickup cab, stuffing a handful of paper flyers in his drop pouch and calling up to me, "Anything?" before I was able to muster a coherent response.

"Yeah," I said, considering a more detailed explanation and settling for a request instead. "Come up here and take a look at this."

Ian climbed into the bed, halting abruptly as he took in the crate's contents.

The pile of homemade body belts with shoulder straps had been crudely sewn with as many pouches as they could accommodate, each pocket bulging with rectangular bricks connected by a leapfrogging assembly of red wires. I didn't need or want to examine them any more closely to know that the explosives were surrounded by ball bearings, each of which would outdistance the blast to fling an omnidirectional swath of death. They were suicide vests, the calling card of local terrorists the world over, designed to be worn by willing martyrs or, in the case of Boko Haram and ISWAP, young women who'd volunteered for the purpose to escape a lifetime of hunger and sex slavery at the hands of the men who'd captured them.

I transmitted over the team frequency, "Doc, how much more time you need?"

Reilly responded after a brief pause. *"I can cut Racegun and Cancer loose, but I'll need a few minutes to finish up."*

"Copy," I replied, then keyed my mic again. "Cancer, Racegun, I need you to collect any mass casualty-producing weapons—RPGs, machineguns —so they're in our hands and not left for the terrorists. As soon as Doc is done, we're out of here."

"Got it," Cancer replied. *"Moving."*

Beside me, Ian gestured to the crate and asked, "What about these?"

"It's too much to blow in place," I said. "We can't spare the explosives, and we'd just scatter the vests anyway."

"So what do you want to do?"

What an excellent question, I thought dryly as I considered our options.

"Probably ten or twelve S-vests here," I said. "We're taking them with us —Cancer can defuse them in the van."

Then I stopped for a moment, scanning the dead terrorists in the street as a new thought occurred to me. I keyed my mic again.

"And let's bag up two enemy bodies with their personal weapons— they're going to join us on tonight's raid."

36

Worthy analyzed his phone screen from the bouncing rear of the media van, calling forward to the cab after he'd made a reasonable estimation of the distance ahead.

"Take a right at the next intersection, 300 meters ahead. We follow that for another three kilometers, then we're back on the highway."

Tolu didn't respond, either verbally or even with a nod; instead he continued steering the van across the dirt road, his gaze fixed out the windshield. The rumbling of tires across the uneven surface made the driver's silence all the more unsettling—he hadn't even turned on his customary rap music, leaving the van interior a more awkward setting than it already was, as if such a thing were possible.

David looked over from the passenger seat and said, "Hey, Mario Andretti—you hear him or what? Right turn ahead."

"Yes," Tolu said quietly. "I heard."

The driver had been uncharacteristically silent since leaving the village, though Worthy was uncertain if that was due to the horrors inflicted by ISWAP, or those inflicted by his own team. After all, narrowly averting an atrocity was one thing. But watching the Agency men you'd been supporting execute an enemy prisoner in cold blood was quite another, and to hear Ian tell it, David hadn't even bothered to send Tolu around the corner before pulling the trigger.

Then Worthy considered the obvious possibility that with a brother in Boko Haram, Tolu's ostensible callousness toward terrorists had been shattered at the sight of one dying up close and personal. Particularly, he thought, when the executed man probably had more in common with Tolu's brother than anyone in the van cared to admit.

But Worthy remained unconcerned over an executed man, particularly one who'd been an active participant in the enslavement and rape of innocent Nigerians. His primary concerns fell not to the dead terrorist or even Tolu, but to the surviving villagers. Had the team saved them, he wondered, or condemned them?

Still, he should have been at least somewhat satisfied—the sight of those wounded civilians was horrendous, but it paled in comparison to how he'd feel if they'd bypassed the village altogether. Almost everything in Nigeria thus far had been one steady steamroll of mission creep—supporting the hostage rescue, raiding the facility in Lagos—but with the village raid, it wasn't Duchess's imperative that sent them into danger but the team's own volition. Worthy was just glad the team had been as unanimous about committing to that intervention as he had felt upon finding the fleeing woman.

Other than that, there wasn't much to get excited about. No new intel, a time delay on their primary mission in Maiduguri, a captured load of demolitions along with the weapons: two RPG-7 launchers with fragmentation rockets, a PK machinegun and its ammo, and two AK-47s. At best, the weaponry had been permanently removed from ISWAP custody. At worst, all of it would be easily replaced by the terrorist force. Regardless, only the two AK-47 rifles would be used by the team as a measure to conceal their identities—as would the van's two new passengers.

He lowered his head, rubbing his temples in silent consideration. Worthy had been a part of some shady, under-the-table dealings in his workings with the Agency, much less during his prior mercenary time, but this was an exceptional brand of fucked-up that he was surprised even David was capable of conceiving.

The two enemy bodies were wrapped in team ponchos and laid out in the center of the cargo area. They hadn't started to smell—yet—but Worthy suspected that would occur long before they reached Maiduguri.

He looked up then, taking stock of his team in the back of the van.

Ian was pale, and rightfully so. If Worthy felt sick to his stomach, he could only imagine what the intelligence operative was going through right now. Reilly sat in muted silence, though Worthy suspected he was mentally replaying his medical treatments in the mosque and wondering what he could have done better.

Either way, Cancer was the only one who seemed unperturbed—he had his boots propped up on an enemy corpse and was merrily puffing away on a cigarette.

Upon seeing Worthy watching him, Cancer quickly reached for the pack in his pocket and extended it to the point man. "Didn't mean to be rude."

Worthy stared at him in disbelief, letting a few long seconds elapse before giving an incredulous reply.

"No, Cancer. I don't want a smoke."

"I hear you," the sniper said, putting the pack away. "I wish we'd gotten there in time to stop the executions, too."

There were times when Worthy couldn't tell if Cancer was mocking him intentionally or inadvertently, and upon seeing the sniper's earnest gaze, he wondered if this was one of those rare moments when the man was actually trying to exude some misguided form of human empathy.

Worthy pursed his lips for a moment, then replied, "How are you cool with this?"

Cancer momentarily ruminated over the question. "Look, you can't win 'em all. I know this isn't ideal. But some people are born with a talent for painting, or piano, or whatever. Fucking hopscotch. Me? I've always been good at dealing violence to the deserving. So as for taking an hour delay off our timeline to stop a lot of rape and murder? I'd call that an afternoon well spent."

Ian spoke Worthy's own thoughts almost to a T. "Until the bad guys come back to the village. Either ISWAP or Boko Haram."

"Like I said," Cancer continued, as if Ian were making his point for him, "can't win 'em all. If you joined this team to save the world, you were sorely mistaken. We did what we could today, and that's enough. If we weren't going to sleep well tonight, then we should now."

Reilly heaved a great sigh before breaking his reverie to say, "We're still a ways out from Maiduguri. No one's sleeping tonight."

Cancer looked irritated, his eyebrows furrowing as he squinted at the medic before taking another lungful of smoke and replying with his trademark indifference.

"Well, tomorrow then. And as for these sorry bastards getting cold in the van"—he waved his cigarette toward the bodies—"anyone who feels bad about them didn't see what I did in the field."

37

Reilly heard Cancer's transmission with a pang of apprehension—the raid wasn't supposed to be this way.

"Take cover, you've got another security patrol coming out."

David was a few paces ahead of him, clearly visible under night vision as he ducked behind a small outbuilding and lowered the cargo from his shoulder, hoisting his weapon as Reilly closed the distance. It was unlikely they'd be spotted at this distance from the compound, especially at night— they were passing through a residential area and had yet to see their objective.

But given the hyperactive levels of guard activity ahead, they couldn't take any chances; and besides, Reilly thought, it was a chance to get the weight off his shoulders if only for a moment. He set down his cargo, readying his HK417 and scanning their backtrail as David covered security to their front.

The muggy night air was thick with the scent of sewage and rotting trash, which mingled with the oppressive heat and his heavy cargo to ensure Reilly had sweated through his shirt minutes after beginning his dismounted infil alongside his team leader. They'd arrived in Maiduguri a few hours earlier to find that, unlike Lagos, vehicle transit was possible at speeds greater than two miles per hour.

But they couldn't risk driving within sight of the target, so a lengthy foot movement ensued—Cancer moving to a rooftop with his sniper rifle, Worthy and Ian flanking to the north side, and Reilly and David approaching the south before kicking off the mother of all diversion efforts.

Their destination was in the northwest corner of the city, equidistant from the airport and the highway. The location was fitting for a logistics hub, though by now Reilly knew that distribution of commercial goods was only a public-facing ruse for what actually occurred in the buildings ahead.

Cancer transmitted, "*Patrol is skirting the western perimeter. Four men, so probably a new team. This is the third patrol in 45 minutes—it's like they're expecting to get hit.*"

David whispered back, "What's your assessment of skill level?"

"*Weapons at the low ready; they're definitely vigilant. They've got one guy whitelighting the ground beneath parked vehicles right now, another checking their six. Everyone's heads are on a swivel. I don't like it.*"

"Well," David offered, "those guards are going to like it a whole lot less in a few minutes."

Reilly hoped his team leader's confidence was well placed—for an objective that Duchess maintained would have a minimum level of overt security, the target ahead had a hell of a lot. You knew things were getting dicey, Reilly thought, when the team's resident sociopath sounded more apprehensive with each transmission from his sniper position.

During his next one, Cancer said, "*I don't know how good these guards will be under fire, but you guys better be ready to rock and roll. Gotta be ten to fifteen security men based on what I've seen so far, and with that kind of manpower they don't need to be good at their jobs to win.*"

Then, before David could reply, Cancer added, "*They just went inside. Get moving.*"

Reilly sighed, then shouldered his cargo once more as David led the way down the row of sporadically placed houses.

Looking past his team leader, Reilly caught his first glimpses of their objective: a tight cluster of rooftops, some far too large to belong to a residential property, that loomed across the street ahead.

Okafor International was ostensibly a food distributor, and if not for the discovery of cocaine being hidden in cans of corn and routed to its commercial address, there was precious little reason to suspect the business of illicit activity.

According to Duchess, Okafor International's records and accounting were in top form, with no digital traces of affiliation to any terrorist organization, least of all Boko Haram, who wasn't known to be involved with any legal revenue streams. That wasn't to say they weren't well funded—extremist donors aside, the group enjoyed a steady income born of kidnappings, bank robberies, and forcibly taxing the population in their area of operations. But there was no evidence of Boko Haram ever using shell companies to facilitate its wider financial goals; and yet here Reilly was, approaching the heavily guarded compound.

Okafor International's corporate headquarters consisted of a partially fenced compound complete with multiple warehouses and subsidiary buildings. It would have been a platoon-sized objective for anyone intending to clear it all, but tonight the focus was on the office building alone, the beating heart of whatever terrorist operation ran out of this seemingly legitimate business.

David halted between the final houses, stopping short of the street before transmitting, "We're at the street—good to move to the drop-off point?"

Cancer replied, *"You're clear. Go."*

Reilly and his team leader broke into a shuffling run, moving as quickly as they could across the dirt side street. Their destination was twenty meters ahead, a remote shed that provided more concealment than cover from small arms fire—but at the moment, concealment was what they needed most given the active guard force. Cancer's assurance that no security men were watching was only as good as his last update, and Reilly adjusted the heavy cargo on his back as he moved, muttering, "Damn you, Johnny."

And while carrying a body was bad enough, it was made far worse by the need for two weapons, one a captured ISWAP AK-47 and the other his Agency-issued rifle. But David was managing the same with a considerable disadvantage in terms of size, and if he wasn't complaining, then neither could Reilly.

Then again, he thought, this whole thing was David's plan in the first place.

David reached the shed and tucked himself around the south side, with Reilly arriving seconds later.

Cancer transmitted, "*You're clear—no movement from the buildings. Hurry up and get them situated before that changes.*"

David and Reilly spread the bodies out by a few meters, the rigor mortis leaving them contorted in awkward positions as they folded the bloody poncho wrappings and tucked them away in cargo pockets.

This was a morbidly gruesome affair, to say the least—though as far as deception operations went, planting dead bodies loaded with a competing faction's propaganda was more or less the gold standard.

Since splitting from mainstream Boko Haram, ISWAP held a checkered past with their former organization. At some points they cooperated; at others, they attacked one another mercilessly. That kind of divisiveness was a dream come true for the counterterrorism community. After all, any effort the factions directed toward harming their counterparts meant energy directed away from the innocent civilians they normally thrived on terrorizing, and if the apparent ISWAP complicity in the wake of tonight's attacks stirred up further infighting, then so much the better.

Still, he thought, there was something uncanny about planting dead bodies prior to a mission. The two ISWAP men had been dead too long to fool any actual forensic investigation, though Reilly doubted that type of thing either existed or would be committed to this part of Maiduguri. But there was nothing about this little deception measure to tie US forces to the action, and that's what really mattered most right now.

Upon getting the thumbs up from Reilly, David transmitted, "Johnny and Walker are in position. Neither of them seem very enthusiastic, but they'll serve their noble purpose. Me and Doc are standing by for our move to the final assault position."

Cancer replied a moment later. "*Wait one, you've got another security patrol exiting the building.*"

Reilly peered out from behind the shed and scanned through his night vision, watching two men with their weapons at the ready making their way across the compound interior. It was yet another confirmation of what the sniper had observed for the better part of the last hour: these guys were well-armed, each man toting an assault rifle and wearing a magazine carrier. His hopes of finding a bored and complacent guard force were dashed—whoever they were, whether Boko Haram or security contractors, they patrolled with a degree of vigilance that came as an unfortunate surprise. It wasn't impossible, of course, that they were chipping some of the cocaine that passed through the facility, and if that was the case, then Reilly and his team were in for some night.

Finally Cancer transmitted, *"Guards just went inside Building Three. You're clear to proceed to final assault."*

I stepped out from behind the shed, darting forward to the low cinderblock wall ahead.

At ten meters distant, I covered the open ground at a sprint—it felt good to finally be unencumbered by an enemy corpse, and I heard Reilly's footsteps behind me before slowing to a halt and ducking behind cover. Reilly arrived in short order, breathing hard as he readied his HK417. I did the same with my Agency weapon, dropping to the prone and peeking out from the right side of the wall to get a clear look at the compound ahead.

Unlike the Gradsek port complex, Okafor International should have been a cakewalk. There were no CCTV cameras or motion sensors, not even a basic alarm as far as the Agency's cyber operators had been able to discern. It made sense in a way; if you were hiding a command and logistics hub for a terrorist organization under the guise of a legitimate business, the last thing you wanted was for the police to be notified and come poking around.

The downside for us, of course, was that Okafor International filled that shortfall with armed security men, and a lot of them.

Our timing on this mission was no accident—at this hour of the night, the facility was abandoned save for the guard force. And if they were all occupied combating what they thought was a major attack on the facility, the office building would be ripe for penetration. At that point, it would be a matter of keeping the security men occupied for as long as possible, a task I would thoroughly enjoy.

While this piece of cover was our final assault position, it wasn't the limit of advance—at least, not for me.

That distinction belonged to the hulking Isuzu box truck parked ahead, just outside the southernmost buildings. Its cargo box was over twenty feet in length, and the fact that it was unattended meant it was surely empty. I had no intentions of searching inside it either way, only instigating a fight with every member of the security force on duty that night.

And to that end, the comforting weight of the small parcel in my drop pouch would be more than adequate.

I transmitted, "Me and Doc are at the final assault position. Racegun, how are you looking?"

Worthy replied, "*Angel and I are set at our final concealment, ready to make entry on your mark.*"

"Cancer?"

"*Still set,*" he answered. "*No movement outside the buildings—better get to that truck while you still can.*"

"Copy, I'm moving. Stand by."

Rising from behind my cover, I took off at a run toward the enormous box truck, making a beeline for the cab. Slowing as I approached, I knelt beside the driver's door, glancing next to the running board to locate the metal cylinder punctuated by a fuel cap.

Then I dipped a hand into my drop pouch to recover the demolition charge, a full block of C4 consisting of a flat brick that weighed in at 1.25 pounds.

It was prepped with an adhesive panel to ensure it didn't slip off before the job was done. I peeled the plastic backing off the C4 charge, and made a move to pocket it before catching myself. In the eyes of Nigerian law I was already a trespasser and a soon-to-be arsonist—what did it matter if I littered as well?

As the scrap fluttered to the ground, I applied the adhesive side of the charge over the truck's exposed section of fuel tank, giving it a firm push to ensure it stayed in place. Then I inserted a cylindrical blasting cap into the

C4 and unrolled the attached wire, taking hold of the fuse igniter and idly wondering how much gas was in the truck.

A partially empty fuel tank would have far better effects than a full one —it was the vapor, not the liquid fuel itself, that would explode. But any dispersed gasoline would spread fire wherever it landed, a good thing for the massive diversion effort I was putting into play now.

Grasping the metal ring, I pushed the firing pin forward and gave it a quarter turn clockwise. Then I yanked it outward as I heard the *snick* of activation, watching closely for the plume of smoke that appeared a moment later. A tiny flame was now traveling through the black powder core of the time fuse, a plastic-wrapped cord that I straightened before setting the fuse igniter on the ground.

Then I turned and darted back to Reilly, keying my radio to transmit one word as I ran.

"Burning."

It was important to clock the elapsed time, but I wasn't about to do it— my only goal in life at present was to retreat to the final assault position and take cover before the blast. Demolition time fuse had a small but not insignificant margin of error, and while I'd cut it precisely to achieve a sixty-second burn time, the last thing I wanted was to tempt fate.

The toe of my boot caught the edge of a hard object—stone, trash, who knew—and I sprawled forward, smashing into the dirt to the sound of my two slung weapons clattering together. I grunted with the impact, considering the possibility of a broken leg before realizing the only damage was to my ego. Pushing myself upright, I charged the remaining distance to the cinderblock wall, rounding the left side and resuming my position next to Reilly, who transmitted for the benefit of the team.

"Forty seconds."

Cancer came over the net, asking, *"You all right there, Suicide?"*

"You didn't see shit," I replied, considering that the sniper was sure to bring up my fall at every opportunity for the rest of my natural life.

True to form, Cancer's next transmission was a humiliating reference to our previous mission in China.

"Relax, boss—at least you didn't go off the side of a cliff this time."

Bastard, I thought, leaving his comment unanswered.

Reilly continued his countdown. "Twenty seconds."

Both he and I slid our Agency rifles to our backs, tightening the slings before bringing our respective AK-47s into a firing position.

"Ten seconds," Reilly transmitted.

The spark of flame that had been working its way up the length of time fuse was about to reach its end, where the final segment was crimped by the blasting cap now embedded inside the block of C4. That narrow metal tube contained its own small charge of explosives, which would detonate to trigger the entire charge—and I could barely wait to see the outcome.

Reilly continued, "Five, four, three, two, one...mark."

Maybe I'd made a mistake in measuring the time fuse, I thought.

Or maybe the entire charge had failed to detonate.

He began counting up. "One, two, three—"

The subsequent explosion was a seismic shockwave of noise and light; the view through my night vision became a blinding glare as the vehicle disappeared amidst the scorching flash. I felt the air being sucked from my lungs, followed immediately by a searing wave of heat blasting over me. A twisted shard of metal clanged to the ground to my right, followed by a rain of small debris that clattered across the compound. Echoes of the blast reverberated as I raised my night vision on its mount, peering through the flickering light to get a closer look at the truck or, more accurately, what was left of it.

A great pillar of flame receded to the sight of a greasy cloud of black smoke as the vehicle chassis became engulfed in a roaring fire. Whatever fuel had been in the tank was now spread in an oblong lake of fire burning fiercely on all sides, the heat so intense even at this distance that I wondered if the security people would come out to play at all—after the sound of that explosion, half of them were probably deaf.

I was so taken aback by the blast's sheer violence that when two men appeared with rifles, it took me a moment to bring my AK-47 into a firing position. When I did, both of the security men responded in unison, wielding their rifles toward me—the downside of the ongoing fire, I realized, was that these people could see Reilly and me plain as day.

Using a thumb to pull the AK selector lever into full auto, I ripped two short bursts in their direction. Whether I'd hit them or not was anyone's guess; the hisses and pops of incoming fire echoed so quickly that I ducked behind cover, alarmed at how fast the security men were responding.

Reilly filled the gap, opening up with unsuppressed gunfire to my left as I angled into a new shooting position, then emerged to acquire a third guard over the iron sights of my rifle before firing another burst.

We'd just stirred up a hornet's nest of enemy activity, and I caught glimpses of guards swarming out of the building as they took up defensive positions. Reilly and I engaged them as quickly as we could, keenly aware that our weapons produced a blinding muzzle flash with each burst, all but a billboard heralding our exact position to anyone who cared to shoot back.

We took our shots accordingly, remaining behind cover to the full extent possible until the volume and accuracy of incoming fire forced us to remain concealed. The men were reacting faster and better than we'd anticipated, and over the crackle of flames I made out the sound of running footsteps approaching to my right—and without any reduction in the incoming gunfire, a knot formed in my stomach as I realized that they were using fire and maneuver to flank our position.

"God*damn*," Cancer muttered to himself, aligning his sights with the front runner in a three-man maneuver element closing with David and Reilly.

His position on a rooftop west of the objective gave him clear lines of sight to the battle in progress, which he now surveilled through his day scope to compensate for the ongoing vehicle fire casting its blazing glow in all directions. The guard force's frequent patrols so far had given him cause for extreme concern, but nothing compared to what he felt now—a deepening realization that his team was in deep shit.

The guards had immediately established a support-by-fire line at the southernmost buildings before sending their runners to flank David and Reilly with astounding speed—these men were no casual employees from the local labor pool. Nor were they Boko Haram, because none of those terrorist shitheads had anything close to the training required to operate this effectively.

That left one explanation: his team had just picked a fight with a guard force of professional mercenaries, meaning that for once they might just have bitten off more than they could chew.

Cancer achieved a shot to center mass, dropping the lead runner in place as the other two responded by wildly spraying the cinderblock wall as they moved. Amid the flames and gunfire, they had no way of knowing a sniper lurked in the darkness, and at this point they probably assumed that David or Reilly scored a lucky potshot.

But those remaining two fighters presented an obstacle of sorts; maybe David and Reilly would be able to tag them first, or maybe not. The bigger issue for Cancer was that the second those guards suspected a sniper, they'd retreat inside the buildings, which would be a very bad thing for Worthy and Ian, tasked with penetrating the inner offices. And for the pre-staged bodies with all their incriminating ISWAP propaganda to have the desired effect, David and Reilly first had to reach them and draw enemy fire at that location.

But a ten-meter gap lay between his two teammates and the shed where they'd deposited the bodies, and if Cancer didn't respond with immediate and deadly force, they'd never make it.

He released his left palm from the handguard of his G28, pivoting his aim on the bipod as he continued to track the remaining fighters through his scope while keying his mic to transmit.

"Two pax, ten seconds out from your right side. You better hit them before I need to."

Then Cancer resumed his grip on the rifle, watching David and Reilly sprawl into the prone almost shoulder to shoulder, their weapons angled toward the approaching fighters.

Cancer held his index finger taut against the trigger, squeezing a shot on one guard as both fell in a collective hail of gunfire from himself, his team leader, and the medic. Those latter two were lucky he'd been able to warn them, he thought, transitioning his aim left to scan for the security force's next move now that their first maneuver element had been effectively reduced to a pile of bodies.

The sight caught him off guard at first—the guards should have sent a second maneuver element in the wake of the first, albeit in a more distant line of approach to the known attackers.

Instead, the next men to move did so toward defensive positions around a central warehouse inside the main compound, taking up vantage points to cover the front and side entrances.

Cancer transmitted, "They're massing around Building Three. Probably a major load they're trying to protect. Entry team, if you're still able to move, now is the time."

Ian keyed his mic and replied, "Entering now."

Releasing his transmit switch, the intelligence operative watched Worthy complete the final steps in his lockpicking effort.

He heard the deadbolt click open, his suppressed rifle poised at the ready to enter, but before he could, Worthy did it for him, flinging the door aside and stepping into the dark hallway.

That wasn't entirely unexpected, Ian thought as he followed, closing the door behind him and locking it shut.

The fact remained that as the team's sole intelligence operative, Ian was by duty description the least equipped to deal with any emerging threats. That was why Worthy had been assigned to safeguard the collection effort inside the building—as the team's quickest shot, he was more than capable of slinging subsonic bullets to great effect before withdrawing.

Ian desperately hoped it wouldn't come to that, however.

No matter what else occurred tonight, the undetected collection of intelligence was at the forefront of the entire operation, and Ian considered that for the first time in a long time, he was now the main effort of a team incursion.

He watched Worthy moving stealthily down the hallway, sweeping his barrel from left to right as he relied on an infrared floodlight to illuminate the building's interior. With no requirement for rear security short of hearing the deadbolt unlatch behind him, Ian resigned himself to ducking inside the doorways on either side of the hall, using his own infrared floodlight to bring the rooms into stark relief in his night vision.

Most were discountable at a glance, the various crates and dollies distinguishing each as a setting for manual labor, however illicit.

But the fourth room he encountered was a different story altogether—its door was closed, and when Ian tested the handle, it held fast.

"Need entry," he whispered, stepping out of the way to assume a point of aim down the hallway as he and Worthy switched places.

The point man set to work on the lock, a difficult process under the best of circumstances and more so with a lack of ambient light. Ian stared into the abyss of the hallway ahead, a dual row of doorways presenting a tantalizing number of options for intelligence gathering. But given the firefight in progress, he'd only be able to perform a partial search of one room; and his instinctive commitment to the secured door could either result in a total jackpot or a wasted lockpicking effort that expended what little time they had left.

He felt a wrenching tension in his gut as he listened to Worthy manipulating the lock tumblers behind him, small metallic clicks interspersed with a few frustrated grunts. Every second that ticked away seemed to span an eternity—when Ian received the order to flee the building, he'd have to leave whether he obtained anything useful or not. Come on, he thought, come on...and then he heard the clack of the lock disengaging, followed by the door swinging open as Worthy entered to clear the space.

Ian held fast, now the only security standing between him and the corridor, waiting with his rifle poised until Worthy appeared beside him and said, "Go."

He spun and dashed inside, seeing that he'd chosen wisely: this was certainly a main office of some kind, its lone desk facing the doorway. Ian had the gratifying realization that if the facility had any command post, then this was it.

Worthy retreated inside the doorway and continued pulling security as Ian rounded the desk, lowering his rifle on its sling as he activated the headlamp around his neck before taking a seat in the chair.

He ignored the desktop computer—for once in his intelligence career, he wasn't interested in digital media. The Agency hackers had already scrubbed all they could of Okafor International's official and unofficial business records, finding nothing that would suggest illegal activity. It had been much the same with Gradsek, whose only true records of their smuggling activity had been coded, handwritten notes on a whiteboard.

That much was no surprise, at least not to Ian. As intelligence agencies became more sophisticated, criminal and terrorist organizations had managed to survive by taking their communications to decidedly lower-tech measures—prepaid phones rotated out of service every few days, written or memorized messages transported via courier. Ian had no doubt that while there was likely information worth finding here, nothing on the computer had escaped the scrutiny of the Agency's hackers.

Instead he pulled open the desk drawers from top to bottom. The first held office supplies, with the notable exception of a half-full bottle of vodka. But the second drawer held a stack of ledgers, the hardcovers a uniform shade of light green. Instinct told him that these were the hand-written records of things that couldn't be documented on digital media, and that a comprehensive search of the stack would reveal illicit activities going back for months if not years.

But he didn't have the time or, frankly, the interest for a thorough dissection. He withdrew the top ledger in the stack, knowing that if he was right, it would be the most current.

Setting the ledger on the desk, he flipped it open and prepared his phone to photograph it as he visually analyzed the first page.

The contents were in handwritten Arabic—a contradiction of sorts, until Ian considered that it was once the official language of Nigeria. It had influenced several local dialects and was still being spoken in its pure form in some parts of the north, if only as a second or third language. More importantly, if Boko Haram had been augmented with a hardliner from the wider terrorist world to manage some strategic-level imperatives, it was statistically logical that individual would speak Arabic.

Ian photographed the first page, not yet resigning himself to partial failure just because he wasn't fluent in the language. The important thing was that he knew the alphabet, which allowed him to phonetically pronounce the script—many of the characters were shared with other languages he'd come into contact with over the years, such as Farsi, Dari, Pashtu, and, on their last mission, Uyghur.

Ian scanned the first header from right to left to see if he could decipher it. If it was a true Arabic word, the answer was overwhelmingly likely to be no. But if it was transliteration, the spelling of an English word using the Arabic alphabet, he at least had a shot.

The header line consisted of a scant five characters, which would appear to the average Western eye as a series of squiggles with sets of one to three dots above and below. Ian recognized the characters without issue, piecing together after a half-second's consideration the phonetic pronunciation of the Arabic characters *sheen, ayn, fa, ra, waw, noon*. That spelled a combination of SH, F, R, OO or W depending on the usage, and N.

Shifrun?

Beneath that was an extensive list of six-digit numerals, many of which had their rows ticked off. Ian recognized these as latitudes and longitudes of specific grid locations but didn't yet understand the import.

As far as the header went, there was considerable margin for error. This realization was all the more apparent as he flipped to the second page, snapping a picture before analyzing the top line. The Arabic language denoted short vowels with small dashes above or below the primary letter, a consideration typically omitted by native speakers. That meant he was looking at an indecipherable string of consonant pronunciations, some of which didn't exist in the English language.

Those differences may not amount to much over the course of a single vowel or two per word, but when you were trying to decipher a written text without context, it was the difference between instant insight and total confusion. Were you looking at the name of a vegetable, an animal, a person? There was no way to tell, and Ian tried to make sense of the characters *ta, kaf, seen, alif, kaf, seen, kaf, waw*. That was the equivalent of writing the English letters T, A, K, S, K, W.

Trying to account for the unseen short syllables, Ian thought, *Taksasku?*

The real solution didn't occur to him until he considered the phonetics when combined with the discovery of Gradsek smuggling in Lagos.

But when the idea took hold, he knew beyond a doubt that he wasn't wrong. Each successive page confirmed the same, and the previously indecipherable Arabic words now made perfect sense. And the key, as was all too often the case in America's foreign relations, was oil.

Shifron was Chevron, and *Taksaku* was Texaco.

After that realization, Ian was able to instantaneously discern the headers on the pages that followed: the Arabic characters *ra dal seen* equated to an acronym for RDS, which in context meant Royal Dutch Shell. Likewise, additional photographed pages indicated AGIP, Italy's Nigerian Agip Oil company, and TPNL, or France's Total Petroleum Nigeria Limited.

Under each heading was a set of rows discernable as latitude and longitude, some crossed off with a date annotation.

The final page in the ledger bore a header that translated roughly to *'Iksoon Mubil*.

ExxonMobil.

After that singular recognition, Ian assumed a laser focus on the page's contents.

Once he did so, he understood that his team's findings went way beyond the one oil company that didn't have a dedicated page in the current ledger: Gradsek. He already knew they were snatching up market share as other oil companies withdrew from Nigeria, and faking reports of attacks on their own locations—but now he realized Gradsek was actively targeting their competitors, providing Boko Haram with detailed intelligence on the locations of drilling operations and exposed pipelines for tasking to pirate and vigilante groups, all without getting their hands dirty. This went way beyond an economic conspiracy—it was a terrorist one as well, a carefully orchestrated web of strategic targets to guide bombings, illegal siphoning, and even, he realized upon reviewing the ExxonMobil page in the ledger, kidnappings.

A line reading *Lagos* harbored an additional notation: the Arabic numerals for eleven, the number of hostages captured five days ago, followed by another latitude and longitude. Ian didn't need to verify this one; it was the camp in the Sambisa Forest, discernable at a glance because it had been crossed off.

But that led him to keep reading, and the instant he saw what came next, Ian felt a rush of euphoria that suddenly justified his team's every action in Nigeria.

There was a scrawled word in Arabic, which read phonetically as Gwoza—a town just 80 miles southeast of Maiduguri—written not over a single grid location but a trio of them.

The three remaining hostages were being kept at separate locations in Gwoza. Now, Ian had exactly what he'd come for.

He snapped a picture of the page, followed by a close-up of the three grid locations just to be certain. The last thing he noted was a dashed series of numbers he recognized from memory: the phone number of Malu, the Permanent Secretary for Nigeria's Federal Ministry of Petroleum Resources.

Just before he turned the paper to reveal blank pages beyond, Cancer's voice crackled over his earpiece.

"I hear cop cars—get out of there, now."

Speaking in a harsh whisper, Worthy called out from the doorway, "You're done. Let's move."

Reilly was midway through firing an AK-47 burst when Cancer's call came over his team frequency, followed in short order by Ian's response.

"I've got what I need."

David transmitted, "Angel, you've got a thirty-second head start—exfil, exfil, exfil."

Then, to Reilly, the team leader shouted, "Go!"

Reilly emptied the remainder of his magazine, then stripped the mag and hurled it as far as he could to the left—if nothing else, it would help inflate the perceived number of attackers in the imminent post-battle analysis, which, with a little luck, would only occur after his team reached a position of relative safety.

After reloading, he called out, "Moving," and waited until David resumed firing to begin his sprint back toward the shed to their south.

He was two steps into his run when David's fire fell silent, a momentary lapse between bursts that allowed him to hear two shouted words from the security force. And while he couldn't discern what those words meant, he knew without a doubt that they were spoken in Russian—meaning they'd been fighting Gradsek security men. The Russian oil company had directly outsourced protection to this critical site for Boko Haram's continued reign of terror.

For Reilly, the knowledge brought with it a surge of validation; he was a medic by trade, and to date he'd never been able to contribute a single facet of information to the team's intelligence picture. He wanted to inform his team immediately, to shout his discovery to anyone who could hear him.

But first, he had to get out of here alive.

He scrambled behind the shed, resuming a firing position off the left side of the structure and opening fire toward the muzzle flashes still flickering inside the compound.

His shots were as effective as a radio transmission in signaling David to end his current burst of gunfire and bound back toward the medic. The flames licking the box truck and its surrounding vicinity were dying down now, and between automatic bursts Reilly could hear the approaching wail of police sirens—Cancer hadn't been exaggerating, he thought. By the sound of it, they were only a minute or two away, and Reilly emptied his current magazine as David skidded to a stop beside him.

"Last call," David shouted, and Reilly stripped his empty magazine, once again hurling it sideways before reloading and firing a final burst.

Leaving his weapon on full automatic, he pulled the sling over his head and dropped his still-smoking AK-47 beside Johnny's body. David did the same for Walker, and both men transitioned to their suppressed Agency weapons before flipping their night vision devices back over their eyes.

Reilly said, "I should wait until you're sitting down, but..." He drew a breath. "Those guys were Gradsek."

"No shit," the team leader replied angrily, as if that much was so obvious it needn't be spoken. "I assumed that when the guys who flanked us were white. You good?"

Reilly swallowed. "Yeah. Yeah, I'm good."

David took up a firing position toward the compound, this time without shooting. This was Reilly's cue to move, and the medic took off southward, completing the next bound of their dismounted exfil.

Worthy came to a halt at the edge of the building, pausing to look both ways down the street. The police sirens were screaming in now, and the glance to his right revealed the distant gleam of a flickering light bar.

This was do-or-die time, his last chance to cross the street before it was illuminated by the headlights of the first cop car to arrive. He launched into a desperate run, his boots slamming across the dirt road. What he needed now was to immerse himself in darkness, to slip into the shadows between the houses ahead and rely on night vision to escape.

He arrived between buildings, skidding to a stop before pivoting backward to check Ian's progress.

And while the intelligence operative was running across the road, his body half-lit by the incoming headlights as Worthy searched for any security guards trying to pursue, the sight beyond gave him pause.

The Okafor International compound was highlighted in stark relief, its rooflines silhouetted against the dim glow of orange flames consuming whatever was left of the box truck—not much, if the volume of David's demolition charge was any indication.

As Ian finally cleared the road and made his way into the shadows, Worthy harbored a sense of disbelief that this thing had, against all probabilities of success, come off more or less as planned. He'd heard Ian's radio call—*I've got what I need*—but Worthy had no idea *what* the intelligence operative had found. He'd only been in the office for a few minutes, tops, and it seemed unlikely that anyone, even Ian, could uncover a landslide of valuable information in that short time period.

No time to consider it now, though—if those lead cops had caught sight of a man or two darting across the road at the periphery of their headlights, he could be looking at a long race ahead, trying to weave his way across neighborhoods to lose any pursuers before linking up with Tolu.

Worthy spun to face the alleyway, moving once Ian was a few meters away. His infrared floodlight cut a blazing swath through night vision, highlighting the obstacles to be avoided as he ran: piles of trash, abandoned cinderblocks, a water pump rising three feet from the ground that would be life-changing if he struck it at a full run.

Another issue were the homes' occupants. No one had yet demonstrated the poor judgment to step outside in the wake of an explosion and audible gunfire, but he couldn't rule out the possibility of having to negotiate a nonlethal encounter with members of the populace. As things stood now, an unsettling number of windows were lit as citizens reacted to the early-morning raid, and Worthy threaded his way between the pools of light they cast on the ground, ducking beneath window frames when the need arose.

He cut left after the next row of homes, beginning a westward dogleg to his route and pausing momentarily to ensure Ian was still behind him.

They continued running for another fifteen minutes before Worthy gave any thought to halting; but at this point, having cleared two-thirds of their circuitous route away from the objective, he needed to confirm or deny that anyone had managed to follow them.

He ducked into the space between two metal dumpsters planted beside a building, pulling Ian behind him before kneeling and peering left and right around the corner. If he was going to ambush any pursuers, this was as good a spot as any. Then he observed their backtrail in a visual search for any flashlight-wielding cops or civilians—nothing.

Satisfied, he whispered to Ian, "Find anything worthwhile?"

"Fuckin' A," Ian replied, a rare segue into gratuitous profanity for the intelligence operative. "All three hostage locations."

Worthy's reaction to this news was a conflicted sense of celebration. On one hand, the very act of leaving this place alive was an achievement, much less doing so with information on the current status of the captives. On the other hand, any hostage rescue would be conducted by professionals who specialized in that kind of thing, and not his own team.

But he had bigger problems at present—namely, safeguarding his and Ian's passage to their pickup site. Until they arrived, every other consideration was futile if not a distraction from the immediate task of surviving long enough to inform the CIA.

Rising from his crouch, Worthy turned and continued their dismounted exfil north, toward the van where Tolu was waiting.

38

I watched the sun rise from the van's passenger seat as the highway extended endlessly on its southerly course to Gwoza.

Ever since the hostages had been captured, this mission had turned into a virtual open season against Boko Haram. Gone were almost all requirements to operate within the Agency's exceedingly narrow parameters, to include submitting every minor adjustment to the preordained plan for Duchess's scrutinizing judgment.

And after Ian had uncovered the Maiduguri ledger, my team had once more managed to stay gainfully employed during the festivities.

This time it wasn't Duchess's request but my own that sent us southbound on the A13 Highway toward the three new grids in the town of Gwoza. I'd pitched our CIA handler on the relevance of this mission not to conduct close target reconnaissance, per se—after all, if we got too close we could alert the Boko Haram captors of our presence—but rather to do some drive-bys of the target grids while remaining within the normal flow of civilian traffic. We could then obtain video footage to effect a rescue by a larger and more specialized element of the US military.

Duchess had approved my proposal in record time, though whether because she agreed with our assessment of the ledger contents or because she had no other way to justify our continued presence deep within Boko

Haram territory, I had no idea. Nor could I begin to speculate how useful the upcoming reconnaissance effort would be—but Ian's instincts on new intel were very rarely wrong. If there was the slightest chance of locating the remaining three hostages, then we needed to act on it at once.

Reilly spoke from the cargo area, addressing no one in particular.

"You have to appreciate the irony."

Ian asked, "What's that?"

"We came to Nigeria so we could hit Usman in his camp just outside Gwoza. Since getting here we've been everywhere in the damn country *except* Gwoza, and now that we're headed there, Usman is locked up in Abuja."

"It's not ironic," Ian corrected him, "it's genius."

Reilly snorted. "Taking the hostages to a military-controlled town? Yeah, real smart."

"It's the only government-owned area anywhere around here. That makes it the last place anyone would think to look."

"Or," Reilly countered, "the hostages aren't there at all."

But Ian was adamant. "Bin Laden was hiding out half a mile from the Pakistan Military Academy, remember? As long as Boko Haram paid off the Nigerian Army to smuggle the hostages into town, they'd effectively disappear from everyone's radar."

"Well with that logic, I guess we can disregard the fact that everything we've done has been one snowballing shitstorm of mission creep."

Turning to face the rest of my team, I asked incredulously, "Mission *creep*? You've got to be kidding me—at this point we're practically coining the term mission *sprint*."

Cancer leaned forward in his seat and shot me a jagged grin. "Would you rather we went home the day after missing Usman? Because that's what would have happened if those hostages didn't get rolled up."

I shook my head. "Don't get me wrong, I'm glad we're staying busy. And that may change if I find myself, or any of you idiots, bleeding out on the streets of Gwoza. But the longer we've been in Nigeria, the less I understand what we're doing, or who we're doing it for."

Worthy agreed, "David's right. And let's not pretend everything we do has the patina of nobility to it."

"Which part?" Cancer asked. "Killing terrorists, or helping to rescue hostages? Both sound pretty solid to me."

"Equipping the Taliban against the Soviets sounded pretty solid to the Agency back in the eighties, too. Can you look me in the eye and say there's no chance we'll find out something about our missions five or ten years down the road?"

Cancer gave a short laugh. "I wouldn't say that. But as long as it doesn't involve us justifying our actions in a secret court, I'll look you in the eye and say that I don't really give a shit."

"Well," I said, "let's hope it doesn't come to that. Besides, we have to survive long enough to worry about the possibility."

Then I turned back to face the road ahead, and the van fell silent once more.

For nearly three hours we'd been traveling along Highway A4 under the constant risk of enemy contact, with every mile south of Maiduguri stretching through wild territory that was controlled by Boko Haram, if it was controlled at all.

Now that the sun was rising, that risk increased exponentially. Fighting with the benefit of night vision was one thing, but when every dickhead with a gun could see just as well as we could, the playing field was considerably more level.

Which was ludicrous, in a way, because the terrain around us was anything but.

To our right, the ground sloped off in a rocky expanse stretching to the fringes of the Sambisa Forest. To the left were tree-covered hills rising to astonishing heights, the greenery lusher than anything we'd seen since departing the mangroves on infil. These were the Mandara Mountains, a volcanic range that extended over a hundred miles.

Cancer stuck his head into the cab to take in the landscape with a low whistle.

"Jesus," he muttered, "look at those mountains."

Ian spoke up behind him.

"When Boko Haram took over Gwoza, a lot of residents took to the hills. Now that the military is in control of the town—more or less—those mountains belong to the terrorists as much as the Sambisa Forest on the opposite side of the highway. Probably more so; the high ground has miles of caves and caverns, and they extend all the way into Cameroon."

Cancer moved back to his seat, commenting, "Sounds like the Afghanistan-Pakistan border."

"It sounds," Ian corrected him, "like a lot of insurgent-infested areas. Inaccessible terrain combined with porous borders are a nightmare for any government and a dream come true for any bad guy."

"After our last mission," Cancer said, referencing China, "I really, *really* don't want to climb any more mountains."

Chuckling in agreement, I said, "Then be glad the hostages are in Gwoza. If we can support another rescue, the hostages could be recovered without Usman—or his predecessor—going free in exchange."

Cancer sounded ambivalent about the prospect.

"So? We still wouldn't get to kill him."

I shrugged. "At least he'd remain in custody."

"Sure, until the next time Boko Haram nabs any civilians considered important enough for the Nigerian government to trade for."

Worthy dealt himself into the exchange then, speaking with a cynicism that I'd rarely witnessed from the normally pragmatic Georgian.

"You guys are missing the point. Or severely overestimating our impact on global events."

"Meaning?" I asked.

He said, "Meaning that even if we smoked Usman, someone else would step up and the terror would continue in one new flavor or another. Just look at how many groups have spun up since Boko Haram got started in, what, 2001?"

Ian corrected him, "2002. And there's only been two spinoffs, technically. One faction—Ansaru—broke off and pledged allegiance to Al Qaeda, while the main group became loyal to ISIS and flagged themselves as Islamic State West Africa Province. After Baghdadi demoted their leader, he split from ISWAP and became Boko Haram again. Now we've got three terrorist groups with the same origin: Ansaru, ISWAP, and Boko Haram, with various links to Al Qaeda, ISIS, and"—he heaved a dreary sigh—"God knows who else."

I shook my head. "That's nothing new, though, just the usual terrorist bullshit. ISIS came from Al Qaeda, right?"

"Not quite that simple." Ian leapt at the opportunity to recount his encyclopedic knowledge of terrorism. "Al Qaeda was founded in 1988. But Zarqawi founded Al Qaeda in Iraq in '04, shortly after the second US invasion. Two years later, Zarqawi was killed in an airstrike. Abu Ayyub al-Masri took the reins, and was killed in 2010. Then Baghdadi took it over, reflagged the organization as ISIS, and took over a swath of the Middle East bigger than the state of Indiana. They recruited 40,000 fighters from over a hundred countries, and started making somewhere around a million dollars a day through the sale of black-market oil. After Delta killed Baghdadi, a new leader emerged and the organization restructured along the lines of Al Qaeda, which it came from in the first place."

"Exactly my point," Worthy said. "As long as there are disaffected and poverty-stricken populations ripe for extremist ideology, there's going to be an endless succession of terrorist groups. And as for our team? We're just one small cog in a very large machine that's got to keep running 24/7, 365, to keep these assholes from getting too powerful—or too effective."

I pointed out, "That doesn't mean we can't make a difference."

"No," Cancer agreed, "but it doesn't mean we get to pick and choose what we accomplish, either. Selecting the targets is up to them, but killing those targets is up to us. I gotta say, I won't be thrilled if Usman gets a free pass."

I considered my next contribution to this meandering disaster of a conversation. Ian's facts were correct, of course, and Worthy's sentiments not entirely unjustified—nor were Cancer's. But just because global terror was more cancer than pneumonia didn't mean that our involvement in the Agency's targeted killing program was without merit. After all, we existed to target the next generation of terrorist leadership before they became a bin Laden or Zarqawi or Baghdadi—and with every tier-one counterterror unit overtasked with more targets than time, I felt confident that my five-man team served a noble if humble purpose in the grand scheme of things.

At that moment, Tolu spoke up for the first time since we left Maiduguri.

"There is a difference," he said dryly, "between killing terrorist leaders and executing the ones they prey upon."

I spun my head to face him—Tolu was practically a different person after our raid against the ISWAP fighters. No more rap, no more casual Pidgin English phrases, and while his latest comment was in reference to the previous conversation, he may as well have been reading my mind.

But before I could voice a response to his sudden outburst, our van rounded a corner in the road and I was staring at a sight that was somehow equal parts peaceful and intimidating: the town of Gwoza.

"All right," I said, "town is coming up. Let's get into character."

I stripped off my tactical vest and passed it back to the cargo area along with my assault rifle. Worthy took them and stashed both along with the rest in the van's false bottom—no small task, given that much of the space was now taken up with the captured ISWAP weapons and disabled suicide vests. That left us attired in civilian clothes, just five gringos and a local driver. Everything we could use to defend ourselves was now concealed from all but the most dedicated search, and after three hours of travel under constant threat of a terrorist checkpoint, I now felt more vulnerable than I had at any point on the mission.

Gwoza was an uncanny sight—the loose sprawl of buildings nestled between forest and mountains had a population matching that of New Orleans, many of them outsiders who'd fled Boko Haram violence elsewhere in the region. Surrounded by danger on all sides, this relative outpost cast a shadow of having been the headquarters of a failed terrorist caliphate for seven long months before any response by the Nigerian military.

I could make them out on either side of the road ahead, armored personnel carriers clustered in a vehicle checkpoint with one blocking the road. Around the vehicles were fighting positions made of stacked sandbags and occupied by groups of soldiers. Pulling out my notepad, I briefly reviewed my notes for the verbal portion of this upcoming interaction and felt a bottomless uncertainty about how it would turn out. Duchess had done all she could to secure our safe passage into the town, but if any military leadership harbored connections with Boko Haram, we could easily be pulled out of the vehicle for detailed questioning or worse.

My eyes darted across the checkpoint as we approached, trying to gauge our odds. The Nigerian soldiers appeared well-organized, attired almost to a man in desert camouflage uniforms complete with flak vests and tan helmets. I told Tolu to go slow, watching for any order to stop and half-fearing they'd take us for suicide bombers despite the advance notice of our arrival.

Instead a great bear of a man strode to the front of the formation, pointing to a spot in the road with the authority of a laser-wielding state trooper pulling us over with a finger. He wore the same uniform as his comrades, though the lack of a flak jacket and helmet told me he was the man in charge. Whatever our fate in the coming proceedings, it would hinge on his decision.

Tolu slowed to a stop and I rolled down my window, casually draping an arm outside the van and waving a preliminary greeting. The enormous soldier approached my door, six-foot-five with a jagged scar running the length of his right cheek. He peered at me through dark sunglasses as I spoke.

"Good morning, sir. Tom Connelly, Garrett News."

He didn't respond immediately, instead continuing to stare at me, then at Tolu behind the wheel, then back at me.

Finally he replied in a deep, booming voice, his Nigerian accent so thick that I struggled to make out his words.

"Lieutenant Colonel Mamman of the Nigerian Army. I command the 192 Battalion, tasked with all defense of Gwoza."

"Pleasure to meet you," I said amicably, "and thank you for allowing us—"

He cut me off.

"I have allowed nothing. It was very dangerous for you to come here. Very unwise."

At that moment I would've almost felt more comfortable if he'd been an enemy fighter—at least then we would've been within our wheelhouse, not relying on my ability to play the part of a professional reporter.

There was a larger issue at hand as well. If Ian's suspicion of military complicity was even half-accurate, this man may very well be the same one who accepted payment to allow the three remaining hostages to enter

Gwoza. And while Duchess had hastily modified our existing cover to allow for access to the town, I couldn't rule out the possibility that anything I said now would be reported to Boko Haram in short order.

I explained, "We coordinated our travel through the embassy. They were supposed to notify you last week."

He shook his head gravely. "I was notified only an hour ago."

"I'm not sure who dropped the ball on that. But I can assure you—"

"Be quiet," he ordered, and through the windshield I could see the checkpoint soldiers shifting their positions, spreading out in a security posture around their commander and examining the exterior of our vehicle.

Then he said, "Why have you come here."

It wasn't a question, and I took from his tone that any answer I provided would be deemed unacceptable.

I replied, "We're doing a piece on the IDPs, the internally displaced persons. After area orientation for my men, we've got meetings at all three formal camps"—I consulted my notes—"Wukani, 20 Housing, and GSS, along with the informal camp, Dangote. Between UNICEF, the International Organization for Migration, and the camp residents, we plan on being here a few days at least. Maybe up to a week."

He frowned. "You will be here, Mr. Connelly, as long as I say so. No one is allowed to travel more than one kilometer from town without military or vigilante escort. That means you"— he jabbed a finger at my face—"will not depart Gwoza until I arrange a military escort to take you as far as Maiduguri. Is this clear?"

"Absolutely," I said with an easy smile, "and thank you for understanding."

"It is you who must understand. The road you just traveled is one of the most dangerous in Nigeria. Many bad things have happened to Americans recently. You would not wish to join them, would you?"

At this point I couldn't tell if the guy was in bed with Boko Haram or not —was he actually making a veiled reference to having us taken as hostages, or issuing an all-purpose warning? After all the crazy shit we'd seen thus far in Nigeria, neither would have surprised me.

I assumed a remorseful but uncompromising tone. "Of course not. We're happy to remain in Gwoza until an escort can be arranged."

"You have no say in the matter, Mr. Connelly, because every single one of my men know your vehicle description and have orders not to let you out until I approve." He unbuttoned a chest pocket and plucked out a business card, thrusting it at me with the admonition, "You will call me to request an escort. I will not hand Boko Haram any more prisoners."

Accepting the card, I said, "Thank you. I'll touch base in a few days."

But Lieutenant Colonel Mamman was already done with me, striding back to the checkpoint before I'd finished my last sentence.

Oh well, I thought, at least we hadn't been strip-searched and our media van ripped apart.

"What a dick," Reilly murmured from the back.

And with that, the armored personnel carrier blocking the road rumbled to one side as a soldier waved us between the sandbagged fighting positions.

Gently accelerating, Tolu maneuvered the van through the checkpoint and into Gwoza.

Reilly shifted to look through the van's windshield, taking in his first impressions of the town as Tolu steered them deeper into a population center that was, by all appearances, fairly banal.

He saw buildings that were both well-kept and dilapidated, men pushing carts, and women with their hair covered by colorful shawls. As with Lagos, car horns were a constant; but they covered ground quickly, easily maintaining cruising speed down the center of the road while flanked by bicyclists. Reilly examined one of the riders closely—a man in his twenties with bags of rice strapped three high on the back of his bike, pedaling as casually as if he were in a peaceful suburb.

He saw no sense of paralyzing fear among the citizens, and upon hearing music from a clearing ahead, he looked out to see two rows of dancers facing each other. Women in flowing black robes spun before a row of men in light blue uniforms with red skullcaps who responded with a series of synchronized foot movements, some West African form of square dancing unfolding before a crowd that clapped in rhythm with the squawking horns played by a nearby quartet.

He asked no one in particular, "This whole place seems a little too...I don't know, peaceful."

"Don't be fooled," Ian assured him, craning his neck to take in the view. "Not so long ago, Boko Haram turned this entire town into a slaughterhouse."

Before Reilly could reply, David issued his next command to Tolu as he angled a small video camera over the dash to analyze at a later time.

"Left turn in one block."

Reilly decided not to offer any more idle observations. Ian, Worthy, and Cancer were crowded around him, each man vying for a firsthand view through the windshield.

Dusty streets were lined with telephone poles and roadside shops with English signs, a detail that surprised Reilly. While English was Nigeria's official language, many of the rural areas relied on a combination of the hundreds of local dialects to communicate.

If Lagos was Times Square and Maiduguri was Compton, then Gwoza seemed something akin to Omaha, Nebraska—a nondescript, peaceful town that seemed like the last place on earth they'd find a bloodthirsty gang of terrorists holding American hostages at gunpoint.

Yet there was no mistaking the three grids that Ian had uncovered—if none of the other locations in that ledger had been elaborately coded, and the Agency confirmed they hadn't, then neither had these. At any rate, they'd find out soon enough. The team was rapidly approaching the first location, which overhead imagery indicated to be the northernmost of the trio, located just outside a marketplace at the base of the mountains.

Like the other two points, the grid was located in a small field at the eastern fringes of Gwoza. Not a building, but a clear patch of ground. That minor wrinkle didn't seem to unnerve anyone else on the team, and Reilly had dismissively listened to various explanations ranging from GPS margin of error, to possible buildings being erected since the satellite imagery was obtained, to Boko Haram hedging their bets in case they needed to quickly exfil the hostages east into the mountains.

To Reilly, however, the real answer was far simpler than that—he harbored a deep suspicion that his team was in the process of reconnoitering three dry holes.

This assumption was based, in large part, on Duchess's response to his team leader's request for approval in a reconnaissance effort. Her reply didn't take long, which couldn't possibly be a good thing. They were approved to move into Gwoza, but there were some steadfast rules that they couldn't waiver from in the least. Do not get close. Conduct a very loose reconnaissance while remaining in the flow of traffic. Do nothing that would spook the captors. And above all, do not get caught.

Part of Duchess's approval was that she wanted some further confirmation of enemy presence before focusing JSOC elements on the town. To Reilly, that wasn't a good sign—if the Agency was as confident in this new intel as Ian was, they wouldn't allow his team anywhere near those grids.

Instead, they'd send in the ISA guys, for whom things like locating hostages using the full gamut of intelligence measures was a bread-and-butter mission tasking.

David said, "Left turn up here—guys, we're coming up on the market. The grid will be less than a hundred meters off our right side. Thirty seconds out."

Once Tolu made the turn, Reilly saw that twenty of those thirty seconds would be redundant.

He could clearly see the area David had indicated, could easily orient himself based off of the overhead imagery. Beyond a cluster of small buildings at the southern edge of the clearing was a perfectly flat patch of dirt, barren of any life or buildings until a row of trees that preceded the rocky slope of the Mandara Mountains.

He heard Cancer mutter beside him, "There's no way. Nothing there, not even a spider hole."

David said nothing, continuing to film the scene as they passed. Reilly looked to the others for some reaction, but the only one to speak was Ian, sounding cautiously optimistic despite what should have been a devastating blow to his assessment of the hostages being here.

"Maybe the grids were just options, and all three Americans are being held at one of the others. Let's go to the palace."

Worthy felt his shoulders sag as they passed the market objective, which was about as promising as a chastity belt and twice as confusing.

But David reacted without loss of enthusiasm, instructing Tolu, "Left turn at the next intersection and get us back to the road at the center of town. I want to take it south and thread our way back in to minimize our exposure time by the objectives."

Worthy didn't know what to make of the fact that the first grid had been exactly as it appeared on the overhead imagery—namely, an open field—but he knew it couldn't possibly be good. Boko Haram had gone to great lengths to conceal those locations from being intercepted, going so far as to handwrite them in a secured facility for, presumably, later transmission over a series of burner phones if not an actual courier. So if the hostages weren't here in Gwoza, then where were they?

The next sight only deepened his sense of despair—a city of white tents erected inside a chain link fence, one of the camps for those displaced by terrorist violence in Nigeria.

Long rows of people were standing along the fence—hundreds of men, women, and children filing slowly forward, clutching plastic plates and bowls as they proceeded toward a daily ration of rice being scooped out of vats by aid workers. The children in particular stared at the van as it passed, their eyes not desperate and pleading but merely curious, no different than Worthy's own nieces and nephews back in the States.

David said, "That's the Wukani Camp on the right."

Worthy asked, "How many are there?"

"Four."

"Not camps," Worthy clarified. "I mean, how many internally displaced people here?"

Ian responded before David could. "Ten thousand in Gwoza. But if you're asking about Nigeria overall, it's three million."

"All from terrorism?" Worthy asked.

"Terrorism, warlords, tyrannical governments—the lines blur here as much as they do in the Middle East."

Worthy fell silent at that. Suddenly Project Longwing didn't seem like nearly enough—more evil was perpetuated by madmen and lunatics than the sum total of civilized militaries could stop, too many tyrants to kill. And rather than growing more troubled by that realization, Worthy instead felt a redoubling of his determination to see Usman dead before his team left Nigeria.

David announced, "Emir's Palace is up ahead. Tolu, take a left at the T-intersection and then the next right. Two minutes out from the objective."

Worthy looked at the compound to the left, a two-story building with arched doorways and a long balcony beneath minarets. Compared to everything else they'd seen in Gwoza, it was a pinnacle of luxury.

Reilly said, "Pretty nice digs. All you have to do is become the emir?"

"Yeah," Ian answered, "that's a dicey career choice, though. Boko Haram assassinated the last one shortly before they invaded. And the current emir can't set foot outside Gwoza without a target on his back."

A series of turns took them through a residential area and a patchwork of storage units before the road emerged onto a sandy patch of ground, flat as a pool table for five hundred meters before reaching the base of the mountain.

The road ran abreast of the clearing, leading southeast along the periphery of town. As the team scanned the area, Cancer asked, "So where the fuck is it?"

David hesitated before replying, "Two hundred, 250 meters to our ten o'clock."

"Strike two." Worthy shook his head. "Not only are the hostages not there, but there's no place for Boko Haram to put them even if they wanted to."

Ian's confidence sounded dashed as he muttered, "There's still one more grid to go."

Ian fell into his seat in the back of the van, mind swirling as David gave Tolu his next instructions: back into town, south along the main road, and then thread a course east to the third and final objective.

Retrieving his Android phone, Ian hastily scanned the screen. The grids near the market and palace had been exactly as they appeared on the satellite imagery, and he examined the final one in the hopes of finding some new detail. After all, his theory that the grids represented hostage locations was only as good as the existence of a place to keep them. While Gwoza was certainly an ingenious and unlikely location to relocate captured Americans, if the final grid yielded nothing more than the first two, then he had no alternate explanation, no secondary theory that would give his team any hope of effecting a rescue.

The third location was the southernmost of the trio, this one in a clearing a few hundred meters south of a secondary school. He struggled to make any sense out of this—he'd been expecting to note some suspicious structure in the grid vicinities, if not one that had eluded their outdated satellite imagery altogether.

He considered the possibility of a coded offset—some uniform metric such as 300 meters due west of the provided grids, a master key that only a few in Boko Haram's leadership would know. But he sensed in his heart that wasn't the case; he'd held the Maiduguri ledger in his hands, photographed every page. It was debatably the most compartmentalized record that Boko Haram possessed, tucked away in the confines of a secure shell company. If the answer was anywhere, it was within those pages. Yet Ian had analyzed every scrap of intel on the drive to Gwoza, and he knew that Duchess's staff of analysts was doing the same back at the Agency. If they hadn't found anything that would help his team by now, it was unlikely they would.

Besides, he thought, there was an elegant uniformity to the pattern: each location was on the east side of town, in a field at the base of the Mandara Mountains. Not only could that not be accidental, it indicated a level of premeditation whose purpose Ian simply couldn't decipher at present.

But until they got eyes on the final location, all hope wasn't lost.

Keeping his phone in hand, Ian rose from his seat and resumed his position beside Cancer, Worthy, and Reilly. The view had shifted dramatically in the past few minutes; instead of a bustling population center packed with civilians carrying out their normal pattern of life in the only military-controlled bastion of safety within a hundred miles in any direction, the van now traveled down an empty street. The area appeared abandoned not only by the town's many residents but by any form of life whatsoever.

A row of buildings extended to their left, the doorways empty, rooflines scorched with black soot—evidence of the devastation that Boko Haram had inflicted when they controlled the town. Piles of sheet metal were scattered in the street, and Tolu steered around a long line of burned-out vehicle carcasses: cars, vans, and commuter buses, all set aflame long ago in what would become their final resting place. The largest building on the street was reduced to rubble, its roof caved in atop the few remaining support beams. On the walls around them were uncountable bullet holes.

David asked, "What the hell happened here?"

Checking his phone imagery, Ian confirmed their location and then said, "This is ground zero of the Boko Haram invasion. They came disguised as soldiers, marshalled the villagers here, and then massacred three hundred. The ones who fled the village ran into an outer cordon where they were gunned down, and whoever survived was subjugated to systematic rape and executions until the army finally got here."

Reilly asked, "Seven months later?"

"Yeah." Ian nodded. "More or less."

The occupants of the van remained silent after that, save David giving Tolu periodic directions on where to turn as they threaded their way toward the secondary school. Ian saw the Mandara Mountains looming over the rooftops ahead, an ominous reminder of where Boko Haram had fled to and from where they would return.

He felt an odd, simmering suspicion at the thought, some detail that remained beyond his grasp. Whether it was part of his omnipresent second-guessing of the tactical situation or some clue that he should be picking up on, he couldn't tell—but the sensation was quickly swept aside as they approached their third and final grid.

David said, "Government Day Secondary School is coming up on our left. The grid is two hundred meters south of the campus."

Ian held his breath as they passed the low green roofs of the classroom buildings, then caught his first glance of the field beyond.

Like the first two, it was barren and flat, the only distinguishing features being a few patches of grass before the field ended at a parallel road. Past that was the mountain vegetation, trees and brush filling the view and sloping sharply upward. No building had been erected since their overhead imagery was constructed, no low-visibility entrance to an underground lair and, therefore, absolutely no way the hostages could be there.

At that moment Ian realized he'd committed the cardinal sin of his profession—he'd fallen in love with his intel, warping the clues around his hopes to locate the hostages. In the never-ending battle between solid facts and informed assessments, he'd seen what he wanted to from the three grids pulled from an office in Maiduguri, and now that his hopes were dashed, he was left bearing the full responsibility of having subjected his team to immeasurable risk in traveling to Gwoza.

But he spoke none of this aloud, and when David posed his next question in the form of four exasperated words—"Ian, what the fuck?"—the intelligence operative struggled to formulate his reply.

"I don't know, guys," he said with a rueful shake of his head. "I just don't get it."

39

Duchess rubbed her eyes wearily, unable to suppress the urge to yawn.

The OPCEN was at half-capacity, with each staff section rotating their members out on rest cycle. One of the many problems inherent in supporting a ground team on the far side of the world was the time difference; while David and his men were completing their sunrise examination of the Gwoza sites, Duchess and her staff were staring down the barrel of a graveyard shift.

She flicked her eyes to the digital wall clock display with a variety of time zones from East Africa to Greenwich Mean Time, finally settling on Eastern Standard to see that it was quarter after three in the morning.

Closing her eyes, she rolled her head in a full circle clockwise, then counterclockwise, to stretch her neck before blinking and reaching for the mug of lukewarm tea. She'd been on a steady drip of caffeine and sugar for longer than she cared to calculate, while most of the OPCEN staff had consumed enough coffee in the past few days to keep a small Starbucks operating profitably.

Not that it mattered, she thought as she took a sip and replaced her mug on the desk. It wasn't like the ground team was getting much rest, either. Those five men and their indigenous driver had been on the move almost nonstop since arriving in Nigeria, and Duchess considered that the results of all that near-constant activity were both heartening and dismaying.

On one hand, they'd been in the right place at the right time to serve as the lynchpin for a rescue of seven hostages. And after that, they'd managed to secure a windfall of intelligence, enough to keep her J2 section in a continual cycle of analyzing the content and farming out documents to various regional specialists within the Directorate of Analysis. The combined effort was required to translate the snapshots of drugs, shipment numbers, and destination information spanning multiple continents into a solidified intelligence assessment. Just as that herculean exertion gained traction, David's team had obtained photographs of the Maiduguri ledger, which was, in terms of intel, if the initial read on its contents proved remotely accurate, something akin to winning the lottery twice in two days.

And now, Duchess waited to see if the team could strike gold a third time.

Her chance to find out came in the form of a burst of static from the speaker box on her desk, followed by David's voice. "*Raptor Nine One, Suicide Actual.*"

She lifted her hand mic and keyed it. "This is Raptor Nine One, go ahead."

"*Be advised, we have completed initial reconnaissance of all three locations.*"

"And?"

A pause. "*There's nothing there. Not at any of them. All are open clearings, exactly as they appear on the satellite imagery—no visual evidence of spider-hole entrances or the like, although we'd have to go boots-on-the-ground to confirm or deny for sure. We're still uploading the video footage to transmit, but it looks like we've hit a brick wall on those hostages.*"

Duchess felt disappointment, but not exactly surprise. Granted, it wasn't inconceivable that military complicity had allowed the hostages to be relocated inside their security bubble of Gwoza. After all, corruption in Nigeria was practically a competitive sport: the politicians alone drained millions from the national bank every year, and their salaries were substantially better than those of the military leadership.

That raised the question of whether Boko Haram would risk such a partnership with the Nigerian Army. Again, the answer was very conceivably a yes. Doing so would protect the hostages from all but the most comprehensive rescue effort, one that would take a hell of a lot longer to plan than the comparatively simple raid against a single camp in the Sambisa Forest. And the amount of effort such a rescue would take to plan, let alone execute, not only bought Boko Haram substantial time to communicate their terms, but exponentially increased US willingness to negotiate a release, albeit through Nigerian government proxies.

All that notwithstanding, the real reason Duchess expected this outcome wasn't a matter of facts or logic, but instinct. Upon hearing the outcome of the Maiduguri raid and its intelligence yield, she knew in her gut the hostages weren't at those grids. But she'd approved the team's relocation to Gwoza all the same because she didn't know what the grids *did* represent, and in lieu of any meaningful purpose for her ground team in the interim, a comparatively low-risk reconnaissance in a protected town was the best means of keeping them in play as the situation continued to develop. After all, they couldn't exactly hang out around Maiduguri after raiding the Okafor International compound.

Keying her mic, she transmitted, "Copy all. Don't beat yourselves up too bad—the intel you've gathered so far is going to have a significant impact, just not to the hostages. For now I want you to lie low in Gwoza and await further guidance, is that clear?"

"*Crystal,*" David replied. "*Sorry we don't have better news for you. Suicide Actual, out.*"

"Raptor Nine One, out." She set her mic on the desk, then looked up to see her J2 rise from his desk.

She watched Lucios closely as the intelligence officer moved to the laser printer beside his workstation, then collected a sheaf of documents that he slid into a manila folder before approaching her.

Duchess made eye contact and hooked a thumb toward the empty seat beside her. Jo Ann was on rest cycle, and Lucios reluctantly lowered himself into her chair before speaking.

"Ma'am," he began, "forensic accounting has returned some preliminary results on the analysis of that politician, Malu."

"The oil guy?" she asked.

"His official title is Permanent Secretary for Nigeria's Federal Ministry of Petroleum—"

"Duly noted. What have they found?"

Lucios laid a sheet of paper on the desk before her, yanking a mechanical pencil from his breast pocket to use as a pointer.

"First off, he's been receiving a lot more from Gradsek than we initially suspected—it just took them some time to run down the accounts he maintains under separate names." He slid the tip of his pencil to indicate a block of numbers. "These are his total deposits from Gradsek for the last six months, spread over seven accounts. As you'll see, they range between 2.6 to 3.7 million, depending on the month."

"Beyond bribery," she noted.

Lucios nodded. "Most likely, ma'am. I believe these figures represent a fixed percentage of the income from Gradsek's oil and cocaine import business, paid to Malu in exchange for continued political top cover, as well as protection from the pirate and vigilante groups. The disparity is that Malu only accumulates a small percentage of it, roughly ten percent, and an additional fifteen percent gets distributed to outside accounts, which I presume route to terrorist and militant groups."

She twirled an index finger to indicate that he should get on with it and asked, "And the other 75 percent?"

Lucios didn't answer, instead shifting his pencil lower on the page and continuing, "Here, you'll see his illicit withdrawals from the national bank. These range from 4.2 to 5.6 million each month. Again, not unusual for Nigerian politicians. What *is* unusual is that these withdrawals follow the same pattern. He keeps 25 percent, and transfers the remaining 75."

"So three-quarters of his income from Gradsek and the national bank gets sent to...where, exactly?"

"A single recipient, ma'am. It's an account in Mozambique, but the forensic accountants are still trying to penetrate their cybersecurity to see where the money goes from there."

She frowned.

"Mozambique...why?"

"Roughly two trillion dollars are laundered globally each year, and

Mozambique is number one on the list of major money laundering countries."

Duchess felt a tic in her left eye as she processed the information, focusing on the one logical conclusion that emerged from her spinning thoughts. "So we're talking what, six to nine million each month of income?"

"Yes, ma'am."

"Seventy-two to over 100 million annually, of which 75 percent goes to Mozambique..."

"Correct."

She looked at him blankly. "This seems indicative of a payout to someone who connected the pieces between Venezuela and Gradsek, who brokered and orchestrated the entire arrangement so he could profit..."

"I agree, ma'am."

"So this means that Mozambique is—"

"Erik Weisz," he finished for her. "Or at least, one of his bank accounts."

Duchess went silent, pausing to draw a long breath before she said, "You're sure about this?"

"It fits all the criteria. Based on the connections between the Uyghur resistance and ISIS in Syria, we've been looking for someone, or more likely a network, that's bridging international connections on a scale we've never before seen. The organizations are all over, of course, but no one has ever pieced them together in such a manner to achieve global effects. I believe Erik Weisz used Malu as the touchpoint to link Gradsek, and thereby Russia, to an unknown contact in Venezuela. Weisz put this together, and now he's reaping the lion's share of the profit."

She nodded. "Which is indicative of not only international reach, but the muscle to enforce the arrangement if necessary."

"Which is in turn indicative of significant manpower, or at least influence over local groups capable of armed response. Extrapolate that to multiple countries, and I think—I assess—this could be bigger than we thought."

Duchess wasn't tired anymore, her pulse soaring with the news and, more importantly, her gut feeling that it was accurate. She wanted to order a full-court press into this issue, to begin personally typing a formal report of these conclusions. The sheer volume of payments made it inconceivable that she and Lucios were wrong on this, and she sure as hell wanted the intelligence community to be aware of the threat.

But she forced herself to take three steady breaths, tempering her initial response to the necessities of the present moment. She still had to disseminate the full reports from both Lagos and Maiduguri, to say nothing of supporting a ground team currently staged in Gwoza.

She spoke in a level tone. "I want all further information conveyed to me as you receive it. What else do you have?"

"Just one more thing, ma'am... the draft of Lagos intel dissemination ready for your review."

"Is it comprehensive?"

He nodded quickly. "Venezuela, oil, cocaine, heroin, Gradsek and the Russian connection—it's everything."

"You ensured the source of the intelligence was safeguarded in every possible manner?"

"Yes, ma'am."

"Recommended a random customs inspection on a key shipment to expose collusion between Russia assisting Venezuela in bypassing international oil sanctions?"

Lucios blinked. "Of course."

"And did you," she continued in a low tone, "emphasize in no uncertain terms that this report remains close-hold until Project Longwing's involvement in Nigeria has come to a close, so as not to risk spooking the players and compromising our ability to action any late-breaking intelligence?"

"Absolutely, ma'am." He procured a stapled packet from his folder and extended it to her. "It's all right here."

She snatched the packet from him, scanning the first page before flipping to a second, then the third.

Handing it back to him, she said, "Cleared for release to the seventh floor. How do we stand on the Maiduguri report?"

Before he could respond, the phone on her desk rang. She held up a finger to silence Lucios and brought the receiver to her ear.

A switchboard operator said, "ISA rep in Abuja."

"Wait one," Duchess replied, putting the call on hold and returning the phone to its cradle. Then she cut her eyes to Lucios. "The Maiduguri report?"

"The ledger photographs are on round three of translation. Once that's complete, I'll have the full assessment turned within two hours."

"Then get back to work. Away with you, Lucios, and nice job."

He pushed back his chair and rose, reaching for Malu's financial assessment until Duchess slapped a hand atop the page and said, "Can I hang onto this copy?"

"Of course, ma'am."

Then Lucios was gone, strolling back to his workstation as Duchess lifted the phone and pressed a button on the console.

"Patch him through," she said.

There was a click on the line and she said, "Duchess here."

A familiar voice spoke with a New York accent. "Duchess, it's Ben Bailey. Is Jo Ann on the line?"

"She's on rest cycle. Any luck with monitoring Malu's communications?"

He gave an audible sigh. "Not much. Most of his calls have been cleared as routine so far."

"You think he's using burner phones for the rest?"

"I *know* he is," Bailey responded with exasperation. "The problem is, we haven't been able to identify them remotely. So short of a physical penetration, which I don't have the personnel or approvals for, I'm not sure what else will turn up. We'll continue to monitor, but I'm not optimistic."

Duchess looked at the ceiling. "Well, we're not doing much better over here—the three grids in Gwoza have been reconnoitered by our ground team, and they're open fields. Nothing more."

Lowering her gaze, she continued, "Forensic accounting of Malu's financial activity has been interesting, however." Duchess lifted Malu's financial assessment from the desk, scanning the rows of numbers. "This stays between us for now, but there are major muscle movements of cash changing hands with the vast majority disappearing to a bank in Mozambique."

"Number one in international money laundering," Bailey said knowingly. "No surprise there. You have any idea who's on the receiving end?"

"More like a working theory."

She said nothing after that, prompting Bailey to ask, "Care to elaborate?"

Duchess frowned. Reluctantly, she set the paper down and replied, "We've seen some indicators of a new element that brokers deals between various bad actors around the world. Could be big, if we're right, so please spare us no details on anything you find."

She felt eyes upon her and scanned the OPCEN to see Gregory Pharr watching her from his seat, apparently waiting for her call to end. She waved him over impatiently—when her assigned Agency lawyer gave any indication that he needed to speak, however subtle, Duchess found herself unable to focus on anything else. Covert operations were subject to so many political guidelines that even a slight misstep could end Project Long-wing altogether, to say nothing of tanking her career.

Pharr collected a tablet from his desk and rose as Bailey replied, "We'll keep you in the loop on whatever we find, and please let me know if there's anything else I can provide your people with from here. I appreciate all the transparency so far, I really do."

"You gave us the facility in Lagos. It's the least we can do."

"Yeah, well, in my experience with the Agency, the least you can do usually amounts to a lot less. No offense."

Duchess gave a half-smile at that not-inaccurate remark. "None taken. Stay in touch."

Bailey clicked off and she hung up the phone, looking over to see Pharr standing a few steps away.

He clutched a tablet in one hand, holding the other aloft in feigned surrender as he said, "I'm low priority, ma'am. If you have any other business to—"

"When a legal representative says 'low priority,'" she interrupted, gesturing to Jo Ann's empty chair, "I take it to mean that we're getting shut down in a week instead of today."

He smiled, taking a seat as he assured her, "Just some atmospherics, ma'am. May be pertinent, may not."

"Let's have it."

Setting his tablet on Jo Ann's desk, he referenced it and said, "Leak from an unnamed Pentagon official. Media is tracking that the administration has blessed a hostage exchange through Nigerian proxies. The press has already latched onto this as proof of the president's willingness to negotiate with terrorists, and it's hitting multiple news networks as we speak."

"Are you telling me we're sitting in an operations center for a targeted killing program established under executive authority, less than four days removed from a flawless hostage rescue executed with practically zero notice, and the president is being accused of being lax on terrorism?"

Pharr chuckled in agreement. "Right now it's just initial reports, but I'd say we're a day out from a major smear piece hitting *The New York Times* or *Washington Post*. All of it will be fodder for the next election."

Duchess lifted a pen from her desk and began tapping it against the side of her neck as she thought.

Then she said, "This is good for us. It'll make the administration more likely to authorize further covert action as it pertains to the situation in Nigeria, wouldn't you say?"

"I'd say that's an understatement. More like it will put them on a hair trigger as far as our approvals go. The question is—"

"What can we request approval for?"

Pharr nodded politely. Duchess tossed her pen on the desk, effecting her best *your guess is as good as mine* expression with eyebrows raised, before Lucios shouted, "Quiet in the OPCEN!"

Every conversation in the room halted mid-sentence as all eyes swung to Lucios.

"Boko Haram has just released a statement to the Nigerian government. They want to exchange the three remaining hostages for three members of their detained leadership, Usman included. They state this is a take-it-or-leave-it offer, with no recourse for alternate negotiations. Any complications will result in the execution of all hostages."

Duchess gave him a curt nod of understanding. "Where and when for the exchange?"

Lucios turned back to his screen, watching it as he called a response over his shoulder.

"It's not one exchange, it's three. All to occur simultaneously in 24 hours' time, each at a separate location. They've stated that exact exchange points will be provided thirty minutes prior—right now all they've given us is the town."

Duchess felt a languid smile playing at her lips, the explanation for every conundrum over the past few hours unraveling in one fell swoop.

"And let me take a wild guess," she said, "as to which town they specified."

40

I walked deeper through the wreckage of the building, whose roof had long ago been transformed into the rubble under my boots, leaving a clear blue sky visible overhead.

The walls were scorched with greasy black smears, and the sections of brick that remained had been covered in a patchwork of graffiti—crude charcoal drawings of AK-47s, RPGs, the occasional tank—all interspersed with Arabic script spelling *Allah,* or *Allahu Akbar*—God is greater. Along with the structural damage to the area around us, these markings were the everlasting reminder of Boko Haram's occupation of Gwoza.

Cancer followed behind me, attired as I was in civilian clothes with a concealed pistol, our radios in a cargo pocket connected to our earpieces. The rest of the team remained with the van, backed into an alley outside. We'd get hotel rooms later in the day; for now, however, I needed some time to stop and think, to remain stationary for more than five minutes and consolidate my thoughts.

And most importantly, I needed to confer with Cancer.

We hadn't gone far, stopping just two rooms deep in the eviscerated building before I turned to lean against the wall. Cancer followed suit beside me, saying nothing as he found his pack of smokes and lit a cigarette.

I asked, "Can I get one of those off you?"

He offered me the one he just lit, then sparked a new one for himself. I took a pull off the cigarette, then exhaled with an appreciative nod.

After a beat of silence between us, he asked, "Laila know you're smoking?"

"You tell Laila and I'll fucking kill you." He shot me a skeptical glance, and I nodded in affirmation. "Try me and see."

"Now you're talking crazy. Remember: 'Beware of an old man in a profession where men usually die young.'"

"I'll second that," I said.

We took a drag off our cigarettes in unison, then blew our smoke upward at the brightening sky. Today was going to be a hot one, I thought. In Nigeria, they all were.

"So what do you think?" I asked.

"About what?"

"Any of it."

He drew another lungful of smoke and said, "We've had a good run this trip. Everyone's performed, and for a team that's not designed to collect intel, we've uncovered one hell of a lot of it."

"Three hostages are still out there."

"And seven are back with their families," he pointed out. "You gotta take the good with the bad, boss. We can only do so much. Those grids were the best shot we had, but nothing's guaranteed in this business. You of all people understand that."

Shaking my head absently, I said, "It's just that—I mean, after China, I thought we were on the brink of something big. Erik Weisz and all that. Everything we've found in Nigeria is well and good for stopping an economic conspiracy, but it's not exactly counterterrorism."

"All we can do is feed the beast. Who knows what the Agency is working on as a result? Remember, they gotta earn their pay too."

My earpiece crackled to life at the end of his sentence.

"Suicide Actual, this is Raptor Nine One."

Keying my mic to respond, I transmitted, "Suicide Actual, what have you got?"

Duchess sounded like she was smiling. "The answer to all your questions."

"Wait one," I replied, pointing a hand toward the doorway and telling Cancer, "Get the guys."

He was off in a flash, leaving me to pinch my cigarette filter between my lips as I knelt, pulling the radio from my pocket and using both thumbs to program it in speaker output mode. Whatever Duchess was about to say, I wanted us all to hear it together.

Cancer appeared with Reilly, Worthy, and Ian in tow, and they formed a tight circle around me as I laid my radio on the ground between us and transmitted, "Raptor Nine One, go ahead."

Duchess's words were tinny but discernible over the radio speaker, and I fiddled with the volume as she spoke.

"*You can stop beating yourselves up now. You didn't find anything at those grids because there was nothing to find.*"

"Meaning?" I asked.

"*Meaning they weren't hostage locations at all,*" she said, "*they were helicopter landing zones. Three simultaneous hostage exchanges, one for each of the Boko Haram leaders to be released.*"

I tossed my cigarette to the side and yanked the phone from my pocket to pan across the imagery of Gwoza, locating the three marked grid locations before zooming in on each one.

Duchess continued, "*The exchange will occur in 23 hours and 46 minutes, at 0800 West Africa Time tomorrow. Thus far Boko Haram has only confirmed the exchanges will be in Gwoza. They'll provide the exact grids thirty minutes prior to the exchange time, but everyone here agrees that this explains the open clearings you reconnoitered earlier today.*"

It seemed so obvious now that we had the answer. Three clearings, all on the east side of Gwoza... and, shifting the image right to see why they'd chosen that cardinal direction, I found my answer in what lay beyond.

The Mandara Mountains began as a wrinkled mass of foothills on my screen, rising toward a seemingly impassable ramble of trees, rocks, and slopes, with only narrow trails penetrating all the way to town.

My mind flashed back to Tolu's assurance to me as we approached the vigilante checkpoint: *Boko Haram uses motorcycles, and that is why the govern-ment has banned them in the northeast.*

"Of course," I transmitted back, "they're going to come out of the moun-tains on motorcycles. Provided the exchange goes off without a hitch, Boko Haram is safe as soon as they hit the high ground—with all the caves and caverns in the Mandara Mountains, they'll be able to hide from airstrikes. And given the number of people they'll be bringing to cover the exchange, the Nigerian military isn't going to risk pursuing them."

"I'd say that's more or less the size of it, yes."

"So what's our play?"

"That's the Catch-22. There have been some leaks that the US will play ball to exchange the hostages, and the administration isn't happy with that kind of press. But the safe return of those hostages outweighs the PR risk, and with them likely being held at three unknown locations in the mountains, there's no way for us to find and rescue them in time to stop the exchange. The prisoner swap is being greenlighted as we speak, and I'll have to pull you out of Nigeria immediately afterward—there's no more political appetite for bad news. I regret to say there's nothing we can do to stop it now nor, I would think, anything we should do."

I keyed my mic. "So Usman goes free, along with two other key leaders."

"What can I say?" she answered unapologetically. *"That kidnapping changed everything. At this point, getting the hostages back safely is the lesser of two evils."*

"Tell that to the Nigerians who will suffer as a result. And once he's out, Usman won't return to his previous camp—he knew someone had a bead on him the second we had our close call with him on the highway. He's going to disappear; they all will."

"But the hostages will be safe, and your team will live to fight another day. In the scheme of things, this is a win."

I didn't know how to respond, instead turning my attention to my teammates.

Ian looked like he'd had an ice cream cone smacked out of his hand, his expression a mixture of shock and anguish that he hadn't surmised the true significance of those three grids before Duchess told us. Cancer's jaw was set—anger, as per usual with him. Reilly was placid, seeming resigned to this turn of events.

Only Worthy's reaction stood out among the rest.

He leaned forward, flashing a wolfish smile as he nodded slowly and fixed me with a predatory gaze.

"What?" I asked.

"We can do it," he replied. "We can still take Usman."

For once, it wasn't me trying to pitch a suicidally ludicrous plan. But Worthy was nothing if not a tactician, and a pragmatic one at that. I thought he'd redact his statement after a moment of consideration, and when he didn't, I pointed out, "Boko Haram is going to bring an army of terrorists out of those hills. We're five guys with peashooters by comparison, and I'm not going to risk—"

"Not peashooters," he cut me off.

"Compared to what they'll bring to support the exchange, yes, Worthy. Fucking peashooters."

His smile didn't fade in the least. "ISWAP, man. Don't forget what we took from ISWAP."

I felt a flush of heat as realization dawned on me, then I looked at the other team members to see them nodding as they reached the same conclusion—first Cancer, then Reilly, and finally, even Ian.

Keying my mic, I said, "Duchess, I think we've got a plan."

41

The next morning, Reilly heard the Boko Haram element before he saw them: over the whisper of wind through the tree-covered foothills around him came a low, grumbling snarl that could only be motorcycle engines.

"I've got audible," he whispered.

To Reilly's left, Ian shifted in his prone position, perching on his elbows to raise binoculars as he replied, "I hear it too. Should have visual any second now."

The medic did the same, aligning his binoculars as he awaited his first sight of the Boko Haram fighters.

His magnified view was blurred at the edges, the effect of wrapping burlap over the lenses to eliminate the morning sun's reflection and, consequently, compromising their position. Each strip of burlap had a slit cut in it to allow a reduced field of view, which now spanned a 250-meter path due north.

Reilly tilted his binoculars low, seeing the sharp drop of the ravine to his front before following the view up the opposite side, from landmark to landmark, just as he'd done dozens of times since morning nautical twilight had begun three hours earlier.

First he found the jagged, moss-covered boulder at the base of the ravine. Then he worked his line of sight upward and slightly left until he located the gnarled trunk of a small tree growing from the side of the rock wall, followed by a dark crevice etched in a near-vertical streak near the high ground on the opposite side.

Then his view settled on a narrow wisp of dirt trail emerging from the forest, carving a twisted path before flattening out in a ten-meter stretch as straight as any mountain path could be. The straightaway was almost perfectly aligned with Reilly's body, both oriented north in a position that he had worked hard to attain. For Boko Haram, it was little more than a flat stretch of trail on their way to the hostage exchange.

But for Reilly and Ian, it was a nearly ideal kill zone.

He held his binoculars steady, listening to the snarl of motorcycle engines grow louder as they approached his field of view.

While the three grids Ian had recovered in Maiduguri gave the team a head start in planning this little excursion, the real key was *why* those grids had been chosen by Boko Haram in the first place.

And the answer to that, as a cursory examination of satellite imagery revealed, had little to do with the clearings themselves. After all, there were numerous other spots along the eastern edge of Gwoza where helicopters could land just as easily.

But the three grids shared one thing in common: trail access from the mountains.

While an endless spiderweb labyrinth of such trails crisscrossed the cave networks of the Mandara range, they congealed into a very limited number of pathways leading down the final foothills and into Gwoza itself. So while Boko Haram could come from virtually anywhere on the high ground, they would undoubtedly divide along the three single trail stretches leading to the exchange points—and that vital assumption had allowed Reilly's team to orchestrate a three-way split to cover each in the interests of slaying Usman minutes after the Nigerians freed him.

The first Boko Haram fighter came into view then, a lone rider atop a dusty black dirt bike with his face covered by a balaclava. A slung rifle rested across his torso, and Reilly had no sooner identified it as an AK-47 than the second bike appeared, followed by a third as he began his mental count.

The drivers had rifles slung across their front, angled barrel-down across their chests; several, however, had passengers who kept their weapons pointed upward with one hand, balancing the buttstocks on their hips as the row of motorcycles threaded across the narrow trail. Reilly caught sight of one RPG, then another, and one driver with not one but two rifles slung across his chest.

His passenger, however, had no weapon at all.

Reilly felt his breath hitch as he took in her features—she was blindfolded, her head wrapped in a shawl with traces of straw-colored hair falling out in tangled disarray. Both her upright head and the tight grip of her arms around the driver's waist indicated she was alive, though as her dirt bike turned north and headed away from Reilly, he could see bloody streaks across the back of her beige shirt. She'd been beaten or whipped or both, and Reilly's instinct to administer medical treatment was relegated to a dull background noise against the burning desire to annihilate her captors upon their return trip.

As a final dirt bike blocked her from view, Reilly considered that the task of ambushing these men would be as easy as it was gratifying. They'd just ridden past with no thought to tactical spacing—their motorcycles were clustered almost end-to-end as they negotiated the path, a tight formation ripe for the picking.

Except, he thought as they passed out of sight around the next turn, there might be no chance to ambush them at all.

After a pause, Reilly asked, "Was that Hostage Two or Three?"

Ian whispered back, "Hostage Three, and I counted seven men, five bikes. Want me to send it?"

"No," Reilly said. "I got it."

Then, keying his radio, he transmitted, "Enemy just passed through Objective North en route to the market. We have PID on Hostage Three, I say again Hostage Three, along with five motorcycles and seven enemy."

David replied over his earpiece, *"Copy all, will relay to Duchess. Be advised, the birds are approximately one minute out."*

It was frustrating not to have eyes-on the landing zones, instead relying on Duchess's updates for a modicum of information. But they didn't have the manpower to confirm which trail Usman would be taking back into the mountains, and couldn't even use Tolu for that vital purpose—in the interests of surviving this thing, they needed the driver staged with the vehicle, ready for a pickup effort that, even if everything went according to plan, would have to occur with every possible urgency.

Reilly could make out the sound of distant rotor blades to his left, the three Nigerian Air Force helicopters ferrying Boko Haram leaders now on final approach to their landing sites in Gwoza. He'd barely detected the noise when Cancer transmitted over the team frequency.

"*Exchange element just passed Objective South, they're continuing toward the secondary school. Eight men, six motorcycles along with Hostage One, I say again, Hostage One.*"

That particular designation belonged to the last remaining ExxonMobil oil executive, and Reilly considered that left only a single remaining female at large.

David replied a moment later, "*Copy Hostage One—I can hear motorcycles approaching Objective Central, stand by.*"

His next transmission came within thirty seconds, and Reilly felt his heart thudding dully as he awaited word on the fate of the final American captive. If she was alive, this exchange might actually play out more or less as they anticipated, but if not, the Nigerian Army forces tasked with securing Gwoza could just as easily end up in a shootout with the arriving Boko Haram teams.

David said, "*Objective Central is in business, seven fighters and six motorcycles headed for the Emir's Palace exchange point along with Hostage Two. The Nigerian birds are wheels-down at this time. Will transmit updates from Duchess as I receive them, we are weapons hold until I get confirmation that all hostages are safely aboard the helicopters and en route to Abuja.*"

Reilly keyed his mic and replied, "Objective North copies, weapons hold."

A moment later Cancer responded, "*Objective South, weapons hold—but we better not be for long.*"

The team leader answered with a single admonition.

"*Patience, boys. This one is all about patience.*"

Sure, Reilly thought, unless they all died of heatstroke before the enemy made their return trip through the hills.

For the second time in Nigeria, the team was making good use of their ghillie suits, and while Reilly was grateful for the concealment they afforded at this range from the target area, the effect on comfort in this near-equatorial heat was devastating.

It didn't help that they'd been in position since roughly midnight, and were going on eight consecutive hours of lying in wait. Nor was killing Usman as simple as a unified team ambush—because Boko Haram hadn't transmitted the final exchange grids until the three helicopters transporting their soon-to-be-freed leaders were in flight toward Gwoza, there was no way of knowing which helicopter would land where. That meant Usman could be arriving at any of the exchange points, forcing the team to divide into three elements in an attempt to kill him shortly after his release.

That much would have been nigh impossible to consider, save for their captured ISWAP hardware. As it turned out, David's decision to confiscate the most casualty-producing weapons opened up a broad range of possibilities for ingenious ambushes, and the team would be making full use of them.

The background noise of idling helicopters at the base of the mountains rose in volume, and Reilly could hear the throttle increasing as the sound shifted upward: they were taking off now, though David had yet to relay any insight on the proceedings from Duchess, who was in turn monitoring the Nigerian air frequencies.

But the team leader came over the net then, speaking quickly.

"All hostages have been exchanged, the birds are now wheels-up and headed home. Do not engage targets unless you have positive identification of Usman at your objective—he's worse than both of the other leaders combined. If either of the other primaries passes through your kill zone, let them go unless you've heard one of the other split teams clack off their ambush. That audible will serve as the all-clear for everyone to engage as able. Until then, straight from Duchess: we are cleared hot, I say again, cleared hot."

With a thin smile forming at his lips, Reilly reached down to pull aside the sheet of burlap before him. Beneath it was the long steel PK machinegun.

Reilly had disassembled the weapon and inspected each component alongside Worthy, Cancer, and David. All had deemed them free of defects, and after thoroughly cleaning and reassembling the machinegun, it had passed a full functions check with flying colors.

That much was no surprise—these Soviet bloc weapons were designed to perform in the worst possible conditions with minimal maintenance, and while precision machinery it was not, the machinegun had probably been rolling around Africa inflicting terror for the past 20 years, and would have been for another 20 years if the team hadn't interdicted it.

They'd ended up spending almost as much time cleaning the ammunition belts as the weapon itself, using toothbrushes and gun oil to scrub the links and remove every trace of rust. A malfunction at this late stage in the game could be worse than the machinegun not functioning in the first place, and he was confident they'd done everything possible to mitigate the chances of that happening.

Still, the real test lay ahead, and with that moment of truth rapidly approaching, Reilly glanced left to ensure Ian was ready for his role in the proceedings.

The intelligence operative was positioned before an ammo bag where close to three thousand rounds of 7.62 by 54mm bullets were linked in an S-folded belt. Ian propped the belt aloft to form a slight dip before the rounds vanished beneath the feed tray cover of the enormous machinegun. Once the shooting began, Ian's only role was to extract the remaining ammo belt from the bag, section by section, and keep the rounds feeding into the weapon that would send them into the kill zone at a rate of ten bullets per second.

But for now Ian used his free hand to perform the same action Reilly did, lifting his binoculars to get a view of their target area.

The ensuing wait was only a minute and a half, perhaps two, although it seemed to span a veritable eternity for the medic. Reilly saw the first motorcycle appear, a single rider with his face still covered by a balaclava now heading up the trail, followed by a second dirt bike with two men aboard.

He feverishly scanned the motorcycles that followed for any indication of a newly-released Boko Haram leader, finding with delight that identification was the easy part—he was in a blue prison jumpsuit that stuck out like dog balls among the camouflage fatigues of his comrades, operating a motorcycle whose previous driver was now a passenger on one of the other bikes. The leader also had a rifle slung, which explained why one of the men had carried two weapons on the way to the exchange.

But the real problem turned out to be determining which leader he was. Two of these fuckers looked virtually identical, and the team couldn't afford any mistakes in making a positive identification of Usman lest they reveal their hand too soon. To make matters worse, this particular leader wore a scarf that partially obscured his face.

Ian whispered, "I can't make PID from here."

In the final second, Reilly's thoughts turned to the implications of letting Usman slip through the ambush unhindered, and then he convinced himself that the man before him was, in fact, their primary target.

"It's Usman," Reilly replied, tossing down his binoculars and lifting the PK buttstock onto his shoulder. "Get ready."

The intelligence operative didn't question him, ditching his own binoculars to lift the ammunition belt in preparation for a seamless feed.

Thumbing the manual safety to the firing position, Reilly aimed the iron sights toward the kill zone 250 meters away.

This process only took him a moment's effort—he'd already propped the buttstock's lower edge atop a sandbag and etched the bipod into the dirt in a near-perfect alignment with the stretch of trail ahead, and now needed only to rock the huge weapon forward slightly, bracing it with his arms to ensure maximum accuracy.

By then the motorcycle convoy was rounding the last turn they'd ever make, angling their bikes directly toward Reilly as they entered the kill zone.

The sight was a dream come true: the Boko Haram fighters maneuvering ducks-in-a-row on the narrow trail. Reilly held his fire until the blue jumpsuit was centered in the kill zone, then depressed the trigger as the machinegun jolted to life in his grasp with the first long burst of fire.

A streak of green tracer rounds indicated the bullets' path over the ravine. Reilly's view of the terrorist leader vanished along with almost everything else—men and motorcycles were concealed by long clouds of sand as the opening salvo found its mark with deadly accuracy.

Releasing the trigger, Reilly let the weapon momentarily settle before resuming his point of aim with the knowledge that his target was unquestionably dead. Then, he unleashed a second and third burst to seed the casualties with new armadas of 7.62mm rounds.

Only when there was no hope of survival within the kill zone did he divert his attention to the periphery, where fighters were ditching their motorcycles to take cover and assume firing positions in a response to the ambush that was far too late to save their leader.

They'd barely managed a few opening potshots before Reilly stitched them with the machinegun, launching burst after burst of automatic gunfire from left to right. At this point, he was merely thinning their ranks —the primary mission was accomplished, and the men wouldn't be able to give effective pursuit given the enormous ravine between victim and attacker.

Nor, he thought with a grim sense of resolve, would Reilly need to conserve his remaining machinegun ammo. He'd be leaving the weapon where it rested, along with some ISWAP propaganda that had been selectively emplaced, before fleeing on foot along with Ian.

Before that occurred, however, Reilly was going to kill as many of these fuckers as he possibly could.

Ending his current burst of fire at the far reaches of the Boko Haram line, Reilly swung his barrel left to begin the process anew. As he did so, the medic caught a glimpse of the kill zone, now visible as a rolling dust cloud lifted away. In the dead center of the trail stretch, lying askew atop his felled motorbike, was a motionless body in a blue jumpsuit.

Reilly aligned his sights with the body, dead beyond all measure of doubt, and loosed another long burst just to be sure as a tremendous explosion erupted to his south.

***

I heard the sound of approaching dirt bikes through the trees to my left, then took a final glance at the trail ahead.

The path was only partially visible twenty meters ahead, my view blocked by a swath of trees that allowed select lines of sight. Fixating on a thick trunk with three interconnected knots in the bark, I oriented myself to the center of my kill zone for a final time before cutting my eyes left to the shred of trail that would mark Boko Haram's return path into the mountains.

A dirt bike slid into view, the rider rising to a half-crouch as he throttled his motorcycle over a tangle of tree roots in his path. The second bike was just behind him, topped by two fighters. The passenger was scanning the woods around him, looking for any threat to the leader now being escorted uphill by the convoy—though which leader that was, I couldn't yet tell. I was confident the lead passenger wouldn't be able to see me in my ghillie suit, and if he did it would be too late: he was entering the far reach of my kill zone now, trailed by a third bike with one fighter atop it.

As the fourth motorcycle crossed my view, I wondered how the rest of my team was faring. There was no need for radio communications, as the first element to identify Usman would clack off their ambush with plenty of auditory fanfare to alert the others.

And in the next few seconds, I saw that initial ambush now belonged to me.

Usman was the sole rider on a motorcycle at the end of the convoy, his bearded face unmistakable over a blue prison jumpsuit. I considered notifying my team of the positive identification just to be safe, but there was no time—at the convoy's current rate of speed, he'd be in the center of my kill zone within mere moments, and once that occurred, I would deal him the last surprise of his misspent and exceedingly violent life.

But then I heard a sound that made my heart seize up—machinegun fire from the north. Reilly had initiated his ambush for no reason I could discern, the echo of his opening burst unmistakable even over the growl of dirt bike engines.

The Boko Haram fighters heard it too, though their reactions differed greatly.

Their lead rider stopped his bike in place three-quarters of the way through my kill zone before he looked rearward for guidance. A second driver had no such intentions; instead he swerved around the stationary dirt bike in an attempt to race toward the high ground. The convoy lurched forward behind him, gunning their throttles to speed past the section of trail to my front.

Usman, however, brought his bike to an abrupt halt. He reappraised the path ahead with a look of wild-eyed terror, and rather than proceed, he began turning his motorcycle back the way he'd come. Despite his position just outside my kill zone, I knew he'd be gone before I reached for my rifle, so I did the only thing I could to stop him.

Ducking my head, I squeezed the firing device in my hand three times in quick succession.

I winced with the thunderclap of a tremendous detonation as over two hundred pounds of explosives from the dozen suicide vests buried along the trail decimated the convoy with a wall of fire and smoke. The ground convulsed beneath me, a shockwave of overpressure rattling both earpieces as scorching air whipped overhead along with thousands of steel ball bearings slicing through the trees. Once the initial concussion passed, I grabbed the rifle at my side and brought it into a firing position.

The kill zone was a hazy blur of smoke and flame, the echo fading to cries of agony from those who had somehow survived the blast, unintelligible screams mixed with groaning death rattles. I ignored the casualties, some of whom were visible in the form of bloody and partially dismembered bodies blackened by the explosion, and swept my gaze left to search for Usman.

He'd been thrown from his bike and was rising from the ground, one arm greased with blood. I brought my sights to bear and opened fire, loosing three suppressed shots as he darted downhill and vanished in the trees to my west.

Pushing myself upright, I broke into a run in a race to pursue him, cutting left alongside the trail, outrunning the screams from the kill zone before entering the cluster of trees where Usman had disappeared. Threading my way between the trees as fast as I could move, I keyed my mic to transmit as I heard the first explosion from Objective South.

At the first sounds of an approaching motorbike, Worthy heard Cancer whisper beside him, "Get set."

Both men assumed their firing positions then, popping up over an oblong clump of earth and rock they'd selected for the best possible cover and concealment. For Cancer, the effort was as simple as setting his sniper bipod atop the mound, then dropping forward on the slope as he writhed into a stable shooting posture.

For Worthy, however, the process was considerably more involved: first he had to adjust the rifle slung on his back, then hoist the RPG-7 onto his shoulder and crouch near the top of the slope with the heavy rocket launcher precariously balanced. He probed the ground with his knees, searching for patches of dirt free of sharp rocks before glancing to his side.

A second RPG-7 launcher rested there—once the ambush kicked off, there would be no time to reload—and he verified its position a final time before taking in the view before him.

The slope rambled downhill for four hundred meters, then flattened out to reveal a long stretch of winding trail that faded away at a narrow angle from the two shooters. The angle meant that the targets would be approaching almost head-on, which was great for the purposes of accuracy; likewise, the sparse vegetation between them and the kill zone ensured that their visibility would be clear enough to positively identify which Boko Haram leader was on his way uphill.

But both factors had their drawbacks: visibility worked both ways, and it wasn't inconceivable that an alert motorcycle passenger looking in the right direction could identify a rocket launcher perched atop the otherwise formless shape of a ghillie suit. And the sparse brush extended for a full twenty meters of rockfall behind them before a stand of trees would provide sufficient cover for a running escape from Objective South.

Since the trees didn't afford a clear line of sight to the center of the kill zone, the two men had settled on the only compromise they could. After Cancer delivered his fatal shot against the Boko Haram leader, he'd have to take off running while Worthy covered his movement with the rockets. After that, Worthy would likely be pinned down at the initial firing point until Cancer was able to get a sufficient vantage point over the kill zone's eastern edge; then, he could deliver effective fire to cover the point man's retreat.

"I'm set," he said to Cancer, adjusting his grasp on the twin pistol grips of his rocket launcher. As the motorcycles continued to approach, Worthy aligned the RPG scope to his eye and angled it toward the farthest visible reaches of the trail.

The crosshairs were misaligned, skewed ever so slightly off center and rotated clockwise, in a way that made Worthy doubt the precision of his shots. That was fine with him—this wasn't a precision weapon. Each rocket impact would inflict high explosives and shrapnel in a blast powerful enough to kill anyone within a 23-meter radius—at least, if they worked as advertised.

The first dirt bike came into view, the driver's gaze fixed on the trail before him. At the sight of a passenger atop the second motorcycle, Worthy feared he'd be seen at once, ghillie suit or no—but the man wasn't looking uphill, instead scanning the opposite side of the trail with his rifle propped upward.

The third and fourth bikes had a single rider, while the fifth was operated by a man in a blue jumpsuit, a rifle slung across his torso. It was Salafi, Worthy recognized at a glance, Usman's predecessor in Boko Haram's command structure before he was captured by the Nigerian military eight months ago.

Neither Worthy nor Cancer said a word as they heard the first rattle of machinegun fire to the north, followed almost immediately by a second burst, then a third, as Worthy watched the Boko Haram convoy's reaction to this new development.

Salafi began shouting over the sound of the bike engines, and his order culminated in the best possible outcome as far as Worthy and Cancer were concerned—the convoy sped forward, plunging into the kill zone at an oblique angle to their firing position.

Then an enormous blast rocked the earth to the north: David firing his payload of interconnected suicide vests, putting these bastards on the receiving end of the same IED tactic they so loved employing against Nigeria's military and civilians alike.

The riders didn't break stride, continuing up the slope in an effort to outrun the danger. At this angle, it didn't matter; they were only making themselves a bigger target.

With the echo of the blast still rolling over the hills and the dirt bike engines closing the distance, Worthy never heard Cancer's suppressed shot.

Instead he saw the newly released leader's blue shirtfront flash red from the sniper round before he fell forward, twisting the handlebars sideways and crashing his bike. The motorcycle behind him was skidding to a halt just short of impact as Worthy squeezed the trigger on his RPG-7.

His optic flashed white with smoke, the launcher becoming light in his grasp before he tossed it aside.

It hadn't made landfall before the streaking, hissing rocket found its mark, exploding in a fireball ten feet in front of the downed bike. The blast preceded an angry cloud of black smoke that cleared to reveal a smoldering mass of motorcycles and human bodies—the latter third of the convoy was fairly well obliterated as the survivors ahead of it dumped their bikes in the trail and scrambled for cover behind the trees while trying to locate the source of the shot.

Cancer was gone, racing toward the trees with his sniper rifle in hand as Worthy shouldered his second rocket launcher, searching for the remaining fighters through its scope as two radio transmissions crackled over his earpiece.

First was Reilly, panting with exertion as he triumphantly announced, *"Objective North is finished, we're moving to linkup. I got Usman."*

Then, as Worthy's sights settled just behind a cluster of fighters taking cover behind a boulder, David responded breathlessly.

"No, you didn't."

Worthy squeezed the trigger, listening to the deafening *pop* of the RPG before he dropped the launcher and reached for his rifle. The rocket screamed over the boulder and struck the trail on the far side, erupting in a blast of high explosive and shrapnel.

He grabbed his HK416 and was crawling sideways behind cover as he heard the first pop shots of return fire, followed by Reilly's stunned voice over the team frequency.

"Yeah, I did."

"*Well that's interesting,*" David shot back, "*because I'm chasing after him now and he has a beard.*"

Worthy shifted right around the mound of earth to his front, no sooner taking aim in the search for targets than incoming fire kicked up great sprays of dirt not five feet down the slope.

He rolled back behind cover, waiting for Cancer to arrive in position as Reilly transmitted, "*I thought Salafi had the beard, not Usman.*"

"*No,*" David replied hotly, "*it was fucking Usman!*"

Worthy heard a scream from the trail below, followed by renewed shouting from the convoy of survivors a moment before Cancer came over the net.

"*Racegun, you're clear to move.*"

With the sniper providing effective fire against the entrenched Boko Haram fighters, Worthy took one more look to verify the route behind him before pushing himself upright and running across the partially wooded slope.

David was transmitting in panted gasps, the voice of a man running as fast as humanly possible.

"*I'm in pursuit of Usman, following a blood trail down the mountain fifty meters west of Objective Central. Fuck the linkup—I need everyone to start moving this way.*"

* * *

Ian plunged through the forested hills in pursuit of Reilly, who seemed to have gained a superhuman burst of energy after throwing the entire operation into disarray. His determination was completely understandable—if Usman got away now, Reilly would be entirely at fault.

They'd shed their ghillie suits, which made rapid foot movement exponentially easier, but the combination of rugged terrain and thick vegetation kept them from proceeding at anything more than a partial jog. Meanwhile, Ian's frustration at the medic's utter failure to positively identify Usman prior to engaging fell second only to his desire to see the terrorist leader slain before his team had to flee the mountains. Because whatever Boko Haram's reaction to the death of two major leaders and a whole lot of foot soldiers in the past few minutes, it was going to be significant and arriving sooner rather than later.

David transmitted, "*Usman is headed for Gwoza, moving west-southwest from Objective Central. Need everyone to set up a picket line to intercept my direction of movement.*"

"Got it," Reilly replied. "Heading due south."

But Ian felt a twinge of doubt at this course of action, not because his teammates couldn't improvise a tactical plan in the most fluid of situations, but because he doubted David's assessment in the first place.

He transmitted, "Suicide, you're sure Usman is running *down*hill?"

"*Yes, I'm sure,*" David almost growled, furious at the unnecessary distraction from his single-minded pursuit.

Ian didn't reply, instead considering the obvious contradiction—to him, at least—inherent in this course of action by a seasoned terrorist leader. Those three Boko Haram convoys had a limited number of bad guys, many of whom had been obliterated by the team's near-simultaneous ambushes.

But the Mandara Mountains had a hell of a lot more enemy fighters, and the Sambisa Forest had more still. All had total freedom of movement outside the town, and all would be converging on the ambush sites as surely as a swarm of yellowjackets reacted to the pheromone from one member of the colony being crushed. Usman needed only to survive annihilation until they arrived; yet he was running downhill, toward the only military-controlled town in the area. Why?

Nigerian Army corruption was one possible explanation, but Ian brushed that aside. No one in their right mind would risk a panicked flight into Gwoza without some prior coordination. The risks of being shot by some trigger-happy private were simply too great, and Usman would be much better off hunkering down during the minimal time remaining until his organization reacted.

That's when Ian realized that Usman had a destination in mind, someplace he could hide until the cavalry arrived to save him.

"Hold up," Ian said to Reilly, "I need to check something."

The medic responded angrily, "Do it later. Usman's getting away."

"It doesn't matter where he *is*, it matters where he's *going*."

"We don't have time."

Ian raced up to Reilly and grabbed his sleeve, yanking the huge medic to a stop as he spoke in an urgent whisper.

"Listen, fucker—you were wrong about identifying Usman, and you're wrong about this. So believe me or not, but I'm stopping."

Then Ian knelt beside a tree trunk, pulling out his phone and grappling to manipulate the screen as he zoomed in on the satellite imagery between David's ambush site and Gwoza. Reilly reluctantly took up security to cover him with the muttered admonition, "Make it fast."

Ian said nothing, instead searching his phone screen for a needle in the haystack of mountain terrain.

He knew innumerable caves and miles of caverns ran throughout the Mandara Mountains—they were a key element to Boko Haram's survival strategy here. Now he just had to try and identify some in the direction of Usman's movement.

Ian found his answer in a dark crease of tree-lined shadow paralleling one of the trails to Gwoza. It appeared to be a sharp linear depression in the terrain, a small canyon of sorts, almost directly in line with the movement of David's icon. Ian tapped his screen to drop a marker there, an inverted teardrop shape with the default title of X1 that would be visible to the others on their shared mission software, before zooming out to see which of the team's three elements would be first to arrive.

Based on current proximity and the terrain between the team members and the canyon, Ian and Reilly would likely be last. They'd arrive shortly after David, which meant Usman had a better-than-passing shot of making it into a cavern and disappearing before he was interdicted.

But the canyon paralleled the trail leading to Objective South, which meant Worthy and Cancer stood a chance of getting there before Usman could.

Putting his phone away, Ian rose and extended an arm southwest. "Take us this way."

Reilly objected, "David said to set up a picket line—we need to go due south, not southwest."

"David's following a blood trail that will vanish any second now. He doesn't have time to gain situational awareness—that's why he needs us. Trust me."

There was a split second of hesitation as Reilly tried to assess who to believe, and whether because he trusted Ian or doubted David, he turned to face Ian's pointed instruction before moving out.

Ian resumed the grip on his rifle and followed, giving a rearward glance to scan for threats before transmitting at a jog.

"Racegun, I need you to head for the X1 marker I just dropped on the phone."

Cancer replied, "*I sent Racegun to get the van in case Usman beats us down the mountain. It's just me—what's at X1?*"

"A small canyon," Ian replied, struggling to keep Reilly in sight. "That's where Usman is headed, not Gwoza. If I'm right, there will be a lot of caverns and cave entrances and he's going to duck into one of them. You're the closest one to it, and if Usman makes it there before you do, we'll lose him for good."

"*Copy,*" the sniper answered, sounding as if they were discussing some routine bureaucratic matter. "*I'll redirect and set up overwatch. If he shows up, he's getting popped.*"

Cancer took cover behind a rock formation, checking his six o'clock before withdrawing his phone to confirm his distance from the canyon.

He saw his own icon hovering within a hundred meters of the canyon's western edge, while those from Reilly's and Ian's phones were slowly ticking downward from the northeast. David would be arriving before them, his tracker moving toward the opposite side of the canyon at a range of four hundred meters, while Worthy, bless his heart, was nowhere close: his icon was far west, almost to the base of the mountains where he'd link up with Tolu and be able to flex for a possible interdiction on the outskirts of Gwoza.

Pocketing his phone, Cancer rose and brought his G28 to the low ready, proceeding through the trees toward a sniper position overwatching the canyon. He moved at half-speed now, scanning for threats in the undergrowth as the remaining distance ticked down with each footfall.

The canyon wasn't a massive diversion from his previous course, though the default labeling of XI seemed appropriate for the situation——a total unknown, a place he was entering alone with little more than his wits and a sniper rifle. The weapon would be ideal for surveying the canyon once he got there but absurdly ill-suited for any close-range engagements prior to that point, and Cancer found himself questioning the sanity of ordering Worthy to recover the van prior to Ian's revelation.

Cancer was covering ground as quietly as he could when he heard a twig snap in the forest to his front. He ducked behind the nearest tree, its trunk wide enough to conceal him, at least for the time being, and readied his rifle as he listened.

A male voice called out, *"Man yadhab hunak?"*

He must have been ten meters or more from Cancer's hiding spot, and the sniper was racked with a momentary sense of disbelief—he knew there were survivors from the ambushes, but how could any have gotten here so fast?

That question had a simple explanation, one that occurred to Cancer along with the somewhat grim realization that he may have just overcommitted himself. The survivors hadn't come here at all, not yet; instead there was a pre-staged element, probably too low-level to be involved in the exchange.

But that didn't make them any less lethal.

The verbal challenge was repeated, and Cancer heard footsteps approaching through the brush. Whoever this man was, he wasn't certain he'd heard something—but he was going to find out. The sentry's voice on that second command was desperate, quavering with fear. Why wouldn't it be? He'd probably been expecting a glorious confirmation of three leaders from his command, and instead heard explosions and automatic gunfire all around his outpost followed by radio silence. Cancer was fortunate not to have been shot at already. If he didn't find a way to get the man's guard down, that streak of luck was seconds away from ending, possibly for good.

Fuck it, he decided. If Usman planned to stumble in here unannounced, then he could too.

Cancer had only an elementary grasp of Arabic, and none of the many local dialects used in Nigeria, so he sided with the universal greeting before transitioning to an outright bluff.

"*As-salamu alaykum,*" he quietly replied, then added, "*ismee*, Usman Mokhammed."

The footsteps continued to advance, and after a moment Cancer heard the tentative reply, "*Wa alaykumu s-salam, qayid.*"

The man sounded as if he'd relaxed somewhat—not entirely, of course, but hopefully sufficient for the sniper to drop him before he knew what was happening.

Cancer turned behind the tree, then eased out from beside the trunk while raising his barrel in a swift upward arc, aligning with the chest of a teenage boy coming to a halt not ten feet distant.

His eyes went wide, hands shakily grasping a wood stock AK-47 as he opened his mouth to yell.

Cancer looked over the top of his scope to take reflexive aim, firing his first shot before the boy could make a noise of protest. The subsonic round punched clean through his upper abdominals before Cancer followed it with two more, a choking gasp fleeing the sentry's parted lips before he collapsed, dropping to his knees and falling forward amid a tangle of low brush.

Advancing with swift steps, Cancer delivered a close-range headshot to eliminate any possibility of a death rattle, then swept his rifle in a half circle that confirmed the sentry was alone. A quick scan of the body revealed an Icom radio clipped to the boy's waist. Cancer quickly reloaded and then knelt to recover the radio, using his free hand to turn off the device before sliding it into his cargo pocket.

Then he continued moving forward, his caution tempered by the knowledge that three of his teammates would be racing toward the canyon whether Cancer had cleared it or not.

He saw the trees thinning out ahead, an indication that the ground fell away to a depression. Weaving his way forward, Cancer took his first tentative glances into the abyss below.

Ian had been perhaps too quick to classify the landscape feature as a canyon; it was more of a tight, deep ravine, possibly the remnants of some long-expired river. But the intelligence operative had been right about the rest—its rock walls were dotted with dark crevices leading to caves, or caverns, or both.

And while Cancer's line of sight was limited to the northern side, already he could make out three figures standing below.

He wouldn't be able to maintain visual on them from the prone, but a seated firing position would work just fine. The range was right around 180 meters, he estimated, and if he couldn't get the drop on them after neutralizing their early-warning sentry, then it was time to hang up his spurs as a sniper.

Cancer selected a patch of ground and sat cross-legged, resting his triceps against the inner edges of his kneecaps to avoid bone-to-bone contact. Then he leaned forward to decline his barrel and looked through his magnified scope to assess the men.

They were conversing in an animated fashion, probably debating what to make of the recent sounds of battle or arguing their course of action amid the ensuing lack of guidance. Cancer briefly debated whether to prolong his assessment, but within a moment the debate was over. There could be any number of fighters in the surrounding caves, but the certainty of three kills now trumped the possibility of more than three later.

Steadying his grip on the G28, he took aim at the leftmost man in the group. While it was impossible to discern the highest ranking member, this particular terrorist dirtbag actually held his weapon in both hands—the others had them slung over one shoulder like Davy Crockett—and was therefore the most likely to get a shot off.

Taking a final exhale, Cancer waited for the natural respiratory pause between breaths before taking the slack out of his trigger and squeezing off a shot. It was a clean hit, a through-and-through to the heart, and Cancer transitioned to his second target and delivered a fatal round before the third man processed the sight and began to run.

When he did, however, it was commendable—adrenaline had turned him into a speed demon, and he now loped toward the nearest cavern entrance with surprisingly rapid strides. And while his response was the best one available to him, his estimation of where the shots came from could have used some work. His path took him not into Cancer's blind spot along the ravine's southern wall, but instead northward as Cancer tracked his movement, squeezing off another shot that flung the man to the ground but didn't kill him.

Instead he rolled partially to his side, facing away and in the process of dragging himself to cover when Cancer drilled him through a shoulder blade, the bullet tearing into his chest cavity and probably blowing out a lung in the process.

Cancer swept his sights across the first two casualties, then back to the third, as he scanned for any signs of movement. Then he lifted his eyes from the scope, watching for any more fighters to appear as he listened for sounds of alarm from the valley below. Nothing. He executed a reload without taking his eyes off the ravine floor, then used his non-firing hand to retrieve the Icom radio from his pocket.

Rotating the volume knob just past the click required to turn it on, he set the radio down and listened for transmissions—any remaining enemies would be wise to stay hidden, though they'd likely be calling for reinforcements by now. When the radio remained silent, Cancer transmitted to his team.

"In position at the western edge of the canyon. Four EKIA, no Icom chatter. I only have eyes on the north side—southern edge remains a blind spot."

The moment he released his transmit switch, the relative silence of his surroundings was shattered by automatic gunfire.

I slipped through the forested hills with all the stealth I could muster without falling behind, secure in the knowledge that my quarry was within reach.

Since following Usman away from Objective Central, I'd managed to strip off my ghillie suit between sightings of the precious few indicators guiding my path. At first great splatters of blood had traced a route for me to follow, though they'd trickled off to a few sporadic droplets. Beyond that point, the majority of my clues were audible—the rustle of brush, the clatter of small rocks underfoot, and on one occasion, a pained grunt as Usman tripped and fell.

But I had yet to actually see the man since my failed ambush attempt, and that struck me as nothing short of ridiculous. This shouldn't have been hard. Usman was fleeing in a blue prison jumpsuit, for Christ's sake. The vegetation was thick but not *that* thick; he'd had a head start, but not *that* much of one. He was wounded and I wasn't, and yet he'd been a ghost for the duration of my pursuit—and no matter what was about to unfold, that pursuit was quickly approaching its bitter end.

Any second now, Boko Haram reinforcements would be streaming in from the far reaches of the Mandara Mountains, to say nothing of the terrorist hordes located in the nearby Sambisa Forest. Whether my team managed to interdict Usman or not, we had to get back to the relatively safe confines of Gwoza or we'd be wiped out in these hills.

I scanned the terrain to my front as I moved, hoping for Usman's next misstep to guide my trajectory. My radio earpieces were invaluable in that regard—in addition to providing communications, they amplified sound until a decibel cutoff kicked in to preserve hearing. They were probably the only reason I'd been able to pursue Usman this far.

But when I found the next evidence of Usman's passing, it wasn't a sound at all.

As I bypassed a cluster of low scrub brush beneath the treetops, I entered a small clearing and caught sight of a shoulder-height branch with leaves marked by a dark slick of fresh blood. Orienting my path toward this new clue, I broke into a run. If the majority of my pursuit was any indication, I might not detect another trace of Usman for another twenty meters if at all.

I was halfway to the blood-marked leaves before it occurred to me that this could be a trap; after all, I hadn't seen his blood in some time, and even then only in small droplets on the ground. The branch was like a billboard by comparison, and I was heading straight for it, entering the middle of a clearing and oblivious to any possibility that Usman was smarter than I was, that he could have planted the sign and was lying in wait.

Already in motion, I feverishly searched for the nearest cover and found a partially exposed boulder rising three feet from the forest floor to my front right—just enough to hide me, provided the attack didn't come from the left.

But by then I had no other options. I altered course in a desperate sprint to the rock, closing the distance as Cancer transmitted over my earpiece. "*In position at the western edge of the canyon. Four EKIA, no Icom chatter. I only have eyes on the north side—southern edge remains a blind spot."*

My final two footfalls propelled me in a lunging leap toward the boulder as I tried to consider from which direction the attack would come.

It was too late.

The burst of automatic gunfire erupted to my right as I dove behind the boulder, a fiery muzzle flash igniting in the periphery of my vision before I landed. By what margin Usman had missed, I couldn't say, but it wasn't much, the snap of the bullets shredding through the space overhead so loud that I initially thought he'd hit me.

I rolled to my side, pushing off the boulder with my boots before lying flat on my back with my knees spread wide and the HK416 aimed above the rock to my front. There wasn't enough cover to rise to a knee, so this was the best defensive position I could manage for now—but it wouldn't last long.

Usman had selected a remarkably good ambush spot. The boulder was squarely in the center of the small clearing, with no cover for fifteen feet in any direction. There was no place to move without him shooting me first, leaving me in a precarious position that he could easily outflank, using the trees for cover to attain a vantage point to deliver the fatal shot. I couldn't even call upon my team to save me and stall for time. I wouldn't last that long.

The plus side of this situation was that I felt reasonably confident Usman only had one magazine—the weapon had probably been handed to him as a largely ceremonial gesture, and it was unlikely they'd expected him to be using it in self-defense minutes after his release.

The downside, of course, was that he needed only one bullet to turn my wife into a widow.

I considered all the information at my disposal in a few panic-stricken seconds. Usman was ruthless and smart, and had laid a brilliant trap to kill me before escaping to the canyon. Why? Cancer said he'd smoked four bad guys there, which meant Usman presumed he'd soon be protected by an element that would defend his escape into the caverns. That meant he didn't *have* to kill me at all—he was doing this out of sheer rage, a deep, unrelenting anger at having been bested upon his release.

And that rage was his only Achilles' heel at present; it certainly wasn't lack of intelligence. Any second now he'd begin a simple flanking maneuver to get me in his sights, and the only defense I had was not to keep him at bay, but to taunt him closer—at least that way I'd know where he was.

I called out, "Your other two leaders are dead."

There was no telling if he would answer me or not; a coldly rational opponent would slip into the trees, stealthily crossing a semicircle in one direction or the other to kill me before I could react. Then again, I thought, a coldly rational opponent wouldn't have risked stopping on the way to the canyon.

Usman replied in a low, heavily accented voice, "As you will be."

He sounded perhaps twenty feet distant, probably just within the trees to my front.

"Maybe," I said, "maybe not. You're running out of bullets."

"And my people will be here any moment, so you are out of time. Tell me, which is the greater asset?"

He had me there, I thought, forcing confidence into my tone as I replied.

"It was my men, you know. The attack on the highway, finding your camp in the Sambisa Forest. Allowing the hostage exchange just so we could ambush you on your way out. We've had so much fun stacking Boko Haram bodies that I'm starting to wish there were more of you to kill."

"You will get your wish any moment now. But the pleasure of killing will be ours."

He was closer now, edging nearer my lone piece of cover, confident that he could best a prostrate opponent. He wasn't wrong; in the battle between my training and his wildly advantageous position, he held the upper hand by a long shot. And each step he advanced removed critical distance where my marksmanship could make a difference.

I looked left and right, searching for any way to turn the tables and finding nothing but leaf litter and brambles, save a fist-sized rock on the ground beside me.

If only it were a grenade, I thought bitterly.

The boulder I hid behind was in the middle of the clearing, open ground that I couldn't negotiate without getting shot—and then I realized that if I was exposed in the clearing, then so was Usman.

Picking up the rock at my side, I called out, "You know what? You're probably right. Here, have a grenade."

Then I whipped the rock over the top of the boulder, a low, fast arc to present a blur of motion that, combined with my words, I hoped would cause him to run for cover.

No sooner had the rock left my hand than I heard him scrambling on the forest floor, and I curled one leg beneath the other to rise into a seated shooting position.

My view cleared the boulder top to reveal a flash of blue disappearing into the trees, and I opened fire as fast as I could pull the trigger.

But Usman was gone, having cut his losses in a race toward the canyon's southern edge, directly into Cancer's blind spot. If he made it into one of the many caverns, then our mission in Nigeria was a failure. It was a miracle this area wasn't already crawling with Boko Haram reinforcements, and their arrival was fast approaching.

I pushed myself upright, darting after Usman as I transmitted.

"Usman is headed for the southern edge of the canyon—Doc, Angel, need you to get there now to cut him off. Cancer, relocate to get a vantage point."

I was plowing northward through the trees when Reilly responded, "*We're still a hundred meters out. Going as fast as we can.*"

Then Cancer added, "*Moving, but it's going to take me a few minutes to get an angle on the south side.*"

Shit, I thought, it was up to me now. I ran as fast as my feet could negotiate the terrain, suppressing my fears of a second ambush. If Usman so much as ducked behind a tree and waited for me to pass, I was done for; but if he reached the canyon before I did, he'd get away forever. With no further US appetite for action in Nigeria after the final hostages were recovered, it was now or never to claim the life of the man we'd been sent here to kill.

I could tell I was approaching the canyon, could see the trees thinning out ahead. But not until I'd passed through a dense swath of leafy bushes did I catch sight of Usman's blue prison jumpsuit.

He was running toward the precipice, about to disappear into the void of Cancer's blind spot as well as my own. I skidded to a halt, raising my rifle in the final second and flicking my selector lever to fully automatic as I shouted a single word.

"*Usman!*"

The cry caused him to make the slightest half-stutter of a footfall, his head cutting partially left to look over his shoulder as my sights aligned with him and I squeezed a long burst.

My rifle spat the subsonic bullets without fanfare, a quiet *twirp twirp twirp* of suppressed gunfire until my magazine went empty.

Usman was gone.

Reilly increased his speed as the vegetation became more sparse, the ground beneath his boots increasingly composed of stone rather than dirt.

As the trees cleared out he could see the rocky slopes of ravine walls rising to his left and right, their craggy faces dotted with dark cavern entrances. No wonder Usman was running here, he thought—a man could hide from all but the most determined and exhaustive search, much less the ten minutes or so before the hordes of his Boko Haram compatriots came tearing down from the high ground.

The medic advanced quickly, almost recklessly; any one of the caverns ahead could hold unseen enemies, and with only Ian trailing him and Cancer still in the process of relocating, Reilly couldn't possibly be more vulnerable than he was now.

He raced into the low ground without so much as confirming that Ian had kept pace, sweeping his HK417 left and right as he moved. A cluster of bodies was visible ahead—three of Cancer's kills, none moving—and he was scanning the ravine's southern wall when he heard the clatter of rock-fall overhead.

Then he registered a sight that was equal parts miraculous and absurd: a body in a blue jumpsuit tumbling down the slope, limbs careening wildly as an AK-74 fell from his grasp. Reilly tried to aim but the body was moving too fast, one dull pop of a bone snapping followed by another. Throughout the rolling fall, the man didn't make a sound. He must have been dead already, Reilly thought.

The body made landfall a short distance to the medic's front, landing in a heap like a gift-wrapped present from God. Reilly advanced with his weapon raised to the sound of a low, primordial groan from the man who was somehow, astonishingly, still alive.

Usman Mokhammed was on his back, one arm coated in blood, a gunshot wound on the opposite shoulder. The splintered fragments of a broken femur emerged from his left thigh—as a patient his wounds would have been a nightmare to treat, and Reilly was glad he wouldn't have to.

Reilly came to a stop a few feet away as Usman's eyelids fluttered open, an attempt to speak eliciting a bloody froth that ran down the side of his face. Broken rib must have punctured a lung, Reilly thought as he addressed the terrorist leader.

"Huh," the medic said idly. "You really do have a beard."

He fired two rounds into Usman's sternum, then a third shot to his face.

The subsonic jacketed hollow points thwacked off the stone beneath Usman's body, pools of blood spreading as Reilly transmitted, "I got Usman. For real this time. He has a beard and everything."

Ian ran up from behind, stopping beside him with a look of stunned disbelief.

Reilly said, "See? He has a beard."

A sound overhead caused both men to look up—David had arrived at the south wall, looking down at them from thirty feet as his voice came over their earpieces.

"Doc, Angel, meet me on the high ground. Cancer, we'll pick you up on the western edge of the canyon. We've got to get the hell out of these mountains."

Worthy leaned out the media van's open passenger window, directing his gaze backward as he called out, "Another five meters, straight back."

Tolu obeyed, reversing the van up the perilously steep slope as Worthy continued, "Three meters...two...one...stop."

That final command was redundant for both men—just before Tolu came to a full halt, they heard tree limbs scraping against the van's sides and roof. Even if the trail weren't getting too steep for the van to reverse up —which it was, rapidly—the path had now narrowed to a point where it was traversable only by foot or dirt bike.

Tolu cranked the parking brake and looked to Worthy with an expression a half-step removed from blind fear.

"Now what?" he asked.

"Now we wait. Leave the engine running," Worthy said, keying his radio to transmit. "All right, fellas, I got the van in position about two hundred meters west of Checkpoint One on the Objective South trail. We can't push any farther back."

David's reply was spoken with all the feverish intensity of a man running for his life, which at this point he most certainly was.

"*We're five, maybe six minutes out. Be ready to haul ass, and make the call now. We can hear motorcycles coming down the mountain—I think they're going to hit Gwoza.*"

"Got it," Worthy confirmed, pulling out a local cell phone and hitting the speed dial.

A deep Nigerian voice answered, "Who is this?"

"Lieutenant Colonel Mamman, this is Jake Brady from the Garrett News team. Listen, we got a tip about the hostage exchange and tried to film it from the high ground. We're going to be driving back into town from the mountains in the same van you saw yesterday—it's just our team, so please do not shoot us."

The army officer's response was spat with incredulous disdain. "How could you be so stupid?"

Undeterred, Worthy continued, "There's something else, sir. We can hear motorcycles coming down the mountain, and think there may be an attack on the way. Recommend you strengthen your defenses on the east side of Gwoza immediately."

"I strengthened my defenses there," Mamman shot back, "as soon as I heard gunfire and explosions in the hills. But I suppose you know nothing about that."

"I'm afraid I don't, sir, but we heard them too. We'll be on our way in the next few minutes. I repeat, the white media van you saw yesterday, coming down the trail next to the Government Day Secondary School. Again, please do not shoot us."

Worthy could hear shouting in the background as Mamman said, "Goodbye, Mr. Brady."

The call ended, leaving Worthy to wonder whether Mamman would inform his men or leave their arrival up to fate. And regrettably, at the present moment it didn't matter much either way—Worthy had more pressing matters to attend to.

He clambered into the back of the van, transmitting, "Battalion commander is tracking our arrival."

"*Two minutes out,*" came David's breathless reply. "*Have the cargo doors open and make sure Tolu is ready to fucking floor it. Sounds like the motorcycles are getting close.*"

Reilly added, "*So many motorcycles...it sounds like a biker rally up here.*"

"Copy," Worthy replied, "going off comms."

He pulled out his earpieces, stripped off his tactical vest and boots, then began the frenzied choreography of changing into his pre-staged set of civilian clothes. The problem with the team's cover as reporters for Garrett News, he thought, was that they couldn't exactly pop out of the van in full combat regalia when they reached Gwoza, *if* they reached Gwoza at all.

Once he'd completed the transition and pulled his boots back on, Worthy pocketed two magazines from his kit, snatched his rifle, and opened the rear cargo doors. He scanned the woods on either side of the trail before kneeling at the rear of the van.

Tolu called back, "*Wahala dey-o?*"

"Yeah," Worthy replied without averting his gaze, "we've definitely got a problem. The boys will be here any minute, but so will Boko Haram. When I tell you to go—and not one second sooner—I need you to drive this thing down the hill like you just stole it."

"I am ready, Mr. Worthy."

"I know you are, Tolu. I know you are, but—"

Worthy ended his sentence abruptly, hearing his first indication of the team's approach—hammering footfalls from up the trail, a noise that preceded his first visual by a full ten seconds.

But what a visual it was.

Reilly was in the lead, the huge medic sweating as much as a human being possibly could. His face was beet red, weapon held in one hand as he charged forward, locking eyes with Worthy and shouting, "Get out of the way!"

And while Worthy started to move toward the passenger seat, he was momentarily awestruck by the file of men following Reilly down the trail. David was second in line, almost at Reilly's heels as he gasped for breath. Behind him was Ian, looking over his shoulder like the Mongolian horde was at his heels, which, in a sense, it was. Cancer appeared the most composed of the group, and even he was running with his eyes laser focused on the ground before him, as if a trip and fall now could be the difference between life and death.

Above it all, even amid the sounds of their trampling steps as they careened down the trail, Worthy could hear dirt bikes approaching.

His reverie was broken by Reilly, whose shrill cry took on an uncharacteristically high pitch as he repeated, "I said GET OUT OF THE WAY!"

This time Worthy complied, scrambling into the cab, where he stepped atop the passenger seat and transitioned to a left-handed grip on his rifle so he could lean out the open window while aiming backward.

The van rocked furiously as his teammates piled inside, Cancer shouting from the back, "We're up!"

"Go," Worthy said, and Tolu dropped the emergency brake before accelerating down the trail.

Combined with the effect of gravity on the heavy van, this resulted in the vehicle practically catapulting downhill, painfully flinging Worthy's chest against the window frame as he searched for targets. It wasn't easy—between the vehicle bouncing over rocks and ruts in the trail and his precarious firing position half-perched on the passenger seat, operating his weapon off-handed was the least of his worries.

He could hear David shouting something in the back, heard unsuppressed gunshots behind them, and knew his team was returning fire through the open cargo doors. But he couldn't see what they were shooting at until Tolu followed a curve in the trail, allowing Worthy a momentary glimpse of a motorcycle following them down the path. The driver couldn't shoot but his passenger was making a go of it, crude though the attempt was. With one hand holding onto the driver, he used the other to balance his rifle atop the driver's shoulder as he took wild shots. This was some real backwoods terrorist effort, Worthy thought, an A+ for enthusiasm but an F for tactical feasibility.

The motorcycle driver was probably deaf by now, and before Worthy could align his sights the man was dead, struck with multiple bullets to the torso before falling over the handlebars as the dirt bike fell to its side and skidded, both riders now rolling into the trees. Another bike swerved around these new obstacles, replacing the first while attempting the same maneuver.

This time Worthy was ready. He ripped three suppressed shots, uncertain of his accuracy as his view jostled violently on the uneven path. Whether by Worthy's hand or his teammates', the driver's head lurched and he toppled backward, dislodging his passenger as the motorcycle continued unimpeded, covering another ten feet before hitting a tree root and crashing into the woods.

Then Tolu called out, "I can see the town."

Worthy flipped his selector lever to safe and slid back inside the passenger window, carefully angling his rifle into the cab. He announced, "Weapon," passing his HK416 to Ian in the cargo area and tossing back the two spare magazines. His last glimpse of the cargo area revealed total chaos —Cancer was pulling the rear doors shut while the remaining members feverishly stripped off their tactical kit, preparing to stash the gear and change into civilian clothes. Worthy slid the folding partition shut, encapsulating the rest of his team from outside view as he turned in his seat, facing forward to take in the view of Gwoza.

Mamman hadn't been kidding when he claimed to have bolstered his defenses: the terrain flattened out to a row of military trucks and armored personnel carriers, their heavy weapons oriented at the van as it barreled out of the mountains and into the low ground.

Worthy flinched in anticipation as the wind howled through his open window—Tolu was speeding them toward a perimeter of soldiers who'd spent the better part of each working day beating back Boko Haram attacks, and so much as one gunshot from a panicked member of the formation would incite the entire line into a free-for-all. Within the next few moments, Worthy saw that his worst fears were coming true.

Automatic gunfire erupted from the Nigerian line, muzzle flashes sparking from heavy machineguns before a truck-mounted launcher emitted a puff of smoke and sent a rocket screaming toward the van. Worthy's final thought wasn't of family or even a rapid-fire slideshow of his life to date—instead, he imagined the Nigerian soldiers picking through the van's charred remains, perplexed to find that several occupants in the back had inexplicably died without pants.

But no bullets shattered the windshield, and the rocket soared just over Worthy's side of the van; he pulled his torso through the open passenger window, tracing its smoke to the trailhead they'd just departed, where the munition detonated in a fireball amid a cluster of dirt bikes following the van out of the mountains.

Worthy dropped back into his seat just as Tolu steered between two army vehicles, continuing along the dirt path leading into town. The road ahead was blocked by an APC bristling with radio antennas, and a group of three dismounted soldiers signaled them to halt by way of aiming their weapons at Tolu.

The Nigerian driver hit the brakes, decelerating sharply to a full stop as Worthy caught sight of Lieutenant Colonel Mamman beside the APC. He was wearing a flak jacket adorned with pouches below a Kevlar helmet, shouting something into a radio mic whose cord led to the backpack of a kneeling radio operator.

Worthy wrenched his door open, stepping outside the van with his hands raised. He had to buy his team just a little bit of time, perhaps one or two minutes for them to transition themselves and the van's visible contents to civilian appearance.

Seeing that the nearby soldiers were ignoring the van altogether, their eyes and weapons fixed on the gun battle playing out on the eastern edge of Gwoza, Worthy lowered his hands and strode up to the enormous officer with a scarred cheek who ended his radio transmission to glare at him through dark sunglasses.

"Lieutenant Colonel Mamman," Worthy began, "I think we're ready for that military escort out of Gwoza."

42

Two Days Later

Duchess manipulated the digital map on her computer, panning the view from one side of Africa to the other, then back again. Never before had this God's-eye view of a single continent made her feel so small, yet she repeated the process in large part because there was nothing else to do.

For once the situation was entirely under control; for once a Project Longwing mission had concluded without risk of political reproach, without some potentially catastrophic fallout that threatened to tank the program and take her career along with it.

The OPCEN at present was a direct reflection of such a victory, if you could call it that—her staff was beginning to trickle in, arriving with thermoses of coffee as they replaced the early-morning shift of personnel who'd been on duty since midnight. Duchess herself had been at her desk for over an hour, not due to any pressing crisis but because of the opposite: she'd awoken early simply because she was unable to sleep any longer. Everyone was well rested, fully recovered from the long nights on the wrong end of a time cycle catering to target areas on the far side of the world. Normally a bustling center of activity, the OPCEN was now filled with the quiet murmurs of staff members working a normal humdrum of routine tasks, all the administrative minutiae of preparing a formal after-action report to submit upon the team's safe return stateside.

All in all, the scene mirrored her experience with successful Agency operations—no back slapping and high fives, no calls from the president to congratulate them. When everything had gone as well as it could on some overseas venture, the reward was more often than not characterized simply by the lack of a crisis to deal with.

Now two cups of tea into her morning routine, Duchess considered that she should have felt far happier about the whole situation than she did. After all, all eleven hostages had been returned to US soil, and only one in a closed casket after being decapitated by Usman. Her ground team had come out of Gwoza alive less than 48 hours ago after killing not just their original target but also the other two released Boko Haram leaders. Now David and his men were safe in Abuja, awaiting only a final exfiltration that night in accordance with the administration's directive to get all American forces out of Nigeria before some terrorist effort tarnished what had been an almost flawless resolution to the hostage crisis.

She continued scrolling across the overhead view of Africa from the west coast to the east, from Nigeria to Mozambique, considering the massive payouts from one Chukwuma Ndatsu Malu to, presumably, Erik Weisz and his compatriots.

Whoever they were.

But Mozambique wasn't the real issue; it was merely a laundering point, and her real interest lay in where the money went afterwards. Until forensic accounting succeeded in tracing the destination, she wouldn't know—and as she zoomed out until the map depicted half the world, she realized that she couldn't narrow the possibilities down to a hemisphere, much less a single continent.

And while those answers would come eventually, she'd still be left with a black hole of information surrounding Malu. Someone, possibly Weisz himself, had contacted the powerful politician and set up a masterfully elaborate network between Venezuela, Gradsek, the Nigerian government, and Boko Haram, and had done so with seemingly no agenda beyond profiting from it. The intelligence concerning that initial contact with Malu, to say nothing of the communications required to sustain the arrangement, was the real key, one that, regrettably, fell so far outside the charter of Project Longwing that she was powerless to pursue it any further.

It wasn't due to lack of effort, of course. Duchess had spent the better part of six hours yesterday trying to rally interest from other divisions within the CIA before reaching out to her contacts at the DIA, NSA, and even the Office of Terrorism and Financial Intelligence to conjure up outside support for the inquiry. The answers had been uniformly predictable: everyone's time and assets were too tied up with known terrorist networks to commit to pursuing an unknown one that may not even exist. They'd more or less agreed to take a look at the report once forensic accounting had returned hits on the Mozambique transfers, but to Duchess the lack of enthusiasm was palpable. There were simply too many bad guys in the world, and every facet of the US intelligence community was working around the clock already.

Now the best she could hope for was some continued surveillance over Malu, but if the ISA had come up dry on his communications over the events of the past five days, it was unlikely anyone would approve a protracted surveillance effort. The hostage crisis was over; everyone had gotten what they wanted, and Washington was more interested in taking that fact for a victory lap of self-congratulation than igniting some deeper probe into the illicit activities David's team had uncovered.

Beside her, Jo Ann asked, "What's wrong?"

Duchess looked over in alarm to see the Navy officer watching her, holding a cup of coffee by a hand bearing her glittering gold class ring.

"Nothing's wrong," Duchess said. "Why?"

Jo Ann raised her eyebrows skeptically, then took a sip of coffee before she replied, "You've been fiddling with that map for fifteen minutes."

"So?"

"So there's no reason to beat yourself up. The hostages have been recovered and the team will be on their way home tonight. Meanwhile, three terrorist leaders are dead. I'd call that a tactical victory on every possible level."

"As would I," Duchess replied, folding her arms. "But it's a strategic failure any way we slice it."

"How do you figure?"

Duchess felt a pang of irritation in her stomach. "How do you not? I'm talking about Venezuela, Gradsek, Malu, everything. The payouts to Mozambique are linked to Erik Weisz and we both know it."

Jo Ann shrugged. "The Gradsek conspiracy with Venezuela will be shut down, in time."

"And what about Malu?" Duchess shot back. "You're honestly telling me he's not the single most important piece of this? If we could take him down, we'd have it all: Weisz's communications, how he links bad actors on an international scale, maybe even what else he's running, to say nothing of what he's planning next."

Jo Ann set her coffee on the desk and turned to face Duchess.

"I'm not arguing that, Duchess. But there's nothing else we could have done. I mean, think about it—if Bailey hadn't been leading the ISA team, we might never have gotten the tip on Lagos. If we didn't have that, we wouldn't have gotten Maiduguri, and without that ledger, Usman and those other two leaders would be free men right now. Try and look at the bright side."

"The bright side," Duchess repeated, her words sounding hollow. "Right, Jo Ann. I'll try to consider that when—"

She stopped speaking as Jo Ann's eyes flew to the front of the OPCEN. The central television screen had just come ablaze with a muted news feed.

The sight made Duchess feel nauseous and enraged at the same time.

It was an overhead view of a container ship at sea, surrounded by Nigerian Navy vessels as the cameraman aboard an orbiting helicopter zoomed in to show uniformed officials swarming over the deck.

The banner headline read *INTERPOL SEIZES NARCOTICS DESTINED FOR VENEZUELA*, while a subtitle beneath it continued, *Russian oil company Gradsek implicated in international drug trafficking.*

Duchess searched for someone to yell at, with her intelligence officer being the obvious choice, but Andolin Lucios, of course, had put the news feed on in the first place, and he was now jogging up the tiered levels of seating with his tablet in hand.

As she waited for his arrival, Duchess felt a flash of heat running down her chest, the onset of uncontrollable anger.

She'd provided that intel in good faith that her superiors would release it only to parties who knew better than to act before the time was right, had clearly *specified* that Gradsek not be persecuted until the Agency had more information on Malu's financial activity. And now someone—God forbid she ever find out *who*—had moved too soon, eager to further their own agenda by leveraging the conspiracy.

Her mind raced through the fallout that would ensue, speaking the ramifications aloud as Lucios came to a stop beside her.

"Malu is going to run—now, today. He knows there will be reprisals from Weisz. Contact the ISA, let them know Malu is going to make arrangements—"

"Ma'am," Lucios interrupted, angling his tablet screen to read the contents, "the ISA just sent us the transcript of his calls. Malu has already scheduled a private jet, leaving the Abuja charter terminal at 1800 tonight. Stated destination is Addis Ababa, Ethiopia, but it's safe to say the pilots will change course once they're wheels-up. Malu also contacted Gradsek and asked for an armed transport to pick him up in three hours for transit to the airport. And he's traveling with diplomatic immunity, so even if we knew where he was ultimately headed, we can't legally interdict."

Pausing to clear his throat, he asked, "What do you want to do?"

The anger faded in one fell swoop, replaced by a sense of crushing despair as Duchess replied, "Right now, Lucios, what I *want* to do and what I *can* do are two very different things."

With a resigned sigh, she concluded, "Continue to monitor the situation. At this point that's the only option we've got left."

Lucios turned to depart as Duchess fell back in her seat, pinching her eyes shut.

Jo Ann sounded inexplicably optimistic as she asked, "What do you think?"

Duchess left her eyes closed, trying to blot out the news report playing out on the massive flat-screen before her.

She said, "I think tonight will be a drinking night. After letting Malu escape, I'm going to need it."

"The ground team is a few miles away in Abuja."

Duchess's eyes flew open, then narrowed as she spoke. "If I so much as suggested action against a foreign politician, the Agency would have me on the street before I had time to blink."

"But Malu holds the link to Weisz, and Weisz orchestrated the July 4th attack."

Turning her head slowly to face Jo Ann, Duchess muttered, "No shit. What's your point?"

"My point is," Jo Ann said quickly, "that Malu's dead whether he knows it or not. If we don't find him, then Weisz will."

"Concur. So what?"

"So if he's dead anyway, and no one can prove it was us"—she turned up her palms suggestively—"why not act?"

Duchess lowered her voice and said, "Even if I, you know...every method of communication with the team is monitored, every contact with them scrutinized for the purposes of legal oversight."

This detail didn't appear to concern Jo Ann in the least.

The Navy officer leaned forward and whispered, "If you're serious about this, I might know a way."

43

Ian stepped out the back door of the safehouse, shielding his eyes from the blazing afternoon sunshine as he felt his body get pummeled by the stifling heat.

He scanned left and right, knowing that no man in his right mind would be sitting in the open right now given the selection of shaded spots in the heavily planted yard; and sure enough, he located a single figure to his left, seated with his back propped against the rounded trunk of a corkwood tree.

Tolu didn't appear to notice Ian's approach, instead drawing smoke from the stump of a cigar whose scent the intelligence operative could detect right away. It was a sweet, aromatic pepper smell, free of any trace of marijuana, and right now that latter point served not as a relief, but a point of concern.

The driver had barely spoken a word since the team's departure from Gwoza with full military escort two days earlier. Even after the convoy reached Maiduguri and turned west toward Abuja, the normally boisterous driver remained quiet and brooding, and once they'd left Boko Haram territory, Cancer actually had to request he turn on the rap music they were normally asking him to turn off. Throughout the remaining journey to the safehouse, Tolu had maintained an oddly detached focus on his driving, and Ian suspected his mood had more to do with David being in the passenger seat than anything else.

Ian entered the pool of shade beneath the corkwood tree, grateful for a reprieve from the heat, however subtle.

Tolu nodded toward him and asked, "You need me, Mr. Ian?"

"No."

By way of response to the lack of urgent business at hand, Tolu reached into his breast pocket and procured a second cigar, holding it out as an offering. Ian shook his head, and Tolu replaced it.

Scanning the ground, Ian selected a patch to Tolu's right and sat cross-legged beside him, leaning against the tree trunk so they sat almost shoulder to shoulder. It was an intimate and non-confrontational posture, one that allowed the participants to speak or remain silent without the potential awkwardness of eye contact when discussing sensitive topics. Ian had enough experience setting up interrogation room seatings to under-stand that facing Tolu head-on could be a dealbreaker right now.

Ian lifted a long, thin stick from the ground beneath him and began snapping sections off the end in quarter-inch increments, tossing the first aside as he asked, "What's on your mind, Tolu?"

He heard the driver blow another cloud of smoke, the cigar's scent renewed in his nostrils.

"Nothing, sir."

"Listen," Ian began, "I'm the closest thing my team's got to being a touchy-feely guy. David shouldn't have executed that man in front of you."

Tolu responded hotly, "He should not have executed him at all. You heard his story—he was kidnapped. Brainwashed. This was the truth, *abi*?"

Ian knew he could contest that point on any number of grounds, starting with the not-unreasonable counterpoint that professional terrorists weren't the most honest brokers.

But to do so would be to lie—Ian didn't doubt the captive's story, and was in fact almost certain the same circumstances applied to others among the ISWAP fighters killed that day. The simple truth was that this was a dirty business, a fight not between good and evil but between combatants with various shades of brutality. The terrorists were undoubtedly at the extreme end, but Ian's team took their place on the same spectrum.

Targeted killing had a nicer ring to it than words like torture and execution, but the team had at various points done the latter two acts in order to achieve the former.

Instead Ian snapped off another length of the stick and said, "You're right. He wasn't lying."

This acknowledgement seemed to relax Tolu somewhat, his voice quiet and vulnerable as he replied, "Then why did he die?"

Ian didn't answer at first, considering his words as he watched a lizard scamper between bushes to his front. Its head and tail were blaze orange, the body a dull blue-gray, and upon reaching the far bush, it leapt to a perch on one of the branches, then scrambled into the leaves with impossible quickness.

Snapping another section off the branch, Ian said, "You've been driving for some time now. I'm sure you've seen a lot."

"Yes," Tolu agreed, "but nothing like your team. I must say, it has been...not so good."

Ian let that statement fade to silence before he replied.

"The world exists in shades of gray—you of all people know that."

"Yes."

Ian swallowed. "The guy we were after, Usman Mokhammed, well...he works in the black. If we handed that ISWAP guy over to the villagers, the odds were they'd kill him themselves, and face worse recriminations than they already would. And if we took him captive, we wouldn't have been able to continue our mission. It could have meant Usman remained alive."

Tolu objected, "You cannot know that. Only God knows."

"You're right," Ian said, tossing his stick aside in frustration. "I can't give you any hard evidence, but I can tell you this—that ISWAP foot soldier had definitely killed a few people in his day. Maybe five, maybe a dozen. Do you agree?"

"Sure. Yes."

"Well, Usman was responsible for *hundreds* of deaths, and he would have been able to achieve a thousand or more if his promotion in Boko Haram continued. Most of them would have been innocent civilians. That guy David executed was raiding a village, yeah. But Usman would have been the one ordering the raids, expanding their efforts to"—he hesitated a moment—"to recruit more young men like your brother. And believe me, Usman was one hell of a lot smarter than the people who will be taking his place now that he's gone."

Ian saw an object fly through the periphery of his vision, looking left to see the crushed stump of Tolu's cigar landing. The driver rose, circling the tree to face Ian.

Then he extended his hand, a peaceful expression on his face as Ian returned the handshake. Tolu released his grip, nodding as he looked toward the safehouse.

"Thank you, brother."

He left before Ian could reply, his footsteps whispering across the ground. A few moments later, Ian heard the safehouse door swing open and click shut.

Ian didn't move at first, wondering whether his assurance had helped Tolu understand the dire ramifications of his participation in the mission, or if the driver had simply given him lip service to end the conversation.

Pushing himself upright, Ian brushed the dirt from his pants and approached the safehouse, crossing back into the sunlight before turning the scalding door handle.

He locked the door behind him, fully expecting to hear the same bustle of activity that had been occurring all day so far as the team packed all but the most essential equipment in preparation for departing Nigeria that night.

Instead, the safehouse was eerily silent, which could have only one explanation: something major had just happened.

He strode quickly toward the operations center, hearing David speak two words as he reached the halfway point in the hallway.

"Get Ian."

"I'm here," he replied, entering the room to see his entire team clustered around the desk.

David and Cancer were seated, while Reilly and Worthy stood to either side of their team leadership, but all eyes were focused on the radio speaker box atop the desk, which emitted a crackling burst of static at the start of a radio transmission that, judging by appearances, wasn't the first.

A man said in a thick New York accent, "*Suicide Actual, come in.*"

Ian looked at David and asked, "Why aren't you answering?"

"Because it's not SATCOM," the team leader replied. "This is coming in over our encrypted team net."

That comment gave Ian pause, bringing to mind a series of complicating factors—namely, no one knew their team frequency except Duchess and her people. And merely possessing the frequency wasn't enough to communicate over it; the caller would need the encrypted radio key just to transmit, and that was a highly protected code that changed with each mission. Even if an outside party had both the frequency and the radio key, this was an FM net. That meant whoever was calling them was located in Abuja, and judging by the clarity of his transmissions, probably within a mile of the safehouse.

The voice repeated, "*Suicide Actual, come in.*"

David was watching Ian, searching for some guidance on how to react to this highly unusual development.

Ian grabbed a legal pad off the desk, flipping to a clean page and snatching a pen as he said, "Don't answer. Let's see what he has to say."

Cancer asked, "What if he won't transmit in the blind?"

"He will," Ian said, "at least if this is what I think it is."

Reilly squinted at him. "What do you think it is?"

Ian blinked, swallowing hard as he considered his response.

"Duchess has gone full gangster."

Over the speaker box, the New Yorker continued, "*All right, in the blind it is. This is a friend of Duchess. I know believing that is a tall order, so here's some bona fides: her callsign is Raptor Nine One, and your team's radio handles are Suicide, Cancer, Angel, Doc, and Racegun. I'm relaying a prepared message that's too hot for SATCOM, so get ready to copy.*"

Ian had his pen poised on the notepad, and he scrawled quick bullet points as the man continued, "*News broke on the Gradsek conspiracy, and it spooked the most critical source of future intelligence: Chukwuma Ndatsu Malu, the politician we've linked to Gradsek and Boko Haram. Malu expects he'll be whacked by Erik Weisz for failing to keep the wheels on their arrangement, and to keep him from compromising Weisz's syndicate. So he's fleeing the country in two and a half hours, via a private plane out of Abuja. He takes off on that, and no* one's gonna see him again except Weisz's people when they put a bullet in his head."

A lump formed in Ian's throat as he recognized that the message's authenticity was beyond reproach—the name Erik Weisz was known to very few people, and the true import of that pseudonym to even fewer. Ian readied the tip of his pen for the next transmission, watching the speaker box as the man continued.

"*Now here's the most important part: Malu is holed up at his personal residence, address is 116 Buhari Street in Abuja. He's getting picked up there at 1600 local by a Gradsek security contingent that's gonna take him to the airport. They've tasked an armed three-man detail plus a driver, and they'll be arriving in a Mercedes G-Class SUV with a ballistic protection level of B5, rated up to 7.62mm. If you're willing and able to roll up Malu, Duchess believes he's got significant information leading back to Erik Weisz. Anything you obtain needs to be attributed to site exploitation from earlier in the mission. You found a cell phone in Lagos or Maiduguri that you forgot to report, or maybe a terrorist from your Gwoza ambushes spontaneously confessed before he expired. Tailor your story to the information obtained, but keep it reasonable so Duchess can cover for you.*"

Ian jotted the word *story* and underlined it twice, his mind already spinning with the possibilities of intelligence attribution—which, depending on what they acquired, could be more complicated than anyone expected.

Then the man resumed his guidance, speaking casually but quickly.

"*All she wants is the intel. She doesn't need Malu alive and she most certainly doesn't want any details about the event. And since everyone in her shop expects Weisz to kill Malu anyway, you can dump his body wherever you like. Just make sure nothing is attributable to the US—it needs to be a covert kill.*"

The speaker box went silent, and Ian took a moment to appraise his team's collective reaction.

Worthy was squinting at the speaker box like he was staring into the eyes of God, which was just as well—both the instructions and what the team chose to do with them had life-or-death consequences not just for their involvement in Nigeria, but potentially the entire future of Project Longwing. If, Ian thought, there was a future after this. An unsanctioned kill carried not just grievous moral implications, but would set a precedent that the team members were more or less free agents for Duchess to use as she saw fit. Absent any political or legal oversight, the team would be coming perilously close to the same tactics used by dictatorships and secret police the world over.

On the other hand, if Duchess was right about this, they could potentially save a tremendous number of innocent lives.

David was looking back at Ian, eyebrows raised as if he was trying to read the intelligence operative's mind. The team leader would act on this, no question, provided Ian advised him to do so. Beside him, Cancer wore an unsettling half-grin, as if things were finally going to some sinister plan he'd been harboring all along.

Only Reilly appeared outright conflicted, his jaw set, massive arms folded and tense. For him, this breach of protocol was unwise at best and bordering on insanity at worst.

The New York accent was tempered with a casual flair, almost droll as the man continued, "*Now I know you boys don't want to answer me, and hell, if I was in your shoes I probably wouldn't either. But I need to know you received the message before I can get on with my day, so do me a solid—key your mic once if you need me to repeat, and twice if you got it all.*"

Ian set down his notepad and pen, picked up the radio mic, and pressed the transmit button twice in quick succession.

44

Cancer strolled down the sidewalk with his hands in the pockets of his unzipped windbreaker, wishing to heaven or hell that he could discard it amid the heat.

Maitama District was an affluent part of Abuja, and like most urban areas in Nigeria, it displayed a staggering wealth disparity. Ten minutes ago he'd passed through a neighborhood of humble one-story homes with stucco roofs, the trash-laden dirt walkways marked by shoddy fruit stands and crossed by as many loose chickens as people.

But a turn at Buhari Street took him into a whole new city, if not an entirely different universe.

To the left of the wide sidewalk, a pristinely manicured row of low bushes bristled with red flowers, forming a small divider next to a golf-course grade of turf punctuated by palm trees and ferns planted at perfect intervals. This lush median parted to a driveway that Cancer crossed at a casual gait, scanning its length to the enormous solid gate on his right—a black leviathan inlaid with dinner plate-sized medallions of elaborate gold filigree. The gate was flanked by towering stone posts marked by gas lanterns whose flames flickered despite the blinding sunshine, and he continued his walk along the towering stretch of wall topped by decoratively discreet iron fence spikes that would skewer all but the most determined invader.

The wall extended to the next driveway gate thirty meters away, the spacing a uniform division of one-acre lots as it had been since he entered the neighborhood. Despite its impressive height, the long stretches of fence did little to obscure his view of the mansions beyond; the second-story windows looked out over the street between ornate columns and large balconies, the sloping roofs rose to three- and four-story pinnacles whose heights formed sharp pyramids against the cobalt sky.

If he were a corrupt Nigerian politician, Cancer thought, this neighborhood was probably where he'd call home. Between, of course, excursions to his other properties in Dubai or Banana Island in Lagos. When you were able to tap the national bank at will, as Nigerian politicians were wont to do, no excess of spending was too excessive. There was little for such men to fear—after all, a corruption inquiry was unlikely to make headway in a country where everyone in power openly did the same.

Cancer crossed over another driveway before he heard the rumble of a large V8 engine approaching behind him. He slowed his pace somewhat, measuring his progress against the next gated entrance ahead. A sideways glance confirmed the Gradsek vehicle passing along the idyllic street to his left: a gleaming black Mercedes G-Class SUV cruising past him, armored panels causing it to ride low on run flat tires and arriving right on time.

He continued walking as it parked on the street to his front with the engine running, the passenger door aligned with the next gate in his direction of movement. The first two Gradsek men to exit took up positions on the sidewalk, a huge bodyguard facing him and the other looking the opposite direction—east and west side security, he saw at a glance, both of them in suits, sunglasses, and earpieces, ready to stop foot traffic.

The third and final man out of the SUV was identically attired, and looked both ways down the sidewalk before taking up a position between them, facing the gate with his hands folded. This was the shift leader, the man in charge of the security detail, and like the others must have been packing no more than a concealed pistol and some spare magazines. A promising development, Cancer thought—while they surely had submachine guns and assault rifles in the vehicle, the financial elite who employed such bodyguards were loath to see overtly displayed weapons.

Cancer approached to within three meters of the stationary detail before the east flank security man, a big lumbering bastard, held up a hand and called out with a Russian accent, "Sir, remain where you are."

At that moment Cancer realized who this hulking man was—the Gradsek guard that he had confronted in the restaurant. They hadn't considered that one or more of those Russians would be present today, and the sniper felt a rare moment of fear that he'd be recognized as well.

But the residential gate was already creaking open, and Cancer didn't break stride.

"Sir," the man repeated, more forcefully this time, one hand tucking back his suit jacket and reaching for a holstered pistol, "stop."

This time Cancer complied, halting at the left edge of the sidewalk, outside arm's length from the nearest bodyguard. Fields of fire were a major consideration on any objective, but when the target area was a few square meters, the placement of each man as well as his every shot had to be surgically precise. Cancer let his eyes tick across the security men, his expression irritated.

Finally he replied, "I live here, pal. What are you gonna do, gun me down for taking a walk in my own neighborhood?"

"We will depart momentarily, and you can be on your way."

The man scanned him, his eyes invisible behind the sunglasses, but Cancer knew some dim recognition was rising in his mind. The bodyguard must have thought he knew Cancer from somewhere, but couldn't place him —at least, not yet. In the restaurant he'd been too concerned with the threat posed by a much larger Reilly, but the window of surprise was closing fast.

By now the gate was halfway open and a second vehicle was approaching from his rear as Cancer asked, "You picking up Malu? Buddy, we play poker once a month. I don't think he'll mind if I walk past."

Malu appeared then as if summoned by Cancer's lie, rolling a luggage case behind him. He was a slight man in his forties, maybe five-foot-six, and to Cancer's surprise he was fairly casually attired—khakis and a tweed blazer over a pink polo shirt.

Cancer addressed him as an old friend, gesturing toward the security detail as he spoke.

"What the hell, man? Can I get past or what?"

His final words were drowned out by the approaching vehicle, Tolu's media van cutting in front of the Mercedes and braking hard.

No sooner had it come to a stop than David jumped out of the passenger seat wielding a black object in his left hand. Cancer saw the west flank security man make a move to draw until he identified the item not as a gun but something debatably worse: a microphone.

One of the rear cargo doors opened a moment later, and Ian emerged with a bulky video camera atop his shoulder, converging with David as the team leader came to a stop at the edge of Malu's driveway.

"Secretary Malu," David called out, "Tom Connelly, Garrett News."

Malu looked horrified, glancing from Ian's video camera to David's proffered mic. The three-man security element was taxed to its maximum—both flank men facing possible threats, with the armored vehicle's forward movement blocked by a media van—and the shift leader made the wisest move he could under the circumstances.

Grasping Malu's shoulder with one hand, he led him toward the street while reaching for the door handle to his G-Class.

Then David spoke again. "Any comment on the allegations against Gradsek?"

As soon as he said the word "Gradsek," the trigger for initiation, Cancer saw the van's remaining cargo door swing open, revealing two new players in the unfolding drama: Worthy leaping out with his suppressed rifle, and Reilly kneeling in the back, leveling his HK417 at the armored windshield a few meters behind him.

Cancer drew his pistol with blinding speed, firing the first two shots from his waist—both hit the security guard to his front, a pair of gut shots that ended his reflexive move for his own handgun and then Cancer married his nonfiring hand to the pistol grip, extending the Glock as David opened fire on the guard at the western flank.

As Cancer fired another controlled pair, this time into his target's chest, he heard the blasts subside to the crunching *pop-pop-pop* of Reilly's armor-piercing rounds penetrating the Mercedes windshield on their way to the driver.

With his target falling to the sidewalk, Cancer transitioned his aim to the shift leader to see that he was too late—the man was still rushing Malu toward the armored vehicle when Worthy picked him off with a subsonic head shot, causing the man to drop in place.

The engagement was over in five seconds flat, leaving Malu as the last man standing. He released his grip on the luggage, turning to flee toward his residence.

But Cancer was upon him in three sprinting footfalls, using one hand to grab his blazer sleeve and spin him around as the other brought the pistol across his face in a savage blow. The bottom edge of the magazine cracked across his cheekbone with as much force as the sniper could muster.

Malu's body jolted with the impact as David seized him from behind, dragging him toward the van as Cancer followed, stepping into the street with a final rearward glance to verify the post-assault activities in progress.

Ian was snatching up the microphone that David had dropped to draw his concealed pistol, while Worthy advanced toward the three fallen bodies, firing suppressed shots to ensure no witnesses survived to provide a description of the attack. David threw Malu into the back of the van as Cancer holstered his pistol and climbed aboard beside Reilly, who'd turned his attention to their new captive. The medic drove a knee between Malu's shoulder blades to hold him down as Cancer retrieved a flex cuff, looking past the open cargo doors as David entered.

The Mercedes windshield was scarred by spiderweb fractures surrounding a tight cluster of ragged holes, providing a partial view through the sun's glare to reveal the shapeless mass of what had seconds before been a living driver.

Then Ian stopped at the bumper, tossing Malu's luggage inside the van before unshouldering the heavy video camera and setting it inside. He was in the process of boarding as Worthy appeared beside him, sweeping his rifle across the scene a final time before scrambling into the van.

"Go," David shouted, and Tolu accelerated forward as fast as the van could haul. The devastated Mercedes receded along with the Gradsek bodies on the sidewalk as Worthy pulled the first cargo door shut and reached for the second as Cancer caught a glimpse of the gate to Malu's residence, only now easing closed on its electronic timer.

Malu was crying out with incoherent panic, his pleas silenced as Reilly pulled a pre-staged strip of duct tape off the side of the van and plastered it over his mouth. Then he tied a blindfold over his eyes as Cancer and the other team members pulled on their tactical vests, donned their radio earpieces, and reached for the rifles lined up on the floor of the cargo area.

Ordinarily they'd begin their tactical questioning as soon as possible, interrogating the captive before the effect of capture shock wore off. But with the possibility of interdiction by Gradsek security contractors if not the Nigeria Police, the team had to remain poised to react with force. David climbed forward into the passenger seat while Cancer, Worthy, and Reilly took their seats with weapons in hand.

Only Ian was exempt from this security posture; after donning his tactical kit, the intelligence operative procured a large black Faraday bag and reached into Malu's pockets, depositing his findings into the sack that would block digital signals and prevent any interested parties from tracking the politician's cell phone.

Then he moved on to Malu's body, conducting a thorough pat-down for hidden pockets and removing the man's belt to see if it had a zippered pouch before moving onto the luggage to continue his search.

Tolu turned right at the next corner, proceeding north toward the A234 Highway.

45

The van rumbled to a stop on the dirt road, and Tolu killed the engine. I watched him for a moment, his profile glowing sunset orange before he looked over with a neutral expression. Then, subtly, he gave me a nod of agreement.

I opened my passenger door, setting foot on the hard-packed desert beside a mud brick building that now lay in ruins. The nearest farm was half a kilometer away, the swaths of land in all directions a wasteland of dried-out ravines and scrub brush. Abuja was miles to our southeast, the buildings glittering on a horizon that seemed to stretch endlessly as I rounded the vehicle, completing my visual sweep.

Stopping at the van's bumper, I paused to observe the sight to the west —the enormous, rounded monolith of Zuma Rock dominated the horizon, a thousand feet of stone standing in sharp contrast against the peaceful hues of the sunset as a few smoky clouds drifted lazily overhead. This was the real Nigeria, I thought, the scene that preceded the corruption and oil and drugs, the murderous terrorism and loss of civilian life by the tens of thousands. It was the scene that would remain long after my species left the earth.

Raising a gloved fist, I pounded twice on the side of the van.

The cargo doors swung open, and I stepped back as Worthy and Reilly maneuvered the restrained politician out of the back, propping him upright as Cancer retrieved the one item we'd never before carried on mission: a metal foldout chair.

He opened the seat and set it a few meters behind the van, unsheathing his fighting knife as his teammates dragged the captive over and spun him around. Cancer maneuvered the flat side of his blade against the man's wrists, slicing upward to cut the flex cuff.

Worthy and Reilly lowered Malu into the chair, removing first his blindfold and then the duct tape over his mouth before departing.

I approached him slowly, seeing the politician looking about in terror, first observing Cancer and me looming over him, then Worthy and Reilly standing in a loose perimeter, ensuring no vehicles approached this desolate stretch of desert. Then his eyes swept the horizon, locating Zuma Rock before settling on the van's open cargo area, where Ian now sat with his legs dangling over the bumper, analyzing a computer in his lap. I watched Malu's eyes following the cables leading from Ian's computer to the laptop we'd found among his possessions, along with his cell phone that was likewise being scanned.

The intentional positioning of his chair seemed to have the desired effect—he panted for breath, seeing that we had the means to catch him in a lie.

I pulled a bottle of water from my cargo pocket and held it out to him. Malu accepted the offering greedily, unscrewing the cap and dropping it in the dirt before downing half the bottle in four long pulls. Wiping his mouth dry, he looked up to see Cancer extending a pack of cigarettes toward him. Malu shook his head, one cheek grossly swollen and marred by dried blood from Cancer's previous pistol strike.

Then the politician met my eyes, watching me with unease as I smiled.

I couldn't help it; we'd actually succeeded in leaving Gwoza alive, then managed to snatch Malu on our last day in Nigeria. And best of all, there was no way for Malu to know who we were.

Leaning down, I spoke the most fearsome string of words I could.

"Erik Weisz says hello."

Malu's hand lost its grip on the water bottle, which tumbled to the ground to spill a widening puddle.

"I did not betray him. Please, you must believe me."

"You tried to run," I said, "and we had no choice but to keep you from getting on that plane."

Blinking quickly, Malu spoke with wild despair. "I fled to protect his syndicate."

"My syndicate didn't ask for your protection. We asked for your loyalty. What evidence have you betrayed of our arrangement?"

He shook his head quickly, as if his vigor would speak to his truthfulness.

"None whatsoever. Do you think I am mad?"

I gestured to Ian sitting on the van tailgate, his equipment scanning Tolu's computer and cell phone. "If you're lying, we're going to find out in the next few minutes. That won't end well for you."

He shook his head again. "My electronics are clean. The only link to your organization is on the SIM cards."

Ian looked over with a raised eyebrow, his silence and expression confirming the uncomfortable truth: we hadn't found any.

"Where are they?" I asked sternly, as if I knew exactly what he was talking about.

Malu responded by pulling open one side of his blazer, then using both hands to peel open an inner seam. I stepped forward, amazed to see a tiny zipper concealed between folds of fabric. He had to pinch the slider between fingernails just to grab it, much less slide it down the zippered teeth. The hidden pocket was almost impervious to pat-down, and Malu reached inside to produce a stack of multicolored SIM cards.

He held them up one at a time, explaining, "Blue is for Boko Haram. The red is Gradsek. Green, Venezuela. And this one"—he lifted a final black card between his trembling fingertips—"is for Weisz himself."

I turned my palm up, and he eagerly deposited all four. Ian appeared beside me, but I couldn't help staring at the cards for a moment before handing them over—what Malu said seemed to confirm everything we'd discovered so far, but there was only one way to know for sure.

Handing the SIM cards to Ian, I watched him scuttle off to the van to begin his analysis.

Malu continued, "Every cash transfer was accurate, paid in full. I kept up my end of the arrangement until the recent...exposure."

"What assurance do we have that you did not compromise our employer?"

He was taken aback by the question, waving his hands emphatically as he replied, "What could I compromise? You must understand I have not seen Weisz's face, or even the emissary who delivered the SIM cards. I merely followed his instructions exactly. Once the first exchange worked as he said it would, I knew he was a man of his word. I did everything he asked since then, and have made him a fortune."

I looked over at Ian impatiently, seeing his face lit by the computer glow as he continued to analyze the SIM cards. Bizarre as it seemed under the circumstances, we couldn't spend all night out here—Reilly, Worthy, and I would be riding a boat down the Niger River in four hours with all our military equipment, with Cancer and Ian departing by commercial air the following day.

Cutting my eyes to Malu, I asked, "If you didn't expose Gradsek, then who did?"

"Perhaps the Venezuelans had a leak, or perhaps—" He halted abruptly, trying to think of any possible explanation. "Perhaps Boko Haram suspected we betrayed them. But you must understand, I did not even know their names, only the phone numbers, only Weisz's instructions."

Finally Ian called out from behind his computer, "It's all here. He's telling the truth."

"You see?" Malu asked, gesturing wildly. "I only needed to reach a safe area before an investigation could expose your syndicate. Why else would I bring the SIM cards with me? I was going to call Weisz as soon as I reached my final destination."

Cancer lit a cigarette beside me.

"Buddy," he said to Malu, blowing the first cloud of smoke into the darkening sky, "you already have."

NARCO ASSASSINS:
SHADOW STRIKE #4

David Rivers chases an elusive narco-assassin through the jungles of Colombia in this explosive assassination thriller...

Former FARC revolutionary Sofia Lozano has become the world's most cunning assassin, and now she's selling her services to the highest bidder. But when the CIA learns that Sofia's newest client is an international terrorist syndicate with plans to kill countless civilians, her name is placed on David Rivers' kill list.

As David and his team track the elusive operative from Colombia's triple canopy jungles to its Pacific mangrove swamps, his team stumbles onto a larger conspiracy: a narco-sub loaded with cocaine and evidence of a terrorist attack-in-progress.

Faced with a lethal web of drug trafficking, terrorism, and political corruption, David and team must eliminate Sofia before she can complete her deadly plan. And a single mistake could cost them thousands of lives...

Get your copy today at
severnriverbooks.com/series/shadow-strike-series

ABOUT THE AUTHOR

Jason Kasper is the USA Today bestselling author of the Spider Heist, American Mercenary, and Shadow Strike thriller series. Before his writing career he served in the US Army, beginning as a Ranger private and ending as a Green Beret captain. Jason is a West Point graduate and a veteran of the Afghanistan and Iraq wars, and was an avid ultramarathon runner, skydiver, and BASE jumper, all of which inspire his fiction.

Sign up for Jason Kasper's reader list at
severnriverbooks.com/authors/jason-kasper

jasonkasper@severnriverbooks.com

Printed in the United States
by Baker & Taylor Publisher Services